The Perseid Collapse

a novel by

Steven Konkoly

First edition

The Perseid Collapse is a work of fiction. The names, characters, places, and incidents portrayed in the story are the product of the author's imagination or have been used fictitiously. Any resemblance to actual persons, living or dead, businesses, companies, events, or locales is entirely coincidental.

ISBN 13:   978-1493695645
ISBN 10:   1493695649

Dedication

To Kosia—still my number one supporter.

To Matthew and Sophia—two awesome kids who put up with dad's long writing hours

Acknowledgments

To my wife, for encouraging my return to the post-apocalyptic genre. I forgot how much fun it can be to plan the end of the world. She's been invaluable to the transition from writing about hardened covert operatives to "civilians." I need constant reminding that the Fletcher's are not the Petrovich's, as much as I want them to be in certain situations.

To the beta reader crew for another round of rock-solid commentary and edits. Trent, Nancy, Jon and Bruce. I'm not sure what to say after six novels, other than—Thank you!

To the production crew, for another standout effort. Felicia A. Sullivan—once again meeting my "deadline" with grace and precision. Jeroen ten Berge—for producing a killer cover design and encouraging me to pursue *The Perseid Collapse* as a series. Stef McDaid—for the top-notch formatting job. Bloody brilliant as always! To Pauline for proofing the work. She's the final layer, keeping the last of the typos and nasty sentences from reaching the reader.

A special thanks goes out to Randy Powers of <u>Practical Tactical</u>. Earlier this year, Randy interviewed me regarding *The Jakarta Pandemic* (<u>interview here</u>) and general disaster preparedness. I thoroughly enjoyed his questions and the practical lessons he found buried in *The Jakarta Pandemic*. He beta read The *Perseid Collapse* with a prepper's eye and provided me with an early copy of *Practical Tactical's Handbook*. Not only did this guidebook help shape the final disposition of the Fletcher's wide array of survival gear and strategy, it currently serves as the "go to" guide for the Konkoly household.

Finally, to the readers, friends and fellow writers who supported my transition to full-time writing. None of this would be possible without your encouragement.

About the author

Steven Konkoly graduated from the United States Naval Academy and served as a naval officer for eight years in various roles within the Navy and Marine Corps. He lives near the coast in southern Maine, where he writes full time.

He published his first novel, *The Jakarta Pandemic*, in 2010, followed by four novels in the *Black Flagged* series: *Black Flagged* (2011), *Black Flagged Redux* (2012), *Black Flagged Apex* (2012) and *Black Flagged Vektor* (2013). *The Perseid Collapse* is Book One in a planned series of three books. *The Perseid Collapse: Event Horizon* will be available in the spring of 2014.

Please visit Steven's blog for updates and information regarding all his works:

www.stevenkonkoly.com

About The Perseid Collapse

The Perseid Collapse takes place six years after the H16N1 virus ravaged the world in my first novel, *The Jakarta Pandemic*. Feedback and reviews for *The Jakarta Pandemic* exceeded all expectations, with many readers asking me to write another novel featuring Alex Fletcher and his family. I balked at the idea, hesitant to write a true sequel to *The Jakarta Pandemic*.

I buried the idea of a follow-on apocalyptic novel for two years, occasionally unearthed by a new reader with the same request—more Fletchers. In between *Black Flagged Apex* and *Vektor*, I started putting some thought into the possibility of bringing them back.

If I planned to bring the Fletcher's back, I had to accomplish two things. First, I had to create a unique disaster scenario. Not an easy task given the recent flood of post-apocalyptic books. Second, I needed to rain hell down on the Fletcher's world. They would not have the option of "bunkering up" within the confines of their home. The final disaster concept hit me like a meteorite, nearly derailing the publication of *Black Flagged Vektor*. I feel confident that you'll share in my excitement, within the first few pages.

Time in *The Perseid Collapse* world is measured in plus (+) or minus (-) Hours:Minutes from the EVENT. Book One in *The Perseid Collapse Series* chronicles the first 48 hours post EVENT.

PART I

"RED DRAGON"

Chapter 1

Xinjiang Uyghur Autonomous Region
People's Republic of China

Liang Zhen approached the shiny steel door and swiped his keycard, activating the biometric scanner. He pressed a shaky hand to the glass panel and waited for the system to verify his identity. He started to look over his shoulder, but stopped. They would read it on his face. The station's endgame rapidly approached, and he had no intention of going down with his ship.

The pneumatic door opened, and he stepped into a new atmosphere—filtered of rank coffee breath and body odor. His sanctuary. The door hissed shut, and he doubled over, bracing his hands on his knees.

Breathe deeply. Get control.

He straightened up and cinched his tie. Loyalty be damned! His destiny did not include dying 450 feet underground, and he strongly suspected that Station Three would not survive the morning.

Station Three had served a single purpose since he arrived two years earlier: to prevent the world's discovery of "ME8192019." Working in shifts, the men and women of his station held a constant vigil over the vast digital fraud and network manipulation required for Operation Red Dragon to succeed.

Now that the operation had entered the terminal phase, his station remained the only loose end, and he wasn't naïve enough to exclude the likelihood that Beijing would "close the loop" on Red Dragon.

He walked swiftly toward a stainless-steel door at the end of the hallway and entered the daily code into the keypad. Green light. Beijing suspected nothing. He opened the door to a brightly lit concrete stairwell, which rose several levels to a private elevator lobby. From there, Liang could summon one of Station Three's elevators and escape the facility.

He felt like a traitor leaving everyone behind, but someone had to survive, and he was the only member of the crew authorized to leave the station. Any attempt at an unauthorized mass exodus would trigger an immediate response. He couldn't wait to see the Directorate's sour faces when he resurfaced. Shock would eventually yield to relief that the genius behind China's recovery had survived.

Liang Zhen, then second director of the Cyber Warfare Recovery Directorate, had been the first to propose the Republic of China wage a more active, silent war against the West, with the ultimate goal of destabilizing European and North American economies. Liang oversaw the program from 2014 until 2017, when the Future Vulnerabilities Group discovered an "event" with the potential to do far more than temporarily destabilize the United States.

They immediately sent Liang Zhen to Cyber Warfare Station Three to oversee Operation Red Dragon and fulfill China's destiny. He was simply taking measures to ensure that the chief architect of that destiny still had a seat at the table when the dust settled. Thick dust.

Liang reached the ground lobby and scurried up three stories of metal stairs to the surface. The wide stairs ended at a thick iron door, which opened into the center of a vast, empty warehouse. Gusts of wind buffeted the building's thin metal walls as he walked rapidly through the roasting heat toward the door.

The driver better be there.

The station was located in one of the most isolated sections of the former Lop Nur Nuclear Test Range, over sixty kilometers from the nearest inhabited post. He had little chance of surviving an escape on foot, and he had brought nothing to the surface with him, aside from his wallet and identification card.

The door swung open, propelled by a burst of stifling hot wind. Squinting through his fingers, he spotted the SUV. Perfect timing.

He struggled against the gale, pausing once to look behind him at the lone warehouse situated between two windswept ridges. One hundred and eleven Chinese citizens had worked on Red Dragon for twenty months, buried deep below the surface. Dead and buried from the start. They just hadn't known it. None of them had—until recently.

Would they cut the power and let it die slowly? Poison the air supply? Did the station already have some kind of self-destruct failsafe installed? Whatever happened, he planned to be as far away as possible.

Halfway to the vehicle, he shook his head. The damn driver was asleep! He had better be resting for the marathon drive ahead. He found the front passenger door locked and knocked on the dust-caked window. The driver didn't move. He banged on the side of the door. Just his shitty luck. The executive service sent an incompetent fool! He wiped the thick layer of dust off the passenger window and stumbled backward, falling to the hardened clay surface.

How could they know?

He turned on his stomach and scanned the horizon. Several figures sprinted toward him from the left side of the warehouse. He was a dead man. How long had they waited for him? The lead figure penetrated the sandstorm. Chinese Special Forces. Death would be a luxury.

"Director, I need you to return to your post immediately," stated the soldier, extending his hand.

He nodded eagerly. It made sense to him now. If killing everyone had been the plan, they wouldn't send him back down alive. He kept his eyes focused on the soldier's feet. What a fool he had been. He'd flushed away everything. The Special Forces team would report his escape attempt, and the career he had cultivated for the past forty years would be finished. Acceptable in light of his irrational behavior. How could he face Tin and the rest of his deputies below? He would have to come up with an excuse.

An emergency meeting at the surface!

"Please, there is little time," said the soldier, helping Director Zhen to his feet.

Chapter 2

Jewell Island, Maine

The wind rose gently, nudging the campfire's spectral plume toward Alex. He squirmed in the collapsible aluminum chair and turned his head as heated exhaust from the dying fire washed over him. The gust intensified, focusing the column of sparks and gases in his direction for a sudden, uncomfortable moment. Just as suddenly, the smoke drifted skyward on the confused breeze.

The mosquitos returned within seconds, causing Kate to mumble a few obscenities and wave a futile hand above her head to disperse the pests. He took her other hand and squeezed, finally catching her gaze. The soft firelight illuminated her gentle face and exposed the first genuine smile he'd seen since they left Boston yesterday.

"He's really not that far away. We can visit him any time we want," Alex said comfortingly, kissing her hand.

"I know. He's just really on his own now," said Kate, returning her eyes to the fire.

They had dropped Ryan at Boston University in the middle of the afternoon, after dining al fresco in Winthrop Square, a late-summer tradition they had enjoyed since Ryan and Emily were in grade school. The definition of al fresco dining had changed over the years, as the children matured. Lounging as a family, on blankets spread over the trampled grass, had inevitably yielded to scarfing down pizza and subs on the outskirts of the park. Still, they never failed to take time out of their annual Boston pilgrimage to visit the iconic Harvard Square gathering place and its eclectic assortment of musicians and vendors.

This year's visit had been slightly awkward, if not tense for the family. Ryan had been anxious to be ferried across the Charles River, but Kate was in no hurry to surrender her firstborn. She prolonged the stroll through Cambridge, pushing Ryan's barely tested patience to dangerous levels. Alex could sense the strain, and had spent most of the day implementing one subtle intervention after another to keep them from exploding before the inevitable outburst at the foot of Ryan's dormitory building.

Kate remained silent for most of the drive back, punctuated by Alex's occasional failed attempt to distract her from the significance of the afternoon's farewell. Ryan was truly on his own, free to follow the path of his choosing. Every phone call that flashed his name would flood them with a mix of joy, apprehension and ultimately relief. Any conversation from this point forward could instantly morph into a defining moment for Ryan. Anything was possible. He had taken the first steps toward escaping his parents' gravitational pull this afternoon. Ryan couldn't understand this yet, but Kate and Alex had effectively released him, which is why Kate's somber mood was nearly impenetrable.

"He's a smart, cautious kid. Just like his mother," said Alex.

"He has a wild side that worries me," she whispered.

She was right to a certain degree. The events surrounding their experience during the Jakarta Pandemic had drawn out aspects of his personality that might have lain dormant for years, fueling a confidence that more resembled recklessness at such a young age. He didn't have the maturity to temper the confidence that came with saving his father from a brutal psychopath at age twelve and standing guard over their house as the world recovered from the pandemic. He never crossed any lines that landed him in trouble with the school or police, but he was far too comfortable walking the line. Ryan was destined for something important. Kate just wanted to make sure he survived until that point.

"ROTC will keep him in line. There's only so much crazy shit you can get away with enrolled in that kind of program," he whispered back.

"Is that supposed to make me feel better? We'll be at war with Iran by the time he graduates."

"We were supposed to be at war with Iran last year—and the year before that. Nobody's going into battle any time soon. He's Navy ROTC anyway," said Alex.

"He'll switch to Marine-Option the first chance he gets. He was placating me with that song and dance about the navy. So were you."

"Why are you guys whispering?" interrupted Emily.

"No reason. Has anyone seen a meteorite? We shall remain at the mercy of these mosquitos until everyone has spotted at least one. That's the tradition," said Alex.

"It's meteor, Dad," said Emily.

"What is?"

"A meteorite is a meteor that lands on Earth. Up in the sky, they are called meteors."

"It could be a meteorite," Alex argued.

"Maybe, but not until it officially hits the earth," Emily insisted. "That's why they call this a meteor shower."

"Ethan, do you agree with Emily's scientific assessment?" said Alex, trying to draw him into the conversation.

"She's rarely wrong about anything," said Ethan, with a hint of humor.

"I know someone else that is rarely wrong," said Alex, glancing at Kate.

"Rarely? More like never," said Kate.

Ethan laughed at their exchange, which comforted Alex. This had been the first year that they had been able to convince Ethan to join them on the sailboat, or any family trip for that matter. The idea to adopt his brother's children quickly fizzled when Ethan and Kevin had arrived in Maine. The sudden death of their parents during the pandemic had firmly attached them to Alex's parents. The situation was complicated, especially in the aftermath of the pandemic, and the Fletchers didn't see any reason to disturb what little stability and family dynamic the children had left. Alex's parents remained the legal guardians, eventually adopting Ethan and Kevin in 2015, when they could finally obtain the proper paperwork and affidavits from the State of Colorado.

They lived with Tim and Amy Fletcher on an isolated farm near Limerick, Maine, thirty-two miles west of Scarborough. Alex had purchased a large parcel of lakefront property and built a custom-designed, sustainable home for them, with the idea that the farm would serve as the Fletcher family stronghold if another disaster or pandemic ever hit Maine. Alex and his clan spent at least two days a week at the farm in the summer, helping with the massive garden, which required constant attention. Over the course of five years, the two families had turned the twenty-acre parcel of land into a self-sustainable family compound.

"Is Kevin looking forward to starting middle school?" Kate asked.

"He seems pretty excited," said Ethan.

Alex met her glance, but didn't hold it. Their relationship with Kevin had been strained since he arrived with his brother in Maine, playing a major role in the decision to abandon the original plan to adopt their orphaned nephews. Kevin had been openly hostile toward them from the start, which had been an understandable reaction to the loss of his parents. Alex didn't need to read the latest "post-pandemic" psychology articles to understand what Kevin might be experiencing. He was well versed in the broad spectrum of emotions and symptoms related to post-traumatic stress disorder.

A brilliant streak flashed across the dark blue sky, just above the tree line to the northeast.

"There's the first one!" said Alex.

"Where?" Kate snapped. "You're full of shit. I was watching the whole time."

"You see, kids, that's why you shouldn't drink underage. You lose your ability to see meteors," said Alex.

Emily looked at Alex. "Mom isn't underage."

"Really? She doesn't look a day over twenty to me," said Alex.

Kate slapped his shoulder. "Your dad—Uncle Alex, is truly full of—"

"Don't say it, Mom!" yelled Emily and Ethan at the same time.

"I meant twenty years old in the dark. In broad daylight you're clearly thirty."

"Nice recovery. You were about to get a stale beer hat," she said, lifting one of the empty beer bottles over his head. "There's one!" she said, pointing. "Move your chairs, kids. They come out of Perseus Constellation. You can barely see it above the trees. The quicker we each spot one, the sooner we can get away from these mosquitos."

"We're catching the tail end of the shower, so it might take a while," said Alex.

Just as he finished his sentence, two near simultaneous flashes traversed the sky, appearing to head west over the coast of Maine. He was surprised that they had seen this many in such a short period of time. The Perseids typically peaked one week earlier, as the earth passed through the densest part of a debris field left by the comet Swift-Tuttle, on its 133-year orbital journey around the sun.

"That's it for me. You can watch the rest of the show from the boat if you don't mind being eaten alive," said Kate, putting an end to the land portion of their evening.

"It just started," said Alex.

Kate shook her head. "It's past midnight, and I'm done. We'll have to get out a week earlier next year."

Ten minutes later, they plied the calm, moonlit waters on an eight-foot, inflatable rubber dinghy, pushed through the silky black cove by a four-horsepower, outboard motor kept at low throttle. Alex loved navigating the dinghy at night, relying on little more than instinct to bring them back to their sailboat, a dark mass anchored in the middle of the tight cove.

They never bothered to display their anchor light in this snug harbor. Aside from the occasional late arrival in the anchorage, the cove in the northwest corner of the island was protected from marine traffic on all sides, except for its entrance. Any boats entering the cove at night would proceed cautiously enough to spot a boat anchored in these waters. Nine boats now lay at anchor within it, and only the two larger sailboats near the entrance displayed mast lights.

Alex pulled the motor's tiller into his body, taking the dinghy to the right of an illuminated luxury powerboat. They slid past the boat at a distance of fifty feet, giving the occupants as much privacy as possible. Inside the topside cabin, Alex could see four adults watching television. As they pulled astern of the monstrous cabin cruiser, he heard raucous laughter ripple across the water.

They came all this way to watch a stupid sitcom. What a waste.

Watching television or movies was not on the Fletchers' list of permitted activities once they left the mooring field back in South Portland. The boat's digital navigation plotter was the only screen onboard, and it didn't stream a damn thing other than their current GPS coordinates. Kate and Alex insisted that everyone unplug on these trips, with the exception of e-readers. Reading, in any offline format, was highly encouraged. Card games were unavoidable. And conversation was compulsory. Sailing had little to do with the destination for the Fletchers, and everything to do with reconnecting as a family in a natural environment. Sparsely inhabited islands, pristine beaches, quiet coves and mesmerizing sunsets took them all down a notch, closer to their true nature, which was quickly obscured by the multitude of electronic devices and distractions that ruled their lives back on land.

He eased the dinghy alongside the *Katelyn Ann* and placed the throttle in neutral, grabbing the nearest rail to keep them from drifting away. Ethan stood up and gripped the toe rail with both hands, walking the dinghy back to the fixed swim platform a few feet away along the boat's stern. He helped Alex keep the dinghy in place as Kate and Emily stepped on the swim deck and entered the cockpit area.

"Thanks, Ethan. I appreciate the help," said Alex warmly. "I'm glad you decided to come along on the trip."

"I'm glad I came too. This is really cool. Kevin would really like this," said Ethan, stepping onto the platform.

"We'll get everyone out next year, before college starts," said Alex.

He tied the dinghy's bow line to one of the cleats attached to the stern of the boat and climbed onboard, surprisingly tired from a day of leisure. Being out on the water always drained a good portion of his energy, especially during the first few days of any trip. Even in calm weather, the constant movement of the boat took its toll, readying him for bed at sunset. Glancing at his watch, he saw that it was at least an hour past his nautical bedtime. He turned and stared into the northeast sky, hoping to catch another meteor. Nothing.

"Who's planning to sleep under the stars and watch the Perseids?" Alex asked.

"Not me," said Kate. "The mosquitos got enough of my blood tonight. Wake me if the meteors really pick up, and I might watch from inside the cabin."

"Emily?"

"No way. Your mosquito net contraption doesn't work," said Emily.

"Ethan?"

"Don't let him talk you into it, Ethan," Emily said. "You'll be eaten alive unless you bury yourself in the bag. Then you'll overheat. It's a lose-lose situation. Seriously."

"It's really not that bad. The net covers your face, and as long as you stay tucked in the sleeping ba—"

"I think I'll trust the women on this one," said Ethan, stepping into the cabin.

"Smart man. The earlier you start listening to them, the better," said Alex, swatting at the swarm that had already found them.

"I heard that," said Kate. "Close the hatch, Ethan. If he wants to sleep outside, he can keep the mosquitos to himself."

Alex stared into the sky. "The love is gone."

A few moments later, the screen door opened, and his sleeping bag was dumped into the cockpit, along with a water bottle and a can of bug spray.

"The netting is inside the bag. How can you say the love is gone?" she said, quickly closing the screen door.

"Don't I get a kiss?"

Kate pressed her lips against the screen, and he gave her a quick kiss through the thin plastic mesh. He turned his head and pushed his cheek against the barrier, feeling the warmth of her face.

"I love you," he whispered.

"I love you more," she replied.

They held their faces together for a few moments before Kate pulled away from the cabin door.

"I can see the mosquitos swarming your head. Good luck out there."

"You're gonna miss the show," he protested, swatting at his arms.

"Not worth the price of admission. Holler if you need anything else, like a blood transfusion," she said, eliciting laughter from the cabin.

"I'll be fine. I have a plan."

"Just don't fall overboard, okay? I do not feel like taking a midnight swim."

He smiled and went to work. A few minutes later, he nestled into a sleeping bag suspended over the cockpit by a hammock. He lay still for a moment, trying to gauge whether the contraption would work. Previous attempts to hang the hammock had resulted in a series of spectacularly embarrassing failures he didn't care to repeat. Suddenly striking the fiberglass deck at two in the morning was guaranteed to provoke laughter and a well-deserved string of "I told you so's." He'd tested the new hammock arrangement at their club mooring with a few mid-afternoon naps and felt that tonight would mark a new era in sleeping comfort aboard the *Katelyn Ann*.

He adjusted his arms inside the sleeping bag and contemplated the empty cockpit. This would be the first time he had slept out here alone. Ryan never turned down an opportunity to sleep outdoors, especially on the boat. Before the hammock idea took hold, they slept opposite each other on the cockpit benches, watching the stars and talking for hours, mosquitos be damned. He was going to miss having Ryan around.

The faint red strobe light of a high-altitude aircraft distracted him from the thought. Travelling in a northeasterly direction, he assumed it was a red-eye flight bound for Europe. Alex could barely separate the aircraft's lights from the growing field of stars superimposed against the velvety black sky.

Through his peripheral vision, he could tell that the western horizon held stubbornly to a thin cerulean blue aura. He resisted the temptation to look, instead keeping his eyes focused on the Perseid radiant rising above the shadowy rock cliffs that formed the eastern side of the cove. Later in the night, the Perseid radiant would drift over the mouth of the cove and continue west, remaining in full view from their anchorage. As long as the evening's prevailing winds continued to blow from the southeast, the boat's position in the water would afford him with a continuous, unobstructed view of the meteor shower.

The sound of a distant motorboat competed with the lapping water, growing stronger until the ugly racket dominated the cove. Sound travelled deceptively far across the water, with surprisingly little deterioration. The deep rumble reached its peak and faded south, as the fast-moving vessel navigated the narrow pass between Jewell and Cliff Islands and sped toward Portland.

An arc of light raced across the sky, burning brilliantly for the briefest moment. He counted two more streaks of light before the distant hum of the motorboat evaporated, enveloping Alex in the absolute silence he would enjoy for the rest of the night. His hammock rocked gently in the light breeze as he waited patiently for the next piece of cosmic dust to strike Earth's atmosphere, unaware that his breathing had slowed and his eyes had drifted shut.

Chapter 3

EVENT -02:53 Hours

Xinjiang Uyghur Autonomous Region
People's Republic of China

Deputy Station Director Tin Jianyu raced his fingers over the plasma keyboard, pausing only to swipe at images on the 65-inch, paper-thin, curved OLED-T screen wrapped halfway around his station. He added a few more strings of code and raised his hand a few inches away from the screen, hesitant to drag the folder to its cyber destination in his centralized directory. He'd run out of ideas, and if this didn't work, nothing would. He "hooked" the folder and moved it. Gone. A few more keystrokes and—nothing.

"Damn it. They must have physically separated the controls," said Tin.

"How could they have done that? The whole station is connected," said Fan Huning, his direct subordinate within the cyber warfare section.

"They must have designed the station like this. I haven't found a single connection to Zhen's office," said Tin.

"How did we miss this?"

"We never looked for it. Zhen played us like a sheet of music to the very end."

"And there's no way to override the elevator controls?" said Fan.

"Same problem. I can't find a single outgoing connection that gives me access to the elevator system root directory," said Tin.

"The security station? They have direct feeds to the cameras in the elevator. I've seen them panning the cameras. There has to be a connection that can be exploited."

Tin shook his head. He had already thought of this. The security camera feeds were wirelessly linked to the security station servers, and presumably

Zhen's private office, but attempts to piggyback the wireless signal only led back to the security servers. Either Zhen wasn't watching the camera feeds, or he had his own camera feeds from a separate hardwire connection to the elevator. Either way, Tin had exhausted all options to access the elevators at this point.

They were trapped four hundred and fifty feet below the surface, with no way to escape. All they could do at this point was hope for mercy from the lunatics that had dreamed up Red Dragon. He wasn't optimistic. The information he discovered, while sifting through ultrasecret, highest-level government communiqués, painted a very bleak picture of their survival.

A brief "eyes only" message to the Centralized Military Commission from a Second Artillery Corp liaison embedded in the National Space Agency had piqued his attention. The message itself was purely administrative, containing nothing suspicious; however, reference to Red Dragon in a Second Artillery Corps communiqué seemed out of place.

The Second Artillery Corps controlled China's nuclear arsenal, and had never been connected to Red Dragon in any of the ultrasecret meetings he had attended with Director Zhen. With his curiosity raised, he dug deeper within the Second Artillery Corps servers, discovering that a ten-kiloton nuclear device had been delivered to the National Space Agency several months ago. More untraceable snooping yielded a nasty secret that had effectively doomed them from the beginning. Cyber Station Three's two-year mission wasn't the most insidious aspect of Red Dragon.

"We could package up what we've found and bury copies on multiple outside servers, with time-release instructions. We force them to let us out of here, or their secret will be exposed," said Fan.

"They've already shut us down. We're cut off from the surface," said Tin.

"What are you talking about? They're still doing their jobs," said Fan, motioning his hand toward the concentric circle of frantic workstations.

"I think we've been interacting with mimic servers for the past twenty-four hours. Cases continue to stream in at the same rate, but we haven't interacted with a new network or server since yesterday around this same time," said Tin.

"When were you planning to let me in on this discovery? We could have forced Zhen to take us out of here," hissed Fan.

"I discovered it accidentally about ten minutes ago, when I tried to access a private server used by some hackers I know. These guys can design code that makes my stuff look amateur. I thought I might turn to them for ideas. I couldn't reach the server—or any new server."

"What about taking control of the mimic servers? Look for something there? They have to be talking to the outside world," said Fan.

"I doubt it. For all we know, the mimic server farm could be located right above us, hardwired to the station—or connected by satellite to another cyber warfare station thousands of miles away. Either way, it will be isolated from the real Internet."

"So that's it? We just wait for them to pull the plug on this place?" said Fan.

"Unless we can force open the elevator doors and try to climb out of here. I don't think the security section will react very well to that plan."

"Maybe it's time we told everyone the truth about this place, including security. Let them make up their own minds. The security people have families too. Nobody wants to wait around here to die."

Tin touched the screen and tapped a code into the window to unlock its contents.

"According to security protocols, any individual, unauthorized attempt to leave the station will be stopped using a combination of lethal and nonlethal measures. Any attempts to leave the station involving more than one person will be immediately met with lethal force. If any single attempt, or combination of attempts, creates an unresolvable evacuation caucus among station personnel, release of a nonpersistent, lethal nerve agent is authorized at the discretion of the security chief," recited Tin from the screen. "They've planned for this."

"We killed ourselves by sharing this with Zhen."

"We were dead as soon as we stepped off the elevator two years ago," said Tin.

Before Fan could respond, a screen activated in the bottom left corner of his wraparound screen. Tin quickly dragged it into the middle.

"Security feed for the elevator?" asked Fan.

"Yes. Looks like Zhen is returning to the station."

"Maybe we let our imaginations get the best of us."

"We'll know shortly," Tin said resolutely.

They watched the screen for several seconds, observing Director Zhen's impassive, unchanging face as the elevator descended. From his workstation, Tin could hear the elevator machinery humming from the doors located in a small vestibule next to the security room.

"Maybe this is a fake feed too," said Fan.

"He always looks like that," responded Tin.

Tin's hopes faded when he heard the elevator doors open in the vestibule. Zhen had never directly accessed the cyber-operations level using the elevator. It was against security protocol. Expecting a tight formation of black-clad commandos to fan out from the hallway, he was surprised to see Zhen emerge alone. The director lumbered toward them, carrying something dark and heavy on his back. Olive-drab shoulder straps tugged mercilessly against Zhen's dust-coated, black suit jacket. Second Artillery Corps had contributed heavily to Operation Red Dragon. Tin relaxed his shoulders and took a deep breath before asking his last question.

"Did you know from the beginning?"

Zhen shook his head slowly and raised his right hand, which held a gray "dead man" trigger mechanism.

"I should have known. I'm sorry, Tin," said Zhen, opening his right hand.

Chapter 4

Comprehensive Nuclear-Test-Ban Treaty
Organization Headquarters
Vienna, Austria

Romy Nadel took a sip of steaming coffee and leaned back in her chair. As the International Data Centre's (IDC) lead analyst, one of her primary duties entailed preparing the previous day's Reviewed Event Bulletin (REB), which compiled all of the IDC's confirmed and corrected seismic or acoustic events for distribution to member states. Once approved, data from the Reviewed Event Bulletin was automatically screened by the IDC's mainframe system to determine whether the event was natural or manmade.

The automated criteria used to differentiate events had been agreed upon by member states during the ratification phase of the treaty, eliminating any possible accusation of bias against the organization should a violation occur. The IDC simply collected, compiled and disseminated raw data. What the member states did with the information was their own business.

She was seconds away from approving the weekend's report when an "Event Alert" window appeared in the lower right-hand corner of her flat-screen monitor. Events meeting the criteria for immediate review were extremely rare, usually the result of an isolated meteorite strike or massive earthquake with unusual characteristics. The software classifying worldwide events kept these intrusions to a minimum. Her videoconferencing software activated less than a second later, opening another window. Walter Bikel's caustic, angular face appeared in the upper left corner of her screen.

"Romy, have you seen the alert data?" he asked.

"No. It just popped up on my screen," she replied, opening the alert window.

"Magnitude 4.7. Estimated 4-5 kiloton explosion at Lop Nur," he said.

"Hold on. Let me take a look."

Nadel saw several other videoconference requests appear on her screen below the initial data assessment. She ignored them and concentrated on the neatly packaged seismic information. The data screen showed initial waveform patterns with a software generated assessment of the cause. Walter was right. China had apparently violated the nuclear-test-ban treaty.

Fast moving P-waves were off the chart compared to the slower moving S-waves, indicating an explosion or sudden detonation of some kind. They couldn't officially rule out a large meteorite strike, but the geographic epicenter left little doubt in her mind as to the cause of the explosion. Lop Nur had served as China's only nuclear testing facility for nearly forty years. The Chinese government issued a formal moratorium on nuclear testing in 1996, the day after conducting their forty-fifth and supposedly final nuclear test. The site had been quiet for twenty-three years, which struck her as odd. They had no intelligence to suggest the Chinese were in the process of renewing their nuclear testing program. Why would they suddenly detonate a nuclear device?

"This doesn't make any sense," Nadel said. "Maybe they had an accidental detonation. The Chinese keep a sizeable weapons stockpile at Lop Nur."

"Seismic data suggests that the explosion occurred deep underground. They don't keep their stockpiled weapons underground. Nobody does," said Bikel.

"I know; I'm being optimistic. Sorry to cut you off, but I need to make a few calls," said Nadel.

"I imagine you do. Good luck."

Romy Nadel disconnected the videoconference and dialed the International Data Centre's direct line, bracing herself for a busy day.

Chapter 5

EVENT: -00:04 Hours

USS Gravely (DDG107)
Norfolk Naval Base, Virginia

Chief Fire Controlman Warren Jeffries took a long swig of bitter coffee from a worn USS *Gravely* travel mug and stared at the unchanging console screen. Three hours until one of Destroyer Squadron Twenty-Two's teams arrived and resumed responsibility for this watch, allowing his sailors a much-needed break before the start of the work week. As Atlantic Fleet's designated Launch On Remote (LOR) Homeland Ballistic Missile Defense (HBMD) platform, *Gravely* maintained a continuous state of readiness to fire her RIM-161 Standard Missile Three (SM-3) shipboard missiles at ballistic missile threats to key infrastructure assets in Washington, D.C. With an operational range of three hundred miles, the Block IIB version carried onboard *Gravely* could conceivably protect New York City.

Chief Jeffries stepped away from the console manned by Fire Controlman Clark and sat down at a deactivated console station several feet away to rest his eyes for a few seconds. The watch required two qualified fire controlmen, who would conduct last-minute checks and sound the appropriate shipboard alarms in the unlikely event that *Gravely*'s weapons and sensors were remotely co-opted by the Missile Defense Agency. Aside from running system diagnostic checks every two hours, they did little more than keep each other awake. Jeffries settled into a deeply relaxing state, letting the hum of the Combat Information Center's active equipment lull him perilously close to sleep.

"Chief, I think we have something," said Petty Officer Clark from the designated C2BMC console.

"What is it? Another system-wide test? Always at five in the goddamned morning," said Jeffries, opening his eyes and reaching for his coffee mug.

"No. This looks—holy shit! Missiles away in thirty seconds!"

"Bullshit. Get out of that chair," said Jeffries.

He barely waited for Clark to vacate the seat before jamming his slightly oversized body into the fixed chair to scan the display.

"Son of a mother! Activate the general alarm and read this over the 1-MC," he said, unclipping a laminated card from the console and handing it to the petty officer.

"When you're done with that, get over to the VLS console and make sure the birds are ready. I'll take care of the Aegis array. Go!"

Missiles started to cycle out of the forward Vertical Launch System before either of them had completed their diagnostic checks, shaking the ship's superstructure. Buried deep within the ship, inside the Combat Information Center, they barely heard each successive launch over the piercing shrill of the ship's general alarm. Jeffries ran back to the console to see if the C2BMC system had given them any further information regarding the threat that continued to drain his ship's SM3 missiles. Glancing at the screen, his first thought was that somebody or something had fucked up big time.

None of the data made sense. The missiles would arc into a western trajectory to intercept a target identified by the PAVE PAWS (Phased Array Warning System) station at Beale Air Force Base in California. Not a typical threat trajectory for the East Coast. One target parameter stood out as terminally flawed. Target speed. His Mach 7.88 missiles had been sent to intercept a target moving at Mach 58. This had to be a mistake. Russian's most updated ICBMs topped out at Mach 23. He wasn't even sure if *Gravely*'s AEGIS system could provide terminal guidance to intercept a target moving this fast. It really didn't matter, because it was out of his hands.

The missiles stopped firing, and he ran to the active AEGIS tracking console, still shocked to see the digital representations of his missiles streaking west over Virginia to intercept a track originating from the southwest. Not a single BMD training scenario had involved a missile threat from that direction.

Thirteen missiles had been fired without "skin on track" by *Gravely*'s AN/SPY-1D phased array radar, meaning that the ship's radar had not acquired the target. The C2BMC system would guide the missiles until *Gravely*'s powerful sensors picked up the track. At that point, the ship's fire control system would provide terminal guidance to ensure that each missile's Light Exo-Atmospheric Projectile (LEAP) collided with the threat.

The entry hatch to CIC flew open, spilling a panicked contingent of crewmembers into the dimly lit space. Dressed in the digital blue camouflage-patterned navy working uniform, *Gravely*'s command duty officer, Lieutenant Mosely, pushed the first sailors out of the way and ran to Jeffries.

"What the fuck just happened?"

"Our ship remote launched thirteen SM-3s at an inbound target identified by C2. It's moving Mach fifty-eight out of the southwest. That's all I know, sir," said Chief Jeffries.

"You mean Mach five point eight," corrected the officer.

"No, Lieutenant. Fifty-eight. Have you called the captain?"

The lieutenant glanced around for a second, clearly confused by the entire situation. Jeffries could understand the officer's hesitation. Less than a minute ago, the ship had been quiet. Within the span of forty-five seconds, *Gravely* had autofired thirteen antiballistic missiles, and they had very little information. For all any of them knew, they could be on the verge of a full-scale nuclear war.

"I'll call him right now. Are you talking to anyone at IMD?"

"Not yet. We barely got our checks done before the missiles launched," said Jeffries, turning to type into the BMD console.

"Get IMD on the line. They're running the show."

"I'm on it, sir. Petty Officer Clark, start making calls to the Integrated Missile Defense command. Get me anyone that knows what's going on. Numbers are on the card," said the chief.

He stood up from his chair and turned to the half-dozen sailors hovering near the hatch. "The rest of you get out of here!"

Two minutes later, Chief Jeffries and Fire Controlman Ben Clark watched the AEGIS display in horror as *Gravely*'s missiles disappeared one by one over central Virginia. *Gravely*'s fire control system acquired and tracked the target for nine seconds before it vanished in the vicinity of Richmond, Virginia.

"That wasn't a missile, sir," said the chief.

"What are you saying, Chief? Hold on, Captain," said the lieutenant, covering the phone's mouthpiece.

"Radar cross section was ninety-six thousand," he said, his voice trailing off in disbelief.

He still couldn't process his emotions. Everything had happened too fast. Repeating the radar cross section brought a single emotion to the surface. Fear. His family lived ten miles from here, in the direction of Richmond. His vision narrowed, and he barely heard the lieutenant's reply.

"Meters? That can't be right," said the officer, walking toward the AEGIS console. He glanced at the data over the chief's shoulder and shook his head.

"We have to get IMD on the line, Chief!" yelled Lieutenant Mosely.

"Captain, Chief Jeffries just confirmed that the target had a radar cross section over ninety thousand. Something has to be wrong. That would put the diameter over three hundred meters!"

Jeffries waited for the lieutenant to continue, but heard nothing. He looked up at the officer, who pressed his ear against the receiver and squinted.

"Captain? Can you hear me? Chief, I think my call—"

He was interrupted by a complete and sudden darkness. The Combat Information Center went dead for a second before bulkhead-mounted, battery-powered LED "battle lanterns" started to provide illumination. The eerie silence continued.

"Shore power's out. We should get power from one of the generators in a few seconds," said the lieutenant.

Ten seconds elapsed, yielding no change to the eerie silence.

"I think we lost more than shore power," said the chief, starting to get out of his seat to help Petty Officer Clark with the communications console.

Before he reached Clark, the entire ship slid laterally, knocking everyone inside to the metal grated deck. A severe rumbling enveloped CIC for several seconds, followed by silence. Jeffries grabbed onto Clark's seat and began to pull himself to his feet when a panicked voice filled the darkened space.

"CDO, they need you on the quarterdeck!"

Chief Jeffries stood up and walked with Lieutenant Mosely toward the hatch, but stopped when the metal beneath his feet shuddered again. Once the ship settled, he unsheathed a powerful LED flashlight from his belt and illuminated the doorway, finding a wide-eyed Hispanic woman in dark blue *Gravely* sweatpants and a white T-shirt. She wore an expression of terror.

"What happened?" asked Mosely.

"Norfolk Naval Base is on fire—and the ship broke free of the pier."

Chief Jeffries stared at her with disbelief. All he could think about was his wife and two teenagers.

Chapter 6

Jewell Island, Maine

Alex buried his head in the sleeping bag.

Now what?

He peeked out of the bag, expecting to find Kate standing over him with a flashlight. It wouldn't be the first time. The island reflected a rich, sunset-orange hue. Long shadows extended from the trees and clumps of rocks along the granite walls. A strange tingling sensation enveloped him.

Lightning!

He rolled out of the hammock, still encased in the sleeping bag, striking the fiberglass deck. He ripped frantically at the zipper, unable to get out of the polyester body bag. A glimpse of the sky eased his panic. The sky bristled with stars, hardly a meteorological condition conducive to lightning. He lay there for a few moments.

More nightmares? Shit. Back to counseling.

He took a deep breath and gave the zipper another try. When it didn't move, he tore it open.

"Problem fucking solved," he muttered, slipping out of the bag and kicking it aft.

He stood up on the cockpit bench and squinted.

What the hell?

Either the sun had risen in the wrong place, or the fall from the hammock had knocked him silly. Alex had spent enough time at anchor in this cove to orient himself without a compass. He scanned his surroundings one more time to be sure.

His boat pointed southeast, pulling lazily against the anchor line. A typical early morning setup at Jewell Island. The cove's narrow opening lay directly off the port side, and the *Katelyn Ann* faced directly into a tree-lined, rocky cliff. The sun always rose over that cliff, but today it appeared due

23

south, hidden behind the tallest part of the island. He watched as the distant light rapidly faded to reveal something more ominous.

A brilliant, undulating reddish glow appeared in the southwestern sky, high above the visible horizon. He closed his eyes and shook his head, seriously wondering if he might have a head injury. Nothing he had felt or seen since opening his eyes this morning seemed normal. Of course, he assumed it was still morning.

He checked his watch: 5:01 AM. Sunrise was at 5:50. Morning Nautical Twilight began twenty minutes ago. He looked over his shoulder toward the east and could see a slight difference between the blackness above and the sky showing between the trees. The sun was rising where it should.

That's a good start.

He turned back to the surreal lightshow to the west. The reddish-purple spectacle changed shape and appeared to pulse over the entire southwest horizon. He'd seen this before. He shook his head.

"No way," he said, knowing there was only one way to find out.

Alex stepped aft, positioning himself behind the wheel where he could see the boat's magnetic compass dial. He pressed a button on the center console to illuminate the compass, and pressed it again.

Shit.

He took a small LED flashlight out of his pocket and jabbed at the on/off control. A shaky light bathed the compass, bringing the nightmare to life. The compass direction moved slowly from the direction of the fading, red aurora toward what he knew to be the right cardinal settings.

Not good at all.

He fumbled to activate the digital chart plotter and navigation system mounted above the wheel. Nothing. He thought about calling out to Kate, but reached for the engine ignition panel instead. He turned the key, not sure what would happen. The engine sputtered for a moment and started.

"All right. All right. That's a good sign," he mumbled.

The forty-horsepower Yanmar diesel engine hummed, vibrating the cockpit and shattering the cove's tranquility. He pulled the kill lever, secure in the knowledge that they could reach the Portland Harbor without getting wet.

A light from the forward berth illuminated the cabin, flickering back and forth as the source drew closer to the cabin door. He stepped forward in the tight cockpit to intercept Kate at the screen door. Woken by the unexpected engine start, she would no doubt be in a hurry to investigate. The door slid open just as he arrived.

"Why did you start—"

"Shhhh," he said, putting a hand out to stop her. "Let's talk out here."

"Did we slip anchor?" she asked, shining the light in his face.

"Not in my face, please. We're right where we should—"

"Something is wrong with the lights."

She was in rapid-fire mode, no doubt brought on by her sudden maritime wake up. Kate was a notoriously deep sleeper at home, who did not respond well to being jarred awake. On the boat she was an entirely different person. She understood the fluid nature of boating, which required quick decisions and immediate action. Boats slipped anchorages, storms arrived unannounced, and equipment failed—often in the middle of the night, and always at the least opportune time.

"Are you done?" he asked.

"You haven't really answered any of my questions," she said.

Alex pulled Kate through the cockpit door and pointed to the bright red and purple aura to the west.

"What do you think that is?" he asked.

She stared off into the distance, shaking her head slowly before finally shrugging her shoulders. "Looks like the northern lights, but the wrong color. But that's not north, is it?" she asked, finally rubbing her eyes and yawning.

"Southwest," he stated, gripping her hand.

"Why did you start the diesel?" she insisted, her gaze captivated by the lights dancing playfully above the southwestern horizon.

"Because I didn't think it would start. I've seen pictures like that at Quantico. Looks a lot like the atmospheric nuclear tests they did out in the Pacific," he said.

"You don't think that was a nuke, do you?" she asked sharply, stepping off the cockpit bench.

"I don't know, but I saw a massive flash of light from the south," he said, pointing to the island off the starboard side, "then I felt a strange tingling, like I was about to get hit by lightning. Now none of our electronics work. I'd say we were hit by an EMP."

Kate pushed his hand away and descended the cabin steps. Alex heard her try to activate the VHF marine radio at the navigation table.

"The radio is dead. So is everything else at the nav station."

"All of the navigation gear is either connected to the radio antenna or the GPS receiver—all located at the top of our mast. An EMP wave would travel right down the wire and fry everything," he said.

Kate directed the flashlight at his face.

"Will you stop blinding me with that damn light?"

"I'm sure you'll be fine," Kate said. "Have you checked the portable electronics?"

"Not yet. I'm going to see if I can restore electrical power to the lights and a few other systems."

"I wouldn't worry about the lights. It's almost dawn. Get the water pumps and the head working. What about the bilge pump?" Kate said.

"It's hardwired to the battery bank, like the engine. Should be fine, but let's check."

Alex waited for Kate to gather the handheld electronics from a cabinet above the navigation table and move to the small couch across from Emily's bed. Their daughter had begun to stir, but still remained asleep. He really hoped she would stay asleep until they figured out what was going on. They needed a little more time to think before adding a panicky teenager to the mix.

He illuminated the electrical panel and noticed that all of the breaker switches had been tripped. No surprise there. He flipped all of the switches and tried the light mounted to the navigation table. Nothing. He knew it wouldn't be that easy. The electrical surge generated by an EMP didn't give surge protectors or breakers time to react to the change in current.

Beyond the microwave oven, radio and the navigation equipment, most of the gear connected to the boat's electrical system didn't contain any of the sensitive microchips susceptible to an amplified EMP wave. If the breaker mechanism itself had been damaged, they would have to do without the electrical system on the return trip to Portland.

"I'm pretty sure the breaker is fried. We'll have to use the manual pumps to draw water. As for the head, I'm not sure what we can do. I don't think it works without electricity," he whispered.

"Not a big deal. We're not that far from Portland. The handheld stuff seems to work fine. Can you tell if we are getting a signal?" she said, holding up the illuminated GPS plotter screen toward him.

"Let's see," he said, taking the unit.

The small satellite icon in the upper right corner of the screen indicated that the unit was receiving a satellite signal. He navigated through a series of onscreen menus to get more information.

"It says we're tracking six satellites. That's good news. See if you can pick up anything on the radio. Let's take this topside so we don't wake the kids," he said.

Kate followed Alex up the steps and into the cockpit, where a refreshingly cool sea breeze greeted them, evaporating the small beads of sweat that had formed on Alex's forehead in defiance of the chilly, coastal air. Despite his demeanor, he was terrified by the prospect of what might lie ahead for them. If something big had indeed gone wrong, he had little doubt that society would quickly collapse. Confidence in the government's ability to handle a major crisis was at an all-time low.

The 2013 flu pandemic had exposed the nation's essential service infrastructure to a slow burn, which caused a rapid, critical failure across the board, launching the country into chaos. While the northernmost states and the upper Midwest had added freezing temperatures and winter storms to the disaster already unfolding, the warmer regions were hit the hardest. The harsh winter weather dampened and eventually extinguished the widespread rioting, looting and violence that continued unabated in cities like Atlanta, Dallas, and Los Angeles. Even the Mid-Atlantic cities saw their share of the devastating civil unrest that ultimately claimed just as many lives as the H16N1 virus.

Not much had changed on Capitol Hill. The likelihood of another pandemic virus striking in our lifetime was a statistical impossibility claimed the epidemiologists—and they were probably right. Funding for national emergency preparedness remained level and consistent with pre-2013 levels, with few politicians willing to suggest cuts, especially with over twenty-six million deaths attributable to the inadequate pandemic preparedness budget authorized by Congress in the years leading to the Jakarta Pandemic. Of course, with the U.S. economy making slow but steady gains, even fewer politicians were eager to increase disaster preparedness funding or spend money on infrastructure improvement programs. Major natural disasters had been shrugged off for decades, given a flurry of attention for a month and pushed to the sidelines.

Alex and Kate understood that the United States could not weather another nationwide disaster, and had taken the appropriate precautions to ensure the safety of family and friends. They would all converge on the isolated farm in Limerick, Maine, where they could live off the grid indefinitely, until society settled back into a routine.

Alex considered the flash of light. It had come from a different direction than the red aura. Was it possible that the United States had been attacked with nuclear weapons? One flash. That was all he had seen. He expanded the scale on the handheld GPS plotter to make a quick calculation. He created a waypoint over Boston and started the navigation function. The system plotted a straight course from the boat to the waypoint.

Standing in the open cockpit of their boat, staring at the blood-red aura, his vision narrowed. He sat down next to Kate and took a deep breath.

"We have to get back fast. I give it two, maybe three days before all hell breaks loose in Boston. We need to get Ryan out of there," said Alex.

Kate sighed. "If it hasn't been nuked."

He stood up and compared what he saw on the GPS chart to their physical orientation in the cove.

"The flash was centered there," he said, pointing his entire hand directly south. "Boston is almost twenty-five degrees to the right of that. A nuke would go off directly over the city. This is somewhere pretty far off Cape Cod," he said, not completely convinced by his logic.

Alex placed the GPS receiver on the top of the cabin and pulled Kate off the bench. He embraced her tightly, but kissed her neck gently. He drew his face even with hers.

"I'm just as scared as you about Ryan. He's going to be fine. We'll get this boat back to Portland, and I'll bring him home, I promise," he said.

She nodded and met his lips for a brief moment, then laid her head on his shoulder.

"I know it'll be fine. We'll be fine," she said, sitting back down and rubbing her face.

"I think we should wait until there's enough light to see the lobster pots on the water. The last thing we need is to tangle the prop and kill the engine. It's 5:09 right now. Sunrise is at 5:50. We get underway fifteen minutes after that. That gives us plenty of time to get our shit together, secure for sea—maybe try to raise someone on the handheld radio. I wish we had one of the satellite phones. If the GPS satellites are still working, maybe the satphone network is still intact," said Alex.

"Remind me why we don't bring a satphone out on the water?" she said.

"Because we don't go far enough out to need one. We never leave Casco Bay."

"I think we need to add that to the required equipment list," Kate said.

"*If* we take another sailing trip, I'll make sure to throw one in the bag."

Kate stood up. "I'll wake the kids and start tidying up below."

The wind picked up, and the boat started to swing on the anchor line to face due south. Alex heard a few trees snap in the distance.

"Get below!" he yelled. "Now!"

Through the clear vinyl window of the dodger, he saw the leading edge of a powerful blast wave explode through the trees. He pushed Kate down the stairs and ducked his head below the cabin overhead moments before a dark wave of rocks and tree limbs pounded the sailboat. The boat lurched sideways with the initial blast, knocking Alex into the galley, where he tumbled to the deck and smashed his elbow against the counter. Within seconds, the debris shower abated, leaving them in absolute silence. The sailboat's hull creaked against something in the water.

"Ethan! You all right back there?" he yelled through the open hatch a few feet away behind the galley.

"I'm fine. What happened? The lights don't work," said Ethan.

"Grab your flashlight and get dressed. I need you out here in thirty seconds. Emily, change in the vee-berth. All hands on deck immediately," Alex ordered. "We have a problem."

"You think?" said Kate.

"You have no idea. We need to go topside to clear the mess and assess damage. We don't have much time."

Kate looked at him quizzically. "I thought we weren't leaving for another hour?"

"I don't think that's an option anymore. Talk about this topside?" he said, pointing at the open hatch at the top of the stairs.

When Alex's head emerged through the cabin hatch, the first thing he noticed was a half-inch-thick layer of dirt covering every horizontal surface in the open cockpit. Rising further, he scraped his head on something solid. He directed his flashlight upward to see a jagged, two-inch-diameter branch protruding above his head, blocking him from climbing the rest of the ladder. He pushed the branch to the right and squeezed through the opening.

"Be careful coming up," he called behind him to Kate.

The branch had speared the left vinyl window of their dodger, stopped by the thick tangle of smaller branches that struck the dodger's dense, aluminum frame. If he hadn't pushed Kate out of the way to get down the ladder, the shredded edge of the branch could have impaled him. He felt dizzy and wanted to take a seat, but there was no time for it. He pushed the near death experience out of his head and stood on the cockpit bench to assess the situation.

His flashlight revealed the rest of the fifteen-foot branch hanging over the starboard side of the boat, straining the sailboat's lifelines. Kate's flashlight probed the port side of the boat.

"I see a few branches and rocks, but nothing else. How's your side?" he asked.

"Same. This branch is the worst of it," she said, directing her light at the torn end protruding through the dodger window. "Jesus," she whispered, touching the sharp edge of the branch.

"Jesus is right," he said, moving quickly aft to the back of the cockpit.

Their gray inflatable dinghy bobbed in the water along the stern, apparently undamaged. He stepped out of the cabin and onto the swim deck, pulling the dinghy next to the boat.

"Can you clear that branch? I need to check the dinghy and start the motor," he called.

"Got it."

He stepped into the dinghy and pressed down on each side of the craft with both hands. The cold plastic exterior gave slightly to the pressure applied, consistent with early morning inflation levels. The boat was undamaged.

"Now for the fun part..." he mumbled, staring at the motor.

He had battled off and on for nearly four years with the four-horsepower, gasoline-fueled contraption, having consigned it to a watery grave on more than one occasion. It should be simple. Open the air vent. Open the fuel valve. Open the choke. Start the engine. That easy. In four years, he could count the number of times it started without incident on his middle finger, which he often lifted to protest the manufacturer. Alex ran through his mental checklist and took a deep breath.

He pulled the starter cord, and the motor caught, puttering quietly at idle. He revved the throttle for a moment, letting the engine warm, before pushing in the choke. The motor continued to idle.

"Shit," he muttered.

Everything had worked perfectly, which meant that he had wasted his one good start of the year on a test. Brilliant. He stopped the motor, leaving everything in position for a quick start. He heard the branch fall away, followed by a quick scream. He flashed his light forward, searching for Kate, but couldn't immediately find her on the deck.

She fell overboard.

Alex jumped onto the swim deck and reached for the Lifesling preserver attached to the starboard rails, when Kate appeared from behind the mast.

"Fucking thing almost took me in with it!" she yelled.

"You all right?" he said.

"I'm fine. A few scratches," she said, starting to walk back along the deck.

"Stay there. I need to check the anchorage," he said.

He made his way forward and met her at the bow.

"We need to talk while I do this," he said, reaching through the forward rails to grip the nylon line stretched into the water several feet below. "That air blast came from the same direction as the flash of light. Took eight minutes to arrive. Only a massive explosion could create something like—"

"Boston," she muttered.

"I'm pretty certain that's not the case. The wind came from the direction of the flash, which puts the explosion in the Gulf of Maine," he said, tugging on the anchor line.

"I hope so."

"Me too, but if the explosion was over water, we could be hit by a tsunami. We need to decide whether to stay onboard and ride out whatever crests the island, or abandon the boat for the concrete lookout tower near the cove."

"I don't think we should leave the boat," Kate decided. "If it gets swept away, we're stuck here."

"I agree, but we have no idea how big the wave will be. Remember those videos of the tsunamis in Thailand and Japan? Solid walls of water travelled inland for miles."

"How long do we have?" Kate asked.

"I'm not sure. If it took the wind eight minutes to get here, I'd guess we have at least another hour? I have no idea. Could be thirty minutes. The anchor feels fine," he said, standing up on the bow. "We might not have a problem at all, honey. From what I remember reading, tsunami waves are barely noticeable out at sea. The problem occurs when the wave hits shallow water. We're several miles from the mainland, and this is a small island. A tiny blip in the ocean for a tsunami. It might not rise up enough to mess with us."

"Then I say we stay on the boat," she said.

"We'll keep the engine running in case we break free of the anchorage," said Alex, starting toward the cockpit.

"If a wave makes it over the island, I don't think the anchor will matter. It might cause a problem for us if it gets snagged on the rocks," she said.

He flashed his light at the anchor line tied to the forward cleat. He couldn't imagine climbing forward to cut the anchor line while the boat pitched violently. They needed a way to detach the anchor if necessary.

"Start securing the boat for heavy seas. I'll run the anchor line back to the cockpit. We can cut it from here. I'm glad you thought of that," he said.

"I'm good for an idea or two," she said, brushing against him on her way back.

"That's one more than I'm good for," he said, grabbing her hand. "We'll be fine, hon. I'll be in Boston tomorrow, picking up Ryan. Nothing to it. We've been through worse."

"I know. I'm just scared for him. He's alone in a new place. No friends. Nothing."

"He knows what to do. Ryan's the least of our worries. He'll probably be waiting for us at the house when we get back," he said.

She buried her head in his chest and didn't respond. The sound of rustling leaves raised her head, and he let go of her to grab the nearest deck-mounted handrail. They wouldn't have time to get into the cabin if another blast wave hit them. A stiff gust of wind buffeted them for a few seconds, swinging the boat on its mooring to face an easterly direction. No flash preceded the airwave, which told Alex that the explosion had occurred over the visible horizon. The only thing due east of Jewell Island was Nova Scotia. When the wind completely died, he stared in the direction of the first explosion, wondering if his plan to stay on the boat would send them to a watery grave.

Chapter 7

International Space Station

Commander David Stull, United States Navy, drifted away from the Harmony node to the adjoining Destiny Laboratory, using his fingertips to guide him. He was several minutes behind the rigid daily schedule imposed by NASA mission controllers, though his effortless flight down the equipment-packed passageway betrayed no sense of urgency. The draconian NASA itinerary served a purpose: to regulate the astronauts' natural biorhythms in the face of a ninety-minute cycle of light and darkness experienced by the station's low earth orbit.

An unresolved communications glitch had put him behind schedule today. The station's connection to NASA had been interrupted during the final moments of their morning briefing and could not be reestablished. His initial diagnostics check indicated no obvious issues with the communications equipment onboard the station. Of course, he wouldn't know for sure unless he inspected the radio link equipment directly, running a series of sophisticated checks on the transmitters. To do that, he would need to enter an unpressurized section of the Z1 Truss structure above the Unite node. This simple thirty-minute voyage into unpressurized space would require an entire day of planning.

He glided into the Destiny node, where Cosmonaut Sergei Moryakov waited. Moryakov's permanent, good-natured smirk was gone. Something was wrong.

"Roscosmos station in Moscow lost all communications with NASA fifteen minutes ago," said the cosmonaut, in perfectly structured Russian-accented English.

"So it's on their end. Saves us the hassle of accessing Z1," said Stull.

"It's more complicated than that. You need to see something," he said, gesturing for Stull to follow him.

Before either of them moved, the lights in the Destiny node flickered. Moryakov's ice-blue eyes darted around the crowded laboratory compartment. In seventy-two days onboard the station, he had never seen the lights flicker—and he'd certainly never seen the Russian exhibit nervous behavior.

He floated behind Moryakov to the Tranquility node berthing connection, tapping the walls to propel his body through the cramped corridor. The short trip ended over the Cupola, the station's seven-window observatory. A pair of legs dressed in a royal-blue jumper extended into the berthing node.

"Take a look. Then we need to talk. We don't have much time," said the Russian.

Commander Stull pushed off the floor with the tip of his boot and flipped upside-down, squeezing into the Cupola next to Cosmonaut Viktor Belekin, who stared through a spotting scope aimed through the center window.

"What the—"

A thick, orange-black smoke trail stretched from the outer stratosphere to the east coast of the United States. From four hundred and sixteen kilometers above the earth's surface, the smoke trail appeared to penetrate a pulsing red magnetic aura that blanketed the Midwest.

He felt nauseous. His wife and children had flown to Boston on Friday, staying with friends for few days until joining his parents on Cape Cod for their annual vacation. The smoke trail ended in New England. His vision narrowed, and he squinted, shaking his head. He was overreacting. Larger meteorites always left massive trails of smoke when they traveled through the atmosphere, even if they were only a few meters in diameter.

"Can I take a look?" asked Stull.

"This is bad, my friend. Very sorry," said Belekin, handing him the powerful scope.

Stull followed the magnified trail across Mexico into the United States. The single inbound object had separated high over northern Georgia, splitting into four tightly packed, but distinctly separate reentry signatures. The smoke trails terminated in a narrow elliptical pattern beginning in

Virginia and ending in Nova Scotia. He couldn't pinpoint the two additional impact points through the atmospheric reentry stream.

He hoped his wife had decided to spend an extra day with friends in Braintree. The Cape was too exposed. Who was he kidding? All they could talk about last week was getting to Cape Cod. How could Spaceguard have missed something this big? Something else bothered him about the scene below him.

"Where are the lights?" he asked.

"I can't believe I missed that," the Russian murmured. "Most of North America is pitch black."

"That's the real problem," interjected Moryakov, hovering above them.

Commander Stull backed out of the Cupola, along with Belekin.

"Our mission control registered a massive radiation flux on the station-based monitors. X-ray levels spiked, causing a minor system-generated EMP. Everything appears to function as it should, so latch-up must have been minimal." Moryakov ran his hand through his hair. "We'll have to run our own diagnostics, of course, and we'll have to go outside to inspect the solar array coatings. Moscow isn't optimistic about the long-term survival of the station."

Stull shook his head. "What do they think happened?"

"All evidence indicates that a thermonuclear device was detonated in low orbit over the United States, causing a massive EMP event. Most of the United States is dark, consistent with this theory," said Moryakov.

Commander Stull stared back into the Cupola, noting the eerie, reddish, spectral glow in the atmosphere over the Midwest.

"The aura," he whispered. "Could it have been caused by whatever passed through the atmosphere?"

Moryakov shook his head. "Radiation readings were highest on the sensors aimed toward the ground. Moscow strongly suspects the radiation is from a manmade source."

"The arrays?"

"Bad timing. All arrays were in Night Glider mode, pointed straight at the earth when the readings spiked. Another eighty-two seconds and they would have been aimed away from the blast, at the sunrise," Moryakov explained.

"We'll have to inspect the coatings for thermomechanical damage," said Stull. "We can't stay up here if the arrays fail."

"That was Moscow's assessment."

"Is everything all right down there?" asked Stull.

"For now," said the Russian.

He didn't like Moryakov's answer.

Chapter 8

Jewell Island, Maine

Alex sat on the starboard side stern rail and stared at the thick stand of trees lining the island's ledge wall. The damage caused by the air blast was fully visible in the crisp, dawn light, mostly confined to broken tree limbs and flattened grass. The cove remained awash with leaves, stirred only by large severed branches that occasionally bumped up against the hull of the *Katelyn Ann*. He listened intently, trying to pick up any sounds beyond the distant, piercing cries of seagulls.

Only the constant, muffled drum of the sailboat's engine competed with the birds, but he had already filtered this sound out. Alex had no idea what he might hear when the tsunami hit, but with two thousand feet of tightly packed island to cross, he figured they would have plenty of warning.

The large cabin cruiser anchored off their starboard side roared to life, causing Alex to jump up from his seat. The overpowered engine steadied into a deafening growl that masked every natural sound in the cove. He hoped they were getting underway. Compared to his forty-horsepower engine, the cabin cruiser's three- to four-hundred-horsepower engine sounded like a commercial jet liner revving for takeoff. He couldn't blame them for running the engine. He was doing the same thing, in case something went terribly wrong at their anchorage, but with the cruiser's engine drowning out his thoughts, he would have to pay close attention to the island and rely on visual cues. They might lose a few seconds of warning, but it shouldn't matter. All he needed to do was get below and shut the cabin door.

Once the wave hit, they would assess and react accordingly. The decision to stay with the boat hadn't been an easy one. The safest course of action would have been to pack up as much gear and food as possible and ride the dinghy to the cove's southwestern shore. From there, a ten-minute walk would put them in one of the island's towering concrete World War Two lookout posts. While assuring their short-term safety, this option almost guaranteed they would lose their transportation off the island. He had considered putting Kate and the kids in the tower and taking his chances alone on the boat, but he had a feeling that the tsunami wasn't going to give him the option to return.

He planned to ride out the initial impact below deck, scrambling topside when the boat settled. He just hoped it wouldn't be too late to react at that point to save the boat. If the boat were dashed against the rocks before he could take control and engage the engine, they would be at the mercy of the elements, forced to swim back to the island.

Alex looked through the cabin hatchway at Kate, who stared back at him, waiting for any sign that the wave was inbound. She wore one of the boat's self-inflating life jackets over khaki pants and a waterproof sailing jacket. Next to her, on the starboard settee, sat a digital camouflage-patterned rucksack tied to an orange type two life preserver. The kids, wearing custom-fit vest preservers, sat across from her in the portside lounge, hugging their own life preserver wrapped backpacks.

They had stuffed most of their food, medical supplies and survival-related gear in five backpacks, affixing the cheap life preservers to keep them afloat. If they had to jump into the water, the packs would be connected to their respective owner by a ten-foot length of parachute cord. They were prepared for the worst-case scenario, which involved losing the boat right in the cove. All of their essential gear was either attached to their bodies or buried in the packs.

He patted his hand against the drop-leg holster on his right hip, making sure that the pistol was tightly secured under two layers of nylon and Velcro straps. Kate hadn't given him a second look when he removed the pistol and holster rig from his rucksack. Before the Jakarta Pandemic, Kate would have ceaselessly berated him for bringing a firearm on a family trip. Now she understood better than anyone that preparation without security was meaningless, especially in the face of a widespread disaster.

The cabin cruiser's engine throttled higher, drawing his attention away from the island one hundred feet away. He watched the thirty-foot boat pull forward while the anchor line retracted, breaking free of the mud surface below the water. A man dressed in white shorts and a red polo shirt steered the craft toward the mouth of the cove, picking up speed before the anchor appeared. He puffed on a fresh cigar from his perch on the boat's flying bridge, saluting Alex as he passed.

The anchor emerged from the surface and banged against the boat's fiberglass hull before snapping into place on the bow-mounted anchor arm. The cabin cruiser increased speed, reaching the mouth of the cove and turning into the narrow confines of the pass between Cliff and Jewell Islands. Alex watched him take the red navigational marker to port and turn sharply. A few seconds later, the cruiser lurched forward at full throttle, leaving a sizeable wake behind as they rocketed southwest, in the direction of Portland Harbor.

Alex was both surprised and relieved that the cruiser's engine started. His sailboat's diesel engine was directly wired to the battery bank and didn't rely on any type of electronics to operate. The cruiser's gas-powered engine was more complicated, and judging by the relatively new look of the boat, he figured that the engine was connected to a series of microprocessors designed to optimize performance. The fact that the gas engine started gave him hope that recent government-sponsored EMP research and assessment efforts hadn't been bullshit.

The EMP Commission's <u>Critical National Infrastructures (CNI) Revised Report</u> released in 2016 took into account the newer, more sensitive technologies present in nearly every electronic device reliant upon a semiconductor. CNI's 2008 report predicted a 10% failure rate for automobiles, which stood in direct contrast to previous predictions by independent researchers and caused considerable outrage. The revised report admitted the difficulty of predicting the effects of an EMP, and raised the failure rate to 60%—still a rosy picture compared to earliest predictions.

Alex, along with preppers everywhere, cast a suspicious eye on the sudden change, wondering if the whole thing was a government ruse to ease fear in the aftermath of their spectacular failure during the Jakarta Pandemic. Trust in the U.S. government reached an all-time low in 2014, and hadn't improved much since.

Jealous of the cruiser's speed through the water, Alex kept his attention fixed on the boat's rapid escape from the cove. They would probably reach Portland in twenty minutes, maybe less. He wondered if they wouldn't be better off doing the same thing. Tsunamis generated most of their power when they arrived in shallow water. Maybe their chances would be better in open water, and not behind an island. He and Kate had studied the nautical charts closely, noting that the depth in Casco Bay didn't vary much from the water off Cape Cod. The depth decreased gradually on the approach to Casco Bay, but not enough to trigger a plunging wave over open water—or so they theorized. Still, they'd decided to stay in place, not really trusting their Google-powered theories enough to risk an open water transit with a possible tsunami inbound. Maybe nothing would happen at all, and they were wasting precious time.

Alex heard a sharp crack, which drew his attention back to the island. He stood up slowly, scanning the trees. Another snap caused him to take a few steps toward the cabin hatch. Staring through the thick foliage at the edge of the island, he saw the tops of tall pines waver and collapse in the distance.

"It's coming," he said, calmly taking position in the hatchway.

"Get inside, Alex," said Kate.

"Hold on…"

He wanted to see what they were up against before dropping below. A cacophony of snaps rapidly approached, followed by an advancing line of fallen treetops.

Any second now.

"Alex!" yelled Kate.

He stole one more glance at the tree line.

A wall of water crashed through the thick pine forest, reaching one-quarter of the way up several mature trees. Alex dropped below and slammed the hatch shut, quickly sitting next to Kate on the starboard settee. A deafening roar filled the cabin, and the boat pitched aft, rising. The kids screamed, and Kate locked her hands around his arm. The sudden wild motion stabilized for a moment; then Alex felt the boat twist to the right. He knew what would happen next.

"Hang on!" he yelled.

The boat heeled more than forty-five degrees to starboard, launching Emily across the cabin into Alex and Kate. Ethan had managed to grip the wooden handrail above him and dangled in mid-air for a moment, before the boat violently heeled to port in response to the sudden change in the craft's stability. He dropped safely onto the cushions below him. Everybody else was unceremoniously tossed onto the wooden deck in a tangle of life preservers and flailing limbs. Alex pulled his way out of the pile, feeling the boat continue to spin while drifting rapidly through the water. He needed to cut the anchor line and take control of the boat immediately.

"I'm going topside! Grab the handrails like Ethan!" he said, stabilizing himself between the kitchen and the navigation table.

He held the side of the wooden steps tightly with one hand and opened the hatch with the other, preparing for the worst. A solid wall of seawater struck the rear of the boat and continued over the stern, filling the spacious cockpit like a bathtub. Alex pushed against the water pouring through the hatch and reached to the right, pulling a serrated diving knife from the hard plastic sheath he had tied to the cleat holding the anchor line. He swept the razor-sharp knife across the taut line. The line snapped through the hole in the dodger made by the tree branch and disappeared over the bow before he could sheath the knife.

Alex slugged through the waist-high water to reach the wheel, praying that the massive intake of water hadn't somehow killed the engine. Salt water stung his eyes as he tried to gain his bearings. He had seen nothing but forest through the hatch initially, which indicated they had been turned one hundred and eighty degrees to face west. He gripped the wheel and scanned his surroundings, shocked to see the roof of the small cottage on the western side of the cove almost directly off his port beam. As soon as his eyes focused on the object, the roof pitched upward and disappeared under the swiftly moving water.

He engaged the transmission and shoved the throttle forward, feeling the boat respond. He unlocked the rudder and attempted to steer the boat, which turned out to be a mistake. Powerful currents jammed the rudder hard to port, once again twisting the boat parallel to the onrushing water. Alex tried to turn the wheel but couldn't budge it. Realizing the impending consequences of the mistake he had made, he used the last available moment to clip his harness to the rail behind him. The D-ring snapped shut a fraction of a second before the boat heeled drastically to starboard, breaking his wet grip on the rail and flinging him against the lifelines.

An incredible, jolting pain surged through his neck and upper body, radiating down into his left arm. He couldn't tell if he had been thrown overboard, just that he was no longer in control of his body. The D-ring had been attached to a twenty-foot line. Long enough to prevent him from hanging uselessly over the side, but short enough to keep him floating close to the boat. Alex dropped into the cockpit, choking on a mouthful of pungent water, which kept him planted in the water while he coughed uncontrollably. The boat lurched forward and stabilized, giving him a chance to drag himself up by the center console. His first mission was to straighten the rudder and lock it.

While the boat drifted parallel to the wave, he turned the helm and managed to center the rudder. Once it was locked into place, he reduced the throttle to idle and put the engine in neutral. In a few moments, they would clear the cove and reach open water, where the force of the wave would dissipate, giving him the opportunity to maneuver.

"Kate!" he yelled at the open hatch.

"We're fine! We have at least a foot of water!" she shouted back.

Kate appeared in the hatchway and flashed him an uneasy look.

"Your head is bleeding! Holy shit..." she muttered, looking beyond the boat at the wave slamming into Cliff Island to the west.

Before Alex could turn to look, the boat shuddered and rolled starboard, stopping dead in the water, but continuing to heel at a dangerous angle as water slammed the port side of the hull. Kate disappeared from sight, falling back into the cabin. He squeezed the stainless-steel handrails mounted to the center console, bracing his feet against the cockpit seat in an attempt to remain on the boat.

Water poured over the starboard deck while the boat teetered. Just when Alex became convinced that the boat would tip over, the *Katelyn Ann* slipped sideways and returned to a normal angle, turning with the rushing water. They had broken free of whatever had struck their keel. He hoped it had only been the keel, and not the rudder or hull. Damage to the latter would severely jeopardize their chances of reaching Portland Harbor.

His best guess was that they struck the western side of the cove, which was solid ledge, and drifted beyond it into open water. Barring critical damage to the steering or hull, they were in good shape to escape the tsunami relatively unscathed. The *Katelyn Ann* was in open water with a functional engine, which was a start. If their rudder were intact, they would be in business. As the boat settled on the same course as the surging water, the southern shoals of Cliff Island swung into view, rapidly approaching.

Alex put the engine in gear and jammed the throttle forward, deciding to take a chance. He had just added eight knots (9 MPH) of speed to the boat's already ridiculous rate of closure with the island. He needed the propeller wash to steer the boat, not wanting to send them into another uncontrolled spin. Holding the wheel in a death grip, he eased the rudder gently to the left, painfully aware that he may not get another shot at this. They had already crossed more than half of the 1000-foot distance between islands.

The *Katelyn Ann* responded to the change in rudder angle, and he watched the bow start to swing left, pointing the boat into safe water beyond the visible rock barrier. Afraid to spin the rudder any further and lose control, Alex watched helplessly as the turn stalled, and the boat drifted back in the direction of the tsunami. Alex straightened the rudder and let the water carry them, building up speed for the next turn. The short period of time the boat had spent drifting to port had made a difference, and they were lined up a little further south along the island.

He waited a few seconds and eased the wheel a quarter of a turn more than before. He felt the rudder tugging at the helm, trying to wrench it out of his grip. He wrapped his right arm through the thick metal spokes and piled his body against the wheel, knowing that his bones were no match against the force of the current pushing against the rudder. He felt the metal bar press tightly against his right tricep, just above the elbow, creating a pressure that caused him to moan. He just needed a few more seconds before the pain stopped.

The boat eased to port, fighting against the continuous volume of water pouring over Jewell Island into the pass. The pressure on the wheel eased when the boat stopped turning, having reached the limit of its rudder-induced maneuver against the current. He untangled his throbbing arm from the wheel and stared at the approaching shore for a moment.

"You've gotta be shitting me," he hissed. The *Katelyn Ann* faced the rocks, unable to break free from the tsunami's grasp.

He centered the rudder, careful to hold the wheel tight as the boat careened toward the ocean-sprayed ledge barricade seemingly obsessed with claiming the boat as a victim.

"One, two—move you son of a bitch!" he said, yanking the wheel left and sliding his arm between the spokes.

The thirty-eight-foot sailboat executed another strong turn to port, causing him to bite his lower lip as the metal spoke exerted a nearly unendurable pressure against his arm and shoulder. He growled at the wheel, biting his lip as it dug into his humerus, grinding muscle against bone. The pressure eased, and he struggled to his feet. The bow was pointed into safe water, and the visible end of the island drifted rapidly to starboard, less than one hundred feet away. He still wasn't convinced that they would clear the island. Alex had always been good with angles, especially at sea. He did the math, comparing the tsunami direction with their position and shook his head.

"Kate! Get everyone on the starboard side! Heads down! I don't know if we're going to make it!"

He heard a flurry of activity below, accompanied by crying he hadn't noticed during their violent journey out of the cove. He wished they had a more powerful engine. Sailboats were so damn underpowered for their size. A forty-horsepower engine in a sixteen-thousand-pound, thirty-eight-foot-long vessel. *Utterly ridiculous.* At the last possible moment, Alex put the engine in neutral to keep the propeller from fouling, and straightened the rudder with his left hand. The bow cleared the leading edge of the rocks with thirty feet to go, still turning with the current.

"Brace for impact!" he screamed.

He squeezed the wheel as the ledge disappeared beneath the starboard rail next to him. The massive jolt that would shipwreck them on Cliff Island never came.

"That's right! You don't fuck with the *Katelyn Ann!*" he screamed at the jagged obstacle, putting her back into gear and increasing the throttle to three-quarters.

He turned the rudder to port and eased the boat away from the southern shore, with plenty of safe water to maneuver ahead of him. The tsunami's energy had faded quickly, allowing him to steer further port without being pushed back. A mile away, off the starboard bow, he watched the leading edge of the tsunami strike the low-lying, western half of Cliff Island, sending geysers of foamy seawater fifty feet into the air. The water swallowed the inhabited stretch of the island whole, sweeping away homes and dropping wooden utility poles. Everything disappeared. Gone.

"What's going on!" yelled Kate.

"We made it. You have to see this."

Kate emerged hesitantly, scanning around to gain her bearings. Her gaze once again settled on Alex.

"What happened to you?" she said, rushing over to help him.

"I decided to punch myself in the mouth for agreeing to buy a sailboat," he said.

"It *was* your idea," she said, reaching out to touch his lip.

"How are the kids?"

"Shaken up. Emily has a few bumps and bruises. I think we got lucky."

"You have no idea," he said, nodding behind the boat at the rocks.

Kate stared aft for a few moments, no doubt examining the boat's wake through the water.

"You almost crashed us," she remarked.

For the briefest moment, he thought she might be serious. He could tell she was trying desperately to suppress a grin, which in Alex's mind saved her from being pushed overboard. Without warning, she wrapped her arms around him and squeezed, causing him to wince. She released the hug immediately.

"What happened?"

"I think my arm is broken. I used it to keep the wheel from turning with the wave. No lectures, please."

She looked at Cliff Island and turned to him. "I'll give you a pass this time. Where's the dinghy?"

Alex scanned the water behind them, quickly turning his attention back to the open water ahead of the boat.

"Shit. I didn't notice it was missing. I was a little preoccupied."

Kate reached over the stern safety rail and pulled on the orange line tied to the stern cleat. The line flopped onto the swim deck, frayed at the end.

"I hope the pier is still intact back at the club," she said, raising an eyebrow.

"I have a feeling we're in for a little swim," Alex said. "Maybe sooner than later. Our stern hit those rocks. We need to check for leaks."

"I'll inspect the aft berth for damage. We still have a foot of standing water in the cabin. The bilge pump light is on, so I assume it's working," she said and waded through the knee-level water in the cockpit.

Alex leaned back and examined the stern. He saw a steady stream of water pump from the hull into the bay. "I see water coming out of the discharge. If we don't have any serious leaks, the cabin should be dry in a few minutes."

He didn't know the specific output capacity of his bilge pump, but based on talk around the club, he figured the boat had been equipped with a pump that could remove up to twelve hundred gallons per hour. A sizeable hull breach could easily overtake that capacity. All they needed to do was keep the boat afloat for another ninety minutes. They had buckets and a few handheld pumps if the situation became dire. Kate reached the hatchway and turned her head to face him.

"Nobody fucks with the *Katelyn Ann*?" she said.

"Nobody," he said to the boat's namesake.

Chapter 9

The Walker Residence
Scarborough, Maine

Ed Walker poured a cup of freshly brewed coffee and turned his head to look at the clock on the microwave, confirming the same thought he'd expressed minutes earlier, when he started to pull the toaster out of the cabinet next to the stove.

I'm an idiot.

A sudden, massive blast of wind had knocked out the power, along with most of the neighborhood's south-facing windows, roughly an hour ago. This hadn't stopped him from repeatedly flipping light switches and trying to activate every electronic device in the house.

His wife, Samantha, had salvaged their two-burner propane camping stove and aluminum coffee set from the garage after they had finished cleaning up the glass. The microburst had shattered every backyard-facing window in their house. They spent at least thirty minutes picking up the visible pieces, relying on flashlights and the rising sun to identify the most noticeable shards. Without the use of their central vacuum system, they would have to wear shoes.

They still had no idea what had happened. The sky was clear, except for the odd reddish glow that had persisted over the southwestern horizon for twenty minutes. Sarah Quinn insisted that she and her husband had seen a brilliant flash while stretching out on the deck for their daily run. By the time they had walked around the house to investigate, the glow had vanished. She thought it had come from the south, but her husband, George, contended that the light had shone from the east. Ed more or less thought they were full of shit. Who knew? He did know that Sarah and George had gotten lucky. Whatever they saw had delayed the start of their run, keeping them sheltered behind their house when the gust hit.

Ed lifted the mug and took a sip of hot coffee, his eyes spotting something shiny among the apples piled into a bowl on the table. They would have to be really careful around the house. He walked to the sliding patio door, noting its absence. The screen door had been severely warped by the blast, but it remained intact like most of the screens in the house. At least they would be spared the mosquitos. A cool breeze poured through the opening, providing a brief respite from the miserable day that lay ahead. Samantha walked into the kitchen from the mudroom.

"No cell phone signal yet. I'm worried about Chloe. The same thing might have hit Boston," she said.

"This was some kind of microburst. They're usually very localized. Probably knocked out power to the cell towers," said Ed.

"I thought the towers had their own backup generators?"

"Most of them should," he admitted. "If we can't reach her by eight, we'll leave the kids with Charlie and head to Boston. We can bring her back if there's a problem down there."

Ed had a sinking feeling that there was more to the morning's power outage than strange weather. He'd retrieved their emergency radio from a box of camping supplies in the garage and taken it out on the deck, hoping to gain some basic information regarding the wind gust. Instead of the choppy, digital NOAA broadcast, he heard static. He anxiously cycled through the AM and FM bands, still unable to located a signal. Ed checked and rechecked the radio, cranking the hand-power generator for at least a minute before trying again. The radio's LED burned brilliantly green throughout the process, telling him what he already suspected. The radio wasn't the problem.

A sharp knock at the front door caused him to jump, spilling coffee on his hand.

"Damn it. Who the hell…?" he mumbled, setting the mug on the table.

He opened the door to find Charlie Thornton panting on his stoop. Charlie glanced over his shoulder twice, looking at the sky.

"They EMP'd our asses. Both of my cars are dead, and nothing works in my house. We're sitting ducks," said Charlie.

"Who EMP'd us?"

"The Chinese! Who else? They'll probably start landing paratroopers within the hour, like *Red Dawn*!"

Ed regarded his neighbor for a moment, hesitating to invite him inside. Charlie stood there barefoot, dressed in faded jeans and an oversized white Red Sox T-shirt. He clung nervously to a black, AR-style rifle fitted with some kind of scope. Ed wasn't keen on letting him inside, especially given the fact that Charlie had chosen a rifle over shoes.

"You gonna let me in or what? It won't be long before we're under direct attack," he said, looking past Ed. "My guess is we'll be hit by drones first."

"Is the safety engaged on that thing?" Ed asked.

"Do I look like some kind of idiot?"

Ed glanced down at his bare feet and gave him a pained look.

"The safety's on, for shit's sake," grunted Charlie.

Ed let Charlie in, closed the door and followed him to the kitchen.

"What did you mean about the cars?" he asked.

"Oh hey, Samantha," Charlie said. "Sorry to barge in on you like this. Damn. Still glass everywhere," he said, lifting a small piece off the kitchen island.

"The cars, Charlie?" Ed prompted.

"Oh yeah. Both of them are dead. The batteries turn over, but the engine won't start. EMP fried the electronics. Have you tried yo—"

"What EMP?" interrupted Samantha.

"There's no EMP, honey. I'm sure the cars are fine," Ed said.

"You need to check them now," Charlie insisted.

"I'm not running out there to—"

Charlie grabbed Ed's T-shirt, pulling him toward the garage, but something caught his attention through the kitchen window.

"What the hell is that?" he said, releasing Ed's shirt to run to the screen door.

Ed heard the problem a few seconds before he saw it. A thunderous crescendo of sharp cracks approached, violently shaking the tops of the largest trees visible over the row of houses directly behind them. At first he thought it was another wind burst, but the loud snaps sounded more like entire trees falling. The burst of wind that had knocked out their windows was powerful, but it had left little more than leaves and branches strewn across the yard. This was different. Something slower and more deliberate.

Before he fully digested the thought, the top of a young maple tree shook and dropped out of sight beyond his backyard neighbor's six-foot privacy fence. By the time the sound of the tree's death reached Ed's ears, he had figured out what they were up against.

"Get upstairs right now!" he barked at his wife, who reacted immediately, dashing past him for the center hallway.

Charlie glanced at him with a seriously puzzled look. Beyond Charlie, Ed saw the wooden privacy fence disappear, replaced by a solid wall of water. He didn't stick around long enough to see Charlie's reaction, but based on the steady stream of profanities catching up to him in the hallway, he figured that his friend had never moved faster.

Ed caught the banister and swung himself onto the stairway, making room for Charlie, who had closed the gap quicker than Ed had thought possible. Both of them paused to look over the railing just as the wall of water hammered the back of Ed's house, snapping the railings on his deck and exploding through the screen door.

"Get out of there!" said Charlie, pulling him by the arm up the stairs.

A powerful torrent of muddy, debris-filled water slammed against the front door and quickly filled the foyer in a swirling eddy of dirty foam that lapped against the bottom stairs. The volume and speed of the water terrified Ed. In the next five seconds, he watched the water rise halfway up the door, showing no signs of slowing down. Two of his kitchen chairs rushed down the hallway half-submerged, piling up against the door momentarily before breaking loose and spilling through the foyer. The rest of his kitchen furniture had already streamed past in the initial onslaught. Somewhere below, he heard glass shatter over the incredible roar of the unending flood plowing through his house. His wife appeared from his son Daniel's bedroom next to the stairs.

"You have to see this!" she said, with a look of sheer disbelief.

Ed hesitated, not wanting to take his eyes off the rising water below him. Half of the staircase was submerged.

"Dad! The whole neighborhood is flooded!" yelled Daniel from the same room.

Ed stood up, feeling slightly unsteady. "I'm sure Linda and the twins are fine," he said to Charlie.

Charlie continued to stare at the floodwaters below. "They were still sleeping when I left," he replied, nodding absently.

Ed joined his wife and two children at the rightmost, front window of his son's room, nearly falling to his knees again. A surging mass of murky brown water covered the ground as far as he could see, carrying large branches, pieces of fencing, plastic garbage bins—anything that had crossed its path since striking the shoreline. The maple tree that normally blocked his view of the Sheppards' house had been knocked into the street, providing his only direct view of the tsunami's effects.

The Sheppards' front door had been blown inward by the force of the wave. Water poured into the previously shattered front windows, likely creating the same effect he'd seen inside his own home. A quick, nearly inescapable flood. Water continued to push up against the house, creating incredible pressure along fifty feet of solid frontage, but he didn't detect any obvious signs of structural failure. He estimated the tsunami's height to be between five and six feet.

Over a mile and a half inland, the initial wave had retained enough energy to topple young trees and pound open doors, but lacked the punch to collapse homes—so far. Water continued to rush through the neighborhood at an alarming rate, and Ed remembered reading that tsunami waves rarely traveled alone, and the first wave wasn't always the largest.

"What do you think?" asked Samantha.

"I think we're lucky we don't live on the water. I can't imagine what happened to Higgins Beach," said Ed.

"Good God," she mumbled.

"Is my house still there?" asked Charlie from the bedroom doorway.

"I can still see the roof. Take a look. It's un-fucking-believable," said Ed, backing away to make room at the window.

"Language," Samantha warned.

"Sorry about that."

"I don't care," said Daniel.

His daughter Abby, who had moved to another window, said, "Neither do I."

"Well, I do," insisted his wife.

"Sounds like you've been outvoted," said Charlie, turning his attention to the scene beyond the window.

Samantha glared at Charlie. "This isn't a democracy."

"Neither is my house—holy shhhh—moley!" said Charlie. "The whole fu—farping neighborhood is fu—fragged to shhhhmeg. Damn it. Can't they just plug their ears?"

Both of the teenagers laughed nervously.

"Can't you complete a sentence without ten expletives?" said Samantha.

"Not under these circumstances," he said, turning to face them.

"Look at that," Ed said, pointing out of a window on the other side of the room. "Water is gushing out of the Fletchers' windows."

"The water's coming out of the *top* of the windows," said Samantha.

They looked fearfully at each other and nearly collided running for the bedroom door.

"Shit," Samantha mumbled, peering around the corner of the door.

The swirling water had climbed three-quarters of the stairway, passing the first floor ceiling level by a few inches. The volume of water pouring into their house through the wide opening created by the shattered slider door couldn't empty quickly enough through the windows. Ed wondered how high the water would rise within the house. He knew logically that the house couldn't fill up to the attic like a container, but seeing this frightened him on an instinctual level.

"Shit, indeed," he said.

"I'd throw a few f-bombs in there for good measure, but the good lady strictly forbids it," mused Charlie.

"I think the language restrictions have been temporarily lifted," said Samantha. "Are we safe in the house, Ed?"

"As long as it doesn't collapse, we're totally fine—not that we have any other options. The water will start to go down in a few minutes. You'll see. I bet your house is doing a lot better, Charlie. Only the right side was exposed directly to the surge. Probably pouring in the windows, but not sweeping through like a freight train," said Ed.

"I hope you're right, not that it really matters," Charlie said ruefully. "We're all totally screwed."

"How does a tsunami fit into your EMP theory? Can't offshore earthquakes cause wind gusts?" asked Ed.

"I don't think so. Maybe the Chinese threw a nuke at Boston and missed, blew up Cape Cod instead. Everything's coming at us from the south. I think a ten-megaton bomb could cause a tsunami like this," said Charlie.

Ed shook his head. "You totally just made that up."

"It's an educated guess. Sarah Quinn swears she saw a flash, then the wind. Now we have a tsunami? Something big hit us."

Ed had to admit that none of this added up. A sudden gust of wind powerful enough to knock out windows; electronics on the fritz; tsunami; possible flashes of light bright enough to turn night into day? Charlie was right about one thing: Whatever this turned out to be, they were most definitely screwed. And that was the least of their immediate concerns. Their daughter Chloe had just moved into an apartment on the outskirts of Boston College, with three other sophomores. Boston College was several miles from the coastline, which eased his fear of a tsunami reaching her, but now they had no way of reaching Boston.

"I hope you're wrong," said Samantha.

He looked over his shoulder and saw that she had started to walk toward the master bedroom. He caught up with her, and she stopped. He could hear her sniffling, trying to stifle the need to cry. He wrapped his arms around her stomach and pressed his chest into her back, kissing her ear.

"It's going to be fine, honey. We'll figure out a way to get down there and bring her back," said Ed, nuzzling his forehead into the back of his wife's neck.

"What if it's not fine? What if Charlie's right and the cars are dead? Shit. They're probably flooded and useless anyway."

"She'll be fine. Alex's son is a few miles away at BU. Ryan's like a mini-Alex. They'll find each other and survive until we can get them back. Ryan has her address, and unless I've read all of the signals wrong, the kid is still crazy about her. I never thought I'd hear myself say this, but he's probably on his way to her apartment right now," Ed whispered.

Samantha relaxed infinitesimally and nodded, which was a start.

"The water's receding!" Charlie announced.

Everyone piled into the hallway to verify Charlie's dubious report. Daniel pushed past them and walked down the stairs to the waterline.

"This is unreal," he said, plucking their wooden napkin holder out of the water.

"Careful, Danny," cautioned Ed.

The water's retreat was barely noticeable, but Charlie was right. The water sat an inch below the ceiling line and appeared to lower another inch while they watched.

"Samantha?" Charlie called.

They all looked back at their red-faced, crew-cut neighbor.

"You don't worry one bit about Chloe. I'll help you get her back safe. You can count on me for that. If we have to push a shopping cart to Boston to get her, then that's what we'll do."

"Thank you, Charlie. I really don't know what to say," said Samantha. Her eyes moistened, but she held back the tears.

"You don't have to say anything. I consider you guys family. That's just what we do," he said. Ed opened his mouth, but before he could speak, Charlie interrupted. "Don't get all feminine on me, Ed. One thank you from the family is all I can handle," he said, slapping Ed on the shoulder.

"Thanks anyway. That means more than you know. One question, though. Why the hell would we need to push a shopping cart to Boston?"

"I don't know. That's what they do in all the apocalypse movies and books."

Chapter 10

EVENT +03:42 Hours

Portland Harbor
Portland, Maine

The *Katelyn Ann* cut through the debris-clogged water off Portland's Eastern Promenade at five knots, as Alex did his best to steer between the larger obstacles, ignoring the smaller ones. His real concern was the quality of the water. Whatever had reached the outer harbor through Portland's main shipping channel had churned up the bottom, dragging along an incredible amount of seaweed and mud. The seaweed tended to wrap around the propeller shaft, putting an additional load on the engine. The muddy water congested the filter supplying seawater to the engine's cooling system.

He felt a solid thump against the hull, which activated his "boat preservation" instinct. He dropped the throttle and put the engine in neutral, hoping to save the propeller if something large scraped along the boat's hull. He glanced over the side and saw a partially submerged, overturned motorboat, roughly half the size of the *Katelyn Ann*, pass astern.

"That's the kind of shit you need to call out!" he yelled to Kate, reengaging the propeller.

"I didn't think you could miss that!"

"Well, I did miss it! I'm watching the gauges!"

Kate nodded, mumbling under her breath. No doubt a few caustic words, fueled by the tension of their approach to the harbor. Kate had been stationed on the bow for nearly an hour. The hour and a half transit turned into two and half hours when they decided to avoid the main shipping channel, opting to navigate the Hussey Sound between Long Island and Peak's Island.

Studying the charts below deck, Kate had made a sobering observation about the geographic orientation of the channel. The channel ran north to south, partially obscured from direct southern exposure by a long stretch of shoreline off Cape Elizabeth and South Portland. If a second wave arrived, it would no doubt slow down when it swept along the shoreline, piling an incredible amount of energy into the relatively narrow lane. The shipping channel would become the least desirable place to be caught in a thirty-eight-foot sailboat.

They had opted to put a few of Casco Bay's islands between their boat and the next tsunami, which cost them an extra hour of time. If the engine continued to overheat, it might cost them more than an hour. South Portland Yacht Club was a mile away, on the other side of the harbor. Alex tucked the boat as close to the Portland side as possible in case the engine died.

Raising the sails and trying to harness the wind for the rest of the trip wasn't really an option. As usual, the winds were dead in Casco Bay at eight in the morning. If the harbor's surface hadn't been covered with a thick layer of brown foam and trash, the water would resemble glass, interrupted only by the wake of an early morning harbor ferry or returning lobster boat. The harbor was eerily devoid of activity as he approached Portland's first commercial marina along the Eastern Promenade. It didn't take him long to figure out why. The tsunami struck the steep southeastern face of the Eastern Promenade, diverting north over East End Beach and southwest into Portland, sparing stately homes along the edge of Munjoy Hill.

The mooring field off East End Beach was in complete disarray. Most of the boats had been flipped, either sinking in the shallow water or floating overturned nearby, still attached to their mooring balls. A dark blue-hulled sailboat stood defiantly at its mooring, appearing untouched by the morning's disaster, while a similar boat lay on its side, keel exposed on the beach. Off his starboard bow, Portland Boat Service's mooring field and docks looked the same. Devastated. None of the business's shore structures had survived the wave, and nearly every boat littered the flat expanse of ground that previously held the Portland Boat Service's massive storage warehouse. Everything was gone, including the century-old brick buildings that marked the beginning of the Eastern Promenade Trail.

Kate looked back at him from the bow and mouthed, *holy shit*, shaking her head. The wave had continued unopposed, sweeping through Portland's tightly packed "Old Port" commercial district. Many of the older, historical buildings on the outskirts of the Old Port between India

Street and Franklin Street had been toppled, but the visible damage stopped there. The taller, more venerable brick buildings and hotels in the same area still dominated the cityscape like nothing had happened. Alex knew differently.

Without warning, a wall of water had washed down Commercial Street and Fore Street, at an unimaginable speed, taking parked cars with it. Anything or anyone caught in the open would have been swept down the streets and dashed against the concrete structures. Fortunately, the tsunami struck at roughly six in the morning on a Monday. Dozens of people had been tragically killed going about their early morning routines, but the casualty numbers would have jumped twenty-fold if the wave had struck an hour or so later, when the Old Port was filled with thousands of employees.

Kate pointed at the water a hundred meters ahead of the boat and signaled for him to turn to port. He eased the rudder over until she gave him a thumbs-up. He never saw the obstacle she had detected.

Alex had been so focused on dodging obstacles and gawking at the Eastern Promenade that he nearly missed the most obvious damage caused by the tsunami. A massive oil tanker sat high and dry with its propellers and rudder exposed, one hundred feet west of the Maine Oil pier. Listing forty-five degrees on its starboard side, the vessel had been ripped from the concrete pier and stranded in shallow water. He recalled seeing the tanker when they passed by the pier on their way to Jewell Island yesterday morning, which gave him hope that the tanker had offloaded its payload of crude prior to grounding. His next observation rendered the thought irrelevant.

The fuel farm normally visible just beyond the pier, which consisted of several white crude oil storage tanks, had disappeared—swept into Portland Harbor by the force of the tsunami. Their yacht club sat less than two thousand feet away along the same South Portland waterfront, the distance casting serious doubt on his ability to approach their mooring. Each tanker pulling into the pier discharged hundreds of thousands of barrels destined for oil refineries at the end of the pipeline in Canada. If the tanker had already offloaded its payload into the nearby tank farm, a thick layer of crude oil would blanket Portland's inner harbor.

Kate pointed toward the grounded tanker and shook her head. He simply nodded. There wasn't much to say. Portland Harbor was ruined. Every nook and cranny would reek of crude oil for years to come. Given the deeper disaster scenario unfolding, he couldn't imagine the harbormaster or Coast Guard engaging in efforts to contain the spill to the harbor. All of Casco Bay would be contaminated in short order.

He reduced the throttle as they approached the most congested part of the inner harbor and did his best to avoid larger objects that could foul the boat's propeller. An incredible amount of debris had been swept into the water from Portland's commercial district, mostly wood from flattened buildings and plastic patio furniture from dozens of waterfront bars and restaurants. The marinas on the Portland side had fared decently well, spared a direct hit by several major commercial and industrial piers staged along the waterfront.

Most of the boats within the marinas had been ripped from their pier lines, left floating within the protected wooden coves, jammed against each other in one place. Dozens of pleasure boats had broken free from their wooden corrals, set adrift in the calm harbor. Alex passed an exquisitely maintained picnic boat with a deep green hull and considered towing it back to SPYC. If he could start the boat, they could put the *Katelyn Ann* on their mooring, reserving it for future use, and utilize the picnic boat to go ashore. The plan was too complicated, so he continued to motor past the derelict craft.

The next time Kate turned her head to confirm that he received her hand signal, he yelled out to her, "Can you tell if we're cruising through oil!"

The surface of the water was thick with mud, silt and foam, making it difficult for him to determine if they were pushing through petroleum. The engine temperature had spiked into the red zone over the past few minutes. Lowering the throttle hadn't lowered the temperature. Kate lowered herself to the deck and pushed half of her body through the bow rail, examining the boat's waterline along the bow. She sat back on the deck, facing him, and nodded.

"We have a thick layer of oil running down the side of the boat!" she replied.

Shit.

Now he wasn't sure what to do. Reduce speed further to delay the inevitable? Speed up and get there faster? Pull right into Portland and deal with the walk across the bridge? Was the bridge even safe? He envisioned the engine's cooling system circulating oil at this point. How much longer would the engine run?

He decided to go for the club or Coast Guard station. He didn't want to deal with the mess in Portland and the trek to find a passable bridge. The Casco Bay Bridge looked intact, but looks could be deceiving. Bridges further down the harbor would be better options, but would put them miles off track and drag them through some heavily congested industrial and residential areas. If there was one thing Alex knew from previous experiences, it was best to avoid crowded areas in a crisis or disaster—and this qualified as both.

"I'm taking us in! Look for a pier on the other side!" he said.

As soon as she nodded, he turned the wheel, pointing the boat at a tangle of wooden piers and pilings across the harbor. Reluctantly, he increased the throttle, accelerating the boat toward its final destination.

"Kids, I need you topside to help. We might only get one chance at bringing the boat alongside," said Alex.

Emily tumbled into the cockpit first, her auburn hair pulled back tightly by a black scrunchie.

"Do you have makeup on?" he asked.

"Yeah. Why? It's not like I didn't have the time," she said, looking at him like he was an idiot.

He couldn't really argue with her logic, though in the context of their situation, he could have said, *Are you out of your friggin mind?* and satisfied most adults with his response. He let it go, marveling as the "center of the universe" stepped onto the deck and walked carefully toward the bow. He couldn't wait to see Kate's reaction. The two of them had been battling each other like gladiators for the past year. Ethan stepped through the hatchway with his backpack firmly strapped to his back, distracting him from the potential melee between Kate and Emily.

"Ethan, you don't want to have that on your back for this. You might have to jump James Bond style from the boat to the pier," said Alex.

Ethan removed the pack from his thin frame, placing it on the starboard cockpit bench. He adjusted his hunter green ball cap, tucking his hair under the brim, and surveyed the harbor.

"Where do you need me, Uncle Alex? Stern line?" he asked, noting Kate and Emily on the bow.

"Exactly. Why don't you take down the lifelines on both sides and get ready to make the jump when we pull up. I'm taking us wherever we can get alongside a solid-looking pier. Could be either side." Alex peered through the chaotic mooring field ahead. "And make sure to run the lines outside of the stanchions and rails."

"Like this?" asked Ethan.

Alex risked a quick glance and saw that Ethan had run the lines over and along the rails, placing them in a neat coil at the opening on each side. All Ethan would have to do was grab one of the coils, depending on which side Alex would expose to the pier, and jump onto the dock, pulling the stern in for a quick tie off.

"Perfect. Just remember, don't sweat a perfect tie up. Just get the line secured quickly and head down the pier to grab Aunt Kate's line."

"I got it," said Ethan, staring ahead with a serious look. "Are you going to be able to get us in?"

"I don't know. It's not looking good," Alex said, as his view unfolded.

The term "not looking good" was an understatement. Only Marine Corps Gunnery Sergeant vernacular could do the scene true justice. Calling it "a regular shit show" would have been more accurate. Astoria Marina's vast floating pier system had been swept across the mooring field and sat pinned against what used to be South Portland Yacht Club's dock. Boats from Astoria were scattered everywhere, some still floating, attached to the dock, most sunk in the shallow water, their masts or flying bridges standing useless vigil, scattered haphazardly across the waterfront. Thick streaks of black oil were evident on every waterline surface, confirming his decision to seek a solid pier.

At sea level from this distance, it was nearly impossible to determine if any of Astoria's docks were still connected to land. Many of the pier sections had flipped upside down, exposing the massive, petroleum-covered floats underneath the wood, giving him few obvious options for his boat. The eastern half of SPYC's mooring field had been cleared by the long dock, pushed perpendicular to the rock wall by the tsunami. A combination of roughly forty sailboats and motorboats had been pushed into the shallow water between the rock wall and the dock. A few of the shallow draft motorboats bobbed in the water, while most of the craft lay marooned at odd angles. The smaller marina to the left of Astoria Marina had suffered a similar fate, leaving him with zero options along the entire length of waterfront—aside from the Coast Guard station. He slowed as the *Katelyn Ann* entered the empty half of the mooring field.

At least the clubhouse beyond SPYC's rock wall looked intact, along with most of the houses and structures along the shore. The wave that had cleared the petroleum tank farm had been limited to the northeastern tip of South Portland, which made sense given the geography of the peninsula. The tsunami wave released by the blast would strike the southern-facing shoreline, causing the biggest pileups of water along the beaches in Cape Elizabeth and Scarborough, miles away, closer to their house.

"What do you think?" he yelled to Kate.

"You might be able to pull into one of those slips," she said, pointing at Astoria's mangled dock, "but I can't tell if it's connected to land. I can see at least a dozen boats under the water and a ton of other shit! Go to the Coast Guard station!"

Alex steered the boat to port, passing by several empty mooring balls, and increased his speed. A few minutes later, they approached the seemingly undamaged station, which stood on a raised concrete platform that jutted six hundred feet into the harbor. Coast Guard personnel on the easternmost concrete pier waved urgently at him. Oddly, their gestures didn't appear welcoming to Alex. It almost seemed like they were trying to wave him off.

Fuck that. Their job is to help vessels in distress, and this is about as distressful as it gets.

He slowed to bare steerageway and searched for a place along the fifteen-foot-high pier that had a ladder or an access dock lower to the water.

A large Buoy Tender occupied much of the water between the eastern and western piers, blocking his view of the inner pier area. He knew that the station boasted a forty-five-foot Patriot Class Medium Response Boat (RB-M), in addition to at least two twenty-five-foot Defender Class Small Response Boats (RB-S), so it made sense that they would have a lower pier to accommodate the craft, maybe on the outside of the western pier. He altered his course to starboard and edged closer to the station. At this point, he could clearly tell that the station personnel did not want him to approach any closer. Dressed in dark blue uniforms with body armor, at least two of them carried carbines slung across their chests. As soon as he saw the rifles, his mind flashed to the drop-leg holster snugged against his upper right thigh.

The holster faced away from the pier, which gave him hope that it hadn't been spotted. He couldn't imagine that they would be happy to see someone openly carrying a firearm on the water. The state of Maine had no prohibitions against openly carrying a firearm, and he was licensed to carry a concealed weapon in the state, but he had no idea if bringing a firearm on the boat in coastal waters was legal. He'd never given it a second thought. He decided that this wasn't the time to push his luck, so he reached down to start the process of removing the holster.

Before he could pull the first Velcro latch from his belt, one of the Defenders roared into view from behind the western pier. Alex moved his hands away from the holster and placed them at the top of the boat's steering wheel. The Defender's forward-mounted M-240B machine gun remained trained on the *Katelyn Ann* as it closed in on the sailboat's starboard side. Kate raised her hands, which set off a chain reaction of hands-raising throughout the boat. The Defender's roof-mounted loudspeaker roared.

"Put your engine in neutral, and place your hands on your head!"

Alex quickly complied as the Defender came alongside, facing aft, disgorging its armed boarding team onto the sailboat's deck. Dressed in blue digital camouflage uniforms and full ballistic body armor, the four-member team split up. One group moved toward the bow, approaching Kate and Emily, pointing their weapons at them. The second group immediately secured Alex and Ethan, removing Alex's pistol and pushing the two of them into the portside cockpit seat. The petty officer manning the M-240B kept it trained on Alex the entire time. When the boarding officer was satisfied that the boat was in neutral and that everything appeared under control, she signaled for the crew of the Defender to lash the sailboat securely to their craft. Without glancing in Alex's direction, she tossed the pistol over the stern.

"Was that really necessary?" asked Alex.

"None of this would be necessary if you hadn't insisted on approaching the station. You were warned repeatedly," she replied.

"My car is over at the yacht club. We couldn't go pier side anywhere but here. I apologize for putting you in this position. I imagine the station is dealing with a lot of shit right now. Do you know what's happening? I'm pretty sure we were hit by an EMP."

The boarding officer glanced at the other petty officer, who shrugged his shoulders and nodded.

"Boarding team, stand down! We'll tow them back to the station. Let's go!" she announced, turning her attention back to Alex.

"We don't know what's happening, but the National Terrorist Advisory System issued an imminent warning, with no threat specifics. The station went dark at about 0500, damage to the systems onshore and onboard our vessels was consistent with your assessment of an EMP. We have our hands full, so if you don't mind, I'm going to bring you pier side for two minutes to offload. After that, I'm putting her on the nearest mooring."

"So I guess a harbor cleanup isn't high on your priority list?" he said, trying to lighten the mood.

"We have some buckets and a row boat if you're volunteering," she said.

"Don't piss her off, honey. Please. We're very grateful for your help," said Kate, approaching them along the port-side deck.

The petty officer nodded and turned to board the Defender, stopping briefly to address Alex.

"Sorry about the pistol, but the NTAS warning came with orders to disarm civilians on sight. I think it's bullshit, but not everyone agrees with me. Either way, you weren't getting on the station with that pistol. I'd be a little more discreet next time," she said.

"Disarming civilians is a little strange, don't you think?"

"I have the distinct feeling that we haven't seen the beginning of strange yet," she said.

Chapter 11

South Portland, Maine

Kate stood facing the chain-link gate, staring at the water-swept, gravel parking lot. The cars had been rearranged, and damage to the clubhouse appeared more extensive than they had observed from several hundred feet away on the water. Structurally, the one-story building looked intact, but all of the windows had been shattered, and part of the steward's shack had been swept off its foundation. The small wooden shack sat teetering on the edge of the rock wall facing west toward the Coast Guard station. She peered through the fence, scanning the parking lot one more time. They would have to walk home.

Alex removed his backpack and grabbed the fence with both hands, gauging its steadiness.

"I don't think there's any point," Kate said.

She didn't want to waste any more time getting back to their house. The car had been parked along the seawall, several feet from the edge, along with the rest of the cars that were either missing or sitting ass-up in the water. The cars in the lot had all been shifted at least twenty feet by the water, which would put their SUV in the oily soup mixture that now constituted Portland Harbor. She didn't even see its tailgate, so there was no reason for Alex to climb the fence and confirm the obvious.

Just their luck, too. Finding a spot for their SUV in the less cramped, outer edge of the parking lot on a clear Sunday morning had been a stroke of fortune yesterday. Now they faced a wonderful five-mile walk with overstuffed backpacks in the stifling heat that would only get worse as the day progressed. Alex either didn't hear her or was purposefully ignoring her. Neither possibility pleased her.

He'd already put them more than an hour behind schedule by confronting the Coast Guard station's commanding officer about the lost pistol and the fact that they were treated like terrorists while approaching the station in a "sailboat." It didn't matter anymore, but he couldn't let it go.

Under normal circumstances, she appreciated his proactive approach to sticking up for the family, but this was far from an ordinary dilemma. They could have walked right from the pier to the front gate in five minutes, but he kept pushing, and they were detained while their credentials were verified. It was pure harassment, infuriating and unnecessary, but Alex should have known better than to push their buttons.

Now it was hotter outside, and her last vestige of patience was about to be completely erased by Alex's Spiderman routine. The quicker they got home, the sooner they could figure out how to get Ryan out of Boston. They needed to stay focused on that goal. Climbing a fence to confirm the obvious wasn't on her list of shit to do right now.

"The car's gone. We're heading out," she stated, signaling for Ethan and Emily to follow.

She took several steps down the road before hearing Alex's footfalls approach from behind.

"Take it easy, Kate. We're on the same page here. I just thought we might be able to salvage something from the car if it was sticking up from the water like some of the others," said Alex.

She softened the look on her face and turned her head. "We can't carry any more crap. It's hot, it's humid, and I want to get home so we can come up with a plan to get Ryan. We have everything we need at home."

"If our house is still there. These packs might be it. We have to think worst-case scenario," he said.

"Every house is still standing. Even the clubhouse on the edge of the water. I'm sure our house is intact," said Kate, picking up the pace.

"You're going too fast for the kids. A regular walking pace would be best, especially with the heat. These packs will feel twice as heavy by the time we reach Highland Avenue."

Kate sensed that he didn't want to fight, so she accepted his suggestion and slowed the pace. He could have argued the physics of how the tsunami might have reached their house with more force, or continued on the all-or-nothing survivor mentality track, but he had opted for more constructive counsel. After more than twenty years of marriage, subtle shifts in tone and commentary often carried more meaning and significance than an obvious, outward expression. In this case, she interpreted it as a temporary concession. She'd take it. They needed to work together from this point forward.

"Yep. I can feel this damn thing digging into my shoulder already. They're not exactly the most comfortable packs. How long do you think it will take us to get home?" she asked, slowing down to fall into step beside him.

"Five miles? I'd say two to three hours, depending on the burden of these packs and the temperature. That's assuming we can follow the usual roads, which is a fair assumption. Even if the water made it that far inland, we shouldn't be looking at anything more than an occasional downed tree or power line—maybe some debris. We should be home before the day gets ridiculously hot."

"Sounds like fun. This isn't exactly the weight-loss plan I had in mind, but I'll take what I can get," Kate said, adjusting the pack on her shoulders.

Kate wished she had taken the time to pick out a more suitable backpack. Alex had given her the opportunity to look through options, but she had deferred the decision to his judgment. Working through the different choices presented by Alex could occupy most of her waking hours if she allowed it—and it never ended. Out of necessity, she gradually took on more of an observational role and let him run the show. Once Alex formed an idea, he could be relentless and impatient about getting it done. She had decided to go back to work at her accounting firm, and the last thing she needed at the end of each day was another deadline. Less than a quarter of a mile into their trek, she regretted not taking a little more interest in the backpack he had chosen.

He had selected the same design for everyone, opting for an OD green, military-style, three-day assault pack. From a purely practical standpoint, the assault pack met their requirements on every level. The "three-day" designation referred to sustained combat operations, where a soldier would carry large quantities of additional ammunition, radio batteries, and other squad- or platoon-based items, in addition to food and water, taking up most of their "personal" space. Alex had chosen the assault pack for its large cargo-carrying capacity and unique interior arrangement.

Internally, the pack contained over a dozen zippered or snapped compartments, making it easy to organize and access the different categories of gear required for an effective bug-out bag. They had bought two backpacks for each member of the family. One for the house and one for travel.

For the boat, Alex staged each backpack with an imbedded three-liter CamelBak hydration bladder, three stainless-steel one-liter bottles, three full MREs (Meals Ready to Eat), a folding knife, one LED flashlight and a basic first aid kit. Everyone was required to add two full changes of clothing and a pair of running shoes, in a sealed three-gallon Ziploc bag, to the bottom of their pack. The rest of the space belonged to the owner, which left more than enough room to pack clothing, toiletries and other essentials for a week-long trip, if you didn't mind wearing the same items for a couple of days in a row. Kate always brought another bag for trips over three days on the sailboat.

Alex always loaded his own pack with additional survival gear. Fire-starting equipment, signaling gear, a pair of handheld radios, an enhanced first aid kit, water purification tablets and a number of items she had already forgotten. His pack always looked like it was about to burst apart at the seams and had to weigh at least fifteen pounds heavier than the other packs. He purposely loaded his own pack with more of the group items, acknowledging the fact that he was asking enough of them to carry basic survival supplies on every local vacation.

Not many families travelled like the Fletchers. Whenever they journeyed by car as a family, four of these backpacks, filled with the required basics, would be stuffed into the vehicle next to their regular suitcases and luggage. Alex didn't expect the family to walk into a hotel or ski lodge with matching, military-style backpacks, but they had the option of retrieving them for a rapid departure in the unlikely event of a disaster. He had become obsessed with the idea of "bugging out" of every possible situation—an obsession that had paid off handsomely this morning.

"Honey, you should tighten the waist belt a little more. It'll take some of the load off your shoulders. The straps are padded decently enough, but I'd guess that the pack was generally designed to go over body armor or some kind of load-bearing vest system. Kids, if you feel like the pack is rubbing your shoulders too much, tighten the waist belt as much as you can stand. It'll make a big difference an hour from now," said Alex.

Several feet in front of them, Ethan and Emily hiked their packs higher on their shoulders and made the adjustment. Kate did the same, tightening her own waist strap as much as she could stand, which significantly lessened the pressure on her shoulders.

"That's much better, until the straps start digging into my stomach," she remarked.

"Wait until you're drenched with sweat. Once your shirt is soaked, the chafing is ten times worse," said Alex.

"Wonderful. Any other good news?"

"We'll all probably have blisters or a hot spot on our feet within the hour, most likely on the dominant foot. The extra weight on your back changes the friction coefficient between your sock and shoe. We'll stop every forty-five minutes and check, make some adjustments—maybe change socks."

"I don't think we should stop," Kate said.

"Trust me, you'll be glad to stop. We did it during road marches in the Marine Corps. Marines would check their feet and drink water, while the corpsmen ran up and down the column repairing blisters and checking on guys who looked like they were about to pass out. We savored those breaks," said Alex.

"You didn't have a son trapped in Boston, waiting to be rescued."

"Good point, though I have a feeling he's not lying in bed sucking his thumb," Alex said.

"That boy needs his mom," Kate insisted.

"He is sort of a momma's boy," Alex joked. "Kids, make sure you keep sipping water! Don't be afraid to stick that hose in your mouth."

"That didn't sound right," whispered Kate.

"That was the G-rated version of what my gunny would have said."

Chapter 12

South Portland, Maine

A lone car approached from behind, causing Alex to stop on the sidewalk. He stood with his family in the shadow of the three-story, red-brick middle school situated on the southeast corner of the intersection at Broadway and Ocean Street. Since turning onto Broadway, Alex had counted four cars of various makes and models. There was no discernible pattern to what type of car survived the EMP, or whatever disturbance had caused the electrical grid to fail. He had expected to see more cars based on the Critical National Infrastructure's (CNI) revised report findings. Three cars in thirty minutes on a major road didn't support the assertion that forty percent of all cars would remain drivable.

They all watched a gray Subaru Outback pass them and stop at the intersection, which was occupied by a functional South Portland Police Department cruiser and three police officers. The Subaru edged forward, but the officers signaled for the driver to stop the car. Alex was pretty sure that he heard them tell the driver to turn off the engine.

"Keep moving. Cut the corner and keep going down Ocean toward Highland. I'll catch up," said Alex.

He kept walking along the curved sidewalk and stood behind a tree, while his family moved along the front of the school in the shade cast by the tall building. Satisfied that they were leaving the scene, he turned all of his attention back to the unfolding drama. Since there was no other vehicle traffic, or any background noise for that matter, he heard the entire exchange.

"Sir, I need you to step out of the car," said the officer by the driver's-side window.

The second officer had taken position on the front passenger side, while the third officer circled the hatchback, examining the back seat and cargo area of the vehicle, before joining the first officer.

"Did I do something wrong?" asked the driver. "I stopped where I normally would, even though there's no light."

"Can you please just step out of the car? You're not in any trouble," said the officer.

"Well, I don't see why I need to get out of my car. I have my license and registration right here," said the driver, holding up the documents for the officer to see.

The officer calmly retrieved the man's driver's license, barely examining it before continuing.

"Mr. Reynolds, the Department of Homeland Security has declared a national state of emergency. We need to replace vehicles that were knocked out by the EMP. I'm sorry, Mr. Reynolds, but this vehicle temporarily belongs to the South Portland Police Department. Please step out of your car."

The officer standing next to him took a few steps back and rested her hand on her service pistol. The driver saw this subtle shift and received the message, opening the door and stepping onto the pavement. He was dressed in khaki shorts with cargo pockets and a gray T-shirt. Nothing about him raised any alarms or gave Alex concern that this might end badly.

"Officer Harker will drive you home. We're really sorry about this, but we have to get the rest of our officers out on patrol. You're better off at your house anyway," said the officer.

"I need to fill a prescription for my daughter at Shaw's and try to find things—like food. I don't suppose Officer Harker will be on loan for the next hour or so to drive me around?" asked the driver, staring down the police officer.

The police officer shook his head and held up the license, which the driver deftly snapped out of his hand. The driver kept both hands in the air, one holding the plastic license, and walked backward, shaking his head, and Alex knew there was far more to the unassuming man in shorts and a T-shirt than met the casual eye. Based on the speed and dexterity of the man's movement, Alex had little doubt that he could have "repossessed" his car and left the three officers on the pavement in a tangle of limbs.

He had to remember this critical lesson for his own upcoming trek. Make no assumptions based on appearance. There were plenty of people out there who were quicker, stronger and craftier than he was.

"I'll walk from here," the man said and turned to head north on Ocean Street toward the supermarket.

He stopped several steps into his journey and turned to address the officers, who had already begun to set up for the next car that might amble into their trap.

"Hey! We forgot to fill out the paperwork! What, no paperwork? Imagine that. Enjoy the car, assholes!" he said and jogged away.

Alex slipped away from the tree and located Kate sitting in the shade of the furthest entrance stoop from the intersection. He headed in their direction, nervously looking over his shoulder. The police seemed cordial enough, but they didn't hesitate to take away a citizen's property in the name of emergency powers. They would have to be cautious around law enforcement. Within a few hours of the event, whatever it turned out to be, law enforcement agencies had started confiscating cars and disarming citizens.

Given the circumstances, neither of these actions qualified as a sudden decline into a "police state," but Alex couldn't shake distant thoughts about some of the theories popularized by Internet conspiracy pundits. "False flag" came to mind, but based on what he'd witnessed since the initial flash beyond Jewell Island, he quickly dismissed the idea as paranoia.

To conspiracy theorists, the term "false flag" implied an attack or hostile operation conducted by the U.S. government and subsequently blamed on a foreign or domestic enemy. The most common purpose cited for a false flag attack was the erosion or outright suspension of civil liberties. Conspiracy groups insisted that the United States had been repeatedly subjected to these attacks by the government over the course of three decades to soften the people's tolerance of government intrusion.

Many of them believe that the 9/11 attacks were supported or "allowed to happen" by factions in the government looking to expand surveillance and detention powers, in the name of the "War on Terror." Similarly, the pundits surmised that the Boston Bombing was perpetrated to test the citizens' reaction to a martial-law-style lockdown of a major city. Would Boston's population openly tolerate the presence of armored personnel carriers and heavily armed soldiers patrolling the streets, while teams of

SWAT officers went door to door, pulling citizens out of their homes at gunpoint?

Even the Jakarta Pandemic had been linked to a "mystery faction's" overall effort to condition the American people, desensitizing the population to situations that might result in mass casualties and essential services shortages. They claimed that all of these events would be linked to a singular, "mass event" that would tip the scales and invoke a permanent national police state, which we would welcome with open arms.

Alex imagined that the conspiracy pundits were going crazy with theories—made even worse by the fact that they had no Internet to propagate them. On a whole, he didn't buy into these theories, but given what he had just witnessed, it couldn't hurt to keep an eye on the big picture. He reached Kate, who sat on the first step of the doorway, and saw that the kids were hidden deeper in the alcove, seated against the building.

"Everything all right over there?" she asked him.

"I don't know. The cops just seized that guy's vehicle in the name of the federal government."

"What?" said Emily. "They can't do that."

"Federal government? That doesn't sound right," said Kate.

"I agree, which is why I don't know what to think. The officer cited Homeland Security and a state of national emergency. Said they needed working vehicles to get the rest of the police department out on patrol," said Alex.

"That makes more sense," Kate said with some relief. "I'm sure that's all they were doing."

Alex shook his head and checked his watch. "That's the fifth car we've seen on Broadway in what—twenty or thirty minutes? How many cars does the department need to replace? If they just started seizing cars, it makes sense, but it's been over three hours since the tsunami hit. I think we need to avoid any law enforcement roadblocks or checkpoints from this point forward."

"How the hell are we going to get to Boston if the police are stealing cars?"

"Let's get home first," he said, extending his hand to Kate.

She lifted herself off the step and immediately hugged his sweaty frame, burying her head in his shoulder.

"We don't even know if our other car will work," she whispered, lifting her head.

"We'll figure something out. I'll ride a bike to Boston if I have to. Everything will be fine. I promise."

Kate shook her head. "You can't make a promise like that."

"I can promise you that I'll do everything in my power to make it happen. You know I'm good for that," he said, kissing her moist forehead. "Let's get moving. If we're sweating like this at ten in the morning, I'd hate to see us at noon."

They took a few moments to adjust their backpacks and CamelBak water hoses before stepping off on the rest of their two- to three-hour hike. They headed south along Ocean Street for less than a block, crossing the street at the end of the middle school's athletic field. Alex kept his eyes on the police cruiser to the north, wondering how many cars they had added to the department's inventory this morning. He couldn't shake the deeply imbedded suspicion that nothing was as it seemed this morning—and the fear that nothing would ever be the same again.

Turning onto Highland Avenue a few minutes later filled him with a momentary sense of relief. Highland Avenue intersected with Harrison Road in Scarborough, at the Pleasant Hill firehouse located less than a third of a mile from their house. All they had to do at this point was follow Highland Avenue for three and a half miles to the firehouse, where they could pretty much stumble into their neighborhood. They had walked for less than a minute before hearing the distant sound of a vehicle. Alex quickly scanned his surroundings and made a decision that surprised him.

"Honey, take the kids and hide behind that car," he said, pointing at an older model minivan in the adjacent parking lot.

"Are we hiding from cars now?" she snapped, grabbing Emily's sleeve and pulling her toward the minivan.

"Maybe I'm being ridiculous," he said, walking with them.

He barely spotted the white sedan rounding the bend on Highland before a clump of thick bushes blocked his view. He had managed to see that the driver had activated the left turn signal, which meant the car would turn north on Ocean Street, headed right into the police trap. He changed his mind about hiding and moved swiftly to the street, waving his hands over his head.

"What the fuck are you doing?" hissed Kate, holding her hands palms up in an annoyed gesture.

"Get behind the car!" he said over his shoulder.

The car slowed enough for him to yell at a blond woman through the open driver's-side window.

"There's a police roadblock at Broadway. They're seizing cars!" yelled Alex.

The car screeched to a halt several feet before the intersection, and Alex jogged along the sidewalk, careful not to approach the car directly and possibly frighten the driver. The woman leaned her head out of the window. She had a laceration on her forehead above her right eyebrow, which had bled profusely at some point this morning given the amount of congealed blood plastered to the right side of her face. Her hair was matted to her head above the wound.

"What are you talking about?" she asked.

Alex caught up with her, staying on the sidewalk to keep at least a car's length distance between them.

"The police have a cruiser set up in the middle of the intersection at Broadway and Ocean. I watched them stop a car and force the driver out. Emergency seizure," he said.

"What about further down at Cottage and Broadway?" asked the driver.

"We just came from there. It was clear fifteen minutes ago," said Alex.

"Good. Did you notice if any of the stores are open?" she asked, glancing around nervously.

"The variety store on the corner of Broadway and Mussey was open, but they didn't have power. Cash only. We saw a slow but steady stream of people walking down Cottage toward the shopping complex. What's the situation like down Highland? We're headed to Scarborough."

"I heard that the water reached Highland across from Wainright Field, but I haven't confirmed that. We live by the high school. There's all kinds of weird talk out there. EMP, Chinese invasion, volcano erupting in Boston…"

"What happened to your forehead?" Alex asked.

He suddenly felt slightly exposed standing on the side of the road. If the water hadn't reached her house, why did she look like she had been in a knife fight? What else did they face walking down Highland Avenue?

"One of my—*neighbors*—decided that I wasn't entitled to one of the few working cars on the street," she said, staring blankly through the front windshield.

Alex didn't care to press the question. He knew what had likely played out in her driveway, and that the neighbor had lost the fight.

"I'd stash this thing as far from the Hannaford parking lot as possible and walk the rest of the way. You might be able to handle one asshole on your own, but every eye in the parking lot will be on your car."

"There were three of them," she said, "and only one of them wanted the car. Fucking savages."

"Sorry. I assume you…" he paused.

"I took care of them," she said, touching the crusted wound on her forehead. "Keep a tight eye on your family," she added, nodding toward the minivan to the left of Alex.

The sedan pulled away and stopped at the intersection momentarily, while the driver undoubtedly confirmed the information he had passed. She accelerated the car down Highland and disappeared behind the chain-link fence that bordered the middle school's athletic field.

"All right. Let's go," he announced.

Kate rose from her dubious hiding spot near the rear bumper of the minivan and walked toward the sidewalk, joined by Ethan and Emily.

"Ethan, turn around and let Emily grab the knife out of your backpack. Outer left pocket, Emily. Then Ethan gets the one out of your pack, sweetie. Turn around, honey, and I'll get yours," he said.

"What did she say?" Kate asked. "She looked like she'd been attacked."

"She fought off three guys trying to steal her car," he replied quietly.

"Keep the knife in your front pocket, out of sight, and keep sipping water. That CamelBak should be empty by the time we reach the high school," he announced, then whispered the rest of what the woman had told him about the attack into Kate's ear.

Kate's expression instantly sharpened to an angry grimace.

"I really wish that Coastie hadn't tossed my pistol," he said.

"We'll be fine," she said, snapping open the three-inch serrated blade to examine his choice for their bug-out packs. "Just fine." She closed the knife and put it into her front cargo pocket.

Chapter 13

Scarborough, Maine

Kate was starting to have irrational thoughts about ditching her backpack. They were less than a half mile from their neighborhood, and all she could think about was throwing the tan contraption into the bushes and coming back to get it later. The pack's weight had nothing to do with the problem. She was in excellent physical condition and could hike for hours with one of the equally sized internal-frame backpacks they purchased from Eastern Mountain Sports. The pack Alex had chosen for the family bug-out bag simply sucked for walking long distances.

Unless you had grown accustomed to working with disgustingly uncomfortable gear, like most marines, the "three-day assault pack" was a killer. It lacked any kind of rigid frame, rendering proper weight distribution nearly impossible, which had the unfortunate effect of rubbing her shoulders raw. Mercifully, she had consumed most of her water by this point, which, according to Alex, had reduced the pack's weight by more than ten pounds. Small consolation.

Of course, by the time she had significantly reduced the water weight, the damage to her shoulders and psyche had been done. She wanted to lay into him for defaulting to military equipment, but didn't see any purpose to picking a fight. The kids weren't complaining, and Alex wouldn't admit the pack was uncomfortable if his shoulders were visibly bleeding. She didn't want to be the only one to bitch about their predicament. They were almost home, where she could toss the pack in the house and lay on the floor for as long as she wanted. If they still had a house.

The first signs of tsunami damage appeared a few blocks from the Wainright athletic fields. The pattern of damage made sense based on what they had observed during their trek along Highland Avenue, which had ascended gradually from the center of South Portland near the middle school. Roughly a mile from the police roadblock, standing on the sidewalk overlooking South Portland High School's football field, they could see the green of Portland's Western Promenade, which towered above Portland's inner harbor. They looked about even with Portland's high ground, and Alex had guessed that they were at least a hundred feet above sea level.

She trusted his judgment when it came to navigation. Alex had an uncanny sense of direction and an infallible ability to get them to wherever they needed to go, often without the help of maps or GPS. After nearly twenty years of marriage, she was a believer. The man was never lost and could read terrain like the back of his hand.

Even the kids started to believe when another mapping prediction came true a half mile past the high school, near Fickett Street. Highland Avenue peaked and began a shallow descent into the neighborhoods along the South Portland/Scarborough border. Alex estimated that their house sat somewhere between thirty to forty feet above sea level. A fact he leveraged when everyone began to feel the effects of the two-mile uphill hike on their quads. Incredibly, none of them recalled Highland Avenue descending into Scarborough, but Alex insisted that they were very likely approaching the downhill portion of their trip. True to his word, the street leveled off and began to slope downward, ever so slightly. The difference was barely noticeable on their bodies, but mentally, it rejuvenated them. The temperature had climbed well into the high eighties by that point, and any factor working in their favor was entirely welcome.

When the mud and debris appeared on the streets and in the yards, they figured they had reached the bottom of the hill. Aside from the ever-present layer of muddy silt, it hadn't looked nearly as bad as she had expected. Most of the wooden fences had been knocked down, but the high water mark hadn't reached the first-floor windows. People they encountered along the road reported basement flooding as their worst damage from the tsunami, which had rolled through without any warning at around six in the morning. Roadside watersheds and ditches overflowed with dirty, foamy water, giving a good indication that the area's natural water runoff system had been completely overwhelmed. No surprise there, along with the observation that all of the sewer grates visible from Highland gushed muddy water.

Alex had found this to be more alarming than the surface damage. With their sump pump out of commission due to the power outage and the town sewer system flooded past maximum capacity, the water in their basement wouldn't drain. They still kept most of their supplies and equipment in the basement. As they continued along Highland Avenue, closing the distance to the shoreline, the high-water mark on the trees flanking the road rose significantly, along with the layer of mud covering the road and ground.

At first the sludge had been a minor inconvenience, preventing them from simply shuffling along the sidewalk and forcing them to step more deliberately to avoid filling their shoes with the slimy concoction of sand, dirt and sea foam. A few blocks into the tsunami zone, they quickly sank to their ankles, removing dry feet from the very short list of remaining comforts. Upon exiting the neighborhood and reaching the stretch of Highland Avenue flanked by the forest preserve, the mud had reached the middle of Kate's shins, turning the hike into a nightmare.

With the midday sun beating down on her, the past three-quarters of a mile had been difficult physically and mentally. The stagnant sheet of thickening muck had grown deeper, sometimes reaching their knees. The closer they got to their neighborhood, the slower they moved toward their goal of getting to Ryan. Every mud-encrusted, strained footstep stood between Kate and her son.

Standing at the corner of Harrison Road and Highland Avenue, she was thankful to see that all of the houses in the Harrison Hill area appeared intact. With this positive thought in mind, she mentally shelved her grudge against the backpack and trudged forward through the knee-high slop toward their house a few blocks away.

౭∻৶

Alex watched Kate stop and exhale at the intersection. She stepped off in the direction of their neighborhood, without bothering to glance at the lifeless fire station on the opposite side of the street. He knew what was bothering her, aside from the fact that their son was alone and over a hundred miles away in a heavily populated urban center. She was singly focused on throwing her backpack to the ground on their front steps. He should have known better, especially since he'd humped similar packs for hundreds of miles after 9/11. The assault pack had taken a toll on him as well. The pack he'd chosen had a reputation for extreme discomfort, which he had conveniently forgotten until heaving the contraption on his back at the Coast Guard station.

His shoulders had started to chafe several minutes into the hike, when his sweat-soaked cotton T-shirt ceased to provide any kind of useful barrier between his skin and the thick nylon shoulder straps. Three and a half hours later, he wouldn't be surprised to see bone protruding from his shoulders, but he didn't dare show the first sign of wincing or whining. Kate hadn't complained at all, despite the fact that she looked utterly miserable. For her first "forced" road march, she'd exceeded all expectations, leaving Alex humbled. Kate was living proof that the Department of Defense's decision to lift the Combat Exclusion Rules had been long overdue.

Amazingly, neither Emily nor Ethan had grumbled about the hike. He hadn't heard much from them at all, which left him puzzled. They whispered back and forth, but beyond that, they had both gone silent early in the trip. He'd tried to get them talking, but it seemed futile. They appeared slightly catatonic, and their responses were delayed. He was worried that they might be dehydrated, but they'd both consumed nearly three liters of water before reaching the top of Highland Avenue. Kate was convinced they were in some mild form of shock from the morning's events, which served to intensify their "teen distancing" syndrome. Whatever it was, they kept going, which was all he could ask from them at this point.

"Nobody at the fire station?" he asked.

"I guess not," mumbled Kate. "How much water damage do you think we have?"

"Based on the high-water mark here and the fact that most small trees have been knocked down, I'd guess that our basement is completely flooded—and our first floor has been wiped clean."

"There's a lot more standing water here—and mud. It didn't look this bad back up Highland," she said.

"We're almost a mile closer to the beach at this point," he said.

"Everything's been stripped away. This is unbelievable."

He stared down Harrison Road and saw the proverbial "forest for the trees." Aside from the houses, larger trees and utility poles, the landscape had been completely denuded by the tsunami, replaced by a foot and a half deep layer of mud and ubiquitous, randomly scattered piles of debris.

Across the street, he spotted another gray, Town of Scarborough trash bin. They'd seen several along Highland Ave over the past thirty minutes, where evidence of a stronger wave surge became evident. He knew the bins hadn't originated from any of the neighborhoods in Harrison Hill. Trash day was Thursday for this part of town. He'd also seen roofing tiles and splintered sections of cedar siding buried in the mud or stuck in the lower branches of the trees of the forest preserve. A tattered lobster trap lay on the left side of the street, half buried in silt a few feet away from an overturned neon green plastic bucket. The entire landscape was littered with these bizarrely juxtaposed confirmations that humanity had been violently upended further down the line. The tsunami must have obliterated the beach communities.

Fifteen excruciating minutes later, they had reached Everett Lane, one street from Durham Road. Everett ran parallel to Durham and led to a small park nestled into the forest preserve abutting the neighborhoods. Alex wondered if a less conspicuous approach to their house might be a better idea under the circumstances. He didn't feel like parading down the street, attracting everyone's attention. Most of the neighbors would look to him for advice, and he couldn't afford to get bogged down.

If his suspicions were correct, he faced an extremely tight timeframe to rescue his son. In less than a microsecond, this morning's EMP burst had permanently disabled the United States' essential services infrastructure, far exceeding the damage and impact caused by the slow burn of the Jakarta Pandemic. In 2013, it took several weeks of food and water shortages before the riots spiraled out of control, and most people still had electricity! Cities burned, and hundreds of thousands of deaths were attributed to the violence and chaos that ensued. For New England, the extreme winter weather had been a blessing and a curse. The cold undoubtedly killed thousands, but it drove all but the most hardcore to seek shelter, extinguishing the civil rampage that burned entire cities to the ground in the south.

He predicted a forty-eight to seventy-two hour lull in the tightly packed urban and city areas. The pandemic of 2013 had taught the population a thing or two about survival, which would delay the chaos long enough for him to execute a search-and-rescue mission deep into the heart of Boston. "Prepping" took off on an epic scale in the wake of the Jakarta Pandemic, but like every other morning-show-fueled craze, it faded from the greater public consciousness and vanished from the everyday lexicon of most Americans. Thirty-day food and water stashes were slowly incorporated into the household grocery regimen, and sealed buckets of dehydrated food were raided for family camping trips or backyard tenting adventures. Even with this erosion, nobody could deny the fact that the nation was collectively better prepared today than in 2013. Unfortunately, it wouldn't be enough to weather the storm gathering on the immediate horizon.

The "grab and go" survival buckets and two-week stockpiles were designed to alleviate the pressing demands on the food supply system. To bridge the gap, giving the government and food supply distributors time to reallocate current inventories and direct the release of strategic food reserves. Based on the fact that Alex had seen a grand total of five cars on the road in three hours, he wasn't optimistic about the immediate future.

He gave it two days until the collective masses realized that nobody could flip the switch and turn America back on. When this realization took hold, memories of the suffering and misery endured during the darkest hours of the Jakarta Pandemic would flood to the surface, fueling the greatest breakdown in United States history. He wanted to be far from Boston, or any urban area, when that started.

"Honey, let's turn on Everett and sneak in through backyards. We'll pass fewer houses that way."

"Sounds like a plan," Kate said, taking a step forward and stopping.

"Mother fffffuuuuh," she hissed.

Alex saw that her left foot had emerged from the mud without the shoe. At least she couldn't blame him for the shoe selection. He'd suggested packing waterproof hiking boots for the sailing trip, but she'd overruled his decision, opting for more comfortable running or cross-training shoes. Her choice made sense, if you didn't have to fight through knee-high mud. He took her right arm and steadied her while she dug through the muck for her shoe.

"These things are useless at this point," she said, leaning against him to use both hands to retie the shoe.

"They're protecting our feet from a puncture or cut. That's about it. We're almost there, my love. Twenty minutes," he said.

"More like thirty at this rate," she said, finishing with her shoe.

He kissed the back of her moist neck, tasting her salty sweat. "You're doing an amazing job. If it weren't for you, the kids would be sitting in the mud on the side of the road a mile back," he whispered.

She turned and kissed him briefly on the lips. "That's all I needed to hear to keep me going for the rest of the day," she said, flashing the first genuine smile he'd seen from her all morning.

"All right then, let's bring this crazy train home. Kids, I want you guys up here," said Alex, motioning with his hands for them to fill the gap between him and Kate.

"Why?" said Emily.

"So I can watch over you. Come on. Let's go."

"It's just our neighborhood," she said, with a hint of teen condescension.

Alex faked a smile and mumbled under his breath, "Yeah. That's what I'm worried about."

PART II

"DURHAM ROAD"

Chapter 14

Scarborough, Maine

Alex held the rucksack over his head with both hands and pushed through the chest-high mess that filled the water runoff ditch. A similar ditch ran parallel to his backyard on the other side of the neighborhood, emptying into the same retention pond east of the loop. He could only assume that the retention pond had been instantaneously filled by the initial tsunami wave, rendering the entire runoff system useless. He climbed out of the soupy mud, trailing thick strands of seaweed. Neither Kate nor the kids looked eager to step down into the light brown slush. He dropped his pack in the mud at his feet and slid down to the edge of the water.

"There has to be a better way to do this," Kate said.

"You can walk around to the front of the neighborhood and say hi to everyone on the way in," said Alex.

She shook her head and swung her backpack around, hesitating to take the plunge.

"Don't worry," Alex said, smiling, "the water's warm."

"Very funny," Kate said, then mumbled, "I've heard that before."

She stepped down into the water, quickly sinking to her waist, then the top of her neck. She teetered trying to keep the rucksack in the air, nearly toppling into the water. Alex really hoped that didn't happen. Normally, he might find the idea of Kate falling unexpectedly into water utterly hilarious, and if the circumstances were right, he'd consider facilitating the situation. This wasn't one of those times. She didn't look the least bit amused with the situation.

"Are you going to stand there and watch me sink in to my eyebrows, or maybe help me with this pack?"

"I hadn't decided yet." Alex smirked. After a short pause, he waded into the water and grabbed her pack.

"That's yours now, by the way. I'm done with that piece of shit," she said, scrambling up the side of the ditch.

He broke into laughter. "You're lucky I don't throw you back in the water."

"You can try."

"I'll ferry the rest of the packs across," Alex offered. "I didn't realize the water would come up so high on you—though I was really hoping there for a second."

"If I had fallen in, you would be in the deepest shit you've ever been in."

Alex heaved the last pack up to Kate and helped Emily out of the water, pulling her with both hands. He was surprised by the difficulty the group experienced crossing the small ditch. The five-mile hike in the blistering sun had pretty much sapped all of their energy, turning the simple act of crossing a waist-deep ditch into a chore. The water had felt good, though he had never once considered jumping into any of the standing water seen along their route. Hiking in wet pants and shoes was a recipe for disastrous chafing and blisters. Only the promise of dry clothing at the very end of their hike had drawn him across the ditch. He felt a pair of hands on his back.

"You wouldn't dare," he said, without turning around.

"Maybe another day. The water felt good, though," Kate said, pulling him by his left hand.

"It did feel good, even though my pants are filled with mud."

A minute later, they stepped onto the mud-swept street. The storm drain in front of the Murrays' old house gushed dirty water onto the street, creating a shallow swamp that covered the street in front of several houses and crept up the driveways. Between the houses, the entire neighborhood resembled a mudflat, littered with downed trees, seaweed, and persistently scattered debris, complete with a small lake forming at the northeastern edge.

He didn't see anyone standing outside, which struck him as odd. For some reason, he'd expected more activity, but the neighborhood was quiet except for the excited chatter of several birds. He kept forgetting that the wave had hit them over six hours ago. By now, most of them would be exhausted from a combination of fear, stress, heat and humidity. He hoped they stayed inside for the rest of the day. By tomorrow, he would be long gone.

Alex looked up the northern side of the Durham Road loop toward the top of the development. Water pumped less forcefully from the other storm drains he could observe, creating rivulets through the mud that fed the street pond. He stared in awe at the new landscape. Aside from the obvious orientation of the houses, there was nothing to indicate he was standing on a road. Something shifted in the pond, catching their attention. He knew what it was before anyone spoke.

"Is that...a body?" asked Kate.

"I think so. Let's keep everyone moving. Don't stop for—"

"Alex! Alex! Thank God almighty you're here!" yelled Charlie Thornton from his front porch a few houses away.

Dressed in Vietnam-era, tiger-striped camouflage, clutching an overaccessorized AR-15-style rifle, Charlie sprinted down the granite stairs leading off his farmer's porch. He grazed the light post to the left of his red-brick walkway with his left shoulder, nearly tumbling into the mud, and stomped through the slush across two lawns. He screamed their names, along with something about Chinese paratroopers. So much for a stealthy entry.

"I need this like a hole in the head right now," mumbled Alex. "Take the kids home, and start filling containers with tap water. Bathtubs, glasses, coolers, anything that'll hold water. I'll be right there."

"You're alive! You made it! We've got a fucking invasion on our hands. I'll get you a rifle—hold on. Bring everyone up to the house. We're totally screwed, Alex. This is what we've been preparing for! Christ, what the hell happened to you? Looks like you stepped on a landmine. Hi, Kate," said Charlie in a rapid-fire, adrenaline-induced stream of words.

"Hey, Charlie," she responded and immediately turned to Alex. "I'll see you at the house, honey."

"Wait! Let me get you some weapons," said Charlie.

"I think they can make it to our house without an armed escort. I'll be right there, honey. Is the safety engaged on your rifle, Charlie?"

"Why does everyone always ask me about the safety?" Charlie asked, furtively thumbing the safety switch.

Alex put a hand on Charlie's right shoulder. "Because I could see from thirty feet away that it wasn't on, and you just bounced off a light post with your finger on the trigger. Good to see you, by the way. Is everyone all right in your house?"

"Uh, yeah, everyone is fine. The wave scared the shit out of the girls, but it didn't tear through my house like the rest," said Charlie.

"Anyone we know?" said Alex, motioning to the body stuck in the street pond.

"I don't think so. Nobody in the neighborhood is missing. That one must have been completely buried in the mud until the water dislodged it. It's not the first. We cleared a few out of the drainage ditches, and I hear that the Carters found one against the back of their house."

"We saw bodies in the harbor, but none on the road. How is your basement?" Alex asked, knowing the answer.

"Completely flooded," Charlie replied. "Came in through the shattered cellar windows in back. I hauled a lot of stuff up when I saw that glow in the sky to the west and our cars wouldn't start. Mostly weapons and our bug-out bags. We've been hit by an EMP blast. That's why I'm running around with my rifle. Chinese jeeps could come tearing through the neighborhood at any second."

"I highly doubt we're facing a Chinese invasion. We've definitely been hit by something, but I don't expect paratroopers to appear in the skies above Scarborough any time soon," said Alex, starting to walk on the sidewalk toward his house.

"That's the problem, Alex. Nobody knows what's happening. The radio is dead silent. No emergency broadcast. Nothing. We have to assume this is a full-scale invasion until proven otherwise. Where's your pistol?"

"Taken by the Coast Guard. There's really nothing being transmitted?"

Charlie shook his head. "Nothing at all. Hey! What do you mean taken by the Coast Guard?"

"Things are changing rapidly. Give me about an hour to assess the situation at my house; then we'll meet up to figure out a game plan."

"You're going to Boston to get your son, right?"

"Yeah. I may leave tonight if it's feasible. I'll grab Ed's kid too," said Alex.

"You make sure to count me in on that one. I'm serious," said Charlie, grabbing his arm and stopping him.

"I can't ask you to follow me down there, Charlie."

"You don't have to ask."

"I really appreciate that. I'll keep you in the loop. Promise," said Alex.

"I'll keep myself in the loop, if you don't mind. The thought of you and Ed cruising down to Boston on a search-and-rescue mission makes me cringe. Ed's about as tactical as a circus clown."

Alex couldn't help laughing at the image. Charlie had an indomitable sense of humor that was infectious—to a point.

"What are we looking at with the rest of the neighborhood?"

"Everything seems calm for now," said Charlie. "I went around with a few others to make sure everyone filled up on water. The basement flooding kind of fucked up a lot of people's emergency stockpiles. They'll be fine once the water drains—if it drains. Wait until you see the retention pond—I mean lake."

"Looks like I'm in for some snorkeling. I have some shit I need down there, and I don't have that kind of time. Give me an hour, man," said Alex.

"You got it, buddy. Hey, I might need to borrow one of your snorkeling masks. I didn't get all of my toys out of the basement. Forgot the thermal scope."

"Thermal scope? You're crazy. You know that, right?"

"Doesn't sound so crazy now, does it?" said Charlie.

"Unfortunately, it doesn't. By the way, I think you're about five decades behind with your camouflage choice. I haven't seen anyone wear tiger-stripe cammies since—"

"John Wayne. *Green Berets.* The guy was a legend. I watched that movie with my dad when I was nine years old. We watched it every year since. This was the first and only pair of camouflage I've ever used hunting. Well, I've made some modifications over the years, and replaced the trousers, but you get the picture."

"John Wayne." Alex laughed. "He also played Davy Crocket in *The Alamo*, which means you should be wearing that squirrel cover of yours too."

"He wore a coonskin cap, and his had the raccoon face in front. I have a collector's edition in my office, but it's in a glass case. You're talking about this one," said Charlie, pulling his famed coonskin cap out of his right cargo pocket.

"Damn, that thing's ugly. Looks like it's seen better years," said Alex, exaggerating a look of dismay.

"Never missed a shot wearing this baby. You know that better than anyone," he said, proudly donning the cap and creating the most ridiculous-looking outfit Alex had ever seen.

"That I do. See you in a few."

Alex saluted Charlie and picked up Kate's backpack, turning toward the southern side of the Durham Road loop. Kate and the kids had already disappeared behind the Bradys' house, which made him slightly nervous. He wasn't sure why, but Charlie had made a solid point. Without any information, they truly had no idea what they were up against. While Charlie's theories about a Chinese invasion force were too farfetched for Alex's vivid imagination, nobody could deny that they were on the receiving end of a massive, wide-scale "event." Man made or natural, he didn't think it mattered. The result would be the same.

Chaos.

Chapter 15

Scarborough, Maine

The mud wasn't as deep immediately in front of Alex's house, most likely because the house had deflected the initial surge and created a buffer. He stepped between two pine bushes that defiantly protruded from the muck and landed on what he knew logically was the slate walkway connecting the front door to the driveway. He could hear activity in the house, and hoped that Kate would open one of the doors for him. He didn't feel like dragging her pack through the backyard.

The act of finally arriving at their destination had suddenly deprived him of energy, as if his mind had involuntarily dampened his sympathetic nervous system, reducing production of the hormones responsible for his fight-or-flight response to the day's event. It didn't surprise him, considering that he'd been engaged in this mode since five in the morning. There would be no break in his immediate future. Right now, he needed to make an assessment of their situation, starting with their Chevy Tahoe.

He saw Kate's face appear in the mudroom door window and headed for the granite stoop. He had a bad feeling that the word "mudroom" was about to take on a whole new meaning. She cracked the door a few inches, allowing a thick stream of water to pour through the opening onto their porch before pulling it the rest of the way. He glanced at the bottoms of the double garage doors and saw a thin stream of water leaking from the far left bay. Shit. His garage had filled too. So much for their bug-out vehicle.

Kate appeared with a tired look. "I'm estimating that to be about a foot and a half. The family room's the same. The rest of the floors are covered in about six inches of this wonderful shit slime. Be careful once you're inside. It all looks the same depth."

"Have you checked the basement?"

"I came right here to let you in. We had to climb over what's left of the deck," said Kate.

Alex handed over her backpack, and she hung it on one of the empty coat hooks while his eyes adjusted to the shadowy interior of their house. The first thing he noticed was the high-water stain on the drywall, less than an inch from the ceiling. That couldn't be right. He scanned the entire mudroom and saw the same line just below the ceiling. He nearly tripped over one of their kitchen island stools examining the roof. He heard the water pipes running in the house and looked through the doorway to the kitchen.

"The kids are filling up the bathtubs," she responded.

"Good. At least the water still works—what are the chances that the Tahoe still runs?"

"Give it a shot," Kate said. "If it works, we'll have half a chance to get Ryan."

"I'll get him back no matter what," Alex said, stepping over to the door.

"I know. I know. I just...looking around here, I'm not hopeful about his chances if this thing hit closer to Boston."

Alex stepped away from the garage door and held her tight, nestling his head next to her ear and kissing her neck.

"He'll be fine. I'll start walking tonight if I have to. This is nothing. A minor bump in the road. In three days, we'll be eating at a picnic table with my parents in Limerick," he whispered.

"Not if you're walking," said Kate.

"Ten days. Let's check the Tahoe and see what we're dealing with."

Alex opened the door to the garage and was greeted by a foot of mud, which reached the bottom of the truck's doors. Silt and small debris covered the black Tahoe from top to bottom. The deluge of water, which at one point had risen above the Tahoe, had upended the garage. A red plastic gas can sat on the SUV's roof, while the rest of the garage's tools and sporting goods equipment was nowhere to be seen, presumably under the water. He pressed the key fob to unlock the SUV and was rewarded by the familiar chirping sound. He pressed it again and heard the door mechanisms activate.

"Good news, honey," he said, hopeful for the first time since waking up this morning.

He jumped into the mud and splashed across the empty bay to reach the SUV, tripping on something submerged below the surface. Quickly regaining his balance, he yanked the door open, which released a small quantity of foamy water into the muck below.

"That's not a good sign," she said.

He pocketed the key fob and hopped into the truck, pressing the keyless ignition button. The batteries turned the engine over, and for a few glorious moments, he thought the Tahoe might start. He should have known better. The 2018 Tahoe hybrid was one of the most technologically advanced heavy SUVs on the market. The commercials likened it to a fly-by-wire aircraft, where every aspect of its performance was monitored and controlled by multiple onboard computers. It was one of the safest, most fuel-efficient vehicles of its kind thanks to cutting-edge technology. Now this revolutionary beast was simply in the way of the bicycles hanging on the far side of the garage. He looked at Kate and smiled.

"I always wanted to mountain bike all the way to Boston on the Eastern Trail."

Kate stifled a laugh, shaking her head. "I'm just trying to picture Charlie on a hundred-mile bike ride." She chuckled.

Alex hopped into the water and walked to the garage door in the empty bay.

"I remember him doing that trek across Maine thing a few years ago," said Alex, pulling on the red garage door manual release toggle above his head.

"Uh—I'm pretty sure he rode an ambulance most of the way back," said Kate.

Alex pulled the door upward, releasing a flood of sludge down the driveway. He lifted the door all the way and was startled to see Ed standing a few feet away, holding two coffee mugs.

"This is what I get for bringing over fresh coffee?" he said, staring down at his dirtied shoes.

"Is that really coffee?" said Kate, her caffeine instincts savagely activated.

"French roast. Had just enough to make two cups," he said, extending the mugs.

Alex and Kate accepted the mugs and carefully sipped the steaming hot liquid. Alex felt the caffeine immediately, which provided a needed boost to counteract his mental fatigue.

"You're a life saver, Ed," he said, shaking his hand and guiding him into the garage. "Come on in. I'd offer you a seat, but—"

"Our house got it the same. You should have seen it, man. Charlie was over when it hit. One minute I was trying to convince him that the Chinese hadn't invaded, the next we were running for the staircase. The water flattened the fence behind us and slammed into the house a few seconds later. Filled the first floor to the ceiling within minutes—no shit. It was unbelievable."

"We got lucky here. I've seen roofing tile and other debris that must have come from Higgins Beach," said Alex.

"They found a sign for the Higgins Beach Lodge up at the top of the street. That used to be up on the third floor of the hotel. The beach has to be gone," said Ed.

"How's Samantha holding up?" said Kate, taking her lips away from the coffee for the first time.

"All right, given the Boston situation," he said.

"I'm going to supervise the water hoarding and let the two of you plan the next move. Ed—you're a lifesaver," she said, holding up the mug of coffee. "I'd kiss you, but Alex might be mad that I stole his kiss."

"Nice. Get a little caffeine in her and she's ready for improv," replied Alex.

After Kate disappeared into the house, Alex addressed the primary concern of both families.

"We have to get the kids, and it's not going to be an easy trip. The families will go to my parents' farm in Limerick, and we'll head to Boston," said Alex.

"Sam's not taking this well at all. I didn't want to say that in front of Kate, but she's on the verge of a breakdown. We have no idea what's happening out there. Nobody does," said Ed.

"Chloe will be fine. She knows what to do in case of an emergency like this. Ryan and Chloe will link up at one of their places and wait for us. Five days is the plan," said Alex.

"What if they don't wait? This is something different altogether. The city will start falling apart by tonight," said Ed.

"That's why we aren't going to waste any time getting down there. They'll be there when we arrive," said Alex.

"That's what I told Sam. She wanted me to leave earlier this morning. Try to get both of them, but—man, I can't tell you how happy I am to see you. There was no way I could have pulled that off. Sorry, that sounded terrible. I'm just glad you guys made it back. I wasn't hopeful, sailboat and all. You look like shit by the way. Almost as bad as John McClane at the end of a *Die Hard* movie."

"It wasn't good. I think we got lucky, to be honest," Alex said, suddenly aware of the pain shooting down his right arm.

He switched the coffee mug from his right to left hand and tried to extend his arm into the air, barely able to get the upper arm a few degrees over the plane of his shoulder.

"I thought you got that fixed?" asked Ed.

"That was the other side," he said, referring to the multiple surgeries required to restore full mobility to the shoulder destroyed by a marauder's shotgun blast during the chaos of the Jakarta Pandemic.

"This is part of my new suite of injuries. I jammed my arm between the spokes on the steering wheel so—"

"On purpose?"

"It was the only way to keep the wheel from spinning out of control. We almost lost the boat," Alex said.

He raised the sleeve on his T-shirt and saw that a baseball-sized area on his upper tricep had turned a sickening black-purple color that looked more urgent than simple bruising.

"You need to have someone look at that. I'm surprised you can use the arm at all," said Ed.

"It's fine. The more I use it the better."

"Yeah, it'll be fine until you wake up tomorrow and can't move it at all. You need to at least put some ice on that and take some ibuprofen. Check your freezer. You should still have some ice."

"All right. Give me a few—"

His sentence was interrupted by the sound of running footsteps. Charlie Thornton appeared, running full throttle up the driveway, waving a satellite phone in front of his face. Alex glanced at his rifle.

"The safety's on, you fucking nervous nellies," Charlie said peevishly.

"That wasn't an hour. More like five minutes, Charlie," said Alex.

94

"I know, but Samantha said Ed was over here. Take a look," he said, waving the phone in Alex's face. "Damn thing's been quiet all morning, then whammo! Emergency broadcast! Just like they said it would work. Looks like all the money FEMA spent on this didn't go to waste."

"Can I see it?" asked Alex.

Charlie handed the phone to Alex, and they all huddled over the digital screen to read the broadcast.

"The Department of Homeland Security has declared a national state of emergency, effective immediately for the continental United States. The European Space Agency has confirmed that a large space-borne object entered Earth's atmosphere at approximately 0455 EST and broke apart over the United States. Impacts have been registered from Virginia to Nova Scotia. Widespread power outages have been reported. Citizens are encouraged to remain at their residences and avoid travel until further notice."

The information created just as many questions as it answered. If the tsunami was caused by an asteroid strike, what caused the EMP? Widespread power outages? No kidding. Why didn't NASA confirm the strikes? Are they offline? Why mention Homeland Security instead of FEMA? He handed the phone back to Charlie.

"Well, at least we're not dealing with a Chinese invasion," said Charlie.

"Unless the Chinese sent that message," said Ed.

"Ed," Alex warned, "don't screw with him like that. Please."

"He's right, though," Charlie admitted. "None of this makes sense."

"Why would you do that, Ed?" pleaded Alex.

"I love to sit back and watch the two of you argue about this stuff," said Ed.

"Thanks. I think we're fine, Charlie. There's more to what they're telling us, but the asteroid thing makes sense. A second burst of wind hit us from the east, which is the direction of Nova Scotia," said Alex.

"I sure as shit hope so," Charlie replied. "I don't plan on letting them put me into a forced labor camp to make smart phones for the Europeans."

Alex sighed. "All right. I really need, like, thirty minutes to go through the house and figure out where we stand."

"Forget about anything in the basement," said Charlie.

"Unfortunately, I need to retrieve some essential gear for our trip. One of our bikes is down there too. I need that for Ethan," said Alex.

"Why don't you just give him yours?" Charlie asked, pointing at the rack of bicycles hanging on the far wall.

"Because there's four in my group, and I only have three bikes in the garage? I don't plan on walking to Boston."

"Who said anything about biking to Boston? Ed's Jeep survived the EMP."

"Shit, Charlie! Will you keep that down?" hissed Ed, pulling them deep into the garage. "I wasn't going to say anything until we got inside, Alex, but we're taking the Wrangler down to Boston."

"Isn't the fuel system contaminated?"

"I checked it out," said Charlie. "It's fine as far as I can tell, and I know a thing or two about cars."

"I didn't think you could submerge a Jeep," said Alex.

"You can't, but it didn't get submerged."

"How? The water in my garage reached the ceiling. We can't run the risk of that engine seizing up ten miles down the road, Ed."

"It was pure luck. I went into the garage to start the cars, but decided to open both garage bay doors first. After opening the second door, I thought about the hand-cranked radio on one of the shelves. I brought the radio inside and got distracted. From what I could tell, the water never rose over the wheel wells. Just flowed right out of the garage," said Ed.

"Un—believable. You win the EMP car lottery and take it one step further by accidentally saving the car. You need to hit Vegas when this is over," said Alex.

"If Vegas ever goes back online, I'll book the first flight."

"I guess we have some planning to do," said Alex.

"We should probably leave for Boston in a few hours," Ed suggested. "Two hours there, two hours back, give or take an hour or two. We should be back before dark."

"It's not going to be that easy. We have no idea what happened down in Boston or the seacoast of New Hampshire. We could be looking at this," he gestured to the neighborhood wreckage, "times ten."

"We can swing further inland once we cross into New Hampshire, get away from the 95. Between the two cars, I have a full tank. That's twenty-two gallons, more than enough to get to Boston and back to Limerick. We can throw a few extra gas cans in the Jeep to give us more range."

"Distance won't be the problem. There's something else. We watched the police commandeer civilian vehicles in South Portland, and one of the petty officers at the Coast Guard station said they had been instructed to disarm civilians on sight. They tossed my pistol in the water without hesitation. What if the police are doing this everywhere?"

"I would have flattened any son of a bitch who tried to take my pistol," said Charlie.

"I had a 240 'bravo' pointed at my head, Charlie. Not a lot of choice there. I think we need to give the police a day to simmer and replace their motor pool, then set out first thing tomorrow with a solid plan," said Alex.

"That's almost twenty-four hours away. Samantha's gonna flip out when she hears this," said Ed.

"We'll get everyone together and explain the situation. Based on what I've seen so far, putting a functional vehicle on the road today is a risky move, especially considering the type of equipment we'll need to bring with us to ensure our safety in Boston. If they're tossing civilian pistols into the water without a second thought, imagine what'll happen when we try to explain a trunk full of combat rifles."

"What's to stop them from confiscating our car tomorrow? We'd be in the same situation, except we'd have lost a day," said Ed.

"There is no guarantee. Just a gut feeling based on experience. By tomorrow, people will start venturing out onto the roads. Anyone with a car will try to leave the more populated areas. They know it's only a matter of time before the situation explodes. With more cars on the road, the police will have their hands full. The most I expect to encounter is a checkpoint or two along the way. They'll be focused on traffic heading north. We'll be headed south. I've seen this before. Every time we rolled up on a city in Iraq, the same thing happened. The streets went quiet while everyone tried to figure out if we planned to launch a major offensive or bypass the city. The next day? Mayhem. Cars backed up into the city along the main roads, families fleeing on foot, carrying suitcases and valuables. If we wait until tomorrow, we'll be able to blend in and lower our risk of attracting attention."

"I'm going to need you to explain this to my wife. She's ready to drive down to Boston herself."

"Here's what I'm thinking overall. Early tomorrow, we put the families on bicycles and send them out to my parents' place in Limerick. It'll take them four hours tops to get there."

"Longer if the roads are like this across town," said Ed.

"True. They'll have to walk the bikes down Harrison Road at least a mile before it eases up. Maybe longer. Anyway, at the same time, we head south for Boston. If all goes well on our end, we'll be back with the kids in time for dinner. Everyone is welcome to stay at the farm as long as they'd like. It's up to you guys. I don't plan on returning here once we retrieve the kids," said Alex.

"Thanks, Alex. I'll have to talk it over with Sam. A lot will depend on what we see out there."

"I know Linda will want to wait it out, but maybe I can convince her to do the waiting in a less populated area," said Charlie.

"We'll have running water and electricity, if that helps sway your decision," said Alex.

Charlie asked, "Won't the solar panels be fried?"

"We have two banks of solar panels, each fully independent, with its own controller, inverter and battery storage bank. One of the two systems is disconnected at all times. No link to the grid and all cables detached. The solar panels themselves should be fine, according to the manufacturer," said Alex, shrugging his shoulders.

"The prospect of hot showers and cold drinks might sway the vote, my friend. It's going to get really rustic around here—really quick," said Charlie.

"That's a fact. How about we give you some time to dig through the house?" Ed asked. "I'll bring cold beers over in an hour or so, and we'll work out the rest of the details. I should have Sam onboard with the plan by then."

"Sounds good. Hey—does anyone else know about the Jeep?" asked Alex.

"Jamie was in her garage across the street when I started it. I let it run for a few minutes to make sure the fuel system was fine. Both of her garage doors were open."

"I suggest you shut both bay doors and reengage the manual release. Make sure it's locked. How about the door on the side? Looks like mine was busted open by the water."

"Busted, along with the windows," said Ed.

"At some point sooner than later, we need to shore up your garage so nobody can get in and try to steal your car. I'd be willing to bet that Jamie wasn't the only person in the neighborhood to hear the engine start. The only thing I've heard so far is the water spilling out of the sewers."

"I heard him start the car from inside my house," said Charlie.

"Then it looks like we may be spending the night at Ed's house and posting a watch. You're holding the winning lottery ticket, Ed, except your ticket is a thousand times more valuable than any of this weekend's winning mega-bucks tickets. I'll swing by when I'm done taking an inventory here. Stay safe, guys. We all know what can happen around here when things get desperate."

Chapter 16

Scarborough, Maine

Alex started his mental inventory before Ed and Charlie had disappeared down the driveway. He'd have to adjust for their updated transportation situation, which would simplify the process but force them to make some painful decisions. They would have to leave most of their gear and supplies behind, opting for lighter, more practical immediate survival load-outs suitable for bicycle or foot mobile operations. The Fletchers' bug-out plan had always been relatively simple, since they had never anticipated travelling any farther than Alex's parents' farm roughly thirty-five miles away. The comprehensive escape plan accounted for the use of two vehicles, but could be scaled down to accommodate any level of timeframe and transit mode. In this case, they would have to reconfigure for a bicycle trip and a forty-eight-hour, low-intensity urban combat mission. Two vastly different operations, with distinctly different objectives.

The bicycle group's individual load-out would be designed for thirty-six hours, with a focus on additional hydration. He would recommend that each person carry ten liters of water, in a combination of three-liter CamelBaks and additional stainless-steel bottles. Four MREs, a dozen energy bars, a flashlight or headlamp, one change of clothing and footwear stuffed in a waterproof bag, one emergency blanket, and a serrated folding knife would round out the mandatory individual load. Within the group, they would have to carry a first aid kit, road maps, enough camping tents to accommodate everyone, binoculars to scout the road ahead, toilet paper, a satellite phone, and of course—firearms.

His vision for the Boston mission involved a twenty-four-hour tactical kit, for operations in and around the city, and a forty-eight-hour sustainability pack in case they were forced to abandon the vehicle at any point during their journey. They could carry extra gear and "luxuries" in the

Jeep, but Alex would configure their essential equipment for immediate evacuation. If something went severely wrong on the road, he didn't need Charlie and Ed fumbling around the SUV, trying to collect their shit. Vehicles had a tendency to attract projectiles in that kind of situation.

He'd instituted a "five second" rule for his Amphibious Assault Vehicle Company in Iraq. If one of his vehicle commanders gave the order to abandon their AAV, each marine had their essential gear stashed where they could "grab and go" within five seconds. The rule had saved numerous lives on the road to Baghdad. The road to Boston wouldn't be lined with rocket-propelled grenades, machine-gun teams and improvised explosive devices, but it had the potential to be just as deadly. Their Jeep would undoubtedly attract the wrong kind of attention, topping the list of high-value targets wherever they drove.

His group would be heavily armed, but a gunfight before reaching their destination would most likely represent the loss of their vehicle. A numerically superior force would push them away from the SUV. They might escape with their lives, but they'd lose the Jeep. A smaller group could irreparably damage the car, leaving them in the same situation. They would seek the path of least resistance to the outskirts of Boston, even if it meant adding significant mileage and time to their trip. *Detect and avoid.* The complete opposite of his mission in Iraq.

He stepped into the mudroom and moved the stools into the bathroom shower stall, glancing at the sink, which was filled with dark brown silt. The sink burped, splattering a small bubble of silt onto the walls. The sewer system was useless at this point. He wondered what would happen if they tried to flush the toilets.

"Kate?" he yelled.

"Yeah?" she replied from the kitchen.

"Is the sink backed up in there?"

"Sort of. It's filled with mud, but I've managed to clean some of it out. It's draining really slowly."

"How about upstairs?"

"Everything looked normal up there, like nothing happened," she said.

Alex leaned out of the bathroom door. "I think we should restrict our use of the bathrooms to the upstairs, and stop using the toilets at the first sign of a backup. I'm afraid to flush the one down here. The last thing we need is raw sewage in the house."

"I'll let the kids know; then I'm going to start on lunch. I think we can skip the water hoarding. Between the garage and closet, we'll be leaving most of it behind when we head out," she said.

"Yeah, I agree. Sounds like they finished filling the tubs, anyway. That should be enough, just in case something keeps us from leaving."

"So Ed's Jeep works?" she added.

"Apparently. It'll get us to Boston a hell of a lot quicker than biking down," said Alex.

"Why don't we ferry the rest of the group back and forth to Limerick? I don't know about leading a group of nine women and kids on bikes through this crap," said Kate.

"Once you get a mile or two inland, you'll be on dry pavement," said Alex.

"Easy for you to say, cruising by in a four-wheel-drive vehicle. You could at least get us to Route 11."

"I don't think that would be a good idea, Kate. It'll take at least two round trips if we do it that way. That Jeep will have a big bull's-eye on it wherever it goes. We can't have it repeatedly cruising back and forth through Scarborough, or any towns, for that matter. We especially can't bring it back here. The neighbors will be all over us. Once that Jeep drives out of the garage, it can't come back. Which reminds me, before we leave, we have to sanitize the house of any information that could lead people out to Limerick, or we'll have a refugee camp on our hands."

"Could you turn any of these people away if they showed up out there?" Kate asked.

"No, but I don't plan on making it easy for them to find us."

Kate flashed him an annoyed look, which he could live with for now. He crossed the sludge-covered floor to the small study that Kate and Alex used as a temporary refuge from the noise level created by teenagers and the ever-blaring television in the family room. The floor-to-ceiling bookshelf had been emptied of its contents, with the exception of the top shelf, which had stubbornly held onto several overturned picture frames. Hundreds of books lay in various states of damage at the base of the bookshelf, forming a two-foot high, unstable pile of soggy pulp and wilted hardcovers. The brown leather chairs were covered in half-dried filth, one of them home to a mangled, brushed silver lamp and one half of the window's plantation shutters. He remembered seeing the other white shutter under the bench in the mudroom. He opened the study closet to take his first real inventory. In all likelihood, they wouldn't need much more than what he could salvage from the closet—aside from the guns, ammunition and a few select gadgets. Actually, this closet was just the "tip of the iceberg."

The right side of the closet housed built-in shelves that held a dozen 2.5-gallon jugs of spring water, two 120-serving "grab and go" buckets of freeze-dried vegetables and a black nylon duffel bag filled with twenty military-grade MREs. This stockpile represented more than enough food and water to satisfy the needs of his family during tomorrow's exodus. He knew that Charlie and Ed kept similar stockpiles on their first floors, so there would be no need to waste time retrieving additional food or water from the basement. Two dark green, metal .50 caliber ammunition cans sat on the top shelf, below the wall's high-water mark. He pulled both of them down and set them on the antique cherry wood desk against the interior wall of the house.

He opened the canister marked "EG" to confirm that it had not leaked. From what he could tell by visual examination, the waterproof seal had held as advertised, sparing the electronics gear from any water damage. The converted storage can held two Iridium satellite phones, a handheld GPS plotter, a pair of two-way VHF handheld radios, a handheld radio scanner and three thirty-round .223 AR magazines. He reached deep into the canister to feel for water or moisture. Thankfully, it was bone dry. He pocketed the full AR magazines before closing the canister.

The second canister, marked "RG," held each item's charging kit and adapter, in addition to a folding solar panel, battery power pack and AC inverter. Ziploc bags filled with loose AA and AAA batteries sat at the bottom of the can. He quickly checked for water damage, finding the same result. No leakage.

Unfortunately, the same couldn't be said for the individual BOLT (Basic Operations for Limited Time) kits assigned to each member of the family. Stuffed together on the floor to the left of the shelving unit, each rucksack was identified by a strip of duct tape with a name. The mud and water that had reached the ceiling earlier had peeled the tape and faded the lettering, but he still recognized the names. He plucked his pack out of the mud and grunted at the waterlogged weight. They'd have to unpack each kit and scavenge for items they could add to the dry rucksacks hauled out of the sailboat.

He hoped that the national state of emergency had shut down the court system. There was little doubt in his mind that Kate would present him with divorce papers after riding for thirty-five miles with the "three day" pack on her back. Kate was going to kick his ass when she heard the news, but there was little way around it. The larger, infinitely more comfortable internal frame packs he'd chosen for their BOLT kits wouldn't dry by tomorrow morning, and their commercial hiking packs were buried under ten feet of water in the basement.

He carried the MOLLE II rucksack to the kitchen island, and dropped it onto the granite. Kate, who was in the middle of preparing cheese sandwiches on an area of the counter she had cleaned, stared at the pack with a look of disgust. She shook her head.

"I can't ride to Limerick with that piece of shit on my back."

"It's smaller than this pack. Might be easier to balance while riding," offered Alex.

"No. We can dry these in the sun on the patio. I'm not putting that thing on my back again. Mayonnaise on your sandwich?" she said, displaying her patented "I'm happy" smile.

"I love you," he said, unzipping one of the outer sustainment pouches on the pack.

"Really? Even though I fully blame you for ripping my shoulders up with your crappy backpacks?"

"Especially after that," he said, pulling a compressed, lightweight sleeping bag out of the sustainment pouch.

She eyed the dripping, down-filled ball that once qualified as a sleeping bag.

"I have a feeling those won't dry by tomorrow," she said.

He shook his head and removed the other item stuffed in the pouch, expanding the grayish, universal camouflage-patterned Gore-Tex sleeping bag shell and shaking the water from it.

"This is probably all you'll need if you get stuck overnight. Maybe one of the emergency blankets. I'll strip the packs down and hang them on what's left of the deck in the sun," he said.

"I'll have some lunch ready in a few minutes. Sandwiches and canned vegetable soup, plus a bag of barbeque chips that I found in the family room," she said.

"Sounds like heaven," he replied, turning his attention to the basement door.

He pulled an LED flashlight out of the MOLLE pack and tested it, pleased to find that neither the water nor the EMP had knocked it out of commission. As far as he could tell, most handheld electronics or battery-powered devices continued to function, consistent with the CNI Revised Report's assessment of the effects of an EMP burst on portable electronics. Then again, the Revised Report seemed to be all over the place in terms of accuracy. The predicted 60% failure rate for automobiles seemed generous at this point. His own observations supported a rate in the high nineties.

Alex opened the door to the basement and flashed the light down the stairwell. The light reflected a Stygian pool that reached the fourth stair from the top and rose above the bottom of the basement ceiling. He extinguished the flashlight and stepped into the stairwell, closing the door behind him. He was immediately cast into absolute darkness and silence. Peaceful, yet suffocating. He let his eyes adjust for a few moments, peering into the water, searching for any sign of light from the basement windows. Nothing. This wasn't good. He needed a few specialty items locked away in his bunker. Actually, he didn't really need them, he *wanted* them. And he wanted them badly enough to consider taking a swim in the blackness beneath him. He opened the door, grateful for the sunlight.

"The basement is a total loss. Water up to the ceiling. Look at this," he announced, looking back down into the impenetrable darkness.

Kate joined him at the door. "I don't think you should go down there."

Alex shut the door. "Who said anything about me taking a swim?"

"I can tell by the way you're staring down at the water, like your mind was plotting something that it really shouldn't."

"My night vision gear is down there, along with most of the weapons and ammunition," said Alex.

"Uh huh. I thought there was enough ammo in the BOLT kits."

He didn't feel like getting into it with her. She was right, sort of. Each pack held two full, thirty-round AR magazines, in addition to two fifteen-round 9mm magazines for the Heckler and Koch P30C pistol. When you added it to all of the ammunition available in the study closet, it equaled far more than enough to handle a worst-case scenario, "guns blazing" transit from Scarborough to his parents' farm, but Boston presented a whole new level of shit storm to the equation, and he had no intention of underestimating the level of chaos he might need to navigate to find their children.

Even his firearm situation was less than optimal given the circumstances. He had a rifle, shotgun and one pistol upstairs, which once again sounded like overkill, but he'd need the rifle and pistol for Boston, leaving Kate with the shotgun. Not exactly the ideal firearm to haul along on a bicycle. He needed to grab his backup AR and a pistol for Emily, some rifle attachments stored in one of several sealed canisters next to the gun safe, ammunition for the rifles and pistols, and his night vision gear. The night vision would provide a significant tactical advantage inside Boston, allowing him to detect and avoid most potentially hazardous human situations.

"I'll grab the kids for lunch," he said.

Alex removed his shoes once he reached the top of the staircase, wondering why he'd bothered. Judging from the multiple mud prints leading in every direction on the hardwood floor, neither Kate nor the kids had bothered to do the same, and it probably wouldn't make much of a difference. His whole body was still dripping dirty water from their ditch crossing. For tactical reasons, he supposed he should keep them on, especially with the state of uncertainty smothering them from all sides, but he'd already left them at the top of the stairs. He turned left into Emily's room and found her packing a laundry basket of personal belongings. Small items from what he could tell.

"You all right, sweetie?"

"We're not coming back here, are we, Dad?" she asked, tears streaming from her eyes.

"Not until it's safe, which could be a while."

He stepped into her room and touched one of her picture collages on the wall near the bedroom door. They'd given her a framed collage of family photos every year on her birthday, starting when she was three. He loved looking at them, though they visually represented how quickly she had changed from a squeaky little girl to a headstrong young woman. They'd have to leave all of this behind, and hope it would still be here when they returned. He turned around with watery eyes and fought not to say anything about the laundry basket of stuff she wouldn't be able to bring.

"Mom made some sandwiches. Everyone needs to fuel up on some real food before we get to work this afternoon. We still have a long day ahead of us."

"What's happening out there? I mean, what is this?"

"Mr. Thornton got a broadcast on his satellite phone. They say that an asteroid broke up over the U.S. and hit the East Coast. I think we got lucky."

"I don't feel lucky," Emily said, wiping her eyes and walking to the door.

"I do. I've got you and your mom safe. Ethan too. Once we get Ryan back, I'll be the luckiest man on the planet," he said, hugging her tightly.

"You're the corniest dad on the planet. You said Mom made some real food? What's the occasion?"

"Digging on your mom and dad in the face of the apocalypse?" said Alex.

"You know I love you, Dad. I'll get Ethan and meet you downstairs," she said and disappeared.

He glanced at the laundry basket, wondering if there was any way he could sneak the contents into one of the spare rucksacks and stash it in the Jeep. Not likely, but he might give it a try anyway. Alex ran into Ethan and Emily on the way out of her room.

"Tell your mother I'll be right down."

Once they had descended the stairs, he hurried into the bedroom and vanished into the darkness of the walk-in closet to change out of his putrid clothes into shorts and a T-shirt for now. His right arm ached as he lifted the shirt over his head. He'd have to tend to this injury immediately after lunch. Losing the effective use of his dominant arm would be a showstopper for Boston. He pushed the pain aside and finished changing. He reached for the bedroom door, but paused, thinking about what Charlie had said. He didn't expect Chinese paratroopers to drop from the skies, but it couldn't hurt to be ready for trouble.

Alex parted the shoulder-level curtain of clothing at the back of the closet and touched the keypad, illuminating the numbers. He'd felt confident that the keypad would function, but had the option of opening the gun safe manually with a hidden key if the electronics had succumbed to the EMP. Alex punched in the eight-digit code on the keypad mounted on the stand-up gun safe, and heard the mechanisms within the door shift.

He pulled on the handle, activating a small blue LED light within the safe, removed the HK P30 pistol sitting on the shelf above the rifles, and started to move it to his drop-down holster. He stopped, realizing that he'd have to thoroughly clean the holster first. The pistol could wait.

The rifle emerged next, along with a green polymer thirty-round .223 magazine. He inserted the magazine and rapidly pulled the charging handle, chambering a round. He placed the rifle against the side of the safe and took the MOLLE tactical chest rig from a hook on the back wall. He donned the rig over his clothes and filled the eight magazine pouches with spare rifle magazines from the top shelf of the safe, bringing his immediately available total to twenty magazines, or six hundred rounds. He may not have to dive for the additional .223 ammunition from the basement, which suited him fine.

He swapped out the two mud-encrusted pistol magazines from his holster rig and replaced them with clean polymer fifteen-round 9mm magazines from the safe. Three additional pistol magazines filled the smaller pouches on the left side of his modular chest rig. A total of six pistol magazines would be more than enough. Standing in his closet, he carried more ammunition than he'd fielded during combat operations in Iraq. Alex closed the safe and picked up the HK416 rifle.

Closely resembling the M4 carbine, the HK416 represented an improvement over the venerable M4 design, offering superior reliability and durability under all conditions. Extensive field-testing over the past decade consistently demonstrated the advantages of Heckler and Koch's proprietary rifle system over the traditional variants of the M4, leading to its adoption by the United States Army and United States Marine Corps as their primary battle rifle. Alex had chosen to purchase and train with the civilian variant of the HK416 that most closely resembled the standard military-issued rifle.

Featuring a 16.5-inch heavy barrel, quad floating rails, vertical fore grip and telescoping stock, his rifle was nearly indistinguishable from its military counterpart. He had even opted to mount a Trijicon 4X Advanced Combat Optical Gunsight (ACOG) to the rifle, further mimicking standard marine issue. The Marine Corps had long ago equipped every rifle in their inventory with a variation of the ACOG sight, bucking the long-standing tradition of relying upon iron sights. Alex compromised by installing flip up iron sights on forty-five degree angle rail mounts, giving him the option of canting the rifle and using iron sights for close-in engagements.

A minute later, he ran into Kate at the bottom of the stairs, holding a plateful of sandwiches out to him.

"We're already at this point?" she commented, nodding at his gear.

"We were there as soon as the EMP hit. Eating upstairs?"

"We could all use a break from the mud. The kids will bring the rest of the food up. I say we clean up and start over. Wash the day off while we still have running water. Lunch once everyone looks and smells human again," said Kate, handing him the plate.

"Sounds like a plan."

"I'll grab one of the coolers from the garage. I put some beers and sodas in the freezer for now. I'll dump the drinks and some ice in the cooler and meet you upstairs," she said.

"Good. I could use a beer before swimming around the basement," said Alex.

"You're still planning on going down there?"

"Unfortunately, I don't see any other option, unless you want to ride to Limerick with a shotgun."

"No thanks. You still need a shower, by the way—not that I can smell you over myself."

"The whole neighborhood is going to smell ten times worse in a few days. This crap isn't going anywhere," he said.

"Good thing we won't be here."

Chapter 17

Scarborough, Maine

Alex sat on the top stair and splashed his feet in the pitch-black water, desperately trying to convince himself that he didn't need any of the equipment in the basement. He could think of twenty good reasons why he shouldn't submerge himself in the darkness below, most of them safety related, some of them purely irrational. His overly active imagination had swept the worst sea creatures conceivable two miles inland with the tsunami, to be deposited through the basement window.

He wore a blue swimsuit, tight-fitting polyester running shirt, and swim fins. A diver's mask and snorkel, which he'd taken from the boat and stashed in his rucksack, sat on his lap. He'd gotten lucky with that decision. Since the Maine coast wasn't exactly renowned for its crystal-clear waters, the rest of their snorkeling gear was in the basement, where it waited for a trip to Florida or the Caribbean. They'd always carried at least one snorkeling kit onboard the sailboat for practical reasons. Over the past five years, he'd gone over the side more times than he could count to clean seaweed from the propeller or disentangle a lobster pot line from the rudder.

His biggest fear was the electricity. What if the grid was restored while he was submerged? He knew this wouldn't happen, but the thought dogged him. The waterline was well above the breaker box, exposed directly to the house's external utility feed. He pushed this thought as far away as possible, focusing on the more immediate, tangible challenges he'd face underwater. Breathing always came in at the top of his mental list.

From what he could tell, the water pushed up against the basement ceiling. He might find a pocket of air between ceiling joists if the water level was a few inches below the floorboard, but the air would be limited. Using the snorkel to access the air presented a few risks. With only a few inches of dry space, he would have to be extremely careful not to tip the snorkel and inhale water. Low on air deep inside the basement, a panicked moment could kill him. This assumed he could find a few pockets of air. If not, he'd have to take the entire operation slowly, making multiple trips to unlock doors, safes, clear debris—all culminating in a few long, unobstructed trips to haul out his perceived bounty. Fortunately, everything he needed was clearly labeled and conveniently located in one place inside the "bunker."

"Are you sure you don't want to attach a line or something?" asked Kate.

"Are you coming in after me if something goes wrong?"

"Why wouldn't I?"

"Then I'm definitely not attaching a line. One of us has to survive this," he replied.

"I think I'm capable of swimming twenty feet and dragging your ass out of there. I'm a better swimmer than you," she pointed out.

"Then maybe you should be the one making the dive," he said, raising his eyebrows.

"I'm not familiar enough with your system down there."

"Having a line attached is just one more thing I have to worry about. I'll be fine. If I'm having trouble, I'll come right up. Promise."

"All right, but I wish we had a way to communicate," said Kate.

"I'll check the first few joists for an air pocket. If I don't find air, you're going to see me back here every thirty seconds or so. If I find air, I'll try to use the snorkel to clear the whole path in one trip. You can sit in the water with your goggles and watch my light. The water's pretty warm," he said.

"You always say that," she said, taking a transparent pair of goggles off the kitchen island.

"It's at least ten degrees warmer than the beach water. Probably heated up over land," said Alex.

He heard a knock from the mudroom, followed by Charlie's voice. "You guys here?"

"Come on in, Charlie," Alex called. "I'm about to take a swim."

Charlie walked into the kitchen with his AR suspended at chest level by a one-point tactical sling. Alex noticed that he had completely rearranged the attachments on his rifle since he'd last seen him. Instead of a long-range scope, the rifle now featured an EOTech holographic sight with flip-up magnifier, a laser/flashlight combination and a bipod. Alex's rifle lay on the recently cleaned granite island, along with the rest of his tactical gear. Charlie's eyes immediately diverted to the rifle.

"You sprang for an ACOG? Dammit. Now I feel like I cheaped out on this," he said grumpily.

"I think that EOTech combo costs the same. I almost went with that," said Alex.

"But you didn't," said Charlie, still staring at Alex's rifle.

He finally broke the attachment-envy-induced trance and joined them at the basement doorway.

"Christ, it's dark down there," Charlie remarked. "Did you open the bulkhead door?"

Alex looked up at Kate and shook his head. "We're fucking idiots."

"I'm not saying another word," said Charlie, winking at Kate.

Five minutes later, the underwater world below looked vastly different. With mostly clear skies and fierce sunlight penetrating the southeast corner of the basement, he could see the outlines of the bottom stairs and a few of the shelves along the submerged facing wall. He felt better about the situation, though it did nothing to alleviate the oxygen situation.

"You think I should be able to find some air?" said Alex.

"Definitely. I've been marking the water progress on the wall next to my stairs," said Charlie. "It's dropped at least six inches in the last three hours. Before that it didn't move. There has to be a pocket of air. You could always wait until later."

"We don't have another three hours. I need to know if the gear is part of our plan or not. It's almost three. We'll get everyone together when I'm done with this."

"You could always use one of the garden hoses to breathe. I assume it's still connected to the house," said Charlie.

"I'll take my chances holding my breath. That hose has been there for fifteen years."

"How about I stick around while you go swimming—just in case?"

Alex nodded and activated the LED light attached to his mask. He'd used over a dozen rubber bands to tightly affix the waterproof flashlight. He had the option of using several head-mounted lamps scattered throughout their rucksacks, but couldn't convince himself that they would continue to work submerged. He knew for a fact that this light would work, and in the environment below, he needed one-hundred-percent reliability.

The light from the bulkhead opening would illuminate his path to the bunker door, but the area inside the bunker would be pitch black. He wasn't taking any chances. He fitted the mask and adjusted the light to face directly forward.

"I always wanted to go cave diving," he said and slid into the water after a deep breath.

The first thing he noticed was the cut on his forehead, which burned like someone held a match against it. A dozen other cuts and scrapes sounded off for a moment, but nothing could compete with the exhilaration of swimming through salt water in his basement. The cuts were a distant memory by the time his feet touched the concrete flooring.

He propelled himself forward, glancing around for a moment. He was surprised by the clarity of the water, which allowed his LED flashlight almost unlimited range in the basement. It made sense. The basement had more or less been a closed, undisturbed system for the past eight hours, giving most of the sediment time to settle. Alex propelled himself upward, just under the lip of the ceiling, and searched the area between the first two joists. He pressed the mask lens as high as possible, finding a three-inch pocket of air. Craning his neck backward, Alex grabbed the joists and attempted to bring his mouth above the waterline, but found the position to be too unstable. His lips barely breached the surface, which wasn't enough.

He put the self-clearing snorkel in his mouth and used his hands to align the top of the snorkel with the floorboard between the joists. Once nearly flush with the ceiling, he expelled the air in his lungs, purging the snorkel through the valve below the mouthpiece. He tentatively sucked air back into the snorkel, encountering little resistance. Alex breathed deeper, bringing nothing but air into his lungs. He took several breaths, alternating the position of his head and snorkel, until he was comfortable using both hands to steady himself on the joists.

Nothing to it.

He popped up in the stairwell and gave his audience a thumbs-up. "I found air. Three inches at least. No problem. I'll be done with this in ten minutes. Why don't you start gathering the troops, Charlie. Is Ed's house any cleaner than ours?"

"His and mine. We've been moving slop for hours," said Charlie.

"Let's go with Ed's. That way Kate and I can sneak around back so it doesn't look like we're having a big meeting. You've been going back and forth all day. Linda needs to be there. Can you leave the girls behind?"

"I sure as shit have no intention of leaving my house unguarded. They can hold their own."

"Good. I'll haul some extra ammunition and magazines up for everyone," said Alex. "If we have time later, I'll fetch your thermal scope."

"You won't be disappointed with that thing. It's unbelievable. Can't see through walls, but it can pick up heat signatures inside windows, which more or less accomplishes the same thing," said Charlie.

"Infrared reflections or ambient shadowing," Alex corrected. "Unless the windows are closed. IR signatures can't transmit through glass."

"Snipers don't typically fire through closed windows," countered Charlie.

"You guys are out of your minds. Can we get on with this?" Kate snapped, descending the stairs into the water. "Warm water, my ass," she added.

"What a lovely couple. We'll start making our way over to Ed's in about thirty minutes," Charlie said and disappeared.

"Ready?" Alex asked.

"Play it smart. I won't be able to see you very well in the bunker," she said, illuminating her own waterproof flashlight.

Alex sank into the water and swam toward the bunker door. He arrived several seconds later and questioned why he had been so worried. He had two locks to open, which shouldn't take much time. He considered trying to open the door before his next oxygen break, but decided against it. Before committing to any kind of task, he needed to verify that another pocket of air existed above him. He'd do the same when he reached the gun safe.

Repeating the process used near the stairs, he relaxed and breathed through the snorkel, flooding his system with oxygen. Kate floated lazily underwater near the bottom of the staircase, pointing her flashlight in his direction. He smiled with the snorkel in his mouth and gave her another thumbs-up sign. She broke for the surface and returned several seconds later. When she returned, Alex used one hand to retrieve the keys from the zippered pocket on his right thigh. He had removed the keys from his larger key chain and put them on a separate ring, wrapping duct tape around the base of the deadbolt key for quick identification. The third key on the ring was the circular gun safe key, which was easily distinguished from the traditional flat keys used to lock the bunker door. With the duct-taped key in hand, he descended a few feet and unlocked the deadbolt. A few seconds later, he had opened the doorknob lock and gained entry to the bunker, which was pitch black as expected.

The sole window to the backyard was blocked by mud, and the light from the bulkhead door barely penetrated more than a foot or two into the abyss. His flashlight cast a bluish-gray beam across the room, spotlighting the oil tanks, which he suddenly suspected were leaking. Another thing he hadn't anticipated. He swept the beam over the room, taking in the eerily monochromatic scene. Unlike the first floor, the water must have filled the basement slowly through the single one-foot-tall by two-feet-wide window in front of him. Aside from the packages of dehydrated food, MREs, and medical supplies bobbing between the joists in the far northwest corner of the bunker, very little had been disturbed by the tsunami.

He turned to his right to face the gun safe and nearly bit his tongue. All of his air vacated in an attempt to scream, and he bolted out of the dark chamber, swimming as fast as possible toward Kate. He scrambled past her and surfaced, grabbing hold of the handrail and ripping the mask off. He coughed violently as the mask drifted away toward the bottom of the stairs. Kate enveloped him, turning his face toward her.

"What's wrong?" she asked urgently.

He coughed a few more times to clear his airway. "There's a body down there. I wasn't expecting it, and I panicked. It was a little girl, or boy—I couldn't tell. Ripped apart pretty bad—fuck." He exhaled.

"You don't have to go back down there."

"I'm going back down. That won't be the last body any of us sees close up. It was just bad timing. Like a horror movie. One second I was surveying the room, the next I'm staring into a dead child's eyes. It's all good. At least I didn't drop the keys," he said, showing them to her. "I'm fine."

"You don't sound fine."

"I'm good. Seriously. Seeing that body gives me all the more reason to get the shit I need out of there. Ryan needs me to have every advantage possible entering Boston. That's what I'm doing down there," he said, glad that the salt water gave him an excuse to continuously wipe his eyes.

"All right. I think you should move the body to the bulkhead. Get it out of your way and up so the authorities can find it. Someone will be looking for that kid," said Kate.

He didn't want to break the bad news that nobody would be looking for the kid floating around in their basement. At least nobody in her immediate family.

"Back down. You don't have to keep an eye on me. I think I've got the technique mastered at this point," Alex said.

"I can handle seeing a dead body," Kate said, "and you missed hitting your head on the doorframe by about a centimeter. I can't rescue Ryan, Alex. You're the only option we have."

He kissed her forehead and dove into the water to retrieve the mask. Ten minutes later, he had returned with four sealed ammunition cans, an M4 carbine and a 9mm HK USP pistol. One of the cans contained a pair of generation two, head-mountable dual night vision goggles, a small, rifle-mountable generation two, night vision monocular, and a dual-beam IR aiming laser. The other cans contained ammunition and magazines compatible with his rifle and pistols.

He was surprisingly tired from the brief underwater foray. "This should do it."

"I'll start hauling this stuff up," Kate said.

"I'll get the body out of there. I think it might be better to leave it inside the bulkhead doors. Tie it to the stairs or something. I don't like the idea of it sitting in the sun where the animals can get to it."

"I'm not sleeping in a house with a dead body in it. I'll help you drag it to wherever they're putting the rest of the bodies."

"Fair enough. I'll get it out of the house and have Charlie help me move it. You don't want to see this one, Kate. It's someone's baby."

Kate's face softened, and she held him for a minute. "They're all someone's baby," she whispered.

Chapter 18

Scarborough, Maine

Alex sat in the empty seat left for him at the head of the kitchen table. Ed sat directly across from him, in front of the missing slider door. He was slightly concerned with privacy, since all of the windows had been blown out, but none of their options were optimal. He needed a table to lay out a few maps, which limited them to the dining room or kitchen. The dining room faced the street, exposing their conversation to anyone passing in front of the house.

He took a sip of ice-cold beer and observed his team. This wasn't going to be an easy journey. They were probably thinking the same thing about him. He knew he looked worse than all of them combined. The slash across his forehead was held together by a butterfly bandage and slathered with antibiotic ointment. The cut wasn't deep, but it was surrounded by a mean-looking bruise and could easily become infected if ignored. Several smaller, less urgent looking bruises had developed on his arms, face and neck, giving the impression that he had been worked over by a bar mob.

The bruise on his right tricep muscle was by far the worst. Partially hidden by his gray T-shirt, the deep purplish-red contusion drew stares from everyone. His arm had felt markedly better since taking ibuprofen and applying ice, but he strongly suspected that tomorrow would be a rough day. He could shoot right handed or left handed, but there was no comparison between what he could do with the right versus the left. He'd have to deal with it the best he could. That's all he could ask of himself and the ragtag group sitting around Ed's kitchen table.

He glanced at Kate and winked. Her normally lustrous black hair, now matted and dull, was hidden under a light blue ball cap. Despite the added trials of the Fletchers' day, she exuded a confidence that he didn't see in Linda or Samantha. She'd changed since the pandemic. The Sig Sauer P228 seated in the drop holster on her right thigh was one of many testaments to her sharply honed commitment to the Fletcher way of life. She would lead the women and children to his parents' farm. God help anything that got in their way.

The Thorntons and Walkers had readily accepted his offer to weather the storm in Limerick. Charlie and Linda owned a fully stocked camp on the Great Pond near Belgrade, Maine, but didn't have any way to get there. With Charlie accompanying Alex and Ed to Boston, it made sense for Linda and their twin seventeen-year-old daughters to travel with Kate. Running water would fail shortly, and electrical power wouldn't be restored for months, turning their homes into little more than three-thousand-square-foot tents.

Once power returned, a multitude of complicated challenges would surface. They would have to replace all of the electrical components in their furnace, if the furnace was even salvageable after sitting in salt water for several days. Not to mention the fact that they would be competing for parts and service with millions of other households. They all had wood-burning stoves, which could carry them through the winter if they could scrounge enough wood. Most of Alex's wood stack had been washed away by the tsunami. The cord he kept in the garage wouldn't last him through December.

Windows were another issue. How long would it take for them to get replacement windows? Two years ago, Alex had accidentally cracked one of their family room windows with the back of a shovel while digging in a flowerbed. The replacement window arrived two weeks later. With several million windows shattered in New England alone, it could take over a year. Most people would be forced to contend with plywood, plastic sheeting and duct tape, which would be no match for a Maine winter.

Households would compress their lives into one or two rooms and cannibalize unbroken windows from unused spaces. Depending upon the orientation of the house, this could work. For the three families gathered here, it would be a less than optimal experience. They all lost large sliding glass doors, which opened directly into large, combined kitchen and family areas. No amount of makeshift shuttering could keep the cold out, even with a wood-burning stove blazing at full strength.

Mold was another issue, but now he was just pig-piling the list of reasons why their friends should join them at the farm. Especially since everyone agreed with Alex's assessment that the situation on the "outside" would explode within the next seventy-two hours, once again sending the hordes north from Connecticut and Massachusetts to pillage the less populated, resource-rich suburbs.

By the time Boston reached critical mass, they would be securely hidden on a picturesque farm, with most of the comforts and amenities of modern life to which they had grown accustomed. Most importantly, they would be together with their families. Space might become an issue, but they'd make it work for as long as anyone cared to stay, even if that meant permanently.

"First, we've all made it this far—and we're going to make it the rest of the way. We've come together before to save each other's asses. Here we are again," he said, raising his beer.

They all clinked bottles and glasses.

"Second, this isn't my operation. It may be my suggested plan, but we all have just as much at stake here, so the plan is open to input," Alex continued. "Lastly, you're all welcome to stay out at the farm indefinitely. That's an unconditional offer, and I don't expect anyone to ever feel like they owe us anything—now or down the line."

"We appreciate that, Alex, Kate," said Samantha. "I don't know what to say other than thank you."

"Exactly. This is incredible. Thank you," said Charlie, followed by Linda.

"And thank you for letting us use the Jeep," Kate said to Ed and Samantha.

"And to Linda for allowing Charlie to join Ed and I in Boston, although I'd really feel better if he was escorting the group to Limerick," said Alex.

"I ain't going on a bike ride with the women," said Charlie. "I'm more use on the high-speed team."

"He's going to get himself killed," said Linda.

Ed snorted. "If Kate doesn't kill him first."

"Hey, hey. I didn't mean any offense to the women. I just. I just—"

"You should quit while you're ahead, Charlie," said Alex.

Charlie nodded. "Good idea."

"All right. That does it for the thank yous," said Alex. "Now we get down to business."

Alex took several sheets of paper and three maps from a small green backpack he'd carried into the house. "I have a few checklists that each family will need to follow," he said. He handed a sheet of paper to each family, giving theirs to Kate. "The first sheet is for the bicycle group. This is a watered-down bug-out or BOLT kit. The focus is on mobility and balance while riding, so anything not directly related to hydration, nutrition, and short-term survival has been scratched from the list. Under ideal, casual cycling conditions, the trip should take no more than four to five hours. You're looking at thirty-five miles taking the shortest route. Given the circumstances, I think you should plan for the possibility of an overnight. Thirty-six hours at the outside, accounting for detours, roadblocks, hiding out—whatever. I can't imagine any scenario other than capture that would keep you from reaching your destination within that timeframe, and I highly doubt anyone will get close enough to you to do that. Everything on this list will fit into a medium-sized rucksack with room to spare."

"No sleeping bags?" said Samantha. "We don't have Gore-Tex shells."

"If you have some highly compressible bags, that should be fine. I was just trying to keep the weight to a minimum. Water, MREs, first aid and tents are the highest priority," said Alex.

"And weapons," added Kate.

"Recommended weapons and ammunition are listed at the bottom. I'd arm the kids if practical," said Alex.

"What about the Homeland Security mandate?" Linda asked. "I can't exactly conceal an AR-15."

"I think you and Kate should plan to break down the rifles and stash them in your packs until you've cleared Scarborough. Shouldn't take more than ten seconds to put one of the ARs into action from the pack if required. Once you hit the back roads near Gorham, you can reassemble and sling them. Everyone should stash their pistols in one of the easy-to-access pouches on your pack, just in case you run into any immediate trouble before clearing town. Holsters too. No reason to give them an excuse to search you. Make sure you wear long pants with cargo pockets for the spare mags," said Alex.

Kate asked, "What if we're stopped and searched in Scarborough?"

"The police will have too much on their plate to bother with that. As long as the weapons aren't obvious, I can't imagine they'll bother," said Alex.

"What if they do?"

"Then you turn over your weapons without incident. Not much you can do in that situation. The last thing we want is trouble with the police. That doesn't go away," said Alex, and Kate nodded agreement.

Alex flattened one of the maps. "I've highlighted what I think is the best route out of town, with a few alternatives. For security reasons, I haven't highlighted the entire route. This gets you to Route 5, in East Waterboro. From there it's pretty much a straight shot to Limerick. Kate knows where to go from there."

Charlie examined the map and shook his head. "I don't know if this route will be passable."

"The mud is going to be rough getting out of here," Alex told him, "but here's what I figured we'd do to make it easier for them, without making multiple trips back into the neighborhood."

"Not here. I mean along Route 1. The Nonesuch River crosses Route 1 just south of where Harrison Road intersects—"

"It's more of a creek," interrupted Alex.

"True, but water follows the path of least resistance, and the creek lies lower than the rest of the land. I guarantee the tsunami channeled up through the creek and over Route 1, dumping a ton of mud along the way. Hell, the marsh extending past Pine Point Beach extends into half of southern Scarborough—all less than a mile from Route 1. The whole marsh is at sea level. I wouldn't count on them passing through much of downtown Scarborough."

"I think he's right, Alex," said Ed.

"That would be a first," added Linda Thornton, winking at her husband.

"Always busting my chops," said Charlie.

"Good call, Charlie," Alex admitted. "I wanted to avoid routing them toward the Maine Mall, but we might not have a choice. At least the roads should be clear of mud and debris north of the Harrison intersection. Let's rework the route while we're here."

Samantha turned to Alex. "I want to hear more about your plan to get us past this mud."

"Here's what I was thinking…we can't make multiple trips back to the neighborhood with Ed's Jeep. Once that engine roars to life, everyone in the neighborhood will be watching. If it returns multiple times, we're going to have a crisis on our hands. It'll be like the last helicopter out of Saigon."

Charlie chuckled. "That's a great image, Alex."

"Which I don't want to repeat here," Alex went on. "So, the bicycle group will leave first and walk their bicycles to the fire station. Mountain bikes or hybrids only for this trip. Will that be a problem for any family? I have an extra mountain bike in my basement."

Everyone indicated that they could provide enough bikes.

"We'll have to inspect and lubricate each bike. I'll leave it to the bike group to put together a repair kit," said Alex.

Kate nodded. "We'll take care of it."

"Once you've all arrived at the station," he said, nodding to Kate, "call us via handheld radio or satphone. We'll start the Jeep and meet you there to transport the bikes and riders to a dry point along Route 1. You'll have to deal with this nasty shit for about a quarter of a mile, but that's it."

"I can live with that," said Samantha.

"We should all wear throwaway shoes and socks for this part," Linda chimed in. "Have your real boots or whatever stuffed away in the backpacks."

"I couldn't agree more," said Alex. "We'll bring a few towels in the Jeep so everyone can wipe off their feet before the trip. You don't want to start out with wet feet. Once we get everyone in place along Route 1, we'll split up and stay in touch. I think we should check in via satphone every two hours."

Everyone nodded in agreement.

"Do your parents have a satphone, Alex? Can we call them along the way?" asked Samantha.

"They do, but I haven't been able to contact them with mine. They might not even realize there's a problem yet. The farm is at least another thirty miles inland."

"Yeah, but they'll notice that the power is out and the cars aren't working. They'll turn the phone on at some point," said Charlie.

"I don't know. The farm is isolated enough to keep neighbors from walking over to say hi. Nearest house is at least a half mile down the road. They're in their early seventies and don't typically go anywhere during the week. They might not discover their car problem until they decide to grab lunch or dinner in Limerick."

"But the power's out. If they have solar, that should raise some questions," said Charlie.

"They call me with all of those questions, and not by satphone. I guarantee they won't figure out it was an EMP until they try to start the cars. Even then they might think the batteries died or something. Don't be surprised if you deliver the bad news about the EMP when you arrive," Alex said.

"How long do you think you'll be gone?" Linda asked.

"I think we'll try to use the turnpike to reach Kittery, then maybe cross the bridge if it's serviceable. If not, we'll head west along the New Hampshire border and cross at the least crowded point. My goal is to reach 125 and take that until Kingston; then we'll do a combination of 107 and 108 to Haverhill—"

"Haverhill? That's a lot of people in one place," Charlie remarked.

"I don't think we can avoid Haverhill. We need to get over the Merrimack, and I'm not sure about crossing options east of Haverhill. This point," he said, landing a pencil on Haverhill, "is about ten miles from the coast. Up here that wouldn't be a problem, but based on the direction of the wave, wind and flash that I saw this morning the asteroid—if it *was* an asteroid—hit closer to the beach down here."

"Going west would be way worse in terms of population," muttered Ed. "You've got Lawrence and Lowell here."

"What about trying to cross at West Newbury?" Kate suggested. "There has to be a way to get there without going through Haverhill. If the bridge is down, you can drive back to Haverhill."

"Let me check on that," Alex said.

He pulled a softbound map book of New England from his backpack and feverishly searched for the page with a detailed street map corresponding to the area Kate had pointed out on the larger map. He found the map and confirmed the validity of her idea.

"We have a couple of options to reach West Newbury from 108. If the bridge there is down, we could use East Broadway here," he said, pointing to a road along the river, "to approach the Bates Bridge on the outskirts of Haverhill. Assuming the road isn't washed out."

"You're welcome," said Kate, smugly.

"You're thanked," replied Alex. "Correct me if I'm wrong here, Charlie, but I think we can work our way from Groveland to Reading without using Route 28."

"Definitely, but once we hit Reading, we might as well take the 28. It won't matter what road you're on at that point. It starts to get crowded."

"Should we ditch the car before Reading?" asked Alex.

"Ditch the *car*?" said nearly everyone at the same time.

"What? We can't drive Ed's Jeep into Boston. We wouldn't last fifteen minutes," said Alex.

Ed asked him, "How far are we going to walk?"

"I guess it depends on where we stash the car. I was hoping for something between five and eight miles."

"Reading's a lot further than that. We'd be useless by the time we reached the Charles," said Ed.

"We can't risk taking your jeep into a high-density population area. Too many variables we can't control without seriously heating up these barrels," he said, reaching over to his rifle set against the wall, "which would make the situation worse."

"How can it get worse?" Ed asked.

"Shooting solves your most immediate problem, but the problem usually comes back really quickly. We'll be slower on foot, but we won't have a giant bull's-eye painted on us. More people probably live in Medford and Cambridge combined than the entire greater Portland area—and they all want out of the city. Ed's Jeep will quickly become the talk of the town, which is likely to put us in an untenable situation."

"Fuck it. I'm in," Charlie announced, rising over the table to examine the map. "No need to stop before Reading. We're talking mostly suburbs. Stoneham's a little more packed, but it doesn't get really busy until Medford. See this right here?" Everyone stood up and leaned over the table to see where Charlie was pointing. "Middlesex Fells Reservation. We could easily stash the Jeep somewhere in the forest about a quarter of a mile from the northern edge of Medford. If the trees are still standing."

"True," Alex agreed. "We really have no idea how bad it is down there. We'll bring the Jeep to the edge of Medford and figure out how to hide it. If the forest is a no-go, we might have to sit back and wait until dark to hide the Jeep near the city."

"Tomorrow night? Now we're talking about tomorrow night?" Samantha said nervously. "That's more than twenty-four hours. I think you guys should leave tonight. Take the Jeep straight through to the kids. You'll be back by tomorrow morning at the latest. I'm worried that you're overthinking this, Alex. Our kids are waiting. They're probably wondering why we haven't shown up yet. The longer we delay this, the worse it'll get out there."

"We can't leave tonight. If the police confiscate our vehicle, we're screwed. Not to mention all the other gear they're not likely to let us keep," said Alex.

"What if they're still confiscating vehicles tomorrow—and the next day? How long are we going to wait?"

"If they're simply replacing the disabled vehicles in their fleet, we should be safe by tomorrow. If they're still yanking cars off the street tomorrow, then we're dealing with something else."

"That doesn't answer my question. Regardless of their reason, what's your plan if they're not done taking vehicles tomorrow morning?" she demanded.

"I'm headed to Boston tomorrow to get our children. Nothing is going to get in the way of that. Are we all good with that?" said Alex, shifting his stare between Charlie and Ed.

"I'm good," said Charlie.

"Me too. God help us," said Ed.

"We'll get the kids back, Samantha. No matter what it takes. We just can't leave tonight. I need time with your husband and Charlie to work out the details, rig the gear, game plan all of the scenarios. If we were having this conversation at ten in the morning, I'd consider giving it a try."

"Sorry to jump on you like that, Alex. I'm just worried about the kids."

"I'm right there with you, Sam," said Kate. "No need to apologize."

"Samantha, you should have heard Kate on the walk back from the yacht club," said Alex, trying to break the tension. "She wanted me to take a right on Harrison Road and continue walking to Boston. I managed to find a few flaws in that plan."

"You looked like you needed a break, so I relented," Kate said, winking.

Everyone laughed at Kate's comment, including Alex.

"We have a lot of prep work to do. Bicycles, backpacks, and weapons are first priority. The rescue group needs two packs. One BOLT bag and a smaller assault kit—"

"What's an assault kit?" asked Ed. "I don't have stuff like that."

"It's just a smaller backpack, like this," said Alex, lifting up the dark green, nylon backpack from the side of his chair.

"We'll use these when we leave the car to get the kids. Nothing but the basics. Ammo, water, limited food, first aid kit…it's all here on the sheets."

"Why pack two bags?" asked Linda.

"The BOLT bags are for situations requiring us to permanently abandon the Jeep. We'll be able to continue on foot with enough supplies to get us to our destination," Alex explained.

"What if that happens before you reach Boston?"

"The mission remains the same. Get the kids and get back to Limerick. The only parameter that changes is the length of time it takes to accomplish the mission. Could be twelve hours, could be twelve days."

"Are you sure you're up for this, Charlie?" Linda asked her husband.

"Of course I'm up for this! What the hell are you talking about?"

"If the car dies in Sanford, Maine, you're looking at what," she made a quick calculation using the map, "a hundred and fifty mile round trip on foot?"

"Then I'll finally lose that last ten pounds!"

"What about your knee—and your back?"

"I'll bring my knee wrap and back brace, along with plenty of pain meds. I hike through the woods for days on end up in the county looking for deer. I'll be fine. It's these two beach strollers I'm worried about—gotcha there, guys," said Charlie.

"We'll take good care of your husband, Linda," said Ed.

"You better. It's not like I can easily replace him at this point, especially with the Internet down," she said, causing another round of laughter.

Alex took a long swig of beer and gently set the empty bottle on the table.

"One last thing. Actually two last things. First, the backpack list doesn't leave a lot of room for personal items. My daughter has already started to collect stuff to bring along, and I didn't have the heart to tell her that most of it wasn't coming. We're all in the same boat with kids—and ourselves. If things start to normalize, we can always come back for stuff—"

"If the houses haven't been ransacked," said Kate.

"Right. Each family should put together a duffel bag with stuff they want to bring to the farm, beyond the few items you can fit in your packs. We can stuff those bags in the Jeep. Nothing huge. Gym bag or backpack sized," he said, and everyone nodded. "The last thing is the most important. I noticed people outside, and it sounds like Charlie has been helping other neighbors to move bodies. We need to minimize contact with the neighbors, and keep our packing efforts a secret. We'll have to move all the gear over to Ed's at night. Our departure tomorrow needs to remain a secret. I can't stress that enough. It sounds cold, but it's our reality. We all have friends in the neighborhood, and for the most part, they should be fine once the basements drain. We did our part after the pandemic. Most of the neighbors have stockpiled food and supplies. I can't run a neighborhood refugee camp out at my parents' farm. It's as simple as that."

Alex didn't sense any problem with his last statement. They all understood the gravity and reality of the situation. Even with a sizable food stockpile and the ability to filter water, life would be extremely difficult in the neighborhood. Most home foundations were more than likely cracked. Some would collapse. The epic scale of this disaster guaranteed that nothing would be restored or repaired for several months, eventually forcing most people to migrate or face a brutal winter with meager supplies and limited essential services. He could envision massive FEMA camps established to handle the overflow of humanity fleeing New England, followed by disease, starvation and depravity. Nobody at the Walkers' kitchen table wanted to stick around for that end game.

"Then it's a done deal," said Ed decisively. "We pack up and wait for dark to bring it over."

"We'll throw dinner together once everyone arrives. Try to use up whatever's left in the refrigerators and pantries," said Samantha.

"Perfect. We should spend some time talking about Boston before heading back right now," Alex said to Ed and Charlie.

"The other group needs to do the same, but it'll have to wait until tonight. Too many people to gather in one place at one time without arousing suspicion. Durham Road may look quiet, but I guarantee people are watching every square inch of the neighborhood. We should also plan to use the upstairs. I wouldn't feel secure gathering the family at night," said Alex.

He distinctly remembered the fear he had developed of roaming the ground floor of his house six years ago, with murderous psychopaths prowling the neighborhood. The obvious presence of a large gathering might attract attention tonight, as households recuperated from the initial shock of having their normal lives ripped out from under them. From what he could tell so far, the neighbors had kept to themselves, nobody quite certain what to think or do under the circumstances beyond clean out their house and take stock of the situation. Some of them had banded together to remove the bodies deposited on the street by the tsunami, but that appeared to be the limit of cooperation to this point. Tomorrow would be very different, especially after the harsh reality of the EMP's long-term impact had time to sink in.

Chapter 19

Scarborough, Maine

Alex lifted Kate's mountain bike up by the center crossbar and tucked his left elbow tightly against his side, balancing the aluminum monster in his left hand. He'd already ferried Emily's bike across the thickening, bug-infested field of muck separating the two houses. The Thorntons had arrived at the back of their house just as he returned from the first trip twenty minutes later.

"Everyone set?" he asked, glancing at the shadows in front of the closed bulkhead door.

"Lead the way, sir," said Charlie.

Alex stepped out of the garage and into the deeper mud behind his house. "Let's go."

The steps were slow, each threatening to suck the shoes off his feet. He'd stuffed his only pair of hiking boots in his backpack, opting for the running shoes he kept in the mudroom closet. The rest of the family's boots were underwater in a fifty-gallon storage bin somewhere in the basement. The added weight of his assault pack buried his shoes deeper, causing him to cautiously lift his feet out of the greedy muck.

Halfway across the yard, he saw the slow progress and had second thoughts about their plan to have Kate's group haul the bicycles to the fire station. Everyone had given up trying to keep the bikes out of the mud. They would have to rethink this part of the plan.

Ed's hitch-mounted bike rack could take four bicycles. They could throw two on top and try to carry the other three with their arms outside of the windows. It would be a complete clusterfuck, but they only needed to drive two minutes with all of the bicycles. The Jeep had an automatic transmission, so Ed could theoretically hold one of the bikes with his left arm. Alex knew that wasn't going to work.

They'd have to make two trips, which was exactly what he wanted to avoid, but he didn't see any way around it. There was no way this group would make it to the fire station pushing bicycles through the muck without thoroughly exhausting themselves in advance of a thirty-five-mile bike ride.

Kate's group would hike to the fire station with their packs and wait for Ed to deliver the first load of bicycles. Alex and Charlie would guard the rest of the bikes and gear until Ed returned for the final load. Once everything was in place at the station, they could resume the original plan. He'd suggest that Kate's group set out for the station before sunrise, with the hopes of keeping onlookers to a bare minimum. He stopped to let Charlie catch up.

"I think we'll have to drive the bikes over to the station," said Alex.

"That'll mean two trips," said Charlie, straining to talk.

"I'm pretty sure my marriage won't last halfway to the fire station," said Alex.

"Halfway?" Linda jeered. "I'll file for divorce right now if this idiot doesn't start agreeing with you."

"Let's go with two trips, my friend," said Charlie.

"Better," Linda said. "Now if you can convince him to drive everyone to the station, I'll make it worth your while."

"Tonight?" asked Charlie.

"Not tonight."

"I've heard that before. I only take payment in advance these days," said Charlie, laughing at his own joke.

"Mom? Dad?" said one of Charlie and Linda's daughters from the darkness. "We're, like, right here, in case you were wondering."

"Your mom started it."

"We might be able to move everyone in two trips," said Alex. "Does Ed's Jeep have running boards?"

"If it doesn't, he's a cheap bastard," Charlie decided. "Why would you buy the four-door Jeep and not have running boards?"

"If he has running boards, we might be able to get six people out on each run. That would do it," said Alex.

He wasn't sure why he hadn't thought of it earlier. The only problem would be jamming all of the packs and weapons into the Jeep's tight interior space. They'd make it work, even if they had to tie stuff down on the hood.

Ten minutes later, Alex returned to the house to retrieve his own gear. He'd stashed his BOLT pack, tactical chest rig, and rifle in the garage. Unlike the watered-down version carried by Kate's group, his BOLT pack contained most of the items on the original checklist, which translated into twice the weight. His final trip across the mud would be interesting. He stepped out of the garage and collided with someone. He cleared his pistol from the holster, stepping backward simultaneously.

"It's me, Jamie. Christ, will you put that away?" she hissed.

Alex lowered the weapon, but didn't holster it. "Are you out of your fucking mind?"

"Is it that bad out there? You don't trust me enough to put away your gun, Alex?"

"I don't trust anyone right now," he said, glancing at the corner of the garage.

"Looks like you trust Ed and Charlie," she remarked. "When are you heading out?"

Alex didn't reply at first. He had really been hoping to slide out of the neighborhood without having to deal with this.

"We're taking Ed's Jeep down to Boston to get the kids. The rest of them are headed out on bicycles to my parents' place. I don't know what everyone will do after that. Hopefully this will all be resolved in a few weeks."

"This won't get better. We're heading out tomorrow for Jeff's family camp near Bridgton."

Alex remained silent.

"I'm not asking for a ride. The minivan started. I just need to know when you're heading out, so we can leave at the same time. We don't want to drive out of here with the entire neighborhood on our heels," she said.

"We were hoping to avoid the same thing. We'll leave at first light," said Alex.

"That's what we were thinking," said Jamie.

Something was off with this conversation. He couldn't see more than the outline of her body against the side of the garage. He knew for a fact that she owned a compact 9mm Glock. He'd recommended the pistol to her when she'd come to him for self-defense advice after the pandemic. He closed the back door to the garage and walked slowly through the mud toward the Walkers' house. Was he already this paranoid?

"Stay safe on the road, Jamie," he advised. "Don't stop for anything or anyone. Route 26 goes through some crowded areas."

"We'll be careful," said Jamie.

Route 26 didn't go anywhere near Bridgton. Jamie had either completely missed what he had said, or she was lying about the camp. He had to assume the latter and plan for the worst-case scenario. So much for a full night's sleep.

Charlie immediately met him at the back door of the Walkers' garage.

"Was that Jamie?"

"Yeah," grumbled Alex.

"She's out of her skull creeping around at night. What did she want?"

"Intel," stated Alex.

Charlie looked at him pointedly. "Do we have a problem?"

"A big one. We all need to talk," he said, stepping through the doorway.

Alex met Kate and Linda in the mudroom. They had just finished stacking the two families' BOLT bags along one of the walls.

"Where are all of the kids?" asked Alex.

"We sent them upstairs," Linda replied.

He dropped his own pack on the tile floor. "Let's keep them up there."

"We've got a place for the rifles in the family room," said Linda.

"I think I'll hold onto mine for now."

"What's wrong?" Kate asked.

Alex glanced at Linda. "Can you grab Ed and Samantha really quick?"

She stepped out and returned moments later with Ed and Samantha in the kitchen doorway.

"What's up?" asked Ed.

"I just ran into Jamie," said Alex.

"Great. Please tell me you didn't invite them to your parents' place," Kate said snidely. "Her new husband is a little off."

"You thought I was a little off before you got to know me," said Charlie.

Linda didn't hesitate. "I've known you for twenty-four years, and I think you're way off."

"She said something that didn't make sense," Alex said, trying to keep them focused. "Claims that their minivan started and that they're headed out to Jeff's family camp in Bridgton."

"Why would they wait this long?" asked Linda.

"Maybe for the same reason as us," said Samantha.

"They don't know that the police are grabbing cars," Ed said. "They haven't left the neighborhood, and I think we would have heard them start the car. Charlie heard mine from down the street."

"What if their garage doors were closed?" asked Samantha.

"Here's the other thing," Alex said. "I told her to be careful on Route 26. She said they will. Route 26 doesn't go anywhere near Bridgton. I think she was fishing for information."

"Maybe she was nervous?" Samantha suggested. "You look like some kind of mercenary. *I'm* nervous right now looking at those guns."

"I know the two of you used to be close…" began Alex.

"She's been through a lot, Alex," Samantha interrupted. "Now that asshole husband's knocking her around."

Linda grimaced. "When did that start?"

"Apparently all along," said Samantha. "He's a piece of sh—crap."

"Maybe he put her up to it," said Alex.

"Up to what?" Samantha asked.

"Trying to find out our plan to get out of here. Why else would she ask when we were leaving?"

"What did you tell her?" asked Ed.

"Sunrise."

"We'll be long gone by then."

"They'll make a move on the Jeep long before that," said Kate knowingly.

Samantha blanched. "What do you mean?" she demanded.

"The Michaud family camp in Bridgton was sold at auction in 2016. The Michaud's were clients of my firm for decades. Jeff pissed away all of the money after his parents died in the pandemic. Apparently, a latent gambling gene surfaced," said Kate.

"Followed by a wife-beating gene," said Samantha.

Kate shook her head. "I'm sure that one has been around forever. How bad is the abuse?"

"I don't know," Samantha answered. "He's got her under tight control." She turned to Alex. "I know Jamie. She wouldn't do this if she had a choice. She hasn't forgotten what we did for her girls."

"We still have to plan for the worst. I can set up outside and watch the back of the house. He'll probably try to break in and steal the Jeep. That's what I'd do."

"Then what?" asked Linda.

"If he shows up, I'll shoot him," said Alex nonchalantly.

"You can't just shoot him, Alex," said Ed.

"I've been down that road, and it got a lot of people killed—"

"That wasn't your fault!" said Kate.

"I don't see it that way anymore. If either of them approaches the house with a firearm, I'm taking them out."

"What about the police?" asked Ed.

"What police?"

"You have to plan for the possibility that someone will hear the shots and contact the police. You said it yourself that they're probably monitoring handheld radio frequencies," said Ed.

"I have that covered."

"The police?" countered Ed.

"No. The sound," said Alex, to skeptical looks.

"What if they're unarmed?" Kate asked.

"Unlikely."

"You have to plan for the possibility," said Kate.

"What's wrong with all of you?" Alex said in frustration. "She *lied* to me out there. They're either coming tonight, or they'll try to hijack the car tomorrow."

"Then maybe you should storm their house right now and kill everyone!" said Samantha, shaking her head in disgust.

"I'm not suggesting a preemptive strike!" Alex said. "We just need to take a more proactive stance here."

Charlie piped in, "Why don't we just capture whoever comes over?"

"Is anyone here trained to take down a potentially armed hostile?" Alex asked. "Just saying…" he added.

"I don't think it's out of the question," said Ed.

"It's out of the question. Trust me. It'll take all three of us if he resists. What if he has help?"

"You really want to shoot him, don't you?" said Samantha.

"Don't you?"

Samantha shot him a nasty look, and the mudroom fell silent.

"I'll issue a warning," Alex said. "If a firearm is visible, they have to drop it. No exceptions. I'm not sending them back with the tools to try again. That's all the leeway I'm willing to give."

Ed let out a deep breath, "I can live with that."

Samantha nodded. "All right."

"We'll need a lookout with a radio on the second floor," said Charlie, "and someone on the ground level in case they try to get into the main house."

"I'll watch from Daniel's room. Charlie's probably a better choice to have guarding the doors," said Ed.

"We'll switch off, so you can get sleep, or at least try," said Samantha.

"It's gonna be a long night, but we'll get through this. By noon tomorrow, you'll be safe at the compound. We'll join you with Chloe and Ryan the day after that," said Alex.

"Easy as that?" said Ed, finally smiling.

"Easy as that," repeated Alex.

Chapter 20

Scarborough, Maine

Alex swatted lethargically at the mosquitos. What was the point? The swarm above his head was unusually aggressive, relentlessly attacking his sweaty face. Their buzz competed with a distant generator. Annoying, but blameless, the mosquitos could be forgiven. Unlike humans, they lacked the capacity to govern their response to deeply ingrained survival instincts. Alex lay in the backyard as a hedge against their collective bet that Jamie and her husband had given in to their instincts.

Samantha had given him a thick comforter to lay over the mud, which he had placed over an old, supposedly waterproof poncho. The system had kept him dry for roughly seven minutes before the brackish water seeped over and around the poncho, quickly soaking the comforter. At least he wasn't lying in a puddle of shit water. The hastily assembled ground cover had prevented him from sinking far enough into the mud for that.

He'd set up along the edge of the drainage easement behind the Walkers' house, on the downward side of the slope, exposing little more than his rifle and his head to the house. His feet sat less than a foot from the water trapped in the ditch. The easement ran the entire length of the backyards, giving him an unobstructed view in both directions. The dual-tube night vision goggles had turned night into day, ensuring that nobody stood a chance of approaching undetected.

His earpiece crackled. "Alex," Charlie reported, "I have a male with some type of rifle crossing the street between Jamie's house and the house to the left. Looks like he's headed to the Andersons' next door. I need to go to the other side of the house. I'm about to lose him."

"Stay where you are, and keep a close eye on Jamie's house. Make sure we don't have any more surprises. I have it from here. Charlie, did you copy?"

"Copy. Standing by," said Charlie.

Alex pointed his HK416 semiautomatic rifle at the left corner of the house. He figured that Jeff would appear there first and slide along the house.

A darkened shape appeared beyond the corner for a moment. He focused his attention on the white trim, which appeared pale green in his goggles, and waited. Jeff Michaud's head slowly emerged, followed by the shotgun. He pressed the transmit button on his shoulder-mounted handheld radio.

"He's at the corner of Ed's house. Pump action shotgun," he whispered, mentally blocking out the nervous replies.

Several seconds later, Jamie's husband stepped into the open and walked slowly along the back of the house, the mud sucking at his feet.

Alex moved his left hand along the hand guard to the vertical fore grip and double tapped the remote switch attached to the rail. A green light spanned the backyard, striking the house behind Michaud. Invisible to the naked eye, the infrared (IR) beam emitted by the Dual Beam Aiming Laser (DBAL) attached to the top rail of his rifle could only be seen using night vision technology. Alex shifted the laser onto Michaud's head and waited for him to pause at the edge of the Walkers' mangled deck.

"That's far enough!" he warned.

Michaud raised the shotgun to his shoulder and aimed into the darkness beyond Alex, craning his head frantically. The green laser remained centered on his forehead. He took another step forward.

"Stop! Right! There!" yelled Alex. "Drop your weapon, and put your hands on top of your head!"

"Where are you?" said Michaud, shifting his aim in Alex's general direction.

"Last chance, Jeff! Drop the shotgun, or I'll shoot!"

Jeff Michaud paused, looked to both sides, and lowered the shotgun. Not good enough.

"Drop the shotgun!"

"I'll leave! This is all I have to defend Jamie and the kids," said Michaud.

"Either you drop the shotgun, or I'll help you drop it."

"I'm walking back to my house, Alex—and I'm taking this with me," said Michaud.

"I'll kill you if you take a single step with that thing. Last warning, Jeff!"

"You wouldn't do that to Jamie and the kids! She's already lost one husband," he said, lifting his left foot out of the mud.

The rifle kicked, and Michaud dropped. The suppressor reduced the sound of the gunshot to that of a compressed-air-powered nail gun. With no background noise to compete, the sound would be heard clearly throughout the neighborhood and the street behind the Walkers', but it wouldn't register definitively as gunfire. Only someone with experience using suppressed firearms would be able to make the determination based on a single shot—not that anyone could call 911. He turned off the IR laser and stood up.

"You there, Alex?" said Charlie.

"I'm here. Jeff Michaud is dead."

"I'll be right there."

"Come out of the back door to the garage. Are we all clear, Ed?"

"All clear on the street, but something's going on in Jamie's mudroom. It's hard to tell, but I saw some movement inside."

"We'll take care of it. Be careful by the window, Ed. Do like I showed you."

"I'll keep you posted. Are you sure Michaud is dead?"

"One hundred percent. Headshot," said Alex.

"And we just leave him there?"

"Do you want to give him a proper burial?"

"Not really," said Ed.

"Alex, was that a suppressor?" added Charlie.

"Let's not transmit stuff like that in the open. Everyone cut the chatter. I'm headed across the backyard."

The suppressor attached to his rifle was not registered with the ATF, and would most certainly land him in jail if discovered by authorities. He'd purchased it with a thick envelope of twenty-dollar bills after a gun show, hoping never to need it. He had a feeling it would be prove to be worth every penny in the upcoming days.

"Shit. Sorry, man. Probably just the echo or angle of the sound waves," said Charlie.

"You done yet?" said Alex.

"Now I am. Out," said Charlie.

They were using a privacy-coded subchannel within a rarely used public channel that had been silent all evening. He highly doubted anyone was listening, but he preferred they maintain better radio discipline. When they reached Boston, all of the channels would be busy, and finding a clear subchannel might present a challenge. He also wouldn't be surprised if law enforcement officers within bigger departments were monitoring all of the available channels and subchannels.

With the grid down, handheld radios would become one of the only reliable forms of longer-range communication within the cities. Controlling the handheld channels or monitoring them would become critical. It was something they needed to keep in mind when navigating the city.

He replaced the radio and fought the mud on the flat ground above the easement lip. Tactically, the better move would be to use some of the sloped earth for cover and traverse along the axis of the ditch, but the mud was difficult enough on level ground, and the steep gradient led right into chest-high water. He had no plans for a midnight swim. Alex kept his rifle trained in the direction of the garage corner as he approached. Charlie's form appeared in the door, and Alex signaled for him to cover the back of the house.

They had worked out very basic military signals for use on their trip. With Charlie aiming in the direction of the deck, he focused all of his attention on "slicing" the corner, finding the side of the garage clear of intruders. He'd patrol the front of the house, sweeping around back and linking up with Charlie. It was the only way to be sure Michaud didn't have an accomplice lurking in the shadows.

He detected movement across the street, from Jamie's mudroom stoop, but nobody emerged. It was hard to tell, but the green image cast by his night vision goggles suggested that the mudroom door was open. She was probably waiting for the Jeep to pull out of the garage before she started carting luggage into the driveway. Almost on cue, the front screen door opened, revealing at least two figures carrying luggage onto the stoop. Alex slid along the back of the garage to join Charlie.

"Side is clear. It looks like Jamie is pre-staging luggage for a quick departure," said Alex.

"Damn," said Charlie, "what do we do?"

"Send her a message," said Alex, "once I confirm that we don't have any more surprises waiting for us."

Several minutes later, Alex returned to the garage corner with Michaud's shotgun. "Anything new?"

"Nothing. Jamie's sitting deep in the mudroom, watching the garage door. The girls are somewhere close by inside," said Charlie, keeping the night vision scope on his rifle pressed to his face.

"The far side of the house is clear. Let's send the message," said Alex.

Alex followed Charlie into the garage and knelt next to the rear left tire of the Walkers' disabled Honda Pilot. He braced his rifle against the side of the SUV and disengaged the safety. His trip to check the other side of the house had given Charlie enough time to communicate with Kate, who would make sure that everyone stayed clear of the front windows. He had no idea how Jamie would react to this message, and his search of Jeff Michaud's body didn't turn up the Glock 19.

Charlie pulled the toggle line connected to the garage door and stepped to the left side of the door. "Ready?"

"Open sesame," said Alex.

The door jerked upward and started to roll on its track. By the time the door had reached the apex of its journey, Jamie and her daughters had started hauling the luggage off the porch. Alex activated the IR laser and directed the beam at Jamie's chest. She reached the end of the walkway before stopping to stare at the open garage bay. She waved her hand behind her and hissed something at the girls that caused them to leave the luggage and scurry inside.

Alex guided the bright green beam past her head, placing it on the light fixture attached to the garage behind her. The rifle barked, sending a .223 bullet past her head at 3,000 feet per second. If the crack of the bullet didn't make an impression, the sudden obliteration of the glass light enclosure should deliver the message.

Jamie lowered her body. Alex fired another round over her head, striking the top of the garage door behind her with a hollow thump. He hoped the Walkers' garage would channel the sound of his suppressed rifle forward, limiting the directional extent of its detectability. At this point, the repeated sound would draw attention. He waited for her to react.

"I didn't have a choice! He threatened the girls! He's a piece of shit!" she screamed.

"Throw the Glock into the street and walk back into the house, Jamie!" yelled Alex.

"Is he dead?" she said, her voice breaking.

"He's dead. Time's up, Jamie. Toss the pistol and get inside."

Jamie reached behind her back, causing him to tense and press into the SUV's rear tire. He knew she would have to do this to comply with his demand, but it still made him nervous. Alex just hoped that Charlie didn't get any panicky ideas.

"You okay over there?" he whispered.

"Yep. Finger's off the trigger," said Charlie.

"As soon as she turns around, you head out and get the pistol."

"Got it."

Jamie raised the pistol over her head and threw it as far as she could. She stood her ground on the driveway, facing the open garage bay.

"He never found it. Can you believe that? I should have put it up to his head while he was dead drunk and pulled the trigger. He had enough reasons to kill himself."

"You should have warned me," said Alex. "We would have helped you."

"I *did* warn you. Route 26? He was listening to the whole conversation through one of the radios. That was all I could do."

Alex stepped out of the shadows. "Shit. I'm sorry, Jamie. I just found out about what was going on with you tonight. We didn't put it together."

"I got pretty good at hiding it. We'll be fine now. Completely fine. If you don't mind, I'd like to get the shotgun back—after you're gone."

"We'll leave it in the garage. Back door will be unlocked—not that you can't just walk through the sliding door," he said, causing her to briefly laugh.

"Good luck getting your kids back from Boston. I figured you were splitting up between the bikes and the Jeep," said Jamie.

"Help yourself to anything you can salvage. There's a ton of food in our basement if you don't mind snorkeling. Firearms too. Need to get to those quick, before the bores start to rust. I have a cord of wet firewood in my garage," he said.

"Thanks, Alex. I'll take you up on that, and I'll keep an eye on the houses. Can I take the pistol?"

"Yeah. Clean it really well. There's a lot of sand mixed into this mess," said Alex.

"See you around," she said.

"Good luck, Jamie. Hopefully we'll see you shortly."

"Somehow I think this is more of a permanent situation. We're ready."

Alex called Ed down to the mudroom, and helped Charlie secure the garage. They locked the bay door in place and barricaded the back door. Ed met them in the garage.

"I'm thinking we should leave right now," said Ed.

"We can't ride bikes in the dark," said Kate, following him.

"The sun will be up in three hours. 5:50. We should at least start rolling out of here at five, before the neighborhood wakes up. By the time we get everyone to Route 1, they should have enough light to travel safely," said Ed.

Kate nodded and rubbed her eyes.

"All right. We'll let everyone sleep for another hour and a half, then get out of here. I don't think she's a threat, but who knows what she's capable of with kids to protect?" said Alex.

"Why don't you and Charlie get some sleep? I'll take the next shift down here," said Ed.

Alex handed Ed the muddied shotgun and patted him on the shoulder. "It's all yours, Ed. I'm going to take a shower, if you don't mind."

"Use the bathroom at the top of the stairs, and uh—try not to make a mess," he joked.

"Funny man for three in the morning," said Alex.

"More like slap happy."

"This is just the beginning of our fun. Wait until tomorrow night," said Alex.

"Can't wait. Charlie, I got this covered," said Ed.

"You sure, amigo? I'm kind of amped up right now. I don't mind holding down the fort," said Charlie, stepping back into the kitchen.

"All the more reason for you to take a nap. Seriously, we're all going to need as much rest as possible for tomorrow. Don't make me wake up Linda to haul your ass upstairs," said Alex.

∞∽

Kate slipped into the upstairs bathroom after Alex and locked the door. She needed a moment with him alone, and this looked like it might be her last opportunity for a long time. Even when they reunited at the farm, they would be living on top of each other with nine additional people, bringing the total at the 2,200-square-foot contemporary farmhouse to seventeen. Alone time would become a premium, which was important for their relationship. Important on several levels, one of which was Alex's mental health. The mental and physical rigors of their pandemic experience had worsened his post-traumatic distress symptoms, his nightmares, and had surfaced subtle changes to his behavior.

The changes were barely noticeable, but Alex seemed more prone to bouts of melancholy and a negative outlook. He'd always had the nightmares, pretending to wake up in the middle of the night to use the bathroom, when Kate knew he was changing a sweat-soaked shirt and wiping his face. He hadn't been the only one pretending. She would lay there breathing slowly, faking a deep sleep, grateful that he'd returned. Her deep, undisturbed sleep had become a joke in their family over the years, but it was a twisted façade. She slept so lightly at night, constantly waking up to Alex's murmurs and sounds, that she could barely lift herself out of bed in the morning.

She'd kept this a secret from him for years, just like he'd tried to keep the nightmares from her. The onset of depression after the pandemic worried her the most, forcing her to suggest he seek PTSD-related counseling. The treatment had been marginally effective at combating his mood swings, and Kate relied on constant, close observation to guide him through tougher spells of darkness. Prior to the tsunami, Alex had been on one of the longest upward swings she could remember. She suspected that he'd started taking the medication he'd been prescribed, which he'd long been against. The current situation had the potential to send him in the opposite direction, and Kate needed to stay on top of it.

"I don't think this is the right time," he said, leaning his rifle against the wall next to the toilet.

"You wish. They ran out of hot water this afternoon. A cold shower with a stinky man isn't at the top of my romantic encounters list. I just wanted to talk with you in private."

"And I had been led to believe that I was irresistible under any circumstances," he joked.

"I'm not sure a shower will do you any good."

"Sadly, I don't even notice anymore," Alex said. "I know why you're here, by the way."

"That obvious?"

"I'm fine. Pretty clear-cut situation out there."

He lit one of the candles on the marble bathroom counter and started to undress.

"It won't always be that clear cut," she said.

"Anything standing in the way of getting Ryan and Chloe back is a clear-cut threat. We know exactly what's going to happen out there. What people are capable of. No second guessing on my end."

"I know you'll get them back. Tomorrow morning we'll be together again. I'll make a huge pancake breakfast for the entire crew. We'll swim in the lake, kick back and enjoy the hard work we've put into the farm," she said, barely believing her own words.

Alex didn't fully believe it either. He never spoke a word of pessimism about their chances of rescuing Ryan and Chloe, but she could see it in his eyes. See him calculating the odds. They had no idea where the asteroid hit, if it had really been an asteroid. Alex didn't seem convinced. None of them could reconcile the EMP effects with the government's version of what had transpired this morning. The only data point that gave them all hope that it hadn't been a hostile nuclear detonation came from Alex's early-morning observation.

He determined that the fading light from the initial flash had been centered on a true bearing of one hundred and seventy degrees, which was east of Boston—possibly out to sea. The tsunami added credence to this theory.

Asteroid or nuclear weapon, it didn't change the fact that the explosion had occurred much closer to Boston than Portland, and their son lived on the sixth floor of a fifty-year-old, fourteen-floor dormitory tower overlooking the Charles River. The implications hadn't escaped either of them. The tsunami would be bigger, sweeping down the Charles River and flooding the campus. The blast and wind effects of the initial strike would be more devastating, causing serious external damage to buildings, and the seismic effect of the impact would be more pronounced, resulting in structural damage.

Alex would never say it, but his body language betrayed the elephant following them from room to room. Their rescue mission stood a good chance of turning into a recovery mission.

"I wish my parents would use the damn satphone. I'd feel better knowing that everything is all right out there. Is there any warm water at all?" he said and stripped down to his underwear.

"None, according to Sam," said Kate. "I'm sure your parents are fine. We'll be out there soon enough."

"They're not exactly spring chickens, and technology kicks their asses—unless it's the Internet. They're all over that."

Kate laughed. "They have more of a social media presence than I do."

"More than both of us," he said and paused. "This may sound strange, but I hope that both of their cars are out of commission."

"I had the same thought. Driving around isn't a good idea right now."

"Especially for those two. The worst would be if one of the cars started on the first try, and they just drove into town, still oblivious. They'd lose the car at their first stop, or worse."

"Limerick is a tight community. I wouldn't worry about them," said Kate.

"What we saw tonight is the tip of the proverbial iceberg. Ed's Jeep carries more real-world value than the combined bank accounts of everyone in Scarborough. Don't be surprised if we end up walking back from Boston."

"Just stay in touch with the phone. Use your portable solar unit to keep it charged."

"Unless we're talking all day and all night, the phones should last pretty long," said Alex.

"Humor me. If you end up walking back, we might not see you for several days."

"I may have to talk Ed and Charlie into hiking a little further than I suggested. We can't afford to lose the Jeep."

"Good luck hauling Charlie *and* Ed that far," she said quietly.

Alex leaned in, bringing his smelly body closer to hers. She tried not to react to the strong aroma of stagnant, rotting mud.

"Between you and me, I'm not taking either of them across the Charles—unless the situation requires it," he whispered. "If I can convince them to guard the Jeep, all the better. Getting in and out of the city with our kids will require mobility and concentration. They'll slow me down," he whispered.

"These guys came through for you before. You're not exactly a trained commando."

"Compared to Ed and Charlie, I'm Delta Force. I'll bring them as far as I can without jeopardizing the kids' safety," said Alex.

"Yeah, and good luck trying to talk Ed out of rescuing his daughter."

PART III

"ROADS LESS TRAVELLED"

Chapter 21

Scarborough, Maine

A thin line of dark blue light pushed gently against the black velvet curtain, barely noticeable through the distant trees. From the second-floor corner window of the Walkers' house, Alex flipped his night vision goggles (NVG) down and surveyed the green image. The eastern half of the neighborhood was dark. He stared at a fixed point for several seconds, trying to register any movement in the limited field of vision afforded by the goggles. All was still. He moved to one of the front windows and knelt, scanning the houses along their departure route. The green imagery betrayed no signs of artificial light within the homes. He clicked his radio.

"Charlie, you showing anything on thermal?"

"Looks clear," Charlie replied.

"Same here. First run leaves as soon as you reach the garage. Everyone set?" asked Alex.

Ed's voice broke into his earpiece. "Loaded and ready."

"That's it, then. Drop Charlie at the top of the street, then straight to the fire station and back. No lights," Alex instructed.

"Got it."

Alex rested his arms on the rifle attached to his chest by a one-point sling and silently counted the seconds. He heard a deep rumbling by the count of seven and Ed's voice at nine.

"Door is up. We're on our way out," said Ed.

"Route looks clear," Alex said. "See you in a couple minutes."

He scooted back from the window and raised his rifle, scanning over the sight through his NVG set. His left finger rested on the toggle switch for the dual-aiming laser. The garage door slid along creaky tracks, breaking the morning silence, followed by a V6 roar. He panned from left to right, focusing on each house momentarily. Even a small flashlight deep inside one of the homes would show up as a bright green flare. The engine idled for a moment; then Ed brought the Jeep down the driveway without headlights. He wouldn't use them until they reached Harrison Road.

Alex stared over the Jeep, studying each house along the route for light. Clear so far. He checked the Jeep. Charlie stood on the left running board, holding onto the two bicycles bungeed to the roof rack. The Jeep's tires sucked at the deep mud as the vehicle staggered down the street. Ed was playing it safe. Too safe.

"Come on. Get out of here, Ed," he mumbled.

He didn't think the mud was deep enough to trap a 4X4 vehicle, but Ed routinely took the Jeep off-roading, so it was his show. At this rate it would take more than a couple of minutes to make the round trip. When the Jeep disappeared behind one of the lifeless structures along Durham Road, he turned his attention back to the northeast half of the street, drawn to his own house next door. He was too exhausted to process the flood of emotions, so he stared, nearly convincing himself that they would be back to salvage whatever remained. He knew better. They all knew better.

He continued the sweep. The neighborhood represented a mixed bag of memories and emotions. They'd enjoyed a pleasant life on Durham Road, raising two children, tending to the yard, and paying the mortgage on time. Throw in a big vacation each year, and anyone would agree they had a nice thing going. They did—until a microscopic organism changed everything. Changed every*one*.

At least three-quarters of the neighborhood had turned over since 2014, which had been a blessing in many cases. Tensions between the two neighborhood factions reached unbearable levels after a brief post-pandemic "honeymoon" period, with kids taunting kids and adults frequently breaking into screaming matches. Most of the "for sale" signs were welcome additions to the landscape. Nearly all of them had been foreclosures. Financial relief measures authorized by the Pandemic Recovery Act hadn't been designed to help families remain in half-a-million-dollar homes near the beach.

Worsening the crisis, life insurance companies folded en masse during January of 2014. Faced with an astronomical number of projected claims, most companies quietly faded away into the night, their cash assets liquidated and distributed to surviving executive management. Little remained for the Department of Justice to seize. Millions of insurance policies, designed and sold as the ultimate "safety net," rarely yielded enough to pay off one of the family's cars. More "for sale" signs.

Of course, the entire turnover was not finance related. The psychopaths from Massachusetts had murdered two households, using his friend Greg Murray's home as a base of operations for their reign of terror. Greg's wife understandably refused to live in the house after learning what had happened. They'd moved closer to Greg's parents in the Catskills and were never seen again.

Eventually, the neighborhood emerged as one collective group of strangers. Adults avoided eye contact, children were kept close at hand, and doors were locked. The more he thought about it, the less he'd miss the place. His home was with Kate and the kids.

Light bathed the side of Jamie's house, blinding him. He raised the goggles and searched for the source.

Shit. Come on, Ed.

"Ed's on his way," said Charlie.

No shit.

"Ed, turn off your lights," he said, straining not to yell.

"We almost hit a tree on Harrison Road. I'm not taking any chances."

"Copy. We'll be waiting for you in the garage," Alex said, clipping the radio onto his rifle sling.

He dashed out of the bedroom, still partially blinded from the night vision flare caused by Ed's headlights. He hit the flashlight toggle switch on the rifle's hand guard, illuminating the stairs for his descent. Samantha waited in the candlelit kitchen.

"They're inbound," he said, blowing out one of the candles on the kitchen island.

Alex flashed his rifle light toward the mudroom to make sure he didn't collide with anyone lingering in the house. He reached the mudroom door just as Ed's headlights swept through the garage, spotlighting the group waiting to load up for the last trip.

"I can't believe we're just leaving everything," said Samantha.

"I'm trying not to think about it," he said.

"Fifteen years down the drain," she added, following him into the garage.

"Hey, you won't have to pay the rest of the mortgage," joked Alex.

"I'd rather make payments."

"Start bringing everything out," barked Kate.

Daniel, Ed and Samantha's son, said, "We need a light."

Alex lit up the bike carrier with his rifle's LED barrel-mounted flashlight.

"Here, I got it," said Samantha, activating a handheld light. "I'm not comfortable with you pointing a rifle at my kids."

"The safety's on," said Alex, lowering his rifle to help with the bikes.

"Humor me."

When the bikes and gear were safely stowed, Alex stepped into the garage and closed the bay door, reengaging the manual release lever to lock it in the down position. He left through the back garage door, locking it behind him. Standing on the side of Ed's Jeep, he caught the last glimpses of his home superimposed against a thicker, lighter blue ribbon of twilight.

Chapter 22

EVENT +24:47 Hours

South Portland, Maine

Alex stood on the Jeep's passenger-side running board and surveyed the intersection before turning his attention to the rapidly approaching mob. This hadn't work out so well.

Lesson learned.

He'd wanted to stage their departure from a less conspicuous location further back along Route 1, but the water and mud had reached further than he'd expected. By choosing the parking lot, he had traded one problem for another. Human activity.

Tents and makeshift shelters proliferated on the grassy areas surrounding the hotel, spilling onto the sidewalks and edges of the parking lots. A sea of useless cars provided additional shelter to the refugees, who must have arrived yesterday to find that the hotel was full. The remnants of jumbled letters on the hotel's roadside sign welcomed some kind of conference or gathering.

Their initial arrival had attracted attention, which had grown from a few dazed, exhausted, early-morning risers upon the first drop off, to an increasingly agitated mob of thirty by the time he had returned with the third carload of bicycles and family. Like zombies, the entire group shifted its collective attention to the working vehicle, sensing salvation and opportunity. Alex weighed their options and decided for a hasty departure. He activated his handheld radio.

"Charlie, get everyone up and moving while they're distracted. Next rally point is the Maine Mall offramp. We'll keep moving the Jeep until you guys are clear of the parking lot."

"Roger that. Hey, I don't have a bike," replied Charlie.

"Run alongside the bicycles, and make sure they get out of the parking lot. I'll pick you up at the intersection."

"Copy. Moving out."

Alex dropped into the front passenger seat and shut the door. "Pull back from the crowd and reposition near the conference center entrance. That should give Charlie enough time to get them out of here," he said to Ed.

"Make sure the doors are locked back there. Yours too, Ed."

The crowd had nearly reached them by the time Ed shifted into reverse and put some distance between the Jeep and the mob. The crowd continued to press forward, yelling a simultaneous string of incoherent and indistinguishable demands at his open window. In the growing daylight, he could see a few rifle barrels in the crowd, most of them pointing upward—for now. He had no intention of letting this group near the Jeep.

"Samantha, put your packs against the doors and have everyone squeeze into the middle. Stay low," he said, hoping to put a little more than thin metal jeep framing between Ed's family and a bullet.

While Samantha rearranged the back seating area, putting two packs against the door next to Daniel, Alex peered past the crowd.

We aren't moving fast enough.

"Charlie, Kate—get them up and moving. We're running out of time here," he said into the handheld radio, getting no response from either.

"Alex, this is stupid. We need to get the hell out of here," said Ed.

"They're all up on their bikes. Twenty seconds. Move back further, but don't get us cornered," said Alex.

"We don't have a ton of parking lot left. If they grab one of the bikes off the Jeep, our plan is screwed," said Ed, driving them at an angle to the hotel and conference center.

"Slow us down."

"Slow us *down*? Fuck that. We're out of here. Charlie and Kate have plenty of room to get them out of the parking lot." Ed stepped on the gas and propelled the Jeep toward one of the exits for Route 1.

"Stay down back there!" said Alex, hoping that the mob's rifles stayed silent.

He was relieved to be moving away from the mob, which was now running in a futile attempt to catch up with the Jeep. Ed drove them to the southernmost exit, which drew the crowd further away from the other group. By the time they turned north on Route 1, Kate and the other cyclists had reached the gas station and accelerated. Charlie trailed them by fifty feet. Kate's group would be long gone before elements of the mob arrived, but he wasn't so sure about Charlie.

As soon as Ed floored the Jeep, pointing it toward Route 1, the crowd chasing them split apart. While the majority of the group continued in a straight, zombielike path toward the vehicle, a smaller group sprinted toward Charlie. Alex did the math and didn't like the outcome. As their Jeep turned onto Route 1, he began to lose sight of the pack behind loosely spaced rows of thick, flowering bushes along the sidewalk between the road and parking lot. Ed jammed on the accelerator, speeding them toward the intersection. Alex glanced through the windshield and saw Kate's group cross Route 1 headed west onto the Maine Turnpike Approach Road.

"This is guaranteed to get shitty," said Alex.

"I'm not risking the Jeep, Alex—or my family," said Ed.

"If Charlie starts shooting—you'll lose the jeep. The police will be all over us before we get to the tollbooth. We have to get him out of there before he panics."

"I'll wait in the intersection, but that's it," he said, as the Jeep rapidly approached that terminal point.

"Slow down for a second."

"Are you crazy?" Ed bellowed.

"Ed, get us out of here!" screamed Samantha.

"Stop the Jeep, and wait for me at the intersection. Do it now!" ordered Alex.

The Jeep jerked to a stop, giving Alex enough time to jump down onto the street before it lurched forward again. He hit the street in a dead sprint, slicing between two thick sections of beach roses and emerging on a collision course with the man catching up to Charlie. Alex's sudden appearance caused Charlie to lower his rifle, which averted the first of many disasters ripening at the moment. With several hotels in the immediate area, he could almost guarantee a nearby police presence.

He emphatically waved his hands at Charlie, silently imploring him to keep running. As he barreled closer, the first runner caught movement in his peripheral vision and turned his head.

Too late.

He tried to bring the SKS rifle around while decelerating out of a full-speed run, but Alex stopped the man's rifle with his left hand and landed his right elbow into the man's neck. Momentum did the rest.

The controlled collision flattened the attacker, leaving him gasping for air on the gritty pavement. Alex ripped the SKS rifle out of his grip, stumbling to the ground. Loose bits of blacktop dug agonizingly deep into his knee. He scrambled to his feet and reassessed the situation. Not much had improved.

"Keep going!" he screamed at Charlie, who had slowed down again.

The next threat, a mid-twenties, stick-thin guy wearing jeans and a salt-stained black T-shirt, arrived without a plan. Alex swung the SKS by the barrel, smashing the wooden butt stock against the right side of his head. Skinny tumbled to Alex's left, hitting the ground hard. His beefy replacement, half muscle and half fat judging by his stretched blue polo shirt, didn't hesitate to close the gap. Alex barely found the time to shift his grip on the rifle and jam the butt stock into the man's oncoming face. Surprisingly, Beefy managed to deflect some of the rifle's momentum, taking a glancing blow to the head. He collapsed to his knees, out of the fight.

His third threat, a longhaired guy wearing fatigue pants and a white tank top, widened his rapid approach.

Time to gain some ground.

Alex turned and sprinted for the intersection, unfolding the SKS's spike bayonet as he ran. He'd taken several strides when something solid struck the back of his head. The dull thud surprised him more than it stunned him, and he kept running. When he heard a metallic object strike the pavement, he risked a look back. A large hunting knife clattered to a stop on the black and gray pavement several feet behind him.

Wild Man raced toward him at full speed. Even if he could beat the guy to the intersection, which was doubtful, Wild Man would be on the Jeep before they could mount up and leave. Alex saw no other option. He reversed direction and squatted low, thrusting the business end of the rifle up through his outstretched hands. The spike bayonet penetrated the man's upper abdomen, just below the xiphoid process, disappearing deep into his chest cavity. The collision's momentum buried the metal barrel deep into the gap opened by the bayonet. Warm blood sprayed onto Alex's arms.

He released the rifle and ran, drawing his pistol to discourage anyone else. He hated to leave the rifle, but trying to remove it from the man's chest could take considerable time and effort. They'd be long gone before anyone could put it into action against them. He reached the Jeep a few steps behind Charlie, pushing him through the open passenger door and holstering his pistol.

"Christ," he huffed. "I almost beat you to the Jeep."

"I wasn't expecting Olympic sprinters in the group," replied Charlie, out of breath.

Once Charlie was inside, Alex slammed the door and jumped onto the running board.

"I'm on! Let's go!"

The Jeep pitched forward, nearly yanking his bloody grip from the front passenger window. He hugged the side of the Jeep as Ed accelerated down the Maine Turnpike Approach Road, risking a glance behind them at the rapidly disappearing intersection. The bulk of the mob emerged from the bushes and swarmed the far side of the intersection, bringing at least thirty men and women into the open. From what he could tell, none of them crossed the intersection.

"Slow down!" he yelled through the window.

He heard Charlie repeat the request and felt the stiff wind weaken.

"You all right?" asked Alex, leaning his head near the window.

Charlie poked his head partway out of the window, staring at the bright red arterial spray covering Alex's hand. "I'm fine. What about you?"

"Good to go!" he said, forming a scarlet red thumbs-up.

He was far from "good to go." He'd just run a man through with a bayonet, leaving him to bleed out onto a dirty asphalt parking lot. The man represented an imminent threat to their group, just like Jamie's husband.

Both of them had to go.

Emotionally and intellectually, he didn't like his ease of transition into this frame of mind. Rationally, his experiences more than justified the evolution. His reluctance to embrace a "kill or be killed" mentality during the Jakarta Pandemic had resulted in disaster. He couldn't make that mistake again. Threats to his rescue mission would be neutralized with extreme prejudice. Terminated if necessary.

The trick was to avoid these situations if possible. "Force application" was a dual-edged sword, attracting unwanted attention while inviting a similar, violent response. The parking lot was a perfect example.

Staging their final rally point in the Best Western's parking lot had been a bad idea. One that had nearly cost them everything at the very start of their journey. He'd underestimated the number of refugees scattered around the hotel, and should have kept driving when it became apparent. Most importantly, he failed to anticipate the rapid rate at which their reception to Alex's group would deteriorate. This should have been obvious from the start.

His group was well organized, which more than likely gave the mob the distinct impression that they had a plan. It probably didn't take them long to figure out that the plan included a destination close enough to reach by bicycle. Some had been interested in learning more about their final destination. Questions hurled at them verified this. Others were solely interested in acquiring a mode of transportation to achieve their own objectives. Some of the more aggressive and vocal members of the crowd had suggested that they "double up" on the bikes and leave the rest behind.

All of them were hungry for information, and desperation lurked dangerously close to the surface. He couldn't afford to misjudge the immediate and lasting effects of desperation again. He had to assume that everyone outside of his own circle had the worst intentions, and plan accordingly—regardless of the situation. Looks could be deceiving. Sympathies could be played. He hated to think like this, but their short- and long-term survival would depend on it.

Alex's group represented something to everyone, and everything to some. He had to make sure that Kate, Linda and Samantha understood what this meant and adopted the same mindset for their trek to Limerick. A group of nine well-equipped cyclists represented an opportunity, regardless of weapons. Alex wasn't optimistic about their chances of arriving without incident.

❧❦

Kate looked her husband over one last time, making sure he showed no signs of the bloody encounter in the parking lot. She'd taken several minutes and used an entire packet of moist-wipes to thoroughly remove the thickened blood from his hands and forearms before she let him change clothes. He kept trying to rush the process, but she insisted on doing a thorough job. If he changed clothes before she was finished, he might get blood on a shirtsleeve or his collar, which could attract attention. One scarlet smear spotted by a police officer standing at a tight intersection might be all it took to stop and search the Jeep.

Hands shaking, he let her proceed. Whatever had happened at the Best Western had been sudden and violent, and Alex didn't want to talk about it. When she crossed the intersection on her bicycle, Ed's Jeep was gunning toward Charlie, who hadn't reached the intersection. She assumed everything was under control at that point and focused all of her attention on the bicycles, pedaling harder and verbally encouraging the rest of her group to pick up speed.

Generating rapid momentum for their sudden departure had taken significantly more effort and time than she expected. With thirty- to forty-pound backpacks to balance while riding, her crew wasn't exactly the most nimble on two wheels, and they needed to gain more distance to be truly out of danger. Their escape from the parking lot established a painful reality. They were slow, awkward and unable to accelerate fast enough to escape pedestrians. The bicycles would serve one purpose on their trek: ease of transportation. She couldn't forget that.

"You'll pass inspection," she said.

"The Jeep won't. We have enough shit in there to start a war. I'm worried about what'll happen if we get stopped," Alex said, glancing around.

She took his cue and leaned in, pretending to inspect the side of his face. They were shielded from the rest of the group by the Jeep, but with the Jeep's windows open, there was no way to guarantee a private conversation.

"Ed nearly drove off, leaving Charlie behind. I almost had to hijack the Jeep," he whispered.

Kate considered the implications of his comment. "I don't know what to tell you. We're all in this together now. You'll just have to keep a close eye on him, and manage the situation."

"And Charlie? I nearly beat him back to the Jeep after taking down four people," he said.

"His heart's in the right place, Alex," Kate reminded him. "He could have chosen to stay behind."

"I know. I couldn't ask for a better friend in this. I just don't want his heart to explode. He only ran like a hundred yards and—"

"With a full pack on his back. You know what you're working with, so work with it. That's all you can do."

"You're right," he muttered, looking up at her.

"I'm always right," she said, patting him lightly on his right shoulder.

Alex visibly winced, and they locked eyes for a moment. She fought the urge to comment on the injury, knowing that anything she said would be unproductive. He was going to Boston to rescue Ryan and Chloe, regardless of the circumstances. End of discussion. He needed to respect the fact that Ed and Charlie shared this same, singular focus. She took both of his hands and pulled him close, kissing him passionately while they still had a modicum of privacy. He responded, pressing her against the Jeep and kissing her neck. They both knew this could be their last moment together, and for a few seconds, they forgot about everything except each other. When Alex kissed her softly on the lips, she opened her eyes, knowing that the moment had ended.

"You can't pull this off alone. It's too big for one person," she whispered in his ear.

"I'd still try."

"I know you would," she said and kissed him again. "You better say goodbye to Emily and Ethan. We need to get this show on the road."

"Emily doesn't look so good," said Alex.

"She's sixteen—and this is the second time in her life that the world as she knows it has come to an abrupt halt. I'm surprised she's functional at all."

"Built tough, like her mom," said Alex.

"Are you comparing me to a Chevy truck?"

"Uh—I hadn't intended to."

"I didn't think so." She winked. "Get going."

Kate watched Alex walk over and sit next to Emily, who looked up at her dad and forced a smile. They talked for a few minutes, and when Alex tried to get up, she grabbed his arm and cried into his shoulder. He kissed her forehead and hugged her tightly for a long moment. When he let go, she dropped herself to the ground near her mountain bike and pulled her backpack next to her. Alex shook his head at Kate as he passed her to meet Ethan on the shoulder of the road.

"Keep an eye on her," he advised. "She's frazzled."

Ethan lowered his bike to the gravel as Alex approached. A quick hug and a handshake. Kate had no doubt that their brief interaction had met both of their emotional needs. Men were so different. She nodded at Alex, who blew her a kiss and made his way to Charlie and Ed near the back of the jeep. Emily would need more than that. Kate wandered over to her daughter and sat next to her in the mowed grass beyond the gravel shoulder.

"Your dad will be fine, sweetie. He'll bring your brother home," said Kate, putting her arm around Emily's shoulders.

Emily leaned in, sobbing. "What if he doesn't come back with Ryan? What if none of them make it back?" Emily asked tearfully.

Kate squeezed tighter. "They're coming back—*with* your brother. I'm certain of it. Your dad can handle this."

"But *they* can't," she said. "He should go by himself."

Kate looked at her daughter, surprised by the realization that Emily had been paying far more attention to the situation than she had assumed. Acting aloof and oblivious to anything beyond her immediate sphere of influence had become her default mode of behavior over the past year, presumably attributable to her early teen years. Kate wondered if this wasn't more of an act than her personality. Emily turned to face her, tears streaming down her dirty cheeks. She wiped her face with her arm, smearing freshly moistened mud across her ear.

Emily had Kate's deep blue eyes and Alex's darker skin. Her auburn hair was pulled into a tight ponytail that protruded from the back of her pink and gray Red Sox cap. She hadn't been pleased with Alex's insistence that she wear long pants and a long-sleeved shirt. Emily had compromised with a pair of hiking pants made out of a quick-dry material and a light blue running shirt. Neither of them was about to argue with her. Comfort would trump tactical for the bicycle crew. They had a long, hot day ahead of them, and nobody had opted for long sleeves.

"He can't do this alone," said Kate, glancing over her shoulder at the men.

"They'll get him killed. I know it."

"Emily, I don't want to hear you say that again. You're going to see your dad again—*and* your brother."

"If he's still alive," said Emily, standing up and grabbing her backpack.

"Emily," she hissed, "what's going on?"

"I'm just being realistic, Mom."

Her daughter lifted the green pack over her shoulders and tightened the straps.

"I think it's time to go," said Emily.

Kate stood speechless for a few moments as Emily picked up her bike and guided it toward the group forming behind the Jeep. She knew their world would never return to normal, and that the scars of leaving their life behind would run deep, but she didn't want to lose her daughter to a fatalistic outlook that would permanently stain her future. Like Alex, she would have to keep a very close eye on Emily.

"Hold on. Let me grab my stuff," she said, relieved to see her daughter stop and force another smile.

At least she was trying.

Chapter 23

York, Maine

Alex felt the rumble strips pass under the Jeep's tires, barely noticeable under a thin layer of sandy mud. Mud and debris had appeared on the turnpike a few miles past the abandoned Kennebunk rest stop, causing them to slow considerably and engage the Jeep's four-wheel-drive system. Their planned forty-minute trip from the Maine Mall rally point had turned into an hour and a half. At one point Alex started to seriously doubt their ability to reach the York exit. The muck slowed them to ten miles per hour along the ten-mile stretch between Wells and York, where the turnpike passed a point two miles from the ocean.

Beyond the nearly impassible sludge, most of their trip had proven uneventful, yielding little insight into what had transpired the day before. Traffic had been light at five in the morning when the suspected EMP hit, leaving a sparse number of stranded motorists on either side of the six-lane highway. Most of the cars had managed to safely find the emergency lane; however, the occasional mid-highway obstacle kept them vigilant. They passed two single-car wrecks, stopping at both to check for bodies. They found none, which gave them the impression that state police still patrolled the roads.

The Jeep hit another set of rumble strips and slowed. Through binoculars, Alex saw a steeply curved wall of concrete barrier blocks diverting southbound traffic across the center divide, into the northbound lanes. A police cruiser sat at the end of the barrier. Two state troopers armed with shotguns stood on the driver side of the cruiser. Looking past the officers, Alex determined that concrete blocks were set between all of the northbound tollbooths, except for a single gap blocked by a state police cruiser. The purpose of the one gap became clear as the scene beyond the tollbooth unfolded.

"Shit. We aren't getting through this. The entire southern side of the tollbooth is a parking lot. I see a few large tents—like a military command post or something," said Alex.

"Both sides of the highway?" asked Charlie, from the back seat.

"Both sides, but that's not the real problem. State troopers have the entire southbound lane blocked. Shit, I see a JLTV on the other side of the tollbooth."

Charlie shot up in his seat, nearly knocking the binoculars out of Alex's hands. Charlie was like an annoying child when anyone mentioned military hardware. His enthusiasm to share his vast knowledge often eclipsed any desire to hear what he had to say. Still, Alex would gladly take Charlie's near encyclopedic recitation of information over Ed's bare-bones knowledge of anything beyond the caliber and ammunition capacity of his Ruger 10/22 rifle.

"What kind?" uttered Charlie.

"Take a look," he said, pushing Charlie's face back with the binoculars.

"I'm pulling a U-turn," said Ed.

"Hold on. Maybe there's a way," said Alex.

"Why take the chance? What if they have a description of our Jeep from the Best Western? We should double back to the Wells exit and take the back roads."

"I'm with Ed on that," said Charlie. "The less time they spend looking in our car, the better. I'm good with the back roads. By the way, that's an AM General Bravo Blast Resistant Vehicle-Off road. Most likely Maine National Guard. Fifty cal mounted on top."

Alex hadn't considered the possibility that the police might have driven by the hotel within the past hour and stopped in the parking lot to investigate the commotion. He was certain that the angry crowd wouldn't fairly represent his side of the story. Would the police be able to assess the scene and determine what really happened? Would they care enough to issue an APB? Did any of their radios work? They hadn't picked up any local chatter on Alex's police scanner, but most of the police departments had converted to encrypted P25 digital radio communications systems. Too many questions unanswered to take the chance.

If the troopers ordered them out of the Jeep, they'd have no choice but to disobey and speed north toward the Wells exit, praying that they weren't worth the time and effort of a high-speed pursuit. Alex's crew needed to do everything in their power to avoid a law enforcement confrontation. The Jeep couldn't outrun the police, and they had hesitantly but unanimously agreed that harming police officers was out of the question. Alex wasn't convinced that he could abide by that pact, especially if it jeopardized rescuing his son. Turning around before the tollbooth assured that he wouldn't have to test these doubts.

"All right, let's get out of here," he said.

The rear passenger-side/center seat combination directly behind Alex had been folded forward to give Charlie quick access to their rifles and tactical vests, which were hidden underneath a thick plaid comforter. Three black school-sized backpacks lay over the comforter next to Charlie, camouflaging its purpose. The lighter, off-the-shelf daypacks had been stuffed with food, water, medical supplies and emergency basics to last twenty-four hours. Sufficient for their excursion into Boston, but not enough to weigh them down like the heavier packs.

They would hide the sixty-pound, long-term endurance rucksacks in the forest, wherever they decided to leave the Jeep. If the Jeep disappeared while they were in the city, the success of their return voyage to Maine would depend on the rucksacks, especially if the kids were in bad shape. The larger packs were stuffed behind Charlie's seat, on top of a few duffel bags filled with each family's memorabilia. Gas containers, several two-gallon jugs of water and a box of MREs filled the remaining gaps in the rear compartment.

They could have fit twice as much gear into the Jeep, but for tactical reasons, they packed lightly. Alex wanted clear fields of vision in every direction and quick access to their equipment, which prevented them from filling every conceivable nook throughout the Jeep with repetitive gear. He also wanted to configure the Jeep's load-out for the possibility of an immediate and irreversible abandonment of the vehicle while under fire. If an overwhelming threat engaged their vehicle, they needed to be in the forest or bushes with their weapons, tactical gear and MOLLE packs in less than fifteen seconds. His combat experience had irrevocably proven that quickly abandoning your vehicle and finding suitable cover, when the situation dictated, bettered your chance of survival. The Iraqi Fedayeen he'd encountered on the way to Bagdad in 2003 never adequately grasped that concept. They'd died in droves, clustered around their disabled vehicles. He had no intention of letting that happen to them.

Ed slowly turned the Jeep left and guided the vehicle through the orange traffic drums separating the two sides of the highway on the approach to the tollbooth. Alex watched the police vehicles with anticipation as they entered the northbound lanes and accelerated away from the massive roadblock. The only vehicle that followed them was a maroon pickup truck released through the checkpoint, which passed them at high speed less than a minute into their detour and disappeared ahead of them. Alex wondered if the pickup could navigate through the mud ahead.

"I don't see anything following us," said Charlie.

"Good. Let's try to sort out a route to the border before we hit the Wells exit," said Alex, reaching between the front seats to open a spiraled map book.

"We'll have plenty of time with the fucking mud," muttered Ed.

"Route 9 to Route 4 takes us through North and South Berwick to the border—then to Dover, New Hampshire," said Charlie.

"I'm worried that we'll be driving into the same situation we saw at the York tollbooth," Alex said. "There's only one other crossing between that one and the turnpike. My guess is that either the state police or locals will have them sealed up—possibly both ways."

"There are plenty of places to cross further west. We can keep driving until we find one," said Charlie.

"How far do you want to drive? They could have the entire border sealed up."

Alex shrugged. "We have all day to figure this out. It's not even nine yet."

"And this little setback will end up costing us another hour, if we don't get stranded in the mud. The clock is ticking. Did you see the rain clouds in the distance? The ground can't take any more water. We're fucked if this is a big storm," said Ed.

"I'm pretty sure it's not a major system. Looked like a chance of showers on the forecast" said Alex.

"When did you check last?" asked Ed.

"Saturday."

"A lot can change in a few days."

"We'll start with the Berwicks and see what happens," Alex said. "We might be able to talk our way across."

Ed was right about the potential storm on the horizon. Alex had seen a chance of rain on the extended forecast when he checked on the weather for their sailing trip. He vaguely remembered seeing a chance of thunderstorms for today and clear weather for the rest of the week. Kate had eyeballed the distant clouds when they parted ways earlier, raising an eyebrow but saying nothing.

She wasn't a big fan of rain-soaked sailboat trips, and he had purposely glossed over that part of the week's weather report right before packing up the car and heading over to the yacht club. The sailboat's interior space shrank quickly when foul weather trapped them below with the kids for any length of time. Ironically, the decision to withhold part of the forecast from Kate probably had saved both of their lives. Kate liked to walk in the morning, and Alex invariably ran every other day. He usually skipped Sundays, which meant that he would have very likely found himself somewhere between his house and Higgins Beach when the tsunami swept inland.

"I don't think it's a good idea, guys," Charlie said. "Dover is a decent-sized city. We need to avoid high-population centers until we have no choice."

"Dover's not exactly teeming with people," countered Ed.

"I'd prefer to avoid places like Dover," Alex told them, "but we should still be all right in New Hampshire. I'm mostly worried about the outskirts of Boston."

"I don't agree, guys," Charlie insisted. "If you live between Boston and Maine, you're gonna want to get the fuck out of there. Dover and Portsmouth were ransacked by the kind citizens of Massachusetts and Connecticut during the pandemic. I'm just saying we can't let our guard down."

"We shouldn't let our guard down at any time, but we can't take every dirt road from here to Medford in an attempt to slip past any town with more than one traffic light. We need to reach the kids by tonight at the latest," said Ed.

"Barring some unforeseen disaster, we'll be in position to enter Medford around dusk."

"Why can't we just hide the car and go straight to the kids?" asked Ed.

"Because we'll be wearing tactical gear and carrying military-style rifles through a heavily populated, urban setting. If we do this during broad daylight, we'll attract a shit ton of attention. The wrong kind of attention. The only thing more valuable than a car right now is a military-grade weapon. Anyone with a little foresight knows that the situation in these high-population-density areas will implode. Even a rifle like yours will replace the dog as man's best friend," said Alex.

"Easy on the rifle," said Ed.

"I'll have to apologize to her later," Alex said, winking at Charlie. "She did save my ass."

"The rifle didn't save your ass," said Charlie.

"Thank you, Charlie," said Ed.

"Will you sit back in your seat?" Alex grumped. "You're like one of the kids."

"I'm not giving up this front-row seat for anything. The only thing missing is a bag of popcorn. The two of you should keep me entertained all the way to Boston," said Charlie.

"Wonderful. Can you at least breathe on Ed?" Alex complained. "I can smell the beef jerky stuck between your teeth."

"See that, Charlie?" asked Ed.

"See what?"

"Alex goes right to the vegetarian digs when he feels threatened by you," said Ed, grinning widely.

"I always suspected he was a foodist."

"Two against one?" Alex said. "This is going to be a long ride."

"Let's hope not," said Ed, the smile suddenly gone from his face.

Prior to the brief exchange seconds ago, Ed hadn't spontaneously smiled since yesterday afternoon. Unlike Alex, who leaned on humor to mask and cope with stress, Ed became stolid and serious, creating an impenetrable brick wall to hide his emotions. The tactic didn't work very well for Ed, because the impassive facade didn't match his usual range of expressions. Alex could read him like a book, and right now, Ed was close to having a nervous breakdown.

"We'll get the kids back, Ed."

Ed nodded his head and looked like he wanted to say something. Alex didn't push it. He glanced quickly at Charlie, who met his eyes and imperceptibly raised his eyebrows, acknowledging Alex's silent message: *We need to keep an eye on him.*

A few minutes later, they exited the turnpike at Wells and decelerated along the winding off ramp. They found the two-lane road blocked at the tollbooth station by a Wells Police cruiser and several orange traffic drums. A police officer and three armed men stood in front of the drums, signaling for them to pull into the right lane, directly perpendicular to the side of the cruiser. Alex examined the situation and made a quick decision to proceed.

"Get your Maine driver's licenses out for the officer. Registration too. Make sure nothing has shifted back there. All windows down," said Alex.

They had placed the licenses and registration in the front breast pockets of their shirts for quick access and to avoid reaching out of a police officer's sight in case they were stopped. While Ed pulled the Jeep into an area of pavement designated by traffic cones, Alex and Ed unbuttoned their pockets and removed their identification. Alex kept his eye on the civilians that accompanied the officer, noting their weapons. One of them held a semiautomatic shotgun and the two others carried AR-style rifles without optics.

They wore a variety of commercial tactical equipment and pistol holsters, which told Alex that they were most likely volunteers from town. Only the police officer wore body armor, obvious underneath his gray uniform. He tipped his campaign hat and approached the driver's-side window. One of the men with an AR walked across the front of their Jeep and took up a position on the passenger side. None of the men at the checkpoint pointed their weapons at the vehicle. He felt comfortable with the faces he saw. Serious. Solemn. Slightly nervous. If anyone had smiled or grinned at him, he would have felt threatened.

"Keep an eye on the guy to our right," he said out of the side of his mouth to Charlie.

"Got it," whispered Charlie.

The police officer stopped a few feet from Ed's door and examined the interior of the cabin, sweeping his eyes over Ed and Alex.

"Morning, gentlemen. May I ask where you came from and where you're headed?"

As agreed earlier, Ed led the conversation for the group. Alex thought it would appear strange if one of the passengers was the primary spokesperson. Possibly suspicious. If Ed faltered in any way, Alex would interject, but otherwise he'd leave the talking to the driver.

"Good morning, Officer. We're headed to Boston to pick up our kids. My daughter is at Boston College, and his son is at Boston University. We left Scarborough about an hour ago and saw that the York tollbooth was blocked in both directions. We're looking to take the back roads down into the city," said Ed.

"Can I see your license and registration? If you don't mind, gentlemen, I'd like to take a look at your licenses as well," said the officer, nodding at Alex and Charlie.

The officer examined the Jeep's registration and their licenses, handing everything back to Ed for redistribution.

"Not a great time to be out on the roads," said the officer.

"We don't have much of a choice," said Ed.

"I suppose not. You should be good to go until you reach the border," said the officer. "Rumor has it that the locals have shut down all of the crossings. Not sure if that means both ways. Nobody wants a repeat of what happened during the crisis a few years ago."

Alex didn't want to drag out their time at the checkpoint, but he needed more information about the general situation.

"Officer, what's happening at the York tollbooth? It looked like a parking lot," he asked.

"Maine Guard units have secured the far end of the Piscataqua River Bridge. They're letting Maine residents or family of residents through for further processing at the tollbooth. They're being thorough, from what I hear. The governor ordered it," said the officer.

"I'm surprised they can get past Kittery. We drove through nearly a foot of mud between here and York."

"Plows cleared a path from York to the bridge for the guard units mobilized out of Sanford. From what we heard, it took them forever."

Ed asked the officer, "Has anyone heard anything from Boston?"

"Coastal areas from Boston on up were hit hard by tsunami and wind damage. A windblast hit us here, but the damage was mostly superficial. Broken windows and branches on the ground. The tsunami did the real damage. Wiped out everything east of Route 1 in Wells and Ogunquit," he said and paused before continuing. "People are saying it was a lot worse in Boston."

"I'm sorry to have brought it up, Officer. I hope your family is safe," said Alex.

"Thank you. We live west of the turnpike, but a lot of the people we know weren't so lucky. It's…uh…I don't know what to say. I've never seen anything like this. How was it up in Portland?"

"The same. We live two miles from Higgins Beach and saw definitive signs of wreckage from the houses in that area. I think anyone living within a half mile of the water is gone," said Alex.

Officer Jenkins shook his head, fighting to keep his eyes from overflowing with tears. Alex couldn't imagine the impact a disaster of this magnitude might have on a police officer who patrolled the streets of a small, coastal town. Jenkins probably knew most of the year-round residents by name.

"Any official word on what exactly happened?" Alex asked. "I assume we got hit by an EMP."

"People report seeing a massive meteorite streak through the sky south of Boston, heading east. They think it hit somewhere out past Cape Cod," said Jenkins.

"Did they see it hit?" asked Ed.

"Reports are sketchy. Keep in mind that I'm getting most of this information third hand from the York and state police. Apparently there was a massive flash to the east, but nobody they've talked to from the cars actually saw the explosion. There's some talk of fires in Boston and people taken to the hospitals with third-degree burns from the flash."

"Sounds like the effects of a nuclear detonation. Add the EMP thing— I'm not convinced this is a natural event," said Alex.

"They think the meteorites or asteroid fragments might have disrupted the ionosphere and caused an EMP. Something like that. Nobody knows shit, basically," the officer admitted.

"That's the real problem. Everybody is guessing." They needed to get moving. "Keep your family safe, Officer. This is going to get a lot worse. You probably know that better than anyone."

"Yeah. Unfortunately, I know it all too well. I hope you get those kids back," said the officer.

The police officer moved his volunteers back and pulled his cruiser forward, clearing a path for their Jeep.

"Stay frosty!" yelled Alex from his window, earning a few nods from the roadblock crew. "Take a right up here on 109," he directed.

"That was easy enough. He barely looked in the car," said Ed.

"He didn't care. Our paperwork backed up our story, so he had no real reason to dig any further," Alex explained.

"I'm glad the two of you had fun. I was shitting my pants back here wondering what our plan might be if that little interaction had gone fucking south for the winter," said Charlie.

"Our best play is to avoid the police or any kind of checkpoint. If there's no way around it, like back there, we give them our story, identification, and hope for the best. If the police decide to search the car, we can always flee."

"With two AR-15s and a shotgun working us over, I don't think we would have gotten very far," said Charlie.

"I didn't get the sense that his crew would have pushed the issue if we had put the Jeep in reverse and left the way we came," said Alex.

"What about the next crew? What about the group that decides their town needs a four-wheel-drive vehicle more than two dads trying to rescue their Ivy League kids—and I mean nothing by that. Just saying what others might be thinking. We need to come up with a better plan for these checkpoints. This won't be our last," said Charlie.

"I'm not drawing down on the police or National Guard. We either flee or surrender to a search if it comes to that," said Alex.

"What if they start shooting?"

"Then we shoot back. We're well within our rights to refuse a search and turn around without being shot at," said Ed.

"I'm with Ed on that one," said Charlie.

Alex agreed, but he needed Ed and Charlie to come to this decision on their own. He'd already reached this verdict when they turned around at the York tollbooth. The last thing he wanted to do was engage the police in a firefight, but they had every right to defend themselves, especially with so much riding on the success of their journey. Avoidance was their best strategy, but eventually they would find themselves facing another checkpoint—and another. They needed more than a general agreement.

"All right. It sounds like we're all on the same sheet of music. Let's game plan more scenarios and establish rules of engagement. We should have done this last night. That's my bust. I should have known better. I wanted to get a better feel for what we'd be up against out here. We really got lucky back there," said Alex.

"I was ready to rock and roll if that went the way of the taco," said Charlie.

They both laughed at his reference.

"There's more where that came from," said Charlie.

"I don't doubt it. Why don't you chamber a round in both of the ARs and put them on safe. We'll need every fraction of a second possible if things…"

"Rapidly devolve into a clusterfuck?" Charlie said helpfully.

"Exactly," said Alex.

Chapter 24

South Berwick, Maine

Alex scanned the road ahead for the inevitable roadblock. They quickly approached the Overlook Golf Course, which marked the edge of town and the most logical place to stop cars headed into South Berwick's downtown area. He risked a glance at the parking lot, seeing several cars parked in the far corner of the spacious lot. The cars probably belonged to the golfers with the first tee times yesterday morning. He remembered driving through this area during the summer for Biosphere Pharmaceuticals. The Overlook had always teemed with golfers and summer events in the white tent next to the eighteenth green. As they passed the clubhouse and raised barn, Alex saw the tent standing empty next to the green.

He imagined a massive, outdoor wedding reception on Sunday afternoon and wondered if the newlywed couple was stuck somewhere between here and Logan International Airport, their honeymoon a long-vanished afterthought. Alex envisioned millions of scenarios like this playing out across the nation, each one consuming the focus of those involved, creating a desperate tunnel vision to survive. The sudden introduction of this desperate focus to millions of people would create a dangerous world.

"Look at those crazy assholes!" said Charlie, pointing out of the left passenger window.

In the middle of a distant fairway, on a rise past a small pond, two men hopped out of a green golf cart. One of them grabbed a golf club from a bag in the back, while the other opened the red cooler that had been stashed between the two men on the front seat. Alex couldn't see what he pulled out of the cooler, but given the fact that these two were golfing little more than twenty-four hours after a tsunami wiped out the coast and the power grid was taken down, he imagined they weren't messing around with cans of soda. He felt surprisingly ambivalent toward two men golfing at ten in the morning. They obviously didn't have any pressing matters—yet.

"Ignorance is bliss," said Alex.

"Yeah," Charlie said, "until they come knocking on your door looking for shit."

"Fucking idiots," mumbled Ed, concentrating on the road.

"The town starts just past that taller tree line. You should slow down a bit," said Alex.

Ed had just started to decelerate the jeep when Alex spotted the roadblock outside of South Berwick's downtown area. The road curved, gently revealing the distinctive shape and style of a police cruiser perpendicular to the road, blocking the inbound lane and most of the asphalt shoulder. A blue minivan blocked the outbound lanes.

"Slowly stop the car and turn us around. Damn it. I thought we might be able to slip through the outskirts of town. We'll backtrack to one of the local roads a mile or two behind us. Figure out how to break through to Route 9," said Alex, fumbling with the map book between the seats.

"They're flashing us!" said Ed, slamming on the brakes.

Alex braced his hands on the dashboard to keep his head from striking the glove box, feeling the binoculars slide from his lap onto the floor. The police car's red and blue LED strobes ominously pierced the distance between them. He estimated that Ed had stopped the Jeep roughly five hundred feet from the blockade, which put them at a relatively safe distance from immediate gunfire. Ed had unknowingly done them a favor with his panicked stop. Possibly a bigger favor than any of them had counted on.

Unlike the group at the Wells exit, the South Berwick blocking force had chosen to stand behind their vehicles, making it difficult for him to analyze weapons and personal equipment. Four men and a woman. From what he could tell, they were all armed. A sixth person sat behind the wheel of the police car, wearing a campaign hat. One of the men hunched down behind the police cruiser's hood, fumbling with something on the hood. He dug around for the binoculars and raised them to his face.

He shook his head. "Turn left and get us out of here."

Ed yanked the wheel left and drove the Jeep forward, exposing Alex to the roadblock.

"What's wrong?" asked Charlie.

"They're scoping us in with a rifle. Ed, faster, please."

"Do you want your HK?" Charlie asked him.

"No! Keep your hands above the window line. Do not give them any reason to send a bullet in our direction."

Alex took one more look at the roadblock through his binoculars and saw that the man behind the cruiser's hood had stood up, which was a relief. Nobody in the group appeared to be in a hurry to jump in the vehicles. Even better. Ed completed the U-turn and gunned the engine. Alex handed the binoculars to Charlie as they passed the Overlook clubhouse.

"I think they wanted to scare us away," said Alex, handing the binoculars to Charlie.

"It worked," said Ed.

"You can slow down. They're still standing around," said Charlie.

"That was different," said Alex.

"Very different," Charlie agreed. "Do you think they scope everyone that approaches?"

"I didn't see any binoculars. It might be all they have to make a long-range identification."

"Helluva greeting," said Charlie.

"Who in their right mind is going to drive up to the roadblock with a gun trained on them?" asked Ed.

"Maybe that's the point. They don't want anybody approaching."

Ed glanced at Alex. "Where do we turn for Route 9?"

"Up here a little bit. You're looking for Blackberry Hill Road. I might break out the GPS if we get too deep into the back roads."

"You want it now?" Charlie asked.

"Not yet. If Route 9 is a bust, we'll put it to work."

"I say we skip Route 9. We don't need a trigger-happy local putting a bullet through the engine block or one of our heads," Ed said nervously. "As much as I want to move this trip along, I think you're right about finding a less crowded crossing further west."

"Then crack out the GPS, Charlie," Alex said. "We won't bother trying to get through Berwick. There's a crossing at East Rochester and—"

"I wouldn't bother with that one," Charlie cut in. "Rochester is a few miles across the border along Route 11. It might be busier than the Route 4 crossing in South Berwick."

"We don't know how busy Route 4 was," Ed pointed out.

"If they're guarding the ass end of town, trust me, it's crowded. These towns are under a lot of pressure to avoid a replay of the Jakarta Pandemic," Charlie said. "We need to find a road that's not connected to a major city in New Hampshire or a town in Maine."

Alex studied the map for a minute, while Ed searched for Blackberry Hill Road. He traced the border with his finger, shaking his head every time it stopped. He needed something away from Rochester, but options thinned past Milton, New Hampshire. Route 125 intersected with Milton, making it a less than optimal choice.

Long lines at the border crossing in Rochester would push refugees north along the border on Route 125. Milton was one of the last crossing points before diverting several miles north. They were guaranteed to run into a strong local presence on the Maine side of the border near Milton. Tactically, Alex would fortify this point, so they would avoid it. Crisscrossing roads, he settled on the last small-town crossing before Route 109. He paged through the map book for a more detailed look at the town, smiling at what he found on the map.

"Milton Mills, New Hampshire," he said.

"Never heard of it," said Charlie.

"Good," Alex replied. "I think we're looking at about twenty-five miles—probably fifty minutes on back roads—but the town has two crossings, and it's just far enough north to give us some less crowded options for reaching Route 125."

"That far?" said Ed.

"It's the last crossing on the map before Route 109. We all know 109 will be guarded. It's a direct route to Sanford."

"At this rate, we'll be lucky to get to Medford before dark," said Ed.

"If it rains as hard as I think it will, we might not get there at all," said Charlie.

Alex shook his head. "We're too far inland for that to be a problem. Plus, a heavy rain will keep people inside. Fewer idiots checking out our ride."

"I'm worried about the area around Haverhill," said Charlie, "it's right on the Merrimack about ten or so miles to the ocean."

"We just need to get over the border, and we'll have smooth sailing through most of New Hampshire," said Alex, turning to meet Charlie's doubtful eyes. "Seriously. We get to 125 and we're home free until we ditch the Jeep," he said, purposely avoiding eye contact.

Alex stared past Ed at the bank of dark clouds swallowing up the remaining patches of blue sky. He doubted they would reach the crossing before the rain, which suited him fine. The rain would mask their approach. One way or the other, this Jeep would negotiate the border at Milton Mills. The choice between a hard or soft negotiation rested with the people guarding the bridges.

Chapter 25

Sanford, Maine

Harrison Campbell approached the red-sided barn along a worn dirt path, nodding to his second in command, who stood in the barn's open bay door. He glanced momentarily at the assembly of vehicles parked on the worn grass in front of the barn, noting the mix. A few economy sedans and an old Subaru Forrester. They'd need full-size SUVs and pickup trucks to handle regular supply delivery and general hauling. He supposed they should be thankful. None of them had put much faith in the latest rendition of the government's Critical National Infrastructure report. He'd gladly take a few beat-up sedans over nothing.

When he reached the barn door, his deputy commander rendered a salute, which Campbell returned. Glen Cuskelly was dressed in woodland camouflage fatigues, with the York County Readiness Brigade patch displayed prominently on his right shoulder. A second patch was Velcroed to his left breast pocket, identifying him as the brigade's deputy commander. Tan combat boots and a black baseball cap imprinted with the brigade's logo completed the uniform, which Harrison insisted all of the county-level chapter leaders wore in the field or in public.

He had led the York County Readiness Brigade, formerly known as the York County Militia, through a public perception transformation over the past several years. Long gone were the days of mismatched uniforms, public displays of military-style weaponry and weekend tactical assault training. The word militia had become synonymous with gun-toting, doomsday-fearing, antigovernment revolutionaries, which couldn't be further from the true purpose of his group.

Harrison had worked tirelessly, often fruitlessly, with the media to change this perception, which had suffered a major setback during the 2013 pandemic. At the height of the Boston exodus, the Kittery chapter decided to blockade the two major bridges over the Pisqataqua River, in an attempt to stem the tide of violence and looting that had engulfed York County. State police, backed by heavily armed elements of the Maine National Guard, had to forcibly remove the group after militia members fired into a sedan trying to plow through the roadblock, tragically killing a young family.

The unfortunate incident went mostly unnoticed until it was revived in early 2015 by a national magazine, in a two-part exposé on the rising number of armed antigovernment groups "training for revolution." Despite the fact that membership was still on the rise, for the first time in over a decade, the York County Militia was politely declined a place in several important Memorial and Independence Day parades.

The message was less than subtle. The York County Militia was no longer welcome by town hall. Harrison Campbell decided to steer the public's focus away from the guns and back to the organization's core values: self-reliance, preparedness and community service. Efforts to regain community trust moved slowly, but 2019 marked the first year that the former York County Militia had marched in parades through Biddeford, York, Kennebunk and Sanford.

"Brigade leadership is formed, sir," said Cuskelly.

"Thank you, Glen. What are we looking at?"

"Brian showed up a few minutes ago, which puts us at three out of the seven commanders," Cuskelly replied.

"Still no word from the York or Kittery chapters?"

"Nothing yet. Reports from the area aren't encouraging. It looks like a total wipeout east of the turnpike."

"And Limerick?" asked Campbell.

"Randy's radio must be down. We haven't heard from him since about eight last night. He knows about the meeting," said Cuskelly, shrugging his shoulders.

"It's not like Randy to blow off his duties. He'll show up. Let's get this moving along, so everyone can get back out to their people," said Campbell, stepping inside the York County Readiness Brigade's headquarters.

The barn's recently renovated interior contained a single, wide-open, post-and-beam interior from front to back, featuring vaulted arches and struts running the entire length of the ceiling. An unfinished oak-board floor held up several rows of rough-cut timber benches, giving the space the distinct feel of a rural Grange hall. A thick, hand-hewn, pine table sat lengthwise in front of the benches at the far side of the barn, surrounded by the brigade leadership team, all of whom leaned over a map, talking excitedly. Several additional maps adorned the far right corner walls, within easy reach of the ham radio station.

The brigade banner towered over them, draped across the floor-to-ceiling flagstone fireplace anchoring the far wall. The royal blue flag displayed their motto, "Semper Tuens" (always protecting), in gold letters above a simple picture of a colonial minuteman. "YCRB" was printed under the minuteman, representing the only change to the banner in thirty-three years. The American flag and Maine state flags flanked the fireplace, attached to thick wooden poles in black iron stands. The poles were canted away from the fireplace at forty-five degree angles to allow the unfurled display of each flag. From the back of the barn, it was an awe-inspiring sight that filled him with pride.

The Campbell family barn and the two hundred surrounding acres had served as the York County Militia's headquarters and meeting place since its inception, hosting everything from small leadership meetings to the town-hall-style public relations events that had become more common recently. The personally funded renovation effort had transformed the damp, dingy barn into a warm, inviting space for these events. They could hardly transform public perception in the propane-lantern-lit, creaky old barn that had served them for years.

The men around the table stood at loose attention when he walked down the aisle between benches.

"At ease, everyone. Why don't we all take seats for now? We'll get to the maps a little later," he said, pulling a chair out for himself in the middle.

"Thank you for making the trip under less than optimal circumstances. I know you have your own families and people to look after, so I won't keep you long. Obviously, we're missing some folks," he said, and the group murmured. "I want you to stay focused on your own areas of responsibility for now. Once we've sorted out how to make the best impact within each of your chapters, we'll explore ways to expand east and help. Let's conduct a quick SITREP from each chapter and see where we stand for now. Gerry?" he said, nodding to the Biddeford/Saco chapter commander.

"Coastal areas were hit hard, which is no surprise," said Gerry Beaudoin. "Old Orchard Beach is a total loss. Biddeford and Saco downtown areas were relatively untouched, aside from a massive surge of water down the Saco River. Messed up the riverfront areas something fierce. We have trees down and windows shattered all over, but the heavily populated areas were spared the tsunami effects. Downtown Biddeford is nearly four miles from the coastline."

"That's good news, Gerry. I know you live out past the 95, so I assume your outreach supplies are still intact?" said Campbell.

"Yep. I have the stuff split between my deputy commander and a few other trusted members. Tents, tarps, fuel, dried stores—all maintained according to brigade readiness standards."

"Vehicles?"

"I have three working vehicles, including the one next to the barn. Another car and a pickup. We'll get out into the community to try to enlist volunteers with vehicles, but it's still too early. Everyone's way too preoccupied with their own situation at the moment."

"It's not helping that the cops were stealing cars from citizens. Trust is running a little thin out there," said Dave Littner.

"There's nothing we can do about that. A contact of mine in the state police said that some of the major municipalities requisitioned cars to replace their own disabled vehicles. It doesn't sound good, and I'd be rightly pissed if they took one of ours, but we're dealing with a statewide emergency. We have to cut them some slack, but keep an eye on the situation," said Campbell.

"I can tell you right now what'll happen if they try to take one of our cars," said Littner.

"Dave, the last thing we need is a police confrontation of any kind," said Campbell.

"I know. I know. But something isn't right with all of this. The police chief in South Berwick is a good friend of mine, and he told me that the state police hand delivered a Homeland Security bulletin mandating that they disarm citizens carrying firearms. I saw the fucking thing. Homeland has declared a national state of emergency, citing the 2015 Defense Authorization Bill's modification of the Insurrection Act. People are worried, Harry. They're worried that this whole EMP thing is a false flag operation."

Everyone broke out into an argument at once.

"Easy now! We need to stay focused!" said Campbell.

"All I'm saying is that some of what we're hearing over the emergency broadcasts makes sense, but what we're seeing from the government doesn't," said Littner. "There's no reason to start disarming the populace if an asteroid hit, unless…"

"Unless what?" Campbell prompted.

"I don't know. All I know is that I don't like it. There's not a lot of information flowing, and that makes people nervous. Look at the borders. They're jammed with folks headed out of the cities. I'm already getting requests from the local police to help out with border crossings."

"Which you've politely declined," said Campbell.

"Absolutely, though we might have to reconsider this position."

"The brigade isn't a police force. We've promised the people of York County that we'd never serve in that capacity. If the towns need help with municipal duties, we'll commit one hundred percent of our resources, but I won't have members of the brigade manning checkpoints with weapons. Are we all good to go with that?" Campbell looked around at the members.

Everyone voiced agreement, except for Littner.

"What is it, Dave?" said Campbell.

"I'm totally with you, but I think we have a problem."

"Have some of your people already done this?"

"No. The chapter is solid," Littner said with a hurt look. "You know that."

"I'm sorry, Dave. I know you've taken pains to weed out the chaff over there."

"That's just the problem. I know for a fact that Eli Russell has approached the Berwick and Eliot police to offer his group's assistance," said Littner.

"I presume they turned him down?"

"They turned him down for now, but the police are stretched thin. They've started to deputize people they can trust to augment the reserve officers. Just manning the border crossings twenty-four hours a day is taking up most of their manpower, and that's only dealing with vehicle traffic. Once the greater Boston area starts to deteriorate and people start migrating on foot, they'll be hard-pressed to turn down Eli's offer."

"That could spell trouble for all of us," said Cuskelly.

"I'm simply suggesting that it might be in our best interest to beat Eli to the punch here," Littner said. "Get our own people involved in these checkpoints, maybe as unarmed observers or inspectors. That way we'll be in a stronger position to argue against the use of his militia."

Harrison Campbell contemplated the suggestion, frowning at the thought of getting involved in formal police operations. He wouldn't hesitate to employ the brigade to protect civilians from specific threats, but patrolling the streets as a sanctioned arm of government didn't square with the public perception they had worked tirelessly to build over the past several years. Littner's idea of using the brigade as an observer force had potential. As unarmed, neutral observers, they could assist with nonenforcement tasks and sell their presence to the public as a quasi-watchdog role.

"Assuming an observer-only role, how many members do you think it will take to get the job done?" he asked after a moment of contemplation.

Littner grabbed one of the pencils sitting on the map and leaned over the table to examine the border area.

"I would guess three per crossing. They can rotate shifts, with one working the checkpoint, and the other two resting up. We'll pick people that live close by and send them with a tent and some supplies. This could also give us a little community outreach presence. If people come by the tent, we'll explain that the brigade is involved as a neutral observer, to ensure the protection of people's civil liberties. Kind of like UN observers."

"Let's steer clear of the United Nations comparison. That'll clear people out faster than one of Glen's chili bombs," said Campbell, eliciting a table full of laughter and fist pounding.

"I don't think anything could empty a room quicker," said Beaudoin.

"Sorry about that, Glen. I couldn't think of a better way to drive home the point. No UN comparisons, please. With two to three per checkpoint, what are we looking at?" Campbell asked, hovering over the map.

Littner traced the border, stopping at each road over the Salmon Falls River.

"Between the Eliot, South Berwick and Berwick PDs, I know they're covering six crossings from the Turnpike to Route 11. The state police have Route 11 coming out of Rochester and Route 109. I don't know what's happening up in Milton or Milton Mills."

"All right, here's what I want you to do, Dave. Before we commit to this endeavor, I want you to drive the border roads and check out each crossing. Stop and talk to each checkpoint to gauge their interest in having a few of our people help with nonenforcement tasks. Once I get in touch with Randy, I'll send him west to the crossings north of 109 to get a handle on things. Just touch base with the checkpoints and feel them out. Has anyone run into Eli's brother down south?"

"Jimmy's been quiet from what I can tell. Then again, it's barely been twenty-four hours," said Littner.

"It won't take his criminal mind long to figure out some way to take advantage of the situation. Keep a close eye out for him. Eli's bad enough, but Jimmy's nothing but bad news. I'll put the feelers out around Sanford and have Randy do the same up his way. I guarantee he's up to no good, especially if he's running the felony arm of Eli's Maine Liberty Militia," said Campbell.

"I thought they were all felons," said Beaudoin, eliciting some nervous laughter.

"Eli ain't a bad guy overall," Campbell admitted. "We just never saw eye to eye on the main purpose of a civilian militia. Jimmy's a different type altogether. He made a lot of friends up in Warren, during his extended stay as a guest of the state. Too many of these friends landed in Eli's militia."

"I guess I should emphasize that fact when I visit the checkpoints. Keep the police informed," said Littner.

"Might not be a bad idea. Dave, you've got your marching orders and a long day ahead of you, so why don't you get going. We'll finish up the status reports, and I'll pass anything along to you that might come in handy. Head over to the equipment barn to load up on extra tents and blankets, then drive out to Milton Mills. Start there and work your way south through all of the checkpoints. Glen, I need you to assign one of the Sanford chapter members to accompany Dave. Probably not a good idea to have you on those roads alone, especially with Jimmy's people on the loose."

"Got it," said Cuskelly, grabbing the handheld radio on his belt.

"Sounds like a plan, Harry. We'll do a loop and head back here to come up with a more detailed plan for these crossing checkpoints," said Littner.

"Make sure you grab a slicker from the barn. Rain's gonna open up on us any minute now."

Littner saluted Campbell, who returned it. After shaking hands with the rest of the brigade's leadership, he departed with Campbell's deputy commander. Campbell had every confidence that David Littner was the right person for the job. Littner had been with the brigade from the very beginning, and had been one of the most vocal advocates of transforming the brigade from a gun-toting band of weekend warriors back to an organization more in line with the original concepts of civil defense.

Guns and the defense of the citizenry's 2nd Amendment rights would always be a core mission of their brigade, but it wouldn't be the focus. The York County Readiness Brigade, like many militia groups throughout the country, strived to function as a nonmilitarized, grassroots version of the National Guard, focused on preparedness and local disaster relief. Littner had helped him convince the most cynical skeptics that they needed to follow a new path or run the risk of fading away into obscurity. If Littner felt it might be in the best interest of the brigade to help out at the checkpoints, then they would explore the possibility of a shift in official policy. He turned his attention back to the two men at the table.

"So how are we looking in the Kennebunk area, Anthony?"

Chapter 26

Acton, Maine

Thick raindrops smacked the windshield, buoying his hopes that the black and purple clouds would unleash a torrent of rain. A thrashing downpour would discourage a detailed examination of their vehicle. They might sail right through. Or not. Either way, they were crossing in Milton Mills. That much had been agreed upon.

A white, single-steeple church sat burrowed in a plot of trees along the road. The back ends of several vehicles appeared in front of the visible portion of the building, tucked behind the church. Two people walked to a white gazebo, one of them carrying a rifle.

"Did you see that?" asked Alex.

"What?" said Charlie.

"A guy back there had a rifle—at the church."

Ed said, "Maybe it's one of those end-of-the-world churches."

"A lot of cars in—"Alex started.

"Heads up," Ed cut in. "White minivan just took the turn ahead."

Alex squinted to get a better view. "Got it." He noticed the Massachusetts plates. "Slow down a bit," he said, as the minivan drew even.

Two men in the front seats, one wearing a military-style boonie cap, woman and children in the back. None of them turned their heads when the two cars passed.

Charlie followed them with his eyes. "Fucking weird."

"Weird is putting it mildly," said Ed.

"What are they doing?" Alex asked.

"Shit!" Charlie blasted. "They just turned at the church."

"What? How does that make sense?" said Alex.

"Maybe it's one of those militia supply points."

"With out-of-town guests? Something is off around here."

"You just noticed?" Ed snorted. "It's like driving through the fucking *Twilight Zone.*"

"At least they're letting cars into Maine," said Alex. "As weird as it is, I think we made the right call."

"I don't know," Charlie said doubtfully. "Something wasn't right with that car."

Alex stayed silent as the Jeep crossed Edgecomb County Road and pressed forward through the intensifying rainsquall. They were less than a mile from the border crossing.

"Is this it?" asked Ed, slowing the car.

"Not according to the GPS," said Alex.

The road opened into an industrial area, flanked by several warehouses and dozens of neatly arranged semi-trailers on either side of the road. One of the warehouses near the road had open sides, exposing stacks of recently milled wood. Trees swallowed the road again, and the rain intensified.

"Maybe we should wait for this to ease off a bit," Ed suggested, slowing the Jeep even further.

"This might be our only shot. They won't get out of their cars in this shit."

"How far?" asked Ed.

"Not far," said Alex. "Start to slow once we hit the bend. You ready back there, Charlie?"

"Ready as ever."

"All right. Let's go through it one more time. Ed stops the car roughly fifty feet from the roadblock, and I get out. I'll talk to whoever is blocking the bridge and figure out what we're up against. Ed watches me with the binoculars. If I give the thumbs-up, he drives forward, and all is good. If I rub the top of my head, it's a no-go. I'll return to the car, and we'll figure out how to bust through. If I reach for the gun behind my back, get ready for a hot extract. Charlie?"

"Suppressing fire. Over their heads," said Charlie.

"Way over their heads, and only if they fire first. There's no reason for them to fire at me. Over their heads and keep the volume of fire high. Ed, you turn the car around and wait for me to come to you. Good?"

"Got it," responded Ed.

"Your job is the most important, Ed. Charlie won't be watching the roadblock. There's a three-way intersection right before the bridge. I need him to observe the road parallel to the river. It leads north to the other crossing, where there will be more police. Shit. Here's the bend—slow us down a little more."

The bend straightened, and the foliage cleared on the right to reveal a stretch of white picket fence along the road. A yellow bungalow-style house with a wide farmer's porch sat back from the fence. A tall white church spire appeared above the trees beyond the house. Alex didn't have time to assemble the bigger picture. The intersection was less than a hundred feet ahead.

He raised the binoculars, immediately spotting the roadblock. They would have to rethink the plan. This wasn't a police roadblock. The tight, two-lane asphalt road spanning the Salmon Falls River was blocked at both ends by single SUVs. He could see little more than a three- to five-foot gap between the front bumper of the nearest SUV and the metal guard railings. The gap on the far side appeared even smaller. He didn't see any personnel in the open on either side. Alex handed the binoculars back to Charlie.

"Stop us here," said Alex.

As soon as the Jeep stopped, the dark green Toyota Land Cruiser's doors opened. Two men dressed in MultiCam fatigues and boonie hats stepped onto the rain-swept pavement. They wore a variety of mismatched tactical gear, which immediately pegged them as militia. The men carried AR-style rifles attached to one-point slings. Alex was beginning to piece things together. Part of him screamed "get out of here." The other part put his hand on the door handle.

"Make sure your rifle is ready for immediate action. I can almost guarantee this will be a no-go. If this goes bad, shoot for center mass. I'll get out of your way. Three quick rounds at one target, then shift to the next. Keep shifting back and forth between targets until they are down," said Alex, opening his door.

"Militia?" asked Charlie.

"Or locals. Nothing official, I can guarantee that."

He glanced back at Ed, who looked calm. "You good?"

"Never been better," said Ed. "Be careful with these guys."

"Careful would be backing up and trying to talk our way past the state police," said Alex, eliciting a nervous laugh from Ed.

He stepped onto the wet pavement and tucked the HK P30 into his waistband, pulling his shirt over the protruding handle. He had chosen not to wear his drop holster or any tactical gear for the drive, since he had anticipated having to possibly approach law enforcement officers at some point during their journey south. Even the presence of an empty tactical holster could end their trip prematurely.

This decision was quickly validated. Both men shifted into alert carry stances when Alex started walking toward them, pointing their weapons in his direction. They were anxious. The question was whether they were anxious out of uncertainty, or anxious to score a kill. In the deafening rain on this abandoned stretch of road, virtually in the middle of nowhere, he began to seriously question his own decision to step out of the car. He kept moving toward them through the warm rain, with his hands raised over his head.

One of them spoke into a handheld radio and waited for a reply, pressing the radio to his ear. A few seconds passed before he lowered the radio and hooked it onto his vest. Radioman assumed the ready carry position, with the butt stock jammed into his shoulder and the muzzle aimed at Alex. He thought of the pistol behind his back long enough to accept the fact that he'd be dead before he hit the ground if he tried to reach for it.

"That's far enough!" yelled Radioman. "State your business."

"I need to cross over into New Hampshire. My son is trapped in Boston. He's a college student, and he has no way to get back home!" Alex yelled over the downpour.

"Nothing gets across in either direction! Those are my orders."

"Look, all I want is to get my son. I'll find a different way back," said Alex.

"Orders," said Radioman, shrugging his shoulders.

"State police are allowing Maine residents to cross the border in both directions," said Alex.

"Then I suggest you take your car to one of their checkpoints. Nobody's crossing here."

"I just saw a car headed south on the road behind me. Looked like one of your guys in it. Massachusetts plates," said Alex.

"They volunteered to give up their car. That's the only way anyone gets across. We're not having a repeat of 2013, with people driving around looting and pillaging our homes," said Radioman.

"You're making them walk?"

"We take them to Sanford or Springvale. Their choice. They have plenty of options there."

"So there's no way we get across here?"

"We'll make an exception if you're willing to give up your vehicle and everything inside. That's the only way anyone gets across."

With that statement, it all snapped into place for Alex. The men with rifles at the church. The car with Massachusetts plates turning into the church. Nobody was getting a lift to Sanford or Springvale.

He forced a smile. "I guess we'll have to find another way across," said Alex, lowering his right hand enough to scratch his head.

"You don't sound so eager to cross at one of the state police checkpoints. How come?"

"I don't trust cops. Are you guys part of the York County Readiness Brigade?"

"Maine Liberty Militia. The real militia. Not that horseshit bean-supper brigade," said Radioman, causing his sidekick to snicker.

"Never heard of it," said Alex.

"Now you have," said Radioman.

"You guys have a good day," said Alex, half-expecting to take a bullet in the back.

Alex hopped into the Jeep and closed the door, surprised to find the barrel of Charlie's rifle protruding a few inches past the headrest. Careful not to disturb his aim, Alex examined his firing position. Charlie had raised the front passenger seat headrest to its highest point and had braced his rifle in the gap between the seat and headrest. He had propped the three assault backpacks next to him to support the right side of his body, providing a stable platform to aim his rifle through the gap and beyond the windshield. He was relieved to see that Charlie had taken the initiative to cover him, and that he'd chosen a method not easily detectable. He was little disturbed that nobody was watching the road leading to the other bridge.

"I know what you're thinking, but I didn't like the way they looked. Ed was watching you and the road, and I had my eye on those two. I think they're running some kind of racket here. That was one of their guys in the car back there," said Charlie, engaging the rifle's safety before setting it across his lap.

"Maine Liberty Militia. Ever heard of them?"

Charlie shook his head. "Probably one of those offshoot groups. A dozen sprung up after 2013."

"Whoever they are, I think they're running more than just a racket. Let's go back down Foxes Ridge Road."

Ed put the Jeep into reverse and executed a two-point turn. When they passed the industrial site, Ed broke the silence.

"Now where are we supposed to cross? If we keep following the border hoping for the best, we'll end up driving to the goddamned Canadian border!"

"We're crossing in Milton Mills," said Alex.

"How? This isn't SEAL Team Six, Alex. You saw the guys down there. We don't even know how many we're dealing with."

"Probably twelve," said Charlie. "I saw three guys on the other side through my scope, talking to a bunch of bikers. Weapons aimed right at them. Looked like a heated debate going on. We have to assume the same setup on the other bridge. Two cars of three."

"Twelve at the border and more at the church," said Alex.

"That's too many," said Ed.

"We only have to get past six of them," said Alex.

"With the rest of the Maine whatever-the-fuck Liberty gang coming to the rescue? What about the church? How many reinforcements do they have waiting over there?"

Alex glanced at Charlie. "We're headed there next."

"Recon?" asked Charlie.

"If my suspicions are correct? Direct action. No survivors."

"Wait. Hold on. You're going into the church? You're out of your mind. These guys are fucking crazy!"

"Which is why it'll work. I saw two of them up close. They'll never expect this. When the bullets start connecting, they'll break."

"You can't guarantee that. If something goes wrong, our kids are screwed. I'd rather walk to Boston to—"

"Ed! Walking to Boston is not an option! We need to be in Boston *tonight*. I can get us over this bridge."

Ed shook his head and muttered obscenities for a few seconds before turning to Alex. "If this is too much for you and Charlie to handle, we find another way. I'm trusting you to make that call. Why is the church so important, again?" he asked.

"The guy at the roadblock said the only way to get across was to voluntarily give up your vehicle. They take your car and supposedly drop you in Sanford," said Alex.

"The last car turned into the church," said Ed.

"Exactly," Alex stated. "I want to know what they're doing with the families. They're sure as shit not driving them to Sanford. I saw kids in that SUV."

"They definitely didn't take the family to Sanford," said Ed.

"I'm shutting this operation down effective immediately," said Alex.

Ed sighed. "This is going to get us all killed."

Chapter 27

EVENT +30:59 Hours

Acton, Maine

Alex approached the next tree trunk, careful not to snap any of the larger dogwood branches. Charlie trailed one tree behind, following his path through the dense forest growth. They had established an effective pattern in which one of them rushed forward while the other watched for threats.

Charlie crashed down next to him, pointing his rifle across the parking lot. Alex covered the northern door and the pavement area visible beyond the corner of the building. The two men he'd seen when they passed the church on the way to Milton Mills had been headed in the direction of the gazebo. Alex had taken precautions during their approach, stopping and observing for long periods of time. He detected no signs of an organized, defensive surveillance effort.

"I think we're clear to approach the back door. Careful with that corner. I'm pretty sure the gazebo is on the other side," he whispered.

Charlie nodded, watching his sector. Alex had been impressed with his neighbor's ability to move quietly through the forest and follow simple hand signals. Charlie's years of experience stalking animals had paid dividends, and he walked quieter than Alex, when he didn't stumble. He hadn't completely mastered the "ready carry" technique, which required him to aim over his rifle's sights and maneuver without looking at the ground. The last hundred yards had shown a marked improvement since they left the Jeep, with Charlie effectively shifting lines of sight without tripping.

Alex drew his pistol and retrieved a dark cylindrical object, screwing it onto the pistol barrel.

"Jesus Harold Christmas! Is that legal?" Charlie exclaimed.

"What do you think? Swap rifles with me."

"Why?" whispered Charlie.

"Because there's gonna be some shooting, and we need it to be as quiet as possible," said Alex.

"This is crazy," muttered Charlie. He unclipped the rifle from his one-point sling and handed it to Alex, casting a doubtful look.

"We'll be fine, Charlie, as long as you stay close to me and remember what I tell you. We clear one room at a time. I enter the room first, staying low and sweeping from left to right. You'll lean in aiming high, sweeping from right to left. When the room is clear, you enter the room and transition to cover the hallway or whatever open space we just used. We'll clear the building room by room until we find what we're looking for. Clear?"

"Clear. What are we looking for?"

"The families they brought here. Ready?"

"Not really," said Charlie.

"Good. Let's go."

Alex rose to his feet and clipped Charlie's rifle into his own sling harness, shifting the rifle and sling behind his back. Charlie raised Alex's rifle to his shoulder and stared through the ACOG scope, shifting his aim a few times. He nodded at Alex, and they started forward. The back door burst open. Alex pushed Charlie down and furiously low-crawled to the next tree trunk several feet ahead of them, squirming through rain-soaked underbrush. He wasn't worried about noise. Cover and concealment was his primary goal for the moment.

He reached the tree without the hissing of bullets through foliage, confident that they hadn't been spotted. He laid the pistol on the damp ground and twisted onto his left side to wrestle Charlie's rifle forward. Charlie rustled through the bushes a few seconds later, settling somewhere behind him.

Alex stared over the holographic sight on Charlie's AR, dismayed by the scene. Six people walked across the asphalt parking lot toward the tree line at the rear of the parking lot. Two men wearing MultiCam uniforms and boonie hats nudged the family forward with their rifles.

Not on my watch.

He leaned back. "Change of plans. We drop both of the militia guys and rush the corner of the building. You'll suppress the gazebo, and I'll clear the building. Once the building is clear, I'll help you with the gazebo."

"If there's anyone left," said Charlie.

"No adjustment necessary on the ACOG. Start taking them down. I'll meet you at the corner of the building," said Alex, rising to a low crouch.

"I got this," said Charlie, settling in behind the scope.

"Take your shots quickly. If they reach the trees, the family is dead," he said, grabbing his pistol off the ground and sprinting to the next tree.

Alex stopped behind the next tree and holstered the pistol. The suppressed rifle barked twice in rapid succession. Alex dropped to one knee and leaned around the backside of the tree. One gunman lay on the pavement. The other teetered on his feet for a moment. A third shot passed through the man's neck, showering the pavement with blood and dropping him instantly. The family ran for the tree line, screaming.

Alex sprinted for the corner of the building. The heavy rain may have drowned out the suppressed rifle shots, but a quick look at the angles ahead told Alex that the men in the gazebo had a direct line of sight to their downed comrades. Even if they hadn't noticed the men fall to the ground, there was no way they could miss an entire family scrambling across the parking lot. He just hoped that the security team didn't decide to gun down the family from the gazebo.

He was still a few seconds away from the corner when he caught a glimpse of movement and raised Charlie's rifle, snapping two shots at the figure that appeared in the EOTech sight's illuminated reticle. He moved the rifle to the right, finding his second target, but a storm of splinters and supersonic cracks forced him flat against the side of the building. He shifted the rifle to a left-handed shooting position and backed up a few more feet, dropping to the blacktop. Leaning the rifle out at a forty-five-degree angle, he reacquired the target. Both targets.

The first shooter was down on both knees, clutching his neck, blood pumping through his fingers. The second man kneeled next to him, yanking medical supplies out of his vest. Alex fired a single .223-caliber projectile through his head, knocking him over. The next bullet struck the wounded man in the forehead. With the only two visible targets down, he turned to Charlie.

"Don't let anyone through that door! I'm going through the front," he said, waiting for Charlie's acknowledgement.

Satisfied with a thumbs-up and Charlie's choice of position on the right side of the concrete stoop, he quick-peeked around the corner, verifying that the parking lot was still devoid of militia. He assumed the ready carry position and shuffled down the side of the building, crouching at each of the evenly spaced windows imbedded into the white vinyl siding. He passed nine cars, all with out-of-state license plates, before he reached the door and drew his pistol.

The sound of a revving vehicle engine stopped him from opening the door, and he slid between the two closest cars. Staying below window level, he moved to the rear of a Honda Pilot and transitioned back to Charlie's rifle. Shots from the suppressed rifle in Charlie's hands echoed through the parking lot.

We're now on the verge of a complete disaster.

He stayed concealed, watching the visible portion of the driveway through the cargo compartment window. He kept his peripheral vision attuned to the building's front door. With Charlie blasting away into the building, the militia members inside might attempt to flank him. Their most logical path to Charlie came through the door he had almost opened.

When the vehicle appeared, Alex waved frantically, trying to get Ed to stop the Jeep before it became visible to the shooters in the building. Ed turned the Jeep off the driveway, screeching to a halt just past the corner. Alex heard the front door open and stayed low, switching back to the suppressed pistol.

He moved swiftly between the Pilot and the silver four-door sedan, staying low with both hands extended forward in an isosceles triangle. The first figure appeared above the hood of the Pilot, and Alex pulled the trigger twice, adjusting his aim for the head. The hollow-point bullets penetrated his skull, plastering the white siding beyond him with a mosaic of dark and bright red clumps. Alex pressed forward, firing repeatedly over the hood at the second man barreling through the opening. The 9mm bullets struck hard, knocking him against the gore-stained cedar siding with a grunt.

A third figure emerged from the doorway and locked eyes with Alex. Before Alex could line him up in the P30's sights, the militiaman lurched forward, firing his AR-15 wildly over the hood. Bullets snapped overhead as Alex crouched low behind the engine block, windows exploding in a pattern toward the rear of the vehicle. Alex slid in front of the Pilot and fired three shots through the windshield toward the back of the SUV. His pistol volley was met by several .223 projectiles, which showered Alex and the hood with hundreds of milky blue safety glass particles and splintered the cedar siding behind him.

He was effectively wedged between two threat vectors, unable to simultaneously watch and engage targets coming from both directions. He quickly peeked above the hood, spotting the familiar boonie hat through the punctured windshield. Bullets snapped past Alex's head, forcing him down. He detected movement behind him and turned halfway to the left, switching pistol hands. The second man he had shot with the pistol groaned, desperately trying to reach the rifle lying next to him. Alex extended his left hand and fired a single bullet through his face, slamming the man's head into the side of the building.

The shooting stopped for a moment, and all Alex could hear above ringing in his ears was the low din of heavy rainfall beating against sheet metal. He needed to reload the pistol. He dropped to the asphalt and reached along the left side of his vest, searching for a spare pistol magazine, while scanning the space under the vehicle. He could see the man's boots shifting on the pavement beyond the protruding axles.

The sound of fast-moving footsteps drew his attention to the front door. Alex propelled himself forward, slamming into the bloody wall just as a man dressed in MultiCam utilities stepped onto the porch, firing wildly into the cars. Sliding down the wall into a shallow puddle, Alex slammed the fifteen-round magazine tightly into place, depressing the slide-stop to chamber a round. Three 9mm hollow-point projectiles struck the man in a tight pattern under his exposed armpit, knocking him out of the doorway.

By hastily moving against the wall, he had put too much distance between himself and the front bumper, giving the shooter behind the SUV a clear line of fire. If he had more time to consider his next move, he would have been better off dropping out of sight—hoping that he could beat the rounds that would soon be headed in his direction at three thousand feet per second. Instead, he did what most people trained to defend themselves with firearms would do. He shifted and fired—at nothing.

"He's down!" yelled Ed, the barrel of his Ruger 10/22 protruding beyond the edge of the church corner.

Saved again by Ed.

Alex gave him a thumbs-up and raised himself out of the crimson puddle, focused on killing the rest of the militia. Four men had rushed out, bringing the total confirmed enemy casualty count to eight. He had no idea if Charlie had added to that number, or if he'd simply kept them from reaching the back door. A volley of three suppressed rifle shots and a scream from inside the building answered his question.

Not wanting to give away his position by yelling, Alex tried to communicate with Ed using basic hand signals. He pointed at Ed with his index finger, then pointed at his own eyes, following this with a quick hatchet hand in the direction of the road. He wanted Ed to cover the road in case the gunfire attracted attention. Ed nodded and disappeared, leaving Alex to wonder if the message had been received. He transitioned back to Charlie's rifle and slowly sidestepped into the open doorway, staring over his sights for any threats.

The door opened into a large vestibule with several rows of coat hooks, all of them empty except for a light blue child's windbreaker. Beyond the vestibule, a tight hallway crossed the building's central passageway and dead-ended at a window on the far wall. A fusillade of rifle fire erupted from the central hallway, causing him to tighten his grip and focus on the right side opening. Clearing the rest of the building would be tricky.

Alex sprinted down the hallway, keeping his rifle pointed toward the right, in the most likely threat direction. He hit the intersection, spotting at least two hostiles crouched in open doorways down the center hallway. Three crumpled bodies lay beyond them. He glanced in the opposite direction and scanned the doors and floor leading toward the church. The doors on the left side were closed, and the shiny linoleum floor was clear of spent brass. He felt confident that the hallway behind him was clear of threats. Now he just needed to figure out a way to keep Charlie from popping him with his own rifle.

He stepped back from the corner and edged toward the hallway until the first occupied doorway appeared in his rifle's holographic sight. The figure in the doorway leaned out and fired two rapid shots in Charlie's direction. Alex fired, spilling the man into the hallway. Alex pulled himself swiftly back from the corner as a single round skipped off the linoleum floor in front of him and buried itself in the drywall behind him. The sound of three suppressed shots echoed through the hallways.

Alex eased himself toward the corner again, angling the rifle to expose as little of his body as possible to the remaining shooter. He waited a few seconds and dashed across to the other side of the hallway, continuing well past the corner. Several rifle bullets followed him, exploding the drywall on both sides of the vestibule hallway, as the shooter tried to follow the arc of his movement beyond the walls. He heard the sound of his suppressed rifle amidst the chaos.

"I got him!" yelled Charlie.

"I'm coming out slowly. Same plan as before, except you stay in place, centered on the stairs. Got it!" said Alex.

"You're clear to move!" said Charlie.

Alex took a deep breath and moved to the corner, peeking into the hallway. Charlie had moved to the middle of the doorway, aiming Alex's rifle down the long hallway. Alex had four rooms to clear. Two sets of two doors, located next to each other on both sides of the hallway. He stepped into the hall and noted a long, mottled red streak on the gray wall next to the first doorway on the left. A mangled head protruded several inches beyond the bottom of the doorframe, anchored by a thick pool of spreading blood. Alex slithered along the right wall, keeping his rifle focused on the left side doorways. He stopped and listened for movement within the rooms, hearing nothing.

He spun to the right and entered the first room on the right side, immediately determining that it was devoid of threats. The classroom had been stuffed with gear belonging to the owners of the vehicles parked outside. He faced the doorway and quickly slipped into the room next door, finding the same thing. Another classroom stuffed with suitcases, oversized duffel bags, coolers, hiking backpacks, tents and sleeping bags.

There was far too much stuff in these rooms to fit into the assortment of vehicles he'd seen in the church parking lot. These fucks had been at this for a long time. He spotted a light pink child's backpack with the initials *LAH* sewn in white thread on the outer pouch. He didn't want to think about what they would find if they took a walk into the forest behind the parking lot.

Alex cleared the two remaining rooms, one of which was empty, waiting ominously for more refugees to take the devil's bargain being offered at the Milton Mills crossing. The other room contained several cots and a large wooden table. Two car batteries connected in parallel sat against the far wall of the room, attached by black and red wires to a power inverter on the right side of the table. Several handheld radio charging stations lined the back of the table, plugged into a surge protector powered by the inverter.

All but one of the charging stations was empty. He swiped the radio from its cradle and turned to the doorway.

"All clear!" he said, peeking into the hallway.

"All clear!" repeated Charlie.

When he saw Charlie start to rise, with his rifle pointed downward, he stepped into the blood-slicked corridor, checking the three bodies slumped against the walls for signs of life.

"They kept coming," he said, his voice trailing off. "Never saw anything like it."

"Just like Khe Sanh?" Alex asked.

"Very funny," Charlie said.

"You did good, my friend. Really good—and you're not even wearing your squirrel cap," said Alex, patting his shoulder.

Charlie stuffed his hand into the left cargo pocket of this pants. "I have it right here!"

"Not now," said Alex, yanking Charlie down from the top of the stoop.

Charlie absorbed the drop with stiff legs and teetered for a moment. Alex noticed that Charlie's breathing was labored, as if he had just run up several flights of stairs. He'd be willing to write this off as expected stress-induced excitability if Charlie's face wasn't beet red.

"You all right?"

"I'm fine. Just a little excited."

"Your face looks like it's going to explode."

"And you look as white as a ghost. You want your rifle back?"

"I don't know. I'm kind of getting attached to this one," said Alex, eyeing him warily.

"Well, too bad. This ACOG scope is useless for close-up shots, and I don't like these angled thingies you put on this. So if you don't mind," said Charlie, holding out Alex's rifle.

"I didn't see you having any problems," said Alex, exchanging rifles.

"I made it work."

Charlie changed magazines and snapped the rifle back into his one-point sling, hustling to catch up with Alex. "Hey, what about that family that took off?"

Alex stopped for a moment and stared off into the forest beyond the parking lot, grimacing. "We don't have time to chase them down—and I don't expect them to come running to us with open arms," he replied. "I wouldn't."

"Hate to leave them out there like this…" said Charlie, hesitating.

"They got their lucky break. Let's go."

Chapter 28

Milton Mills Crossing, Southern Bridge

Ed's hands trembled on the steering wheel. Alex's plan for getting across the bridge was crazier than the raid on the church. His handheld radio crackled, filling the cabin with Alex's voice.

"I'm not seeing any indication that they are alerted or expecting us. Charlie, you see anything at the northern crossing?"

"Negative," Charlie replied. "The road is clear."

"Ed, how does the road look heading toward the church?" Alex inquired.

"It's clear. I don't buy it, Alex. They're waiting for us."

"We would have heard something on the radio. All we picked up was a report of agitated bikers at the far end of the south bridge. All three of the militiamen are positioned in the open, behind the SUV, aiming their rifles at a group of people assembled about twenty feet away. The guys in the closest vehicle are tucked away nice and dry. This is as good as it gets, Ed."

"Somehow I doubt that."

"I'm moving closer to the bridge, where I can fire at both vehicles. Charlie, I'm going to need your help with the nearest SUV. When I start shooting across the river, I want you to pump at least half of a magazine into the doors. If someone spills out onto the road, they're yours. Once you see me on the bridge, reload and cover the road leading from the other checkpoint. Are we clear?"

"Crystal clear, Alex. Give me a few minutes to crawl into position. I don't have a clear line of sight to the vehicle," said Charlie.

Charlie even sounded like shit over the radio. His breathing hadn't recovered from the first round of mayhem before Alex yanked him out of the Jeep for round two. He was pushing Charlie past his physical limits, and it was going to kill him, if it didn't get them all killed first.

"Ed, I'll radio you when I have the first SUV cleared," said Alex.

"Roger. I have the Jeep running," said Ed, shaking his head.

"I'm moving into position. Out."

Out of your fucking mind is more like it.

Ed put one of his shaky hands around the grip of the .45-caliber Glock 37 lying on the front passenger seat, not feeling any comfort in the cold, utilitarian shape. He turned his head and stared through the rear windshield, catching glimpses of the road beyond the rear wiper's useless arc. The rain had intensified again, drumming the Jeep's sheet metal roof with an incessant staccato. The oppressive sound gave him hope that Alex might be right, that the men at the bridge could hear nothing more than distant, muted gunfire in the rain. His radio burst to life.

"I'm in position. What's your status, Charlie?" asked Alex.

"Give me thirty seconds. I'm almost at the edge of the brush," Charlie huffed.

Ed glanced at the wooden stock of his Ruger 10/22 rifle. Protruding through the space between the front seat backs, he could put it into action much faster than he had at the church. The rifle had been stuffed under the smaller backpacks, rendering it impossible to pull it free from the front driver's seat. He'd hopped out and opened the rear passenger seat, yanking it free in a panic when the shooting broke out. He'd barely reached the corner of the church in time to save Alex—again.

One .22LR (long rifle) Interceptor bullet to the back of the head had dropped the guy hiding behind the SUV. The forty-grain, hypervelocity, hollow-point cartridge didn't pack the same punch as Alex or Charlie's .223 rounds, as Ed was constantly reminded, but it did the job. Twice by his count.

తళుళ

Alex dragged himself through the dirt, squirming through a thick tangle of bushes less than forty feet from the first SUV. Through the driving rain and dense foliage, he caught glints of steel and glass. He could see enough of the SUV to confirm that they hadn't activated the front windshield wipers since his previous visit. Their view of the trees and bushes beyond the guardrail would be a blur of cascading raindrops.

He raised his head far enough off the ground to observe the SUV on the other side of the short bridge that spanned Salmon Falls River. He had a clear line of sight. All three men still stood behind the black SUV, pointing their rifles in the direction of a small crowd gathered in front of several motorcycles. Two of the militiamen stood near the front of the SUV, while the third man lingered near the tailgate, partially obscured from Alex's sight.

He'll be the first to go. ˙

Alex spun his body and took a seat on the mud-soaked ground, splaying his legs and bending his knees. He rested his elbows on his knees to fully steady his rifle. Satisfied with the stability of his firing platform, he took his right hand off the rifle to grab his handheld radio. He hadn't heard from Charlie, and it had been longer than thirty seconds.

"Charlie, are you in position?" A few seconds passed without a response. "Charlie, what is your status?" Nothing.

Damn it, where are you?

"Ed, can you see Charlie?"

"No. He disappeared in the trees. Do you want me to move the Jeep closer?"

"Negative," Alex replied. "Charlie, are you there?"

"I'm here, I'm here," Charlie finally responded. "Damn bushes knocked my fucking earpiece out. Sorry, guys. I'm at the edge of the road with a clear shot at the exposed side of the SUV. Ready to go."

"All right, this is it. Remember, Charlie, don't start shooting until you hear my rounds headed down range," Alex reminded him.

"Got it, Alex. Ready to do this."

"Here we go," said Alex, clipping the waterproof radio to his vest.

He settled into the rifle, nestling the stock deep into his shoulder. Through the 4X ACOG scope, he located the partially obscured militiaman near the back of the vehicle and placed the tip of the red chevron reticle in the center of his head. There would be no need to compensate for bullet drop at this range. At an estimated range of roughly fifty yards, the .223 bullet would retain a flat trajectory, even in the pouring rain.

He took his eye off the scope momentarily, feeling nauseous and warm. Maybe this was a mistake. The plan had just enough moving parts to descend into complete chaos. What if they couldn't break through this side of the bridge quickly enough? They needed to be driving across the river, unopposed, when reinforcements arrived. Everything depended on his ability to accurately shoot three men within the span of seconds. If any of them survived to seek cover and return fire, they'd have to abandon the bridge attack and retreat. Alex didn't have a plan for that.

He put his eye to the scope and breathed slowly for several moments, easing the trigger back. *Crack.* The rifle bit into his shoulder, but he kept the scope's field of view on the target. The man crouched and aimed toward the two-story buildings in Milton Mills, edging into full view. Alex spotted a small, paint-chipped hole at the edge of the SUV. His shot had been off by an inch.

Not a good start.

He sighted in on the confused militiaman and fired three rapid shots. The man clutched his neck and dropped to both knees, teetering forward to fall face first into a puddle.

Unable to determine the source of the gunfire, the two remaining men darted for the edge of the bridge. Alex placed the red chevron on the lead runner and fired another tightly spaced three-round volley. He didn't wait for the results, shifting immediately to the second target. Alex's bullets arrived before the man reached the perceived safety of the metal guardrail, knocking him to the pavement as Charlie's fusillade erupted.

Alex changed magazines and slid down the riverbank to put some earth between Charlie's gun and his approach. He scrambled across the slippery mud and climbed the jagged rocks set against the bridge. He slowly raised his body, aiming the rifle in the direction of the SUV. With both eyes open, he stared through the ACOG scope, processing the entire scene. Movement beside the SUV brought the rifle left, his eyes quickly finding a target. Two trigger pulls punched the militiaman over the far guardrail and out of sight. Alex crouched lower and scanned for additional movement. The gunfire had stopped.

"Alex, this is Charlie. All targets are down. One in the car; one on the road in front of the roadblock; one over the side."

"Roger," Alex replied. "I'm moving up to clear the SUV. Hold your fire."

"Got it."

Alex heaved himself over the guardrail and crouched below the hood just as Ed's voice broke onto the radio net.

"They're panicking at the other bridge," Ed said nervously. "We need to get out of here."

"I'm working on that. Bring the Jeep down, and pick up Charlie on the way," said Alex.

He edged past the bumper, angling his rifle to examine the driver's side of the SUV. A body rested against the side of the vehicle, legs sprawled forward in an awkward pose. Blood and broken glass covered the wet pavement around the inert form. Alex fired a single bullet into the man's head, unwilling to take the chance that he might have one trigger pull left in him as a surprise.

Moving in a low crouch down the side of the SUV, he glanced upward and noticed a head protruding through the shattered driver's window, blood dripping steadily from the brim of the boonie hat attached to it. Alex stood up and opened the door, yanking the body to the pavement and spilling the remains of the man's brains onto his boots. He felt the sudden urge to vomit, which he fought while tossing his rifle inside and jumping into the brain-splattered driver's seat. The keys were in the ignition, thankfully. He didn't relish spending any more time than necessary in this mobile charnel house. He started the Toyota Land Cruiser and put it in reverse, creating a gap large enough to fit Ed's Jeep, which barreled toward the bridge.

"They're coming!" was all he heard from the Jeep's open window.

Alex turned the wheel right and jammed the Toyota into the guardrail, blocking the road. He removed the keys from the ignition and climbed over the blood-slick center console, opening the passenger door. He hit the pavement running, rifle in one hand and keys in the other. A few seconds later, he reached the Jeep, pocketing the keys and grabbing the roof rack bar. With his feet firmly planted on the passenger side running board, he slapped the front door with this hand.

"Go! Go!"

The Jeep lurched forward just as two cars appeared on the far side of the Toyota. Bullets snapped overhead before they reached the SUV on the far side, prompting Alex to release his right hand from the roof rack and swing his rifle over his left arm. Using the crook of his left elbow for stability, Alex fired several rounds in the direction of the cars before Ed eased the Jeep to a halt. He leaned down into the rear passenger window to yell at Charlie, who was halfway out of the rear driver-side window, firing at their pursuers.

"Charlie! Move the roadblock. I got this!"

Alex hopped down from the running board and went prone on the pavement, hoping to present the smallest possible target to the men less than one hundred and fifty feet away. Incoming rounds cracked off the asphalt, forcing him to roll against the Jeep's rear tire. He zeroed in on a man trying to squeeze through the small opening between the rear of the SUV and the guardrail. With the chevron reticle centered on the man's chest, Alex fired three times, dropping him in place.

Were they really attempting to take the bridge on foot?

Staring past his ACOG scope, he saw at least two more men attempting to move forward under covering fire.

Let's see what we can do about that.

A bullet skipped off a puddle less than a foot in front of his head, ricocheting into the Jeep's rear tire, flattening it with a hiss. He rapid-fired the rest of his magazine at the approaching men, then scrambled to the front of the Jeep to shield himself from the incoming fusillade. He changed magazines and looked up to see Ed peeking over the dashboard, waiting for Charlie to move the roadblock, flinching with each bullet impact.

The SUV behind him roared to life and jerked forward, clearing the road into Milton Mills. He stood to give Ed the thumbs-up just as the front windshield shattered in place, leaving a one-inch hole in the middle of an opaque, milky blue screen. Alex jumped out of the way, sure that Ed wasn't about to spend another second in the kill zone. True to his prediction, Ed gunned the Jeep down the road, barely swerving in time to avoid running into the pack of motorcycles parked on the left side of the road.

Alex tucked behind one of the metal posts holding up the guardrail, and turned his attention to the two men advancing across the bridge. His first salvo yielded at least one hit to the closest militiaman, collapsing him against the guardrail. A few of the bikers lying in the grass on the other side of the road rushed up to grab the rifles dropped by the militiamen Alex had killed at the beginning of the battle. Alex expended his magazine, providing cover fire.

Within seconds, semiautomatic rifle fire from the Milton Mills side of the river tore into the militiamen stranded in the middle of the bridge and started to obliterate the SUV on the other side. Alex took advantage of the extra rifle fire to deliver well-aimed, single shots at the sparse targets that appeared behind the Toyota. He struck one of them in the head through the half-shattered rear cargo compartment window, which stopped incoming fire from the Maine side of the bridge. Moments later, one of the cars parked behind the SUV spun its tires on the wet road, tearing off north on Foxes Ridge Road, leaving the Salmon River Falls crossing quiet.

Alex stood slowly, making sure the retreat was genuine. Sensing no movement on the far end of the bridge, he walked over to the dazed bikers, who had just begun to lift themselves out of the gravel next to the road. Halfway across the road, he dropped to one knee and vomited onto the pavement. Charlie jumped down from the SUV a few moments later and braced himself on the guardrail. When he turned around, Alex seriously wondered if Charlie should continue the journey. He wore a pained look across a dark red face, gasping for breath.

"You all right?" Alex asked.

"Better than you," he said, followed by several deep breaths.

"When you're feeling better, grab a few extra magazines for each of us. Leave the rest for them."

"I'm fine right now," said Charlie. "Ed's the one you need to check on."

Alex glanced at the Jeep idling past the bridge. Ed sat upright, motionless. Maybe this would be the end of the journey for both of them.

"Better than shitting your pants," he heard over the rain.

A man with a thick gray beard and hair tied back into a ponytail lifted himself off the road and approached with a smirk. Wearing full leather riding gear, sunglasses and a red bandana tied across his forehead, he looked like a *Sons of Anarchy* recruiting poster. He slung the rifle over his right shoulder and extended a hand, oblivious to the rain beating down on him.

"I brought a change of pants just in case," said Alex, stepping forward.

"I believe a thank you is in order. Jim Koch."

Alex gripped his hand and shook it vigorously. "Alex Fletcher, and the thanks is all mine. Not sure how that would have gone without the backup," he said, coughing.

"Looked like you had it more or less under control."

"I think you'll need these to move that SUV, if it still works. Hope you didn't have a big lunch. The front seat's a little bit messy," he said, holding up a set of blood-drenched keys.

Jim swiped the keys out of Alex's hand. "What the hell are you guys?"

"Nothing, really," Alex said. "Just wanted to get across that bridge."

"Hate to point this out, but you're headed in the wrong direction," said Jim.

"We have kids in Boston. I dropped my son off at Boston University on Saturday for early orientation."

"Dude, Boston got hit hard. Everyone with any sense is getting out of there. We're headed up to my brother's place in Standish. Shitheads here wouldn't let us cross unless we gave up our rides. Not much we could do about it without some serious hardware," said Jim, patting the AR-15 he had taken off the road.

"How long have you been here?" asked Alex.

"Two hours. Figured these idiots would bail when the rain hit. We saw three families take that deal."

"There was no deal," said Alex.

"What do you mean?"

"There's a church about two miles up the road. They take the cars there and execute the occupants in the forest—as far as we could tell," Alex informed him.

"Looks like that's our next stop," Jim said, inserting the magazine in the rifle and pulling back the charging handle.

"We shut it down—hard. Nothing left for you to clean up."

"Sounds like you've had a long day, man. I'd buy you guys a drink, but under the circumstances..." he said, looking around and shrugging his shoulders.

"If I see you again, I'll take you up on that offer," said Alex. "What route did you take to get up here?"

"Came up from Woburn. No problems at all until this shit," said Jim.

"Any news from Boston?"

"National Guard units rolled into the areas north of the Charles pretty quickly—almost too quickly. Cambridge, Watertown and the areas closer to the city are pretty stable. South of the river is a clusterfuck. The military isn't letting anything across the Charles, and nobody north of the river is complaining. Sorry to be the bearer of bad news," said Jim.

"That's the first real SITREP we've received since this whole mess started."

"Ex-military, right?" said Jim.

"Marine Corps. Iraq War. Yourself?"

"Army. First Gulf War."

"An oldtimer," said Alex.

"Watch your mouth, Captain Fletcher," said Jim.

"What makes you think I was a captain?"

"Sergeants can smell an officer a mile away—kind of a pungent, toe cheese odor. You handled yourself a little too well to be a boot LT, so that narrowed the field a little."

"Well, Sergeant Koch," said Alex, "welcome to Vacationland. I suggest you avoid Foxes Ridge Road. I suspect your group won't be happy with what they find at the church."

"I bet they won't," Jim said, giving his crew the signal to mount up.

While the motorcycles filled Milton Mills with a deep rumble, Alex jogged over to the Jeep and looked in the driver's window. With his hands still gripping the steering wheel in a near perfect ten and two o'clock position, Ed stared blankly at the opaque windshield directly in front of him. He slowly turned his head toward Alex.

"Can you please promise me no more of this SEAL Team Six shit? I think we used up all of our luck with this one," he said, meeting Alex's eyes.

"I used up all of mine back at the church. I borrowed heavily for this one," said Alex, patting him on the shoulder through the window.

"Is that a yes or a no?"

"Both," said Alex, unwilling to make a promise he couldn't keep.

"I'm too fucking tired to figure you out right now. Let's get this Jeep back in working order," said Ed, "unless the spare is wrecked."

"Miraculously, the spare is intact."

Ed stared at him for a few seconds, eventually grinning. "You must have borrowed heavily. I hope you left some for Charlie and me."

"You're still alive, right?" said Alex, walking with him to the rear of the Jeep.

"Somehow," he mumbled.

They finished changing the punctured tire while the last of a steady stream of vehicles crossed the bridge. The bikers, who had taken up armed positions at the far end of each bridge, revved their motorcycles and roared away behind the last car. Ed cranked on the last lug nut and raised himself off the gravel, wiping a thick sheen of sweat from his face with his shirt. He surveyed the other side of the bridge and shook his head.

"I'm worried about our families. What if this group is bigger? They could have shit like this set up all over southern Maine."

"I don't think so," said Alex. "An operation like this is too visible to run anywhere else. This was their big score. Sam and the crew will be fine. They're probably in Limerick by now."

"Cooking hotdogs and drinking beer—or eating tofu and salad in your case! Gotcha again!" yelled Charlie.

"You know the saying 'there's no such thing as an atheist in a foxhole?' Well, there's no such thing as a vegetarian in an apocalypse," said Alex.

"I hope you guys are right. Still nothing on the satphone?" asked Ed.

Alex shook his head. "The military must have hijacked the system. A low orbital nuke would take out a few of the company's satellites, but they have over seventy in geosynchronous orbit. Coverage shouldn't be an issue for a satphone to satphone call. I guarantee the government took over the satcom networks as part of their continuity-of-government plan. We're limited to receiving their emergency text message broadcasts."

"One message twenty-four hours ago. Someone made a ton of money selling this crock-of-shit idea," Ed muttered. "Maybe there's a bigger problem out there."

"It doesn't matter. We get the kids and hole up at the farm. That's our only mission. We can worry about the big picture later," said Alex.

"Unless the big picture swallows us up in Boston."

Chapter 29

EVENT +31:46 Hours

Acton, Maine

Dave Littner pulled his Honda Civic off the road, craning his head out of the window. He watched the heavily armed biker gang disappear beyond a stand of trees and reappear several hundred yards beyond, cresting one of several rolling hills along Milton Mills Road.

"Let's grab the rifles," he said to Karen Goodsby, one of Campbell's people.

"Expecting trouble?" she asked.

"Something isn't right. That's more cars than I've seen since this whole thing started."

Littner opened the trunk and dug into a long nylon bag, producing a stripped-down AR-15 for Karen. He pulled back the charging handle and locked the bolt carrier back, handing her the cleared weapon.

"Old school iron sights," she said, examining the bore.

"I don't put any fancy gizmos on my rifles. Let me know if that's going to be a problem."

"As long as it shoots straight, we're in business," said Karen.

"It shoots straight. Front sight is set for one hundred yards," he said, handing her three magazines.

Less than a minute later, they were back on Milton Mills Road, heading toward the border. The northern crossing appeared beyond a small, blue-trimmed Cape Cod home, flanked on both sides by wide expanses of calm water. The road extending to the New Hampshire side was clear, except for a small group of young adults loaded down with backpacks and camping gear, pedaling mountain bikes over the bridge.

"Seems kind of odd that the state police would forget this spot," said Karen.

"York County Sheriff's Department and the state police alternate duty days out here. It's possible, but unlikely," said Littner.

He drove past French Street, which connected the two bridge crossings on the Maine side, and rolled his window down to address the closest cyclist. The group slowed, eyeing each other.

"Did you see any police on the other side?" he asked.

"Something happened at the other bridge, but I didn't see any police," said one of the men toward the front.

"They kind of looked military to me," said the woman next to him.

"Who looked military?" asked Littner.

"The dead guys on the bridge."

"They weren't military," said one of the guys at the back of the group. "Hair was all fucked up, and none of them wore the same gear. They all had those stupid boonie hats on too. Every unit we've seen coming up through New Hampshire is geared up for heavy combat. Helmets, body armor—everything."

Heavy combat? Littner didn't like the sound of that.

"How many are on the bridge?" he asked.

"I saw maybe six or seven of them. Three on the New Hampshire side. More in the middle. Not sure what was on this side. We didn't stick around very long," said the woman.

"Thanks, everyone. I don't want to hold you up any further. Looks like you have a little break in the weather. You guys headed anywhere in particular?"

"Probably try to make it to the Bridgton area. My family used to rent a house on Long Lake every other summer. There's a private school up there. Should be empty."

"Bridgton Academy. It's in North Bridgton, about five miles past town. When you get to the intersection in Bridgton, across from the Food City, keep going straight. You'll see the signs. Good luck," said Littner.

"You too," said the cyclist, fixing his eyes on Littner's hat.

The cyclists had cleared the intersection by the time he turned around and took a right onto French Street, speeding toward the southern bridge. The first thing he saw beyond the white Baptist church was a blue Volvo SUV parked in the middle of French Street near the bridge. The driver's-side doors had been left open.

The scene unfolded slowly as their car crept past the SUV. Several members of Eli's Maine Liberty Militia, easily recognizable by their boonie caps, lay in a grotesque pile at the foot of the bridge. Two more men lay dead toward the middle of the bridge against the left guardrail. He didn't see any weapons on the ground, which didn't surprise him. Whoever had done this would have stripped Eli's men of anything useful. He parked the car next to the mound of bodies.

"Shit," he said, "I guess we better take a closer look."

"I don't see the point. Someone shot up Eli's people. Probably the bikers we saw," said Goodsby.

"Just a quick look and we're out of here."

He pulled the first body halfway out of the pile, disturbing hundreds of flies that had gathered. He turned the corpse on its back.

"Wounds look fresh. I've seen my share of traffic accidents to know that," she said.

Karen Goodsby had worked as a part-time Emergency Medical Technician (EMT) out of Gorham before taking a full-time position at Waterboro Elementary School a few years ago. He didn't know much more than that, but Harrison Campbell constantly sang her praises.

"Two to the chest, one to the head. Mozambique Drill. Looks like the work of a professional," said Littner.

"There's a lot of blood on the Land Cruiser's windows. Maybe an ambush?" Goodsby surmised, pointing at the bullet-riddled SUV backed into the bushes across the road.

"Could be. I'm counting five guys here. Three with headshots. Looks like two more dead on the bridge. A ton of brass on the ground. Whatever happened here was quick and vicious. Probably a coordinated strike against both sides. This is part of something bigger," he said, raising his head to scan the other side of the bridge.

"Think we'll find more on the other side?"

"I don't plan on staying around long enough to find out. I'm going to pull a few more off the pile and take pictures for Harrison."

He gripped another body from the bloody mound and pulled it free of the mess.

"Holy shit," hissed Littner, the body's torso and head thunking against the pavement.

Goodsby raised her rifle and crouched, scanning the open sectors around them.

"What is it?" she whispered.

"We have a big problem," he said, nodding at the body.

She glanced down at the man's face and shrugged her shoulders.

"That's Eli's little brother," he said, staring at the red hole drilled between Jimmy Russell's lifeless eyes.

He pushed the head to one side with his boot, stopping at the exit wound.

"What's the big deal? I thought he was a dirt bag," said Goodsby.

"The big deal is that Eli will go ballistic. We need to get a hold of Harrison immediately. All hell's about to break loose."

"Looks like it already did."

Chapter 30

East Waterboro, Maine

Kate Fletcher leaned into the mountain bike and pedaled up the long hill leading into East Waterboro. She glanced behind to check on her group, which rode in a loose formation stretching fifty feet back.

We're too far apart.

Linda Thornton brought up the rear, keeping watch over the floundering flock. The group moved along at a painful crawl, everyone pedaling lethargically after the rainstorm. The intense cloudburst had shattered what little motivation the group managed to salvage from their extended journey throughout the morning.

Best guess, they had travelled twice the distance originally calculated to reach East Waterboro. Avoiding police checkpoints around the Maine Mall had taken them several miles in the opposite direction, forcing them to use neighborhood roads and business parks to reach Western Avenue near the eerily silent Portland Jetport.

The gradual hills and awkward backpacks started to take a serious toll within the first few miles. Touted by Alex as an easy four-hour ride through the countryside, the trek had morphed into a grueling seven-hour battle. A battle to keep the group moving forward and delay the next break. She wanted to push them straight through to Limerick, fifteen miles away, but her crew wasn't going to last another mile without a long break—and lunch. She'd start looking for a place to stop after East Waterboro.

Kate swatted her neck. Not a good sign for the rest of the afternoon. Nothing sucked the life out of you faster than a steamy August afternoon with Maine's biting flies. Her mind drifted to Alex riding in Ed's air-conditioned Jeep.

Must be nice.

Mercifully, the road sloped downward, allowing them to glide several hundred feet through East Waterboro's only intersection.

ॐॐॐ

Nathan Russell took a long swig of cold beer and crumpled the can, whipping it at a nearby light post. He missed, and the flattened can skittered on the pavement to join a dozen empties already scattered beyond the post.

"I'll take another," he said, keeping his eyes glued to the intersection adjacent to the empty Hannigans parking lot.

"Here you go, Nate," he heard, as another sweaty can of Budweiser appeared within reach.

He popped the tab and took a long pull, lightening the can significantly. Now he felt it. He was getting there. Getting into the zone, where he was unstoppable.

"What do you make of that?" he asked.

David Mullins raised his hand over his eyes and peered at the procession of bicycles streaming through the intersection.

"Looks like a bunch of bitches out for a ride," said Mullins.

Not through my town, they ain't.

Nathan slid off the hood of the silver BMW SUV and reached through the window to grab a pair of binoculars. He scanned the group, starting at the front and working his way back.

What the fuck?

He drained the beer can and took another failed shot at hitting the light post.

"You see this shit? Two of those bitches are carrying assault rifles. Looks like they're escorting a bunch of teenagers. Hot ones too. The bitch in the front ain't half bad either," said Nathan.

"Gimme that," said Mullins, attempting to grab the binoculars.

Nathan snatched them away and glared at Mullins. "You do not fucking grab shit from me. Understand?"

"Sorry, Nate. I got excited," said Mullins, retracting his hand.

"I hate that grabbing shit. You're like a two-year-old. Grab my shit again, and I'll bash your fucking teeth in."

"It won't happen again, Nate."

Nathan stared at his friend, wanting to smash his face in anyway. "Get in the car. We need to have a chat with these fuckers about the new firearms ordinance in town."

"We have a new ordinance?"

"Are you extra stupid today? The new ordinance is what I say it is, and I say nobody rides around with assault rifles through my town. Weren't you listening to a thing my dad said? We're the law around here now, so start acting like it," said Nathan.

"How far is our jurisdiction?"

"As far as we want it to be. When's the last time you saw a county sheriff's car or one of those punk-ass staties?"

"I haven't," replied David.

"Exactly. Dad says it's up to us, so here we go. Get in the truck."

Nathan closed the door and started the engine, sensing that David's line of questioning would continue. He leaned forward to draw the pistol tucked into the waistband of his jeans just as David opened his mouth.

"I thought your dad was talking about the militia being in charge. I don't think—"

Nathan jammed the barrel of the semiautomatic pistol into David's cheek. "You don't think what?" he said, fixing a murderous stare.

David shook his head, mumbling, "I'm sorry, man. I promise—"

"This is your last warning, dude. Dad left me with full authority to do what needs to be done around here. He's a full colonel in the militia, right under my granddad. Why the hell do you think he gave me this car? To run errands? Use your head, man—or fucking lose it. I'm serious," he said, easing the pressure on David's cheek.

"All right. Let's do this," said David.

"I do all the talking. Play this right, and one of those bitches will be bobbing on your knob. Ain't nothing free in this world anymore. Gotta pay a toll to use the roads around here," said Nathan, grinning wickedly.

"I can handle that. I'd love to work those twins over," said David, touching the denim bulge forming in his pants.

"Don't get greedy. You keep fucking up and it'll be one of the boys," said Nathan.

"I don't care who it is," said David. "Let's get this on!"

"That's better," said Nathan, shifting the car into drive.

ॐ

Shit. Kate glanced at the grocery store parking lot again. The sight of two men surveying their group with binoculars made her nervous. They could be waiting for someone to arrive via the same route, or they might be keeping an eye out for trouble. The mess of beer cans near the light post suggested otherwise.

Keep pedaling. The parking lot would be out of view within a few minutes.

"Kate! They're coming!" yelled Samantha.

Of course they were. She slowed her bike and watched the black SUV speed across the parking lot toward the shopping center exit fifty feet ahead of her group.

"Linda?" said Kate.

"Got it covered," replied Linda.

Kate cruised half of the distance to the exit and stopped, dismounting her bike. She swung her rifle forward on its two-point sling, and tried to remember how Linda taught her to transition quickly to a forward position. She knew the strap would switch shoulders, but beyond that she didn't have enough practice with the maneuver to do it correctly on the first try. The BMW SUV careened onto Route 5 and skidded to a halt twenty feet ahead.

Screw this. She pushed her AR-15 back into position on her back and unsnapped her holster. At this range, she could probably do more damage with her Sig Sauer.

She risked a quick glance back at the group. They looked more exhausted than alarmed by the sudden appearance of the SUV. Linda had already transitioned her rifle and was approaching swiftly along the center median line, keeping her distance from the kids. She knew what she was doing, which was more than Kate could say about the situation. She noticed Ethan fiddling with one of the side pockets on his rucksack. He had pulled the pack off one shoulder.

"Ethan, leave it in the pack. Same for you, Emily," said Kate.

She heard Linda give the same warning to her daughters, whom Kate knew for a fact were armed. Even the Walker kids carried firearms, though they had never been trained to fire one. If things deteriorated into a gunfight, Kate and Linda would buy the group enough time to find cover, while Samantha helped the kids put the rest of the group's weapons into action. She turned back to the SUV just as the front doors opened.

Black motorcycle boots and shit-kicker jeans appeared to be the uniform of the day for their welcoming committee. She guessed early to mid twenties, but they both wore that hardened, "up to no good" expression that made it difficult to tell. The passenger swayed a bit after standing. He looked dumber than a rock garden. Drunk and dumb didn't mix well in serious situations, and this was about as serious as any situation would ever get for these two.

The driver stepped around the hood, staring her down with beady eyes and a twisted smirk. A black semiautomatic pistol grip protruded from his jeans. Beady Eyes was the dangerous one. He would be the first to die if this went badly—and she expected it to. She could think of no logical reason why these two dipshits would suddenly pull out in front of them. They wanted something, and five seconds of observation made it clear that they didn't want the bicycles. Rock Garden hadn't taken his eyes off Linda's twins since he blundered out of the BMW. This would definitely end badly, especially if Linda figured out what Rock Garden had in mind.

"Afternoon, ladies. Nathan Russell. Part of the militia in charge of the area," he said, resting his hands on his hips—dangerously close to the pistol.

"We're gonna have to ask you to surrender those rifles and consent to a search. We can't have people running around with weapons—uh—in the area."

"I'm pretty familiar with the state's firearms laws, and there's no problem here. If you don't mind, we have a long day ahead of us," said Kate.

"But there is a problem. We've been given authority to make decisions about these kinds of things," said Beady Eyes, drawing a quick look from Rock Garden.

"Who gave you this authority?" said Linda, straining to keep her rifle barrel pointed down.

"The local commander," said Beady Eyes. "So I need you to clear those weapons, and we'll get you on your way."

"Unless you want to pay the toll," said Rock Garden with an eager look.

Beady Eyes silenced him with a deadly glare.

"We're not travelling with any money," said Kate.

"There's other ways to pay," muttered Rock Garden.

Mouth open, he glared at Linda's twins. Kate slowly moved her hand back along her thigh, feeling the nylon holster and mentally picturing the draw. She'd give them one more chance.

"We're gonna get moving now. I think you should drive back to the parking lot and enjoy the rest of your beers. It's a beautiful day. Be a real shame to ruin it," she stated.

Beady Eyes shifted his right hand toward the pistol. "Nobody's going anywhere until I—"

The blast from Linda's rifle punched a small red dot through the center of his forehead. Kate drew her pistol and dropped to one knee, firing rapidly at Rock Garden's head and chest. His head snapped backward moments before blasts from Linda's rifle punctured his torso and shattered the window behind him. She shifted her aim to Beady Eyes, who remained upright, staring blankly past her at the kids. His mouth mumbled something unintelligible as he slowly sank down the side of the vehicle and tumbled forward to the blistering pavement.

Emily screamed, setting off a chain reaction of panic and hysteria among the teenagers. Kate's vision narrowed to the tiny red hole in the front of his head. The hole was so perfect. The shrieking faded into a high-pitched ringing. Someone grabbed her arm.

"You all right, Kate? We need to get out of here! Can you stand?" said a familiar voice.

She broke her fixation on the trickle of blood flowing from the bullet entry wound, and turned her head to the sound. Linda stood over her, trying to pull her up. Everything snapped back into place. She thumbed the decocking lever on her pistol and holstered it.

"We need to load up right now!" Linda ordered. "We're taking the car!"

"Everyone's all right?" asked Kate.

"Everyone except for those two. Find the keys. I'll get the kids in the car," she said.

Linda glanced behind her and saw the kids cowering behind their bicycles. She pulled at her frantic daughters, urging them to get in the SUV.

Emily threw her bike down and rushed forward, crying. "I want to go home, Mommy!"

"We'll be fine, sweetie," Kate said to her. "We'll be at Nana and Grandpa's house in thirty minutes. I need you to get in the car now. Don't look at anything but the car. Can you do that?"

Emily nodded and buried her head in Kate's right shoulder.

"We need to get moving," said Linda.

Kate kissed her daughter. "I love you. Get your pack off, and get in the car."

Emily nodded, staring past her mother at the dead body. She started crying again and grabbed Kate.

"I'll hold you later. Promise. Follow Mrs. Thornton around the back of the car," Kate said, pushing her daughter toward the rest of the kids.

"Let's go! In the car! Now!" yelled Linda, pulling Samantha, who looked more shell-shocked than her kids.

"Should we hide the bikes?" asked Kate.

"No time for that. We have witnesses," said Linda, pointing to the Hannigans shopping complex.

Kate saw at least a half-dozen people lurking near the intersection, peering in their direction.

"Shit. I'll move the bodies," said Kate, placing her rifle and backpack against the hood of the SUV.

She grabbed Beady Eyes by his dusty boots and dragged him to the side of the road, leaving a slippery trail of gore on the hot asphalt surface. A pinkish-gray lump clung stubbornly to the road, stretching from the top of his skull. She shook her head.

I didn't see that.

Her stomach wasn't convinced, exploding a brownish-yellow stream onto his jeans. She kept pulling. Another involuntary spray hit the gravel on the shoulder of the road. Kate felt grass beneath her and dropped his legs, breathing heavily.

How can you push something like this out of your head?

You couldn't. Not according to her husband. You pressed on and dealt with it later. They were counting on her to do that.

"All right. You can do this," she mumbled to herself.

She removed the pistol from Beady Eyes' waistline, ejecting the magazine and racking the slide to eject the chambered round. She cocked her arm to throw the pistol into the closest drainage ditch, but stopped. No reason to give the weapon back to the same community that had produced these two pieces of shit. Kate tucked it into her belt and searched for a wallet and keys. She examined his license and exhaled. Just what they didn't need. A Waterboro local. And the other one?

"Ethan, you don't have to do that!" said Kate, running on rubbery legs back to the SUV.

Ethan had started to pull Rock Garden away from the car by his armpits.

"I can handle it, Mom—Aunt Kate," said Ethan.

A weak fountain of blood pulsed from a jagged hole in the back of Rock Garden's neck, emptying into the scarlet pool beneath Ethan's boots. He stared at the blood for a few seconds before dropping the body on the pavement. She hugged him while he sobbed.

"It'll be okay, Ethan. We're almost at Nana's."

"I know why you killed them." He sniffled. "I saw them looking at the girls."

Kate searched for a parental line to soften Ethan's harsh induction into their "kill or be killed" world. She drew a complete blank.

"We won't let anything happen to you guys. Understand?" she said, locking eyes with him.

He nodded, wiping his eyes and putting on a tough face.

"Can you help everyone get into the car?"

"I want to learn how to shoot like that," announced Ethan.

"You'll have to talk to your uncle. He taught me how to shoot," said Kate.

"I thought he couldn't hit anything with a pistol?"

"He's better than he cares to admit," said Kate, kneeling next to the body. "Get going."

She fished a wallet out of Rock Garden's back pocket and held up another blood-smeared Maine driver's license. Wonderful. Another local.

"Forget moving that one! They're starting to take pictures," said Linda, pointing at the crowd back at the intersection.

Kate helped Ethan squeeze into place next to Samantha's son and handed him his rucksack. Samantha passed two more backpacks to Kate, which she stuffed into the cargo area against the boys. Less than a minute later, the SUV peeled off down Route 5 toward Limerick.

Chapter 31

Limerick, Maine

Kate had made this trip enough times to recognize the landmarks as they approached, but nothing seemed familiar. Nothing at all.

Linda, who was driving, glanced at her. "You all right?"

"Yeah, I'm fine. Just not sure...we may have passed it. If we see a 'Welcome to Parsonsfield' sign, we definitely missed it."

"We haven't hit that yet," she said. "Let me know if I need to slow down."

Linda could sense that she was off. Kate saw it in her eyes. Maybe they all knew it. She didn't think so. Only Linda would be attuned to what transpired after the shootout. Kate had momentarily shut down. At least she hadn't frozen when it counted most. She pictured the gun draw in her head, and training took over when Linda's bullet evacuated the kid's skull. She barely remembered firing at the second kid—had no recollection of hitting him in the face.

"I know it's .37 miles past the only cemetery on the road," said Kate.

"We just passed that," said Samantha.

"There it is, right?" said Linda, slowing the SUV in front of the entrance to an unmarked dirt road.

Kate squinted. "Yep. That's it. It's the only road on the left."

I can't believe I missed that.

She needed this funk to pass quickly. The group depended on her leadership—or so she had been told. Maybe she wasn't the best person to make decisions for the group. Stupid thought. She couldn't exactly put Linda in charge of the compound—but she would certainly put Linda in charge of their security.

Linda turned the car onto Gelder Pond Lane, taking the dirt road at a reasonable speed. Kate glanced back. They had five people jammed into the

224

rear bench, which was two more than capacity. Samantha, who had given up the front seat to let Kate navigate, was crushed under her daughter on the right side, with Linda's twins compressed on the left. This left Emily stuffed between them in the middle, buried under three of their backpacks.

"You should take Gelder Pond as slow as possible. It's a private road, and everyone that lives back here is private about their money," said Kate.

They turned left at the three-way intersection, a quarter of a mile into the thick forest, and headed down the eastern side of Gelder Pond Road, which formed a rough circle around Gelder Pond. The Fletcher compound had been built on the first of twelve planned lots along the road, facing the pond. Facing difficult economic times after the Jakarta Pandemic, the Gelders—one of the oldest families in the area, finally decided to yield on a five-decade-old commitment to do their part to keep the rich city folk out of Limerick. The Fletchers paid the asking price in cash for two of the plots in late 2014, and started clearing a two-and-a-half-acre area within the twenty-two-acre enclave as soon as the winter broke. The Fletcher family compound was fully operational by the end of the year, housing Alex's parents and their two nephews.

"How far down is it?" asked Samantha.

"Half mile at most. It's the only driveway on the eastern side of the loop. Impossible to miss."

"We'll have to do something about that," said Linda.

She was definitely putting Linda in charge of security. At least until Alex returned.

"There it is," she said. "There's a gate about a hundred feet down the driveway. You can't see it from the road."

"Who plows this road in the winter?" asked Linda.

"Homeowners' association pays the town. You can imagine what we pay to keep the road cleared up to our driveway."

"You better hope the town gets their shit running again before winter," said Linda.

"We have a plow for the ATV and riding mower," said Kate.

Linda cast her a doubtful look.

"And snowmobiles," added Kate.

Linda guided them onto a gravel driveway carved through the thick pines. Peering into the dense forest, she saw no hint of the clearing one thousand feet due west in the direction of Gelder Pond. The opaque stand of conifers would continue to shield them during the winter months when the leaves fell throughout the region. Tree type had been one of their primary considerations in selecting the plot.

The gate appeared after a slight turn, another purposeful design to keep the casual observer from drawing any conclusions about the driveway from the road.

"We're here," Kate announced. "Hopefully they'll have the hot water working, or you can cool off in the lake. There's a dock, a little beach, even a rope swing into the water. Whatever you want."

Nobody said a word. She figured most of them would crash out as soon as they settled into the house. She wished she could do the same, but it wouldn't be an option. Whatever they had left behind on the street in East Waterboro wasn't finished. The apple rarely fell far from the tree. There would be little rest.

"I assume the punch code won't work with the power down," said Linda, lowering her window at the touch pad in front of the gate.

"Try it," Kate said.

Linda pressed a few buttons, but the LED screen remained blank.

"No problem. It's not connected to the auxiliary sources at the house, and power goes out all the time out here," Kate said, fishing a set of keys out of one of the backpacks in her lap.

She stepped out of the vehicle and fought her way through the scrub on the left side of the black aluminum gate, emerging on the driveway behind the gate, and walked to the other side, locating the manual override box on the back of the gate's electric sliding motor. She inserted the key and opened the box, which gave her access to a small handle. Kate pulled the handle to disengage the physical connection to the electro-mechanical operator and slid the gate far enough along its track to allow the SUV through. Once the SUV crossed the threshold, she reversed the process, locking the gate. No sense making it easy for an angry posse to drive up to the house.

Gravel crunched underneath the SUV's tires as they eased left and entered a protracted stretch of shaded driveway. A bright patch of light appeared at the far end of the dark corridor.

"Christ. How far back is the house?" asked Linda.

"About a thousand feet."

"You gotta be kidding me? How much gold did you buy before the pandemic?"

"A lot."

"Wait till you see the compound," said Samantha, uttering her first words since the shooting.

The road brightened as they approached another gate near the edge of the clearing. Through the trees to the right, Kate could see the outline of a gray house and red barn. An occasional shimmer of sparkling light penetrated the tree line toward the back of the clearing. Linda slowed to a stop in front of the gate, and Kate hopped down from the SUV with her keys. She stopped after several steps, craning her head in the direction of a soft rustling sound beyond the gate. She pocketed the keys and eased her pistol out of the holster.

"Kate? You made it!"

A man dressed in jeans and a gray polo shirt emerged from the foliage and stepped onto the road behind the gate. Tim Fletcher slung a scoped M-14 rifle over his shoulder and grabbed a green handheld radio clipped to his belt.

"Amy, they made it! They're here!" he yelled into the radio, running toward them.

Kate holstered her pistol and hurried to the gate.

"Let me get the gate for you! Holy shit, I can't tell you how good it is to see you. Now I'm talking like you. See what you've done. Oh, God—Amy's gonna scream when she sees everyone," he said, fumbling with the key to unlock the gate.

"We tried the satphone and—"

"Alex isn't with us, Dad," said Kate.

Tim stopped for a moment and continued without looking up.

"He left to get Ryan out of Boston."

The gate slid open, and Alex's father rushed forward to crush Kate with a hug.

"Everyone's alive. That's all that matters," he said, his eyes watery and his voice pitchy. "We thought we lost all of you with the boat. We were going to give it forty-eight hours, and then I was heading to Boston on one of the ATVs."

"I don't think you would have made it very far on one of those things," she said, reciprocating tears.

"I would have tried. Alex will bring Ryan back, Kate. He planned for this kind of thing."

"I know," she said, hugging him again. "Ethan's fine. He's in the back."

"How many do you have with you?"

"Nine, including me. Good friends from Durham Road. You've met the Walkers," she said, signaling for Linda to drive forward.

"I remember them. Three kids right around your kids' ages?" he said, pulling her out of the road.

"Right. Samantha and two of her kids are with us. Her husband is with Alex. They have a daughter in Boston, near Ryan."

"I seem to remember Ryan and her having a little thing," said Tim.

"That's not public information, Tim," she said, smiling.

"Really? The kid fawns all over her anytime I see them within a couple hundred yards of each other. Boston University wasn't his only choice of schools," Tim reminded her.

"Boston College would have been too obvious," she said. When the SUV pulled even with them, she made introductions. "This is Linda Thornton. Her two daughters are crammed back there somewhere. Her husband, Charlie—"

"I've heard all about Charlie. It's a pleasure to finally meet one of you, Linda," said Tim.

"The pleasure is all mine. I can't thank you enough for having us out here," said Linda.

"We'll have none of that. Any friends of Alex and Kate's are friends of ours, and you're all welcome to stay here indefinitely. That's an unconditional offer," said Tim.

"That's very generous of you."

"This isn't an offer of charity. Your husband volunteered to go with them to get the kids?"

"Well, he's a little touched in the head," said Linda.

Tim laughed. "I bet he is, but that doesn't change anything. My house is yours. Simple as that. Where's Samantha?"

The back driver's-side window lowered.

"Good to see you again," he said, shaking her hand through the window.

"Call me Sam. You remember my daughter, Abby?"

"Sure do. I'm just surprised Ethan didn't manage to squirm his way into the back seat here with her," said Tim.

"Grandpa!" yelled Ethan from the cargo area.

"Behave yourself, Tim," said Kate. "Sorry, girls. He's really pretty harmless."

"I've been called a lot of things before. I don't remember harmless on that list."

"I'm just doing my best to keep them from turning the car around and taking their chances on the outside," said Kate.

"I'll behave. Promise. Let me get this gate locked, and I'll meet you back at the house. I have one of the two-seaters," he said, raising the handheld radio to inform his wife that they had guests and update her on the missing family members.

"I'll keep him company," said Kate. "We'll be right up."

Tim slid the gate across and locked it, giving it a pull to be sure.

"How did you know we were coming?"

"The camera is out, but the buzzer still goes off when the gate is opened. Some stuff works, some stuff doesn't. Most stuff doesn't. I'm over here," said Tim, motioning toward the olive-drab ATV nestled into the forest on the edge of the clearing.

He cranked the engine, and they lurched in their seats as the ATV broke out of the brush into a brown grass field. Kate grabbed the nearest vertical upright bar with her right hand, but immediately pulled the hand back to her side.

"Hit a rough patch on the way?" Tim inquired, eyeing her bloodied hand.

"We need to keep the car out of sight," said Kate vaguely.

"I figured as much with the out-of-state plates. What happened?"

"Two drunk kids stopped us on Route 5 in front of the Hannigans. One of them mentioned a toll and kept staring at the girls. Claimed to be part of a militia. We didn't wait for them to explain the details."

"I don't blame you. Locals with an out-of-state car?"

"The real owners are probably dead. I took the kids' ID. Waterboro addresses," she said, pausing. "We should sink the car in the pond tonight."

"We might need it in an emergency. Does Alex have a car?"

"They took the Walkers' Jeep. It was the only car working between the three families," she said.

"How did you get out here?" he said.

"Rode our bikes until Waterboro."

"You're kidding me," said Tim.

"We've had a long day," Kate said, stepping off the ATV.

"Well, it's over," Tim said.

"For now."

Tim parked in front of the house next to the BMW SUV. A wide farmer's porch extended the full length of the gray colonial, wrapping around the right corner and connecting to the mudroom stoop. A gray-haired woman wearing jeans and a purple blouse yelled from the door and ran down the front steps. Ethan's brother, a thin, dark-haired boy in swim trunks, followed.

Kate hopped off and opened the back of the SUV.

"Finally," said Ethan, untangling his legs from Daniel's.

"No shit," said Samantha's son.

"Watch your mouth, Daniel," scolded Samantha.

"You can blame that on me. Grab your stuff and drag it inside," said Kate, catching a glimpse of Ethan's hands. "Let's wash those off before your grandma gets a hold of you," she added.

"Wash what off? Where is he? Where is Ethan!" said Amy Fletcher.

"Come on, Nana. Not now," he whispered, glancing into the back seat behind him.

"I won't smother you in kisses in front of your girlfriends," she said.

"Someone help me," muttered Ethan.

Daniel patted him on the back. "You're on your own, man."

Ethan dropped to the crushed rock and grabbed his rucksack, trying to delay the inevitable hug; which hit him before he could turn around.

"Your brother was worried out of his mind," said his grandmother.

Ethan's face flushed red, but he returned the hug and stuck his hand out to grab his brother. The three of them clung together for several moments before Kevin pulled away, examining Ethan's hand.

"What's this?"

Amy grabbed Ethan's hands and gasped.

"It's not his," stated Kate. "We ran into a problem on the way."

"I'm just glad you guys are all right," Amy said, holding her arms open for Kate.

"I'm a little ripe," Kate warned.

"I don't care," said Amy Fletcher, starting to cry. "Thank God you made it!" She rushed forward and held her.

"Alex is on the way to Boston," said Kate. "I'm scared."

"I am too, honey. We're all scared. But he's the best hope of getting Ryan back," said Amy. "He's a very capable man."

"He is," Kate agreed.

"And he has help?"

Kate nodded and walked toward the house, motioning for Amy to follow. Her mother-in-law got the message and joined her near the garage door.

"Ed Walker and Charlie Thornton went with him. They left early this morning. Ed's daughter is at Boston College."

"That's right. Aren't those two an item?"

"That's not something we advertise." She winked.

"I'm not the one you have to worry about," said Amy.

"Believe me, I've already had a talk with your husband," she said, smiling.

"And Charlie's with them?" Amy asked, raising an eyebrow.

"He volunteered. What could Alex say? He's been a great friend," said Kate.

"I know. It's good that you're all together. I just hope they don't slow him down," whispered Amy.

"I'm sure he planned for it somehow," said Kate.

"I wouldn't be surprised. Let's stop looking suspicious and get everyone cleaned up. You guys smell like sewage," said Amy.

"You have no idea."

Chapter 32

Haverhill, MA

Alex studied the GPS plotter for a few seconds, looking up to compare the digital map to the real world. Emerging from the shelter of the dashboard, a stiff wall of air buffeted his face from the damaged windshield, causing him to involuntarily raise his free hand to block his face. He felt a quick sting on the palm of his hand, followed immediately by another on the top of his left ear. At least he could duck down momentarily to escape the onslaught. Ed didn't have that option.

Lowering his hand a few inches, he spotted a break in the road, which more than likely marked the last rural intersection before they turned onto East Main Street, in the hopes of finding the bridge over the Merrimack River intact.

"I think this is Merrimac Road coming up," he said. "After that we only have another mile or so to Rocks Bridge."

Their concern about Rocks Bridge had more to do with the effects of the tsunami than with what happened in Milton Mills. If anything, further concerns about roadblocks and rogue militia units had eroded over the course of two completely uneventful hours of travel. True to what the biker had said, the roads had been mostly empty of vehicles and completely devoid of trouble.

Traffic picked up along Route 125, a few miles past Epping, New Hampshire, but it was still confined to two or three cars per minute, which hardly constituted a problem. The number of vehicles increased as they approached Kingston, doubling by the time they turned onto Route 107 and navigated several lesser-travelled rural roads to arrive at the Merrimack River, where they hoped to find at least one bridge intact.

They decided to start with Rocks Bridge, which was four miles downriver from Haverhill, in an attempt to minimize their exposure to populated areas. With a population of sixty-two thousand, Haverhill wasn't a major city by greater Boston metropolitan area standards, but most of the population was packed in the area along the river, which made Alex uncomfortable. He had a long history with bridges.

His battalion commander in Iraq had affectionately called them "meat grinders," and the bridges they encountered on the road to Baghdad had lived up to that nickname. For centuries, if not millennia, men had fought and died to control bridges, even under the most pointless of circumstances. The incident at Milton Mills proved that under the right conditions, even the most insignificant bridge could spill its share of blood.

They would start with the smallest bridge and work their way toward the city. If Rocks Bridge was damaged, they would drive south to Bates Bridge, which Charlie assured them was much sturdier. Failing that, they could drive into the heart of Haverhill and try to cross the Basiliere Bridge. They had options.

Less than a minute later, conditions along the road suggested they might be forced to seriously consider these other options. Severe water damage appeared before they reached River Road, featuring the telltale deposit of silt and broken debris along the road. Ed switched the Jeep into four wheel drive, and they proceeded through the thick mire, which completely blanketed the landscape around the colonial-style homes that lined East Main Street. The neighborhood looked like it had been extinguished.

Signs of heavier blast damage appeared around Kingston. Denuded trees, stripped branches, roofing tiles torn skyward, and downed trees slowed their progress near the Massachusetts border, forcing them off-road several times. Rural roads approaching the Rocks Bridge had been worse, nearly impassable at a few points. The further south they travelled, the more Alex questioned their plan to approach Boston using back roads.

"This doesn't look promising," said Ed.

"No, it doesn't," mumbled Alex.

A group of several adults picked their way through the mud-covered remains of a collapsed house at the intersection ahead, pushing the larger pieces aside.

"Give them a wide berth," said Alex.

"Got it," said Ed, turning the Jeep toward the right side of the road. "You feel that?" he added.

"Feel what?"

"I think we're driving over wreckage buried under the mud. All the houses are missing beyond the intersection. One nail or piece of glass and we're on foot," said Ed.

"Hold on," said Alex, checking the GPS screen.

"Do you think it's a good idea to stop in the middle of the road like this?" said Charlie. "I'm starting to see a lot of people."

Alex's eyes darted between the GPS screen and the growing crowd of people approaching their Jeep.

"Put us in reverse and turn around. We'll take East Broadway toward Haverhill. Do you see any weapons?"

"Negative. They look more curious than anything. Probably the Maine plates," said Charlie.

"Switch to sectors, Charlie," said Alex.

"Yep," he heard from Charlie.

Ed backed the Jeep slowly through the thick mud.

"Can't you just turn us around?" said Alex.

"No, I can't. We're pushing through two feet of mud. We can still get stuck."

Alex didn't respond. Ed was pissed, and there was no point making it worse. He scanned his sectors and waited, keeping his rifle ready just below the door. As the intersection receded, they picked up speed.

"We clear back there?" asked Ed.

"Looks good," said Charlie.

"I think the mud is thinning," said Alex, knowing the comment would rattle Ed.

"Do you want to drive?" Ed snapped.

"No. I shouldn't have said anything. You've been doing great. I'm just a little fried. Sorry. I think this is the turn for East Broadway," said Alex, pointing to the road forking left.

"Make sure," said Ed, tapping the GPS on the center console.

"Are you two gonna bust each other's balls all the way to Boston?" said Charlie.

"He started it," said Ed.

"I started it?" replied Alex. "This is East Broadway. Watch out for the tree over there."

"Like I didn't see it?"

"I don't know what you see. I point shit out for you. That's my job," said Alex.

"Aw shit," muttered Charlie. "I'm on a road trip with the bicker brothers."

"Careful, or he'll be all over your shit next," said Ed.

"Too late for that warning," said Charlie.

Alex frowned. "What is that supposed to mean?"

"It means you've been acting like my personal physician for the past two hours. I'm fine, Alex. I just get a little winded," said Charlie. "I don't have all day to work out and run on the beach like you do."

"I don't run on the beach," said Alex.

"You run *to* the beach. Same thing. Some of us have to work for a living."

Alex didn't know how to respond to Charlie's last comment. It indicated something deeper than simple annoyance. Resentment? He didn't know, and didn't care. Alex had to keep their unconventional triumvirate together long enough to rescue the kids and get everyone back to the farm in one piece. That was his pact to the rest of them, and he would die honoring it if necessary. He needed to turn this tide of bitterness around quickly, before it swallowed them.

"Can we all agree that we annoy the shit out of each other right now?" said Alex.

"That pretty much sums it up," said Charlie.

"I'll second that," said Ed.

"Good. We agree on something. Can we all agree that we're on track to get the kids out of Boston?"

Ed nodded.

"We're in Massachusetts. That's a good sign," said Charlie.

"Then I say we've all been doing our job, and that's more than enough for me," Alex said. "I'll quit micromanaging."

"It's not that you're micromanaging—" started Ed.

"He's babying us," Charlie interrupted.

"I didn't realize it was that bad," said Alex.

"It's pretty bad," said Ed, "but we're sunk without you. I'm sure as shit not going to get us across Boston."

"And Charlie wouldn't last two city blocks on his own—with his bad health and everything," said Alex.

"Damn it, I'm fine!" Charlie snapped.

Ed broke out into laughter before Charlie finished his tirade.

"I was kidding," protested Alex.

"More trees," said Ed, maneuvering the Jeep into a field to avoid a large Silver Maple that had upended.

"I don't know if we'll be able to approach Boston on anything too rural," Alex said. "We might need to rethink our plan."

"Route 125 is a four-laner. About the best you're gonna do without linking up with one of the interstates. The 93 would take us down to the northern edge of the Middlesex Reservation. There's an exit in Stoneham," said Charlie.

"What do you think?" asked Alex, looking at Ed.

Ed raised an eyebrow without looking in his direction.

"Hey, I'm trying."

"Just messing with you." Ed chuckled. "I think we should try to stay off the interstate system if possible. If the roads become impassible, we might have to reconsider that. The less police attention we attract, the better. A shot-up Jeep might raise some eyebrows heading south," said Ed.

"*Any* car heading south should raise eyebrows—and questions of sanity," said Charlie.

"That's the truth," said Ed.

"Is anyone opposed to me guiding us to the 125 from here, even if it means crossing the bridge at Haverhill?" asked Alex.

"I think you're making a bigger deal out of Haverhill than you need to," said Charlie.

"You're the one that got me worried about it in the first place, Charlie. You said something about too many people."

"Did I say that?" said Charlie.

"I remember it," said Ed.

"Well, compared to what we've seen so far, it's a lot of people," said Charlie. "There's really not that much by the Basiliere Bridge. A couple of apartment buildings and a small industrial area. It's a wide bridge. No way that sucker is down."

"Then it's off to Haverhill—with your approval, of course," said Alex, turning to Ed.

"You're pushing it," Ed grumbled.

"That's what Kate always tells me."

"Maybe you should listen to her a little more."

"Touché," remarked Charlie. "The truce lasted a whole three minutes."

Chapter 33

EVENT +35:04 Hours

Stoneham, Massachusetts.

The outskirts of Stoneham reeked of campfire. Alex swept the southern horizon with binoculars, seeing nothing but scattered billows of gray and white against a sun-bleached sky. If Boston had been set ablaze, they should be able to see it from here.

Ed squeezed the Jeep between a downed tree and a stranded delivery truck. Like most of the trees they had seen south of the Merrimack River, the leaves had been stripped from the few remaining branches. No effort had been made to clear any of the obstacles. Damage to the buildings and houses remained subtle—shattered windows, peeled paint, and an increasing number of roofing tiles on the ground—but Alex could sense there was more. They were getting closer to the impact area.

A red Audi sedan approached from the south, swerving into their lane to avoid a distant tree.

"Slow down," Alex cautioned. "This idiot's all over the place."

"I don't like stopping with all of these peop—Shit!"

Alex slammed against his seatbelt, losing his grip on the binoculars. The Audi veered left across the centerline, missing them by less than a car length. Beyond tinted glass, he caught a glimpse of a young couple arguing over an unfolded map. A rear-facing baby carrier sat stuffed between tightly packed bags and gear. The sedan scraped the branches of the tree behind them, barely squeezing through the same opening Ed had just navigated.

"Fucking idiots," hissed Ed.

A smaller group of people broke out of the thick stream of people several feet away. Alex stuck the barrel of his rifle through the window, making sure it couldn't be missed. The sudden appearance of a military-grade rifle stopped the men at the curb.

"Ed, get us out of here, please."

Beyond the Interstate 95 overpass, Route 28 widened into a four-lane road separated by a grassy median. Trees flattened by the east-to-west wind lay across the northbound lane—only the tallest reaching into the southbound road. They drove unopposed until the road narrowed, channeling them onto Main Street. Three-story, red-brick buildings lined the street, pushing the dense parade of refugees off the narrow sidewalks into their path. Ed drove slowly through the sea of people. The evacuees focused their energy on keeping their families and possessions together, jostling between parked cars and decorative light posts toward perceived safety. An occasional belligerent emerged to find the barrel of a "black rifle" pointed at their head.

An undercurrent of fear and tension crackled just below the surface. Alex had seen all of this before. Furtive looks and quick movements—the body language. He could feel it, and the exodus was in its infancy. Blue and white flashing lights peeked through the swarm of moving bodies. Alex lowered his rifle.

"Police at the intersection," he said.

Main Street opened into a wide intersection bordered by a small common area featuring two green benches under branchless trees. The Town of Stoneham police cruiser sat facing them in the middle of the intersection. Alex passed his rifle to Charlie, keeping it low.

"Bury the rifles fast! Go to the right of the car," said Alex.

"Shouldn't I stop at the intersection?" said Ed.

"The light's been torn off the pole. Just keep going."

The cruiser's siren stabbed the air, thinning the crowd between the two vehicles. Another shrill burst emptied the intersection. Two police officers stood to the right of the vehicle, behind the open driver's door. The closest officer stepped in front of the door and motioned for them to pull up while his partner pulled a shotgun out of the front seat and leaned it against the top of the door. Alex opened the glove box and grabbed his pistol, tucking it behind his back.

"If this goes bad, it's on me. You just get as far away from the shooting as possible," whispered Alex.

"What the fuck are you talking about?" Ed hissed.

"That's good right there!" said the officer, resting his right hand on his holster. The officer walked forward, stopping even with the driver's-side window. "Not a good time to be heading south, gentlemen."

"I couldn't agree with you more, Officer, but our kids are trapped in Boston. We want to bring them home before things get crazy," said Ed.

The cop took a few more steps and looked into the back seat for several seconds. Alex hoped he didn't walk around the Jeep. The back and passenger side sported several bullet holes that would attract far more attention than a full complement of busted windows.

"I'm just keeping these two out of trouble," said Charlie, holding his hands up.

"Doesn't look like that worked out so well," he said, sticking his hand through the window behind Charlie.

"We ran a militia checkpoint at the Maine border," blurted Ed.

"These people are headed for a frosty reception up north," added Charlie.

"Everyone remembers the fires that broke out during the pandemic. The riots. They're trying to get ahead of it this time," said the officer, motioning to the crowds.

"I give it a few days," said Alex.

"I don't know. Take a look around. A quarter of these people are carrying concealed weapons. Some don't even bother to conceal them. We're just here for show at this point. Same with the marines down along the river," said the officer.

"Sometimes that's all it takes. I was with the marines outside of Baghdad in 2003. We did show-of-force missions like this all the time. One Humvee and four marines could keep an entire city block from reaching critical mass," said Alex.

"Yeah, well, I don't have a fifty cal mounted to my police car. When this goes to shit, we're out of here," said the officer.

"You need to be long gone before that, Officer," said Alex.

"We can't leave yet."

"The first rock thrown at your car, the first tough guy that doesn't back down after you've drawn your pistol, the first bullet fired in your direction—you get the fuck out of here. Two pistols and a shotgun will buy you a minute tops if this goes crazy. A fifty cal might buy you two or three more. We learned that the hard way."

The officer stared at him and nodded. "All right. Good luck, guys. You need to be really careful with this thing down past Medford. Someone will blow your brains out for it. No warning. We've seen a lot of cars with blood-splattered windows."

"Appreciate the heads up, Officer—Kennedy," Alex said, studying his nametag. "Any relation to—"

"You think I'd be driving a patrol car?" interrupted the officer. "Be careful down there. Don't flash any of that hardware until you have to. I assume everything you have buried under the blankets is legal in Massachusetts," he said, patting Ed's door and stepping back.

"Perfectly legal," said Alex. "Thank you, Officer Kennedy."

Ed drove them through the intersection, picking up speed on the wider streets beyond the downtown area. Alex twisted and looked directly behind his seat.

"What the fuck, Charlie? I can see one of the goddamn barrels sticking out of the blanket."

"I had my hand over it!" said Charlie.

"You raised both hands—right when the cop looked in your window!"

"Hey, I didn't have a lot of time to hide this shit. You threw your rifle at me. What the fuck was I supposed to do?"

"Uh, I don't know. How about make sure the barrel isn't visible? That's probably at the top of the list."

"Well, nothing happened," said Charlie. "It's over."

"Because we got lucky," muttered Alex.

They rode in silence until the Jeep slowed in front of an empty gas station. Alex compared the GPS map to the street sign next to his window. A vast stretch of naked trees flanked the road ahead.

"This looks like the beginning of the Middlesex reservation. It's less than a mile to the turnoff," said Alex.

"This isn't going to work," said Ed.

"What isn't?"

"We can't hide the Jeep with this many people around. Especially with the trees stripped like this," said Ed, slowing the Jeep.

"Yes, we can," said Alex. "I'm seeing plenty of scrub and smaller trees with leaves. We'll go a half mile in if we have to."

Ed shook his head and repeated, "Not with this many people around."

"We'll be fine."

"If we lose the Jeep, the plan is screwed, Alex," Ed insisted.

"Ed, we'll be fine. The entrance to the parking area is less than a mile away. GPS shows a road off the parking lot heading deeper into the reservation. We'll find a path off that road and hide the jeep. Nobody's out for a nature hike today."

"People will see us turn into the park—and they will look for us. It's hard to hide a Jeep behind twigs."

"Then what do you think we should do?"

"We've gone this far without any trouble. I say we go for it."

"Go for what?" said Alex.

"Try to drive through to the kids," said Ed.

"Are you kidding me, Ed? This is not—no, I'm about to lose it here. Don't take this the wrong way, but—"

"Shit. Here we go," mumbled Charlie.

Alex turned to face him. "Feel free to weigh in on a decision once in a while."

"These are your kids," countered Charlie. "The two of you need to work this out—and fast."

"There's nothing to work out! You heard what the cop said. Marines are running the show north of the Charles. How's that gonna work when we get stopped in our most conspicuous vehicle? 'Just driving a car full of military grade weapons across the river. Nothing to see here, Sergeant.' Add to that a million plus people staring out of their apartment windows, all thinking the same thing: 'Wish I could trade this gun for a car.' Then along comes a four-wheel-drive vehicle with Maine plates! You want to try to drive this thing all the way through, go for it. It's your car. Just drop me off up here with my shit, and I'll walk it. Switzerland back there can stay with you if he wants a bullet in the head. Sorry to force you into a decision, Charlie."

"Charlie?" asked Ed.

"Yes?"

"What do you think?"

"I don't think this is my—"

"Bullshit, Charlie. You're making it worse by not weighing in," said Ed.

"I agree," said Alex.

"First time we've agreed in a while," said Ed. "Charlie, we're coming up on the turnoff. I know you have an opinion."

"You sure you want to hear it?"

"Yes," both Alex and Ed responded.

"We need to hide the jeep, even if it means walking an extra mile or two to make sure it won't be found."

"All right. We ditch the Jeep in the reservation," said Ed resignedly.

"The turnoff should be right—there," said Alex, pointing at a granite slab etched with "Sheepfold Middlesex Reservation."

Ed turned the Jeep and edged forward, clearing people out of the way. A few fists pounded the hood in protest, but nothing serious materialized as they forced their way through the refugees.

"Chandler Road should be on the left, just after the turnoff for the parking lot. Anyone following us?"

"Negative," said Charlie.

Alex handed him the binoculars. "Make sure."

"All it'll take is one downed tree on this road to stop us," said Ed. "There's no room to go around."

"Most of the trees we've seen down are smaller than this," Alex said, failing to hide the doubtful look on his own face.

Chandler Road ran east/west from the parking lot to the reservoir, following the same directional axis as the air blast. Any flattened trees should land within the forest. Alex was more concerned about the eight-hundred-foot north/south stretch along the reservoir, where an upended tree could fall laterally across the road, blocking them from reaching Middle Reservoir Road.

Middle Reservoir Road was the only route he could find on the GPS plotter that could take them west, deeper into the reservation. What were the chances that an eight-hundred-foot north/south-oriented section of road in the middle of a forest preserve would be clear?

"Up there," said Alex, pointing toward an unmarked dirt road. "Watch the road behind us, Charlie. If anyone appears while we're turning, we have a decision to make."

"We're clear," said Charlie, as the Jeep squeezed onto a tight path cut through the trees.

"This is a road?" asked Ed.

"That's what it says. Shit. Can you get by that?"

"Looks like it," said Ed, pulling the Jeep as far to the left as possible without clipping the side mirror on a tree.

Jagged branches scraped against the passenger side of the Jeep, snapping and cracking as Ed coaxed them past a massive, torn branch. A ruler-sized piece popped into Alex's lap.

"Dead?" he said, snapping it with little effort.

"Root system looked fine. Shallow, but healthy," said Charlie.

Alex examined one of the pieces more closely, rubbing it between his fingers. "I think this was singed," he said, passing it back to Charlie.

"I don't know. But it's definitely dried out," Charlie said, sniffing it. "Smells a little smoky."

"Everything smells like that. Right or left at the reservoir?" asked Ed.

Alex looked up at the calm, glittering water ahead. "Left. This has to be damage from the blast," he said, holding up the branch. "I don't see any leaves on the ground—anywhere. I bet the leaves burst into flames from the initial flash, and the air blast extinguished the fires a few minutes later, like when you blow out a candle."

"Look at the bushes. Totally fine," Ed noted.

"The treetop fires would be caused by thermal radiation. Like a sunburn," said Alex.

"A really bad sunburn," said Charlie.

"SPF 1000 bad. The radiation only lasts for milliseconds, so the leaves probably blocked most of it from reaching the ground. I bet we'll find some burnt spots where the trees thin out," said Alex.

"I think this is the end of the road," announced Ed.

The Jeep stopped in front of a one-and-a-half-foot-diameter tree trunk raised two feet above the ground—pitched perfectly across the ten-foot-wide dirt path. The top of the tree lay in the calm.

"No problem. We can get this thing out of the way in a couple of minutes unless it's jammed in the trees on the other side," said Alex, hopping down from the Jeep.

Charlie winced. "We should have brought my chainsaw."

"I thought about it. Charlie, keep an eye on the road behind us. Ed, I'll need your help."

"Got it covered," said Charlie, pulling his rifle out of the pile stuffed under the blanket.

Alex walked to the back of the Jeep with Ed and opened the rear gate. He moved the red gas containers and dug underneath the blankets. His hand emerged holding a thick coil of royal blue boating line.

"I just hope it can handle the strain. We'll have to go really easy."

They tied the thick rope around the tree at the closest point to the water's edge.

"We tie the other end to the bumper and ease the Jeep back as far as we can go until the line starts to slip," said Alex. "You're driving."

"I'm always driving," said Ed.

Ed kept the Jeep's motion smooth, pulling the tree slowly. The tree resisted initially, as it broke free from the reservoir's muddy grip. Alex gauged the strain on the line, guiding Ed with hand signals. When they had finished the first round, the tree lay mostly in the road, branches aimed at the Jeep. Ed craned his head into the passenger seat to gauge their effort.

"I still can't get through without flipping this thing into the reservoir," he said.

"We're not done yet. We'll wrap the line around the thickest tree we can find on the left side of the road—"

"Pulling the tree from a different angle," finished Ed.

"Elementary, dear Watson. Elementary—in theory," said Alex.

Ed smiled for the second time Alex could recall today.

"We're gonna make it," stated Ed, nodding gently.

"Still have a long way to go—but yes. I don't see anything stopping us."

"I wish I had more of your optimism," said Ed.

"I'm just better at ignoring reality," said Alex, slapping his shoulder lightly.

Chapter 34

Acton, Maine

Eli Russell's feet hit the pavement before the pickup truck had skidded to a halt. Dave Connolly, a grizzly, two-hundred-twenty-pound barrel of a man, rushed toward him.

"Eli, you don't want to see this. We'll get to the bottom of it. I promise," he said, holding up two hands.

"Touch me and I'll kill you, Dave. Everyone! Out of the fucking way," he said, parting a crowd of sweaty, MultiCam-clad militia.

"Who moved the fucking bodies?" he said, addressing Connolly.

"Nobody moved nothing, Eli. This is how we found 'em."

"None of us touched shit," added the man closest to the pile of bodies.

"Nobody fucking asked you!" barked Eli, pointing a finger at him. "Get control of your men, or I'll find someone else to run your squad."

"Yes, sir," he said, stepping forward. "Buddy, move them to the other side of the street, and wait for instructions. No dicking around over there."

"Do you want them in formation on the road?" asked Buddy.

"Just get the fuck out of your commander's way!" yelled Connolly. "Sorry about that, sir."

The gaggle of AR-15-cradling Maine Liberty Militiamen scattered out of Eli's way, exposing the scene. Lifeless eyes stared skyward, barely visible under a shifting layer of flies. Two of the bodies lay side by side, pulled halfway out of the blood-caked mound of twisted limbs and contorted faces. The sharp smell of feces permeated the humid air. Eli approached his brother's body. His fists clenched. A faint, gravel boot print appeared on his brother's right cheek.

"Nobody touched my brother?" whispered Eli.

"Nobody. I was with the first group here. Sorry, Eli. I don't know what to say," said Connolly.

"You don't say another word. That's what you say," he whispered, fixated on his baby brother's gore-covered face.

Jimmy had been nothing but trouble from an early age, spending a solid chunk of his life locked up in one of the state's correctional facilities. Eli had spent the same amount of time trying to keep him out. He'd always been a good kid with bad ideas. Really bad ideas—which was why he'd been the perfect choice to run the Milton Mills operation. The militia needed vehicles, lots of vehicles, but they couldn't go around confiscating them from the constituency. Not yet.

Selling safe passage across the border to fleeing motorists had been Eli's brainchild from the beginning, along with a few other flashes of genius. He'd dispatched Jimmy's special-missions platoon on two missions within hours of the blast.

First priority was to barricade the crossing at Milton Mills with a skeleton crew. Traffic would be light for most of the morning, as people struggled with the decision to abandon their homes and flee north. The vehicle-snatching operation could afford a short delay while Jimmy personally handled the second task: a series of targeted assassinations focused on the York County sheriffs assigned to patrol western York County townships.

Three of the deputies had been caught at home, stranded without a vehicle. The fourth died in a gas station ambush, sprawled over a map he'd been examining with three good citizens of West Newfield. Jimmy stuffed the four bodies in the trunk of the cruiser, driving it to one of their secure locations. You never knew when a York County sheriff's car might come in handy. Jimmy was always thinking, which was why Eli liked having him around. Sometimes that thinking got the better of him, which appeared to be the case today. Or was this something else? He couldn't tell yet.

"How many of Jimmy's platoon were killed?" he said, walking toward the nearest bridge guardrail.

"Five here. Three on the other side. Two in the middle. One along the riverbank down there," said Connolly, pointing across the street. "Looks like he was knocked over the side. Eleven in all."

"No sign of the twelfth guy? He had six on each bridge. I know that for a fact," said Eli.

"We've looked everywhere. The twelfth guy could have washed downriver if he went over in the middle of the bridge. River's pretty high from the rain."

"Or he was taken prisoner," said Eli.

"Prisoner?"

"Look around you, Dave. This wasn't the work of a rival militia group or band of locals. Only a military Special Forces unit could pull this off. They bottled up Jimmy's people on one bridge somehow and hit them from both ends. Fucking shooting gallery. We'll probably find the survivor gutted by the side of the road somewhere up the road, tortured to death for every last bit of information about our militia. Jimmy probably gave them a good fight, gave them some wounds to lick. I'd want to know everything about the Maine Liberty Militia too. We're up against something sinister here, Dave, and the government is behind it. No question."

"Shit. Should we even be here?" he asked, glancing around.

"They're long gone. In my experience, they shoot and scoot. No way they'd stick around after a gunfight like this. Get your squad to work loading up the bodies in one of the pickup trucks. Not mine. Bring them back to Shapleigh, and take the back roads. We'll do a proper burial with full honors when I get back. I have a few things—"

A blaring horn disrupted his sentence, snapping his head toward the bridge. A white sedan crept forward along the bridge, twenty feet from Dave Connolly's squad of disheveled, pathetic miscreants. Buddy unenthusiastically waved the car off, turning his attention back to a lively conversation among his squad mates. The driver laid on the horn again, this time fully ignored by Connolly's men. Eli's right eye twitched once, and he walked calmly over to the mess of men Connolly called a squad.

Buddy never saw the butt stock that collided against his right cheekbone, shattering half of his face. Mercifully, the trauma caused by the impact switched him off like a light bulb, and he never felt any of the repeated strikes that crushed his head to a pulp between the pavement and the rifle's composite plastic.

Eli heard the car shift gears and tear into reverse, squealing its tires. He raised his AR-15 and centered the ACOG scope's reticle on the driver's head. Blond hair, woman. He fired methodically, exploding the windshield as he walked across the bridge. The back of the car veered left and hit the guardrail, blocking the road. The engine revved desperately as Eli changed magazines and flipped the selector switch to fully automatic.

Voices screamed from the car, followed by frantic movement in the back seat. He drew even with the side of the car and fired an extended burst through the rear passenger window, momentarily intensifying the shrieks of panic. He switched back to semiautomatic and fired three rounds at the lowest exposed point along the driver's right leg, putting an end to the wild engine acceleration. He noticed that the back driver's-side door was open and listened for several seconds. A low sobbing sound competed with the idling engine. A little hide and seek? Oh, this could be fun.

"One, two, three. Here I come. She'll be comin' around the mountain when she comes," he said, walking around the hood of the car. "She'll be comin' around the—"

A woman in white shorts and a purple blouse exploded into view, hurling herself over the side of the bridge before he could shoot. By the time he reached the guardrail, her body had been whisked thirty feet downriver by the rushing water. He fired rapidly, using the white geysers of water caused by each projectile to guide his aim, until one of them erupted red. She was done. He turned his attention to the car. The few intact windows were splattered red. Perfect. Eli wrenched open the driver's door and pulled the woman out by her sticky, crimson-matted hair. She spilled onto the street. That should be enough to keep traffic off the bridge.

Eli Russell stood up and approached Dave Connolly's squad. "Form them up in two ranks for a promotion ceremony."

While Connolly's men fell into place, Eli changed magazines and shouldered his rifle. He nodded at Connolly and turned to face the squad, noting the look of sheer dread on their faces. He kept searching until he found what he needed.

"Mr. Connolly. Third man from the right, back row. Who is he?"

"That's Jeffrey Brown, sir. One of my best."

"He's just been promoted," said Eli, drawing his pistol.

"To what position?" said Connolly.

"Squad leader," said Eli, firing a bullet point blank into Connolly's head. "Eyes forward. Nobody looks at that piece of trash again. You understand?"

"Yes, sir!" they yelled in unison.

"No more happy horseshit in this squad, Mr. Brown. Am I clear?"

"Clear, sir," said Brown, staring straight forward at a point in the distance.

"Front and center, Mr. Brown. This is your squad. Get these bodies loaded up and back to Shapleigh."

"Yes, sir. Permission to speak, sir?"

"Better be good," growled Eli.

"Can I assume they go in the river?" said Brown, nodding at his dead squad mates.

Eli chuckled and patted the young man on the shoulder. "And anyone else that ain't militia material," he said. "Get it done, Brown. And get it done fast. The fewer people that see us here, the better."

"Yes, sir. No witnesses," said Brown.

Eli smiled. "Looks like I picked the right man for the job."

Eli cocked his head and put a hand to his ear. A car approached from Foxes Ridge Road.

"Ambush positions, both sides of the road!" barked Brown.

When the men didn't move, he physically pushed half of the remaining ten men to the shoulder of the road next to the shot-up sedan. "Cover and concealment. Lock it down!"

Eli led the rest of the men to the downslope beyond the opposite shoulder, taking the position closest to the three-way intersection connected to French Street.

"Wait for my command!" he yelled to Brown, who had his hands full positioning his men.

A silver SUV careened into view a hundred yards away, squealing its tires.

"Stand down! Stand down! It's one of ours," said Eli, jumping up onto the shoulder.

Brown followed his lead, waving his arms and rushing into the middle of the road. The right man indeed. By putting himself between the oncoming vehicle and his men, he took the extra step to prevent a blue-on-blue engagement. Eli joined the new squad leader and waited for the SUV to arrive.

"You have prior military experience, Brown?"

"Yes, sir. Five years in the army. Went in right after the pandemic. Left as a sergeant," said Brown. "Heads up, sir."

The SUV stopped inches from Eli Russell, but he didn't flinch or betray any sense of apprehension.

"Sounds like a perfect match. Connolly never said a word about you being a sergeant. Now I know why. Get your men to work," he said, returning Brown's salute.

Kevin McCulver opened the door and slammed it shut.

"Something wrong with your fucking radio, son! We almost lit your asses up!"

"The church is wiped out," he sputtered with a panicked look.

"Not here," spat Eli, grabbing his sleeve and guiding him behind the SUV. "You out of your mind talking about that in front of them?"

"Sorry, Eli. I'm a little fucking spooked by this. No survivors," he said, spotting the pile of corpses. "What the fuck? Same thing here?"

"Get a hold of yourself," said Eli.

"Jimmy?"

Eli shook his head.

"I'm sorry, Eli. We all—"

"No time for that. We have one guy unaccounted for. Bet he was taken for interrogation."

"What?" Kevin said, shaking his head. "Interrogation?"

"Someone took out Jimmy's entire platoon simultaneously at both locations. This is hard-core Special Forces work, and the only reason we'd have a Special Forces group operating in the area is if this whole EMP thing was a false flag operation."

"The meteorite thing seems pretty real," Kevin said cautiously. "There's talk of that all over."

"You talk with anyone that saw it?" asked Eli.

Kevin shook his head. "It's on the ham radio, and we've been getting reports from refugees and the cops."

"The U.S. Army has entire divisions dedicated to deception warfare. Psychological Operations—Psyops. Disinformation could be spread by agents on the ground. Ham broadcasts could be transmitted by aircraft. They've been softening us up for decades, just waiting for the opportunity to declare martial law. It's happening, Kevin," Eli said with conviction. "We need to go to ground and start phase two. Heavy recruitment, by any and all means necessary. I want double the number of people by the end of the week. I don't care how you get them out to the training compound. We've talked about this."

"Got it," said Kevin. "I'll start spreading the word."

"See you back in Shapleigh. Make sure nobody follows you."

"Understood."

Eli got back in his truck and paused. His driver wore a pained look.

"What?" Eli shrugged.

"I don't know how to say this, Eli," said the driver, trembling slightly.

"Just say it, Dan. I'm not in the mood."

"One of our patrols just found Jimmy's son shot dead in front of the East Waterboro Hannigans. Him and a buddy," said Dan, holding out a quivering radio.

"They know what happened?" said Eli, using every shred of self-restraint not to yank out his bowie knife and stab Dan through his protruding gut until every ounce of fat and blood spilled out onto the seat.

"Witnesses say that a group of bicyclists shot them dead and stole their car."

"Bikers?"

"No," Dan said, slowly shaking his head. "*Bicycles.* They're saying it was a bunch of women. Shot Nathan and his friend in cold blood. Left the bikes behind. I'm sorry, Eli, I know that kid meant—"

"Not another word, Dan. Not unless I ask. Which way did they go with the car?"

"Route 5 toward Limerick."

"Take me to Waterboro first. I want to talk to the witnesses. When I'm done there, we'll gather some folks and take a little trip out Route 5 and see what we can scare up."

PART IV

"JUST A WALK IN THE PARK"

Chapter 35

Middlesex Fells Reservation, Stoneham, Massachusetts

Alex pulled three olive-drab tactical ball caps out of his MOLLE assault pack, and handed one over to Ed.

"Try it on."

"Is this our team ball cap?" Ed quipped, pulling it over his hair.

"In a way. What do you think, Charlie?"

Charlie nodded. "I like the subdued American flag patch on the front. Pretty slick."

Alex donned one of the caps and stood next to Ed. "What is your first impression?"

Charlie squinted.

"Don't study us. What are you thinking right now?" said Alex.

"You kinda look like the guys from that old spec ops show. *Strike Down?*"

"*Strike Back.* Great show. Take this and put it on," said Alex, gripping his weapon and moving next to Charlie.

"Ed?"

"Looks like you're in some kind of a uniform, but not really," said Ed.

"Special Forces," whispered Charlie, straightening himself.

"Khaki pants, hiking boots, chest rigs, drop holsters, and long-sleeved, earth-tone shirts. It's the only way we'll be able to walk around in broad daylight carrying rifles. I guarantee nobody will bother us looking like this," said Alex.

"We're like the A-Team! Except for his rifle. Goddamn, I wish you didn't have a .22," said Charlie.

"Easily explained. Welcome to Bravo Platoon, 1st Battalion, 3rd Special Forces Operational Group," said Alex.

"What's our mission?" said Ed.

"Sensitive material recovery at MIT. End of discussion," said Alex.

"Where did we come from?"

"None of your business. HALO jump if pressed," Alex responded. "The government is taking steps to secure vital technology and research."

"Why not have the marines, or whoever is around MIT, do it?" asked Ed.

"Because it's too early for the government to determine if military units were involved in the attack. EMP is a trigger event for 3rd SFOG recovery-team deployment."

"Nice. So, how are you planning to explain my Ruger?"

"You don't get to carry it. You're the technical liaison, a rare addition to one of these teams. Getting you to MIT is mission critical. Let them wonder why."

"What am I?" said Charlie.

Ed snickered. "You're Murdoch."

"Was that necessary?" said Charlie peevishly.

"At least you're not the science geek," said Ed.

"Charlie is the sniper. That's why I had you switch out the EOTech with your thermal scope," Alex explained.

"I hope we don't have to shoot up close or inside. This thing is useless for CQB," said Charlie.

Ed looked puzzled. "What's CQB?"

"Don't worry about it," interjected Alex.

"Close Quarters Battle, techie," answered Charlie.

"I'd watch it. If Alex is the team leader and I'm mission critical—that makes you the expendable one," said Ed.

"He sort of has a point." Alex shrugged, patting Charlie on the arm.

"Thanks."

"Ten minutes," said Alex, checking his watch.

"We've got about two miles in the reservation. Another seven or so to the river."

"It's only 5:20," said Ed.

"I want to get to the edge of the reservation and rest—watch the outskirts of Medford. We do a little surveillance and enter the city around 7:30. Puts us near Cambridge after dark," said Alex.

"Why don't we just leave from here an hour later? Walk straight through," protested Ed.

"There's a catch. Once we enter Medford, we have to move with a purpose. No window shopping."

Charlie and Ed shook their heads in confusion.

"It's a saying. We can't look like we're out for a stroll. A Special Forces team en route to a critical national objective doesn't stop for breaks. You'll be thanking me for the rest. Trust me."

Alex had an entirely different reason to leave immediately, one that had nothing to do with timing. There was no way Charlie would make it to the Charles River—not at the pace they had to maintain in the city. There was no way to say this without an argument. Charlie would insist he could make it, and they'd be left carrying a two-hundred-pound sack of meat when they could least afford to.

Charlie had more than earned the right to be here. He'd been indispensible so far, but it was time for him to assume a different role in the mission. He needed to stay behind to guard the Jeep. Since there was no way to make this suggestion directly, Alex would take a more subtle approach. Sort of.

"Ed, I don't want to sound too crass, but you should leave your keys with the rucksacks. If we get separated, or I can't reach your body for some reason—"

"Can't...can't reach my *body*?"

"Sorry, man, but we have to think of everything. We have no idea what we might find down there. You could fall through a hole. Get cut off from us in an ambush and killed. The same could happen to any of us."

"The Jeep's not exactly invisible from the road. Someone could find the packs," said Ed.

"Nobody will find the packs. If anyone finds the Jeep and somehow figures out that it's functional, they'll never guess that we hid backpacks on the island. They'll be too preoccupied trying to figure out how to hotwire it," said Alex, kicking off his clandestine campaign.

"Why did you wait until now to bring this up?" said Ed, holding up the keys.

"I just thought of it. Sorry, I'll run them out to the packs as soon as I get all of the backup handheld frequencies programmed."

"I can take care of the keys," said Charlie, swiping them from Ed.

"Thanks, man," said Ed.

Charlie set his rifle against the Jeep and waded through the thick brush. Alex pulled Ed behind the Jeep when the sounds of snapping twigs and rustling branches faded.

"I'm going to book ass through the reservation," said Alex.

"What? What are you talking about? Didn't you just say—"

"That was all bullshit," said Alex, "well, most of it."

Ed paused for a moment. "No. You're not—he'll go ape shit."

"There's no other way. You know how he his. He'll kill himself doing this," said Alex.

"He didn't have to come along," said Ed.

"I understand that, but we have to face some realities here, really quickly. If he drops halfway through the city, we're double fucked, unless you're willing to ditch his ass in exchange for Chloe's safety."

"This isn't all on me," said Ed.

"I didn't say it was. If I have to choose between dragging Charlie along and Ryan?" he said, glaring at Ed.

"All right," he groaned. "What do you need me to do?"

"Do your best not to complain. We have to make this look like a normal speed. I'll keep reinforcing how we're going to pick up the pace once we hit Medford—like hard-core Special Forces operators."

"Was all of that cover story bullshit just for his benefit?"

"Negative. You're still the team's geek. We say our third guy landed in the reservoir. Couldn't get untangled and drowned."

"No way this will work."

"Trust me. It'll work—if we don't kill him by accident in the next fifteen minutes. You didn't see him at the bridge. Looked like he was having a heart attack or something," said Alex.

"You looked a little rough yourself," said Ed.

"You didn't see the inside of the church. I'm running him into the ground. Stay hydrated."

The bushes near the front of the Jeep shook for a moment and parted, revealing a huffing, red-faced Charlie. A dark brown sweat stain formed a thick ring around his neck. Alex raised a thumb in approval, and Charlie nodded, wiping his face with his sleeve. Ed cast Alex a disapproving look, shaking his head.

"Shouldn't you get those frequencies programmed?" he whispered.

"I did that before we left Scarborough," said Alex.

Ed cocked his head. "I hope you're not planning to ditch my ass at some point."

"Not unless you keep pissing me off." Alex winked. "Here he comes."

"I put the keys in Ed's pack. Hot out, huh?" Charlie panted.

"Perfect—and you tied an IR chemlight to the bag. I think we're ready to step off," said Alex.

"Chemlight? Shit—I didn't think to do that," said Charlie.

Alex rubbed his chin and grimaced, weighing the fake decision. "Don't worry about it. If we get here before sun-up and can't find the packs, we'll just set a perimeter and wait until it's light. That should be fine. Right?" he said to Ed.

Ed pretended not to hear Alex's question.

"No. No. We need to be able to make a quick departure. The situation out there is too fluid. I'll run one back," said Charlie, handing his rifle to Alex. "Am I even carrying any?"

"You should have two of them in one of the side pouches on your vest. I wrapped a small strip of duct tape around the center," said Alex.

"Okay. I remember those," he said, patting his vest and turning.

"Better make sure. You don't want to make two trips," said Alex.

Ed shot him a glance, and Alex mouthed, *What?*

"No. I remember you giving them to me," he said over his shoulder. "Be back in a minute."

Alex waited until Charlie disappeared beyond the foliage.

"I give him one mile."

Chapter 36

Middlesex Fells Reservation, Medford, Massachusetts

A droplet of sweat dangled from the brim of Alex's hat, flying over his shoulder when he checked on Charlie. The man had to be close to his breaking point. A dark ring of sweat had formed around the top of his thick nylon tactical vest, spreading past the protruding chest-mounted magazine pouches and extending halfway down his half-rolled shirtsleeves. The shadow of perspiration had even reached his pants, darkening his crotch and upper thighs. Sweat poured in a steady stream from the tip of his hat as he sucked at the CamelBak valve. Alex suspected that Charlie's body had expelled more fluid in the past thirty-two minutes than it had accepted. He couldn't possibly last much longer at this pace.

He tapped Ed on the shoulder and slowed the pace enough for Charlie to catch up.

"How we doing back here, Charlie?"

He knew the answer from the look on Charlie's beet-red, pained face.

"I think...I think I'm going to need a short break," he huffed. "Just five minutes to adjust my gear, catch my breach. Less than that, probably. Just a quick one."

"All right. We should get all of our breaks in now, before we hit the city. We won't be able to stop there," said Alex. "Ed, let's hold up for a few minutes."

Charlie stopped midstride, nearly falling over. He put both hands on his knees and breathed deeply, blowing air out of his mouth.

"Grab some earth for a second," said Alex, lowering himself to the ground.

Ed slid his backpack to the worn, grassy trail and took a seat on the ground next to Alex. He shot Alex a dirty look when Charlie buried his head in his hands and sighed. Alex shrugged his shoulders.

"It's hotter than balls out—another reason I'm in no hurry to hit Medford. Trees are the only thing keeping my undies dry, even with the leaves gone," said Alex, smirking at Ed.

"Too late for that," said Charlie into his hands. "My nuts are chafing like a son-of-a-bitch. That's why hunting season's in the fall. Fuck this weather."

"I think it's still hot down south when the season hits," said Alex.

"Well, they're idiots for living down there," said Charlie, laughing at himself.

"Ed?" said Alex.

"Miserable, but good to go. Pace is about right. I could pick it up if we had to," he said.

"We'll keep the pace where it is. We've got about another mile and a half to the edge of the reservation. Then an hour of rest before we push through to the river," said Alex. "Everyone ready?"

"I guess," said Ed.

"Yep. I'm good," muttered Charlie.

Alex raised himself off the ground using one hand. He readjusted his rifle, positioning it across his chest for quick access. Charlie struggled to get up, and Alex offered him a hand, picking up his pack at the same time. He helped Charlie slide into the pack, pulling on a few of the straps to tighten it.

"Thanks, man. I feel like an old-timer. I really hope I'm not slowing us down," said Charlie, slinging his rifle over his shoulder.

"This is a good pace for now. Remember to drink while you walk. Little sips. You're leaking water like a sieve," said Alex, patting him on the back.

Ed cast him a critical look as he passed them. Alex mouthed a kiss and winked as he stepped around Charlie.

"All right, ladies, step it out," he said, picking up the pace, resigned not to look behind for ten minutes.

Eleven minutes later, Alex risked a glance back to find Charlie more than twenty-five yards behind the group. This had to be it. His walk was labored, and he sucked air through his mouth. One way or the other, Alex would send him back. Another five minutes might kill him.

"Hold up," he said and jogged back to Charlie.

"I'm-I'm good," Charlie barely managed.

"Charlie, look at me," said Alex.

Charlie raised his head, tears streaming down his deep-red face, building momentum with each bead of sweat they absorbed.

"I d-didn't want to let you guys d-down," he stammered.

"You didn't let anyone down, Charlie. Let's get this off you," he said, removing Charlie's backpack. "Come on, let's grab a seat. There's a tree trunk with your name on it right over here."

Alex helped Charlie to a decayed tree at the edge of the trail. He dropped Charlie's pack and opened one of the top Velcro compartments, pulling a spare water bladder from the pouch. He removed Charlie's drenched ball cap and opened the CamelBak spigot, holding the bladder above his head and showering Charlie's sweat-matted hair with water.

"God, that feels like heaven. I'd jump in the reservoir back there if I didn't have to take all of this shit off and put it on again," said Charlie.

"I thought about it too," said Ed.

"You guys aren't the only ones," Alex admitted. "I want you to drink the rest of this water. I think you're a few steps away from heat stroke." Alex paused a moment. It was now or never.

Sorry, Charlie.

"We need to get you rehydrated, rested up—and send you back to the Jeep," said Alex.

Charlie looked down. "I was afraid you'd say that."

"We wouldn't have gotten this far without you, Charlie. There's no doubt about that, but you have to sit this one out. We need you one hundred percent combat effective for the ride back to Maine, and we need the Jeep to be here when we get back. We might need you to bust out of here and pick us up further south. Most importantly, I need to make sure you return to your family."

Alex kneeled in front of Charlie and grabbed both of his shoulders. "Look at me, Charlie."

Charlie slowly looked up, eyes filled with tears.

"I couldn't ask for a better friend, Charlie, which makes this a tough call. I know how much being here means to you."

"I'll still be here," said Charlie, straightening up a little.

"And you're still the team's sniper," added Alex.

Charlie wiped his eyes. "You guys should get going. I can find my way back to the Jeep. The kids are waiting for you."

"We can spare fifteen minutes to make sure you're back in business," said Alex.

"Thanks, man. I'm really sorry about this. I really thought I could make it. I'm glad we figured this out now. Not later."

"Me too, and quit apologizing," said Alex, patting him on the shoulder. "You sure you can get back all right?"

"I'll take it super easy. East Dam Road all the way to the southern tip of the reservoir. We marked off the only confusing point with one of the IR chemlights. I'll be able to find that. It's a no-brainer from there. Follow the reservoir until Middle Reservoir Road—another chemlight—and turn left. The island thingy is right there."

"Sounds like your noggin is working fine," said Alex.

"As good as before," added Ed.

"Nice." Charlie winked.

"We've gone over the radios, but let's do it one more time," said Alex, taking his handheld out of a pouch on his vest. "I have eight channels preprogrammed. One through eight. We'll start out with the first preset. Hit the privacy button and select code 129. If there's too much interference from other users on that channel, go to the next preset channel and do the same."

"Code 129?" asked Ed.

"Yes. Keep shifting channels until we can talk on a quiet frequency. The bad news is that we'll probably be out of range by nightfall. These transmit at three watts, which kicks up the range a bit, but with the urban environment, we'll be lucky to get three to four miles. Each radio has an out-of-range icon here," he said, holding it up and pointing. "They periodically check in with each other to see if they can communicate. The signal ID is unique to the radio set we'll be using, including the spare in the Jeep."

"That's pretty sweet," said Charlie.

"It is pretty sweet. It'll come in handy on the return trip. You'll know when we've wandered back into range," said Alex. "If at any time you feel like you've gotten lost with the frequency shifts, hit the home button, here. It'll send a burst transmission through every frequency, looking for our radio set's signal ID. It'll automatically tune you to the nearest radio's frequency channel."

"Couldn't we just use this function to pick a clear frequency, instead of the presets? One of us serves as the base station and finds a clear frequency, then the others migrate over?" Ed asked.

"The only problem is that it has to search over three thousand channels. It can take time," said Alex.

"How long does it take?"

Alex paused to consider Ed's question. "You know—you're right. It doesn't take that long. Twenty, maybe thirty seconds for a full sweep. Let's start out with the presets, and if that doesn't work out, we'll switch to Ed's method. Ed's radio will serve as the base station. Charlie, you'll need to keep the radio on, with one of the earpieces in at all times—even if you have to sleep."

"I won't be sleeping," said Charlie.

"When's the last time you slept?"

"I think I got an hour last night, or maybe—"

"You're gonna fall asleep. You can snort the MRE instant coffee all night like a junkie, and guess what? You'll still crash at some point. You're better off doing it on your terms. Give yourself three to four hours, and make sure you set up camp away from the Jeep," said Alex.

"No way I'll be able to sleep out there."

"Charlie, if I started singing 'rock a bye baby' right now, you'd be out before I finished. We'd all be out. It's been a long two days. Set up some kind of trip wire on the path leading to the Jeep. There's a spool of yellow wire in the duffel bag. About four hundred feet. Came with the invisible dog fence we never installed. Run it tight around some trees, and tie it to something you keep wedged under your head. Nothing that makes noise. You good?"

"I'm good," said Charlie.

"Spare radio is in the glove box, along with a car charger. You shouldn't need either, but do what you have to do to keep the radio up. I'll leave the satphone with you," he said, digging into his backpack.

He pressed the "on" button and watched the screen, shaking his head. "I don't get it. The phone says it's tracking two satellites, but it won't place a call. Iridium has over fifty satellites in orbit. Even if a few of them got fried, there should be coverage like the GPS—unless they rely on ground stations to function," said Alex, handing Charlie the phone.

"Or the military commandeered them," said Charlie.

"Or that. Give it a try every few hours."

Alex paused, trying to think of something useful to say. He took a long sip of water to kill a few more seconds.

"You two don't plan on babysitting me for the full fifteen minutes do you?" asked Charlie.

"We don't want to run off and—"

"Go get your kids," Charlie interrupted. "I got it from here."

"You sure?"

"Better than waiting around with two nervous Nellies," Charlie snorted. "I'll be back at the Jeep in no time."

"You'll drink plenty of water now and when you get there?"

"No, I thought I'd do jumping jacks until it was dark. Then start a campfire and blare music across the reservoir. Maybe go skinny dipping!"

Alex raised an eyebrow at Ed.

"Holy shit! Will the two of you get the hell going? I've got it under— Oh, hold on! Let me give you the thermal scope," Charlie said, fumbling with his rifle.

"I really can't do anything with it," said Alex. "It's not zeroed for my rifle."

"You can hold it in your hand and look through it, right? Damn. Maybe we should spend the next fifteen minutes building a litter so you can carry me along to do all of your thinking."

"Now that would be a sight," said Ed, laughing.

"Funny," said Alex. "You sure you won't need this?"

"Nope. All set. Night vision goggles should do the trick," said Charlie, patting one of the pouches on his backpack.

"Thanks, bud. This should come in handy," said Alex, wrapping the scope in a T-shirt and stuffing it into his pack.

"So—we're off?" he said, extending a hand.

Charlie took it, and Alex pulled him to his feet, hugging him for several seconds.

"Stay out of trouble," uttered Alex.

"Same to you," said Charlie, pulling Ed into the huddle.

"You're not going to kiss me, are you?" inquired Ed, his head on Charlie's shoulder.

"Well, now that you mentioned it—no. Get out of here before I change my mind," said Charlie, releasing them.

Alex saluted him and followed Ed down the path, glancing back at Charlie a few times, until the trail veered left and their neighbor disappeared.

"We can slow down now," said Alex, taking the lead.

They walked in silence for fifteen minutes, pushing their way through broken branches and climbing over fallen trees, until the trail intersected "Red Cross Path." Alex shifted his rifle to a ready position across his chest and slowed the pace, peering through the trees. A few minutes later, he spotted the faint outline of a neighborhood ahead. He crouched behind a tree on the left side of the trail, signaling for Ed to get behind him.

"I thought we had another hour and a half," whispered Ed.

"What was I supposed to say? We're almost there? We made better time than I expected from the Jeep. GPS has been coming in and out with the trees blocking the signal. I almost choked when I saw how far we had made it on the first half hour."

"Shit. I really thought we had at least an hour to go," said Ed.

"You can walk back and forth for another forty-five minutes if it'll make you feel better."

"That's quite all right. So now what?"

"We move about a hundred yards off the trail and very cautiously approach the edge of the neighborhood. We'll wait there until 7:30 or so," he said, checking his watch. "Eat dinner, take a nap. We have some time to kill."

"You sure we can't press on? Doesn't look like an urban kill zone up there. More like Durham Road," said Ed.

Alex scanned beyond the trees through his riflescope. "White, two-story colonial with attic bump-outs. Red garrison. Three-car garage. I see what you mean," he said, lowering into a crouch and listening.

Dead silent.

"Charlie gave me the impression that this gets crowded really fast as we move south. Hold on," he said, activating his handheld radio. "Charlie. You there?"

"Miss me already?" Charlie responded immediately.

"Not exactly. Quick question. Where does it get really crowded on our route south? We're thinking about pushing through when we get to the edge of the forest."

"You'll probably exit the forest at the top of Governors Avenue. It's pretty swanky all the way to High Street. Nice little downtown area along High. Expect people. The Mystic River is just past High Street. It really starts to get busy over the river. You'll have a lot of people displaced from the areas closer to the coast. Shit. Come to think of it, you might have some trouble getting across the Mystic because of the tsunami."

"Seems like plenty of bridges to get across," said Alex.

"Yeah. Those can be fun," said Charlie.

"Not looking for that kind of fun. Any other places to hole up on the way?"

"Lots of athletic fields and small parks. Tufts University has a fairly large campus. Nothing you can get lost in like the Middlesex Reservation. Once you cross the Mystic, you're in the city."

"Got it. Thanks, Charlie. Let's use call signs from now on. Lots of Eds, Alexes and Charlies out there. Use our former street name followed by street number. If you need to authenticate a transmission, ask for the other person's wife's name, or one of the kids. That should keep any impersonators busy. Durham three-zero, signing out."

"Solid copy, three-zero. Durham one-seven standing by," said Charlie.

Alex shook his head. "Sounds like a no-go on leaving the reservation. Charlie didn't think we'd find anything like this on the way. I miss him already. Never thought I'd say that."

"Me either, but you made the right call. No way he could have made it. Not to Boston and back," said Ed.

"The Best Western parking lot sealed it for me. I knew he'd have trouble once we ditched the Jeep."

"I would have taken off if you hadn't jumped out to help him," Ed said.

"That's why I jumped out. I couldn't leave him like that, and I knew we'd need him later. It was a calculated risk. Sort of."

"Hell of a risk," said Ed.

"We would have been fine," said Alex.

"I didn't mean you and Charlie."

"I know. I wouldn't have blamed you if you hadn't waited. Family first."

"I'd really hate to catch a glimpse of how your mind works," said Ed.

"It isn't pretty," said Alex. "Right now I'm wondering why this neighborhood is quiet when I can hear commotion east of here. I'm thinking there must be a serious roadblock set up at the hospital. Something we want to avoid."

"The Special Forces story feels a little thin to you too?"

"We need a more chaotic environment for that to work. A focused roadblock in a quiet residential area probably isn't the best place to test our new identities. I'll have to carry your rifle when we roll."

Ed shrugged his shoulders. "Why?"

"Because it doesn't look right as a primary weapon. If anyone asks, or looks at it funny, I can say that it's part of a specialized load-out. A .22 equipped with a suppressor can be extremely quiet. Either that or we leave it behind," said Alex.

"How long did it take you to make that up?" said Ed.

"I started plotting this trip when you told me Chloe was going to Boston College," said Alex.

"Chloe?"

"You didn't think I'd let you make this kind of a trip on your own?" said Alex.

"Amazing. You have this whole thing planned out in there. Don't you?" said Ed, poking Alex's hat.

"I've put a lot of thought into it."

"Do any of those thoughts include ditching me along the way?"

"Not yet. Let's find a spot out there and rest up. It's going to be a long night."

Chapter 37

Limerick, Maine

Kate set her beer on the wooden coffee table in front of her and collapsed into the cushioned chair between Linda and Samantha, the constant pain from her quadriceps and thigh muscles governing the discordance of complaints her body had lodged against her. Shoulders, lower back, wrists—all vying for her attention but failing to take her mind off the fact that she could barely walk. The sun had dropped below the tree canopy, casting a shadow over the screened porch and dropping the temperature a few degrees—not enough to bring any real relief to the humid evening. She closed her eyes and thought about Alex. He'd set out with Ed and Charlie soon.

She was jarred out of her thoughts by the sound of a chair scraping along the deck. Her father-in-law dragged a chair over to them from the patio table.

"Mind if I join the ladies' club for a few minutes?" he asked, placing a cooler on the floor next to his chair.

"Not if that's another round of beers," blurted Samantha. "Did I actually say that? I'm sorry, Tim. Two beers appears to be my limit tonight."

"This is the most I've seen her drink since I can remember," said Linda, laughing. "Tim, I have to thank you and Amy again for everything. We're all still a little legless from the ride, but we'll be earning our keep tomorrow," she added.

"Same with my crew," said Samantha. "We'll turn to in the morning and make breakfast for everyone. We should set up a rotation, if that's all right with Amy."

"I don't think you'll get an argument from Amy. Retirement for her meant retirement from all domestic duties. I must have missed that in the original contract," said Tim.

"It's in small print on the back page of your marriage certificate," said Linda.

"I'm pretty sure she added it after the fact," said Tim. "Just as well, between you and me."

"Oh shit, he didn't go there," said Samantha.

"He can get worse. At least Amy's out of earshot," said Kate, finishing her beer.

Tim fished a bottle out of the cooler and set it on the table next to the bottle opener. Kate gripped the ice-cold pale ale and held it for moment. She resisted the beer commercial cliché of lifting it to her sweat-glistened cheek.

"We'll be on our best behavior," he said, holding Kate's glance long enough for her to get the message.

"Me too," she said.

"Refresh on the beers?" he said, placing two more on the table. "I always carry bribes."

Samantha raised her new bottle. "To the Fletchers and the best damn dinner I've had in years. I almost felt like none of this was happening."

"Well, the timing couldn't have been better. Harvest is in full swing," said Tim, with a chuckle.

They all broke out laughing, drawing stares from the gaggle of teenagers sitting by the fire pit behind the deck.

"To the apocalypse!" said Linda.

"I'll drink to that," said Kate.

"You'll drink to anything," said Linda, causing Samantha to cackle.

"Here's to the three of you bringing the kids here safely. That's what really counted today," said Tim.

The laughter died off, and they clinked bottles, settling in for a serious talk.

"Should we grab Amy?" said Kate.

"No," Tim said. "She didn't want to hear all of the gory details, and she's worried sick about Alex. Head in the sand is her preferred mode of operation when it comes to the uncomfortable stuff. So…the SUV is in the garage. Best way to keep it out of sight for now. It might be possible to sink it in the pond if we could get it over there at night—quietly. There's not a lot of water access on this side of the pond, aside from the walking path over there," said Tim, pointing past the barn to the flickering points of light visible through the trees.

"The other side has too many houses. All locals," said Kate.

"Nosy locals," said Tim, "and everybody has known everybody for generations. I don't think the BMW would remain a secret for long—especially if someone saw us pushing it into the pond."

"How about the woods?" Samantha suggested.

"Fine for now, but once the foliage dies, anyone walking the property could stumble across it," said Linda.

"How worried do we need to be?" asked Tim.

"The kid claimed his dad was some bigwig in one of the local militias," said Kate.

"He said his dad put him in charge of Waterboro, which sounded a little crazy to me," said Linda. "They were sitting around the Hannigans parking lot, throwing back beers like, uh—"

"Like it was the apocalypse, and the rules no longer applied to them," said Kate, tipping her bottle back for a swig.

"His ID says Nathan Russell. Does that sound like anyone Alex met in the York County brigade, or whatever it's called?" asked Tim.

"I have no idea. Name doesn't register," said Kate.

Samantha frowned. "Alex talks to those crazies?"

"He got in touch with the York County group to do an interview for his website," said Kate.

"Thesurvivaldad.com?" said Linda.

Kate nodded. "He went to one of their public meetings down in Sanford. Had a long talk with the founder and a few of his deputies, or whatever they're called. Parts of the interview were picked up by the *Portland Times*. Definitely some tinfoil hats in the crowd, but Alex was impressed with the organization. Whatever we ran across in Waterboro felt different."

"Scary," said Samantha.

"We have to assume the kid was connected to something bigger than a dysfunctional family. He was dead serious about being the new sheriff in town. That's why I drilled him between the eyes," said Linda.

"Jesus," said Samantha.

"She's right. He had more than Budweiser coursing through his veins. He had authority. You could see it," said Kate.

270

"Then we better keep the Beemer in the garage and cover the windows. I'm sure someone saw you roll through downtown Limerick," said Tim.

"We saw a few people milling around the variety store," said Kate.

"Let's hope they didn't recognize you," said Tim.

"We have to assume they did," said Linda.

"Then we have some work to do. Alex has several bins filled with stuff like motion detectors, trip flares—"

"He doesn't have trip flares," declared Linda.

"Oh yes, he does," answered Kate, rolling her eyes.

"—security monitors, weatherproof cameras, spools of insulated wire, relays, inverters," Tim continued. "All kinds of shit down there, and I have no idea what to do with it."

"Don't look at me," Kate said. "That's Alex's show. He's the IT guy at our house."

"Same with Charlie," said Linda.

Samantha smiled. "I think I can help."

"Aren't you a lawyer?" said Kate.

"Not me. Abby. She's all over this stuff at home. Seriously. She reconfigured all of our electronics. Ran wires through the floors and walls for speakers. I guarantee she'll be able to figure out how to get that stuff working. It'll be up to us to figure out where to install it," said Samantha.

"That's the easy part. Alex has it all mapped out," said Tim.

"How much time does he spend on this?" said Linda.

"It keeps him busy," said Kate.

"Sounds like an understatement," said Linda.

"Don't get me started..." said Kate.

"But here we are," said Tim, "in the midst of another disaster, and we're ready this time."

Kate raised her beer. "I'll drink to that. He was right again."

"If you don't mind, Samantha, I'd like to show Abby the map Alex produced and let her dig around those boxes. Tomorrow," said Tim.

"Absolutely."

"Maybe she can make sense of the backup solar power system. The battery banks stopped taking any charge after the power went out. Either the EMP fried the panels, or the charge controller got hit. Probably both. Alex has backups for everything, all disconnected from the grid or any wires that could conduct EMP energy. He felt pretty confident that the backup could be used after an EMP attack. The solar panel bank on the roof of the barn is not connected to anything. It should be fine. I didn't want to connect it to the battery bank without Alex's help. If he's a day or two out, it might make sense to try to get the system up and running, especially if we're going to hook up all of this surveillance gear. I have no idea what kind of strain that stuff will put on the remaining battery charge."

"Until we get it figured out, we should run patrols along the perimeter," said Kate.

"Tomorrow. We'll be fine tonight. There's a room for every family upstairs. Ethan and Kevin will share a room. Amy and I will take the small bedroom. We can move some beds around and make it work. We can lock the door at the top of the stairs," said Tim.

"I'll sleep down here, with my friend," Linda said, nodding at one of the rifles set against the screen porch frame.

"Same with me," said Kate.

"I'll take a real bed upstairs," said Samantha, draining her beer.

"You'll be lucky if you make it off the porch," said Linda.

"I think I'm ready for bed right now."

"You've had a long day. Why don't we finish up here and get the kids inside," Tim suggested.

"I wouldn't bother them unless we have to," said Linda.

"Once the sun hits the treetops, the mosquitos take over. Kevin and Ethan are already getting up. Amy will get them situated upstairs, and I'll lock everything up once everyone's inside."

Kate studied her watch, the digital numbers fuzzy for a moment: 7:34. She finished her beer and contemplated another, but shook her head. Three would be more than enough. She'd sleep hard tonight. Linda saw her check the watch.

"Do you think they're heading out now?" she asked.

"That was the plan," said Kate. "Clear the outskirts of the city at dusk."

"I hope Charlie had the sense to stay with the Jeep," said Linda. "He's in no shape to hike that far. Not with all that gear."

"Are you serious? Why didn't you say something when we were studying the maps?" said Samantha.

"I tried. You know how he gets."

"It's all fine," said Kate, stopping the argument and drawing their stares. "Alex isn't going to let him hike into the city."

Linda shrugged her shoulders and squinted. "What are you saying?"

"He told me that he'd make sure Charlie stayed with the Jeep," said Kate.

"How was he going to do that?" said Linda, annoyed.

"I don't know. That's all he said," said Kate, willing Tim to offer her another beer.

"When was he planning to ditch Ed?" said Samantha.

"Come on now. Linda, you just said you didn't want your husband leaving the Jeep," said Kate. "And Samantha, do you want Ed swimming the Charles River?"

"He's going to leave Ed at the Charles?" said Samantha, shaking her head.

"I didn't say that," said Kate.

"But you and Alex clearly talked about the Charles River. Ed's not a strong swimmer. Alex knows that. Anything else you want to tell us? He's still planning on getting both of our kids back, right? Not just Ryan?" said Samantha.

"Samantha," scolded Linda.

"It's not like that. He's just worried that Ed might slow him down in the city. Alex is good at this kind of thing. He's done it before," said Kate. "I'll have another beer."

"I think the bar is closed," said Tim.

"Thanks," she said.

"Alex is good at this kind of thing? How long ago was he in the Marine Corps? He better not put Ed and Chloe in danger," said Samantha.

"Is everything all right, Mom?" asked Samantha's son, Daniel, from the steps leading up to the screened porch.

"Totally fine. We're just talking about what the dads are doing," she said, smiling.

"Trust me. That's the last thing he would want," said Kate quietly.

"I hope you're right. Alex isn't the one-man army he thinks he is," whispered Samantha, as the kids entered the porch.

"He knows that," said Kate, not altogether convinced.

Chapter 38

Medford, Massachusetts

Amber rays lingered on the soot-stained, red-brick chimney and vanished. Only the blackened, naked branches of a maple tree beyond the mangled roof reflected the last vestiges of the sun's arc through the crisp summer sky. Alex shifted his binoculars to the loose stream of civilians wandering up Governors Avenue. Perfect.

He popped five ibuprofen pills into his dry mouth and took a swig of water from his CamelBak hose, choking the pills down. Beyond the throbbing arm, his whole body ached. He leaned his head against the tree trunk and took in the last few moments of rest he could expect for the next twenty-four hours.

"Ready?" he said to Ed.

"Shouldn't we wait until that group passes?" Ed asked, peering through the bushes.

"It doesn't matter at this point. We no longer have the option of avoiding people." Alex stood up. "It'll get worse the further we go."

"But we still try to avoid the military or police?"

"At some point it will be unavoidable. I'd like to postpone that as long as possible. Follow my lead and stick close. Remember, I'm escorting you through the city."

"It's a thin story," said Ed.

"All in the delivery, my friend. You'll see," said Alex, helping him to his feet.

He squeezed the remote radio transmit button attached to his tactical chest rig. He had taken some of their time at the edge of the reservation to tape the radio hardware in place to make it easier to use. A black wire led from his earpiece to the button, which was attached to the radio in one of the chest pouches.

"Durham one-seven. Three-two and three-one stepping off," said Alex.

"Copy. All quiet here at the home base. Have fun in the city."

"Three-two looks thrilled," Alex responded. "Stay on this channel for updates. We'll keep them coming as long as we're in range."

"I'll be here. One-seven out."

"That's it?" said Ed.

"That's it. The kids aren't coming to us," said Alex, adjusting his rifle to sit across his chest.

"You're not scared?"

"I'm scared shitless," said Alex.

He stepped out of the forest onto South Border Road, freezing a group of college-aged backpackers in the middle of the street. A few of them raised their hands. He ignored them and crossed the street, his attention drawn to the white colonial they had watched from the forest. The paint was blistered and peeled on the eastern-facing side, something they couldn't see from their hide site in the reservation. Dozens of the wooden siding strips were cracked.

"What does that look like to you?" said Alex, pointing at the house.

"The whole house is sagging," said Ed.

"No, I mean the…shit, you're right," said Alex.

The broken cedar planks formed a rough, diagonal line that ran from the top right corner of the house and disappeared near the middle of a wall, behind a ragged, charred row of evergreen bushes along the concrete foundation. The thick tangle of small branches blocked a clear view of the concrete.

"We didn't see anything like this in Stoneham," he remarked.

"No, we didn't," muttered Ed. "See how the paint's peeled away? What would happen to someone standing outside?"

"Second- or third-degree burns. Let's keep moving," said Alex, pulling at his pack.

"Good thing this happened at five in the morning."

"That's about the only break anyone got with this."

He led Ed down a side street that would take them past the Lawrence Memorial Hospital and any obvious law-enforcement roadblocks. They ran into a few clusters of refugees, all working their way northeast to Interstate 93 or Route 28. Most of the groups had young children. They hopped a low stone wall and crossed a short lawn to reach the corner of a two-story home at the intersection of Lawrence and Ashcroft.

"Hold up here. Lawrence spans most of northern Medford. High traffic potential," said Alex.

"I think rush hour's over," Ed said ruefully. "Permanently."

"You hear that?" asked Alex. A low hum echoed off the darkened houses. "Outdoor generator units at the hospital. Big, portable stuff. My guess is military. We need to watch our asses."

Alex turned and slammed into a man that had suddenly emerged from the corner, knocking both of them to the ground.

"Back the fuck off!" a female voice warned from the shadows.

Alex struggled to his feet, aiming his rifle at the corner.

"Hey, we're not looking for any trouble. Headed north, that's all," said the man, brushing himself off.

Alex backed up and shifted left, bringing the entire group into view. A black and yellow, overstuffed hiking backpack pulled heavily at the husband's shoulders, stretching his sweat-stained, gray T-shirt. With a dark green ball cap pulled tightly over his head, it was hard to pin down his age. The fading light didn't make it any easier. Mid-thirties to early forties probably.

His wife wore khaki, multipocketed shorts and a black shirt, equally burdened by an overstuffed integrated frame hiking pack. Blond hair spilled over her shoulders from under her maroon cadet-style hat. Solid hiking boots and CamelBak hoses completed the couple's REI look. He couldn't see the kids through the parental shield, but they didn't come up past the husband's waist. They wouldn't last very long on the road. He doubted they would make it out of Massachusetts.

"Are you travelling alone?" Alex asked them.

"Just us. We left an hour ago," said the man. "Put the knife away, honey. He has a gun bigger than you."

"Sorry about that," Alex said, lowering the rifle. "Captain Alex Fletcher, 3rd Special Forces Group. We're part of a surveillance team sent to assess the ground situation. Have you seen any other military units in the vicinity?"

"All over the place. There's a big unit at the hospital. That's probably your best bet," said the husband. "Where did you guys come from?"

"North," said Alex.

"We need to get going. We figured the 93 would be less active at night."

"How far do you plan to go?" said Alex.

"We have family up in Concord. It's a straight shot."

"Honey," his wife whispered, pulling at him, "we should go."

"Do you have maps?" asked Alex.

The man didn't answer.

"Stay off the main roads, and avoid any downtown areas," Alex advised. "They're jammed with plenty of people who wouldn't hesitate to cut your throat in front of the kids to take a peek in one of those backpacks. You should plan to stop by nine in the morning. Start looking for a private, shaded spot well before that. The kids won't last an hour in the midday heat. Replenish your water whenever possible. Can you purify water?"

"We have iodine pills," said the husband.

"Try to strain the water through a T-shirt before filling your CamelBaks. Kids don't like to find sinkers and bobbers in their water. Keep a low profile, and don't take any deals that seem too good to be true. We've had reports of militia units doing some nasty shi—stuff further north."

"Jesus," muttered the wife.

"Trust nobody but family. It's getting bad out there," said Alex.

"That's why we're leaving," said the husband. "We've heard the city is out of control past the Charles, and it's about to spill over."

Alex tilted his head, catching the sound of a diesel engine. Headlights flashed along the bushes across Lawrence Road, headed in their direction.

"Grab the kids!"

Alex grabbed both of the parents by their backpack chest straps and yanked them around the corner into a scorched evergreen bush. The kids screamed, causing the wife to break loose and pull at Ed. Alex jerked her backward by her hair, and she screamed.

"Shut up!" he hissed, clamping his hand over her mouth.

Ed managed to corral the kids into the shadows as a large, wheeled military vehicle rumbled past Ashcroft Road, heading east on Lawrence. The woman bit his hand, and he let go, giving her enough leverage to twist around and punch him in the mouth. He grabbed her wrist before she could pull it back to hit him again.

"What the fuck is wrong with you people? Why didn't you want them to see you?" she demanded.

"Avoid contact with any government units if feasible. Make no assumptions. Can you navigate the Middlesex reservation?"

She stared at him, poised to strike again. "What's going on out there?" she asked.

"Nobody knows."

The woman took both children by the hand and pulled them out of the bushes. Her husband stood there, frozen.

"Are you coming? We need to get as far away from here as possible. We should have left yesterday like I said. I *knew* it. If these guys can't even trust each other," she said, pointing at Alex and the distant vehicle, "we're utterly fucked."

The woman grabbed the hand of one of her kids, angrily motioned for her husband to do the same, and they stalked off.

"That went really well," said Ed when they turned a corner. "How's your face?"

"Still have all of my teeth. She bit me. You see that?" said Alex, picking up the pace.

"Can you blame her? 'Grab the kids'?" said Ed. "We're lucky she didn't stab one of us. Hey, on the bright side, you sounded convincing back there."

"That's about the only thing that went right."

"And we didn't get machine-gunned by the truck. Maybe walking the streets with an assault rifle isn't the best idea with armored personnel carriers cruising the streets," said Ed. "Especially at night. Can you break that thing down?"

"I can't hide your Ruger. It's one piece. Carrying a civilian rifle will look even more conspicuous," said Alex.

"More than your SEAL Team Six gun?"

"I'll try to keep it out of sight for now," said Alex. "Once we get over the Mystic, we won't stick out."

"Except we'll be going in the opposite direction," said Ed.

"People will be going everywhere. We'll be fine."

Alex peeked around the corner, scanning the street toward Governors Avenue. A blood-orange band of sky stretched across the western horizon, hanging above the quiet street. A few stragglers moved up the sidewalk in the distance. They'd have to be extremely cautious crossing open spaces, especially streets.

Just hours after the "event," the Department of Homeland Security issued orders to disarm citizens on sight. Thirty-six hours later, those orders might include "shoot on sight" considerations. Armed men sneaking around at night would go at the top of that list. The M240G machine gun mounted to the Joint Light Tactical Vehicle turret would make short work of them, no matter where they tried to hide.

"Just a walk in the park," he mumbled.

Chapter 39

Cambridge, Massachusetts

Alex leaned against a tree and lifted his night vision goggles to check his watch. Four miles in three hours. The pace was agonizingly slow, but it had kept them out of trouble. After Medford, they strictly avoided commercial or business districts, opting for the quiet, pitch-black neighborhoods that most of the refugees avoided. They couldn't avoid crossing major roads, but the continuous migration east toward Interstate 93 kept the main thoroughfares busy, providing enough urban camouflage to slip across and disappear. They'd seen two police cars and one military vehicle during their journey.

"Let's stop here and take a break," said Ed.

The smell of barbequed chicken wafted into the street, chased by raucous laughter.

"Probably not the best place for a pit stop."

Alex took out the GPS plotter and examined the map. "Point eight miles to the Boston University Bridge. We're almost there."

"Alex, I need to stop. We're about to run out of quaint, cobblestone-sidewalk streets to hide on. We need to find a quiet spot to rest up and eat. Try to learn something from the radio traffic Charlie's been able to pick up. He's been hearing about the marines guarding the bridges. We might be wasting our time headed to the BU bridge. Shit, that chicken smells good."

"Judging by the laughter, I suspect the beer isn't bad either," Alex remarked.

Another round of laughter emptied into the street.

"Pretty careless to advertise like this," said Ed.

"Maybe they don't care," said Alex. "There's a park ahead. We'll cut through and find a place to hide."

Alex dropped his night vision goggles back in place and took a moment to scan the street ahead. Most of the three-story homes were pitch black. A few windows flickered bright green, indicating a candle. Nothing out of place beyond careless laughter and the smell of mesquite. He started forward, but the sudden appearance of green glow on the southern horizon stopped him. A deep, distant thumping reached his ears several seconds later, reminding him of a sound he hadn't heard in over fifteen years. The eerie glow flickered and disappeared, replaced moments later by a similar, over-the-horizon shimmer.

"Hear that?" asked Alex.

"Can I say no?" said Ed.

"It's usually not a good idea to ignore heavy-machine-gun fire. Probably the marines, or whoever is down there. I think they're using aerial flares."

"What could possibly require the use of a fifty-caliber machine gun?"

"Zombies," said Alex.

"That's not even funny."

Alex approached the three-way intersection cautiously, weaving them between parked cars. The military vehicles they had spotted in Somerville didn't use headlights, the drivers relying on night vision equipment to navigate the shadowy streets.

"Stay here," Alex instructed. "Sennott Park should be across the street. Sounds too quiet to be another triage center or refugee camp."

He slid along the remaining cars, crouching low and searching for signs of activity beyond the stripped bushes and trees on the other side of Broadway. He could identify a children's playground directly ahead, and something to the left of it that looked familiar. Two bright green lines reached out from the edge of the park, terminating somewhere directly in front of him. He let his rifle hang loose in its sling and raised his hands high above his head.

"Ed?"

"Yeah?"

"Put your hands as high as possible in the air, and step into the street," said Alex.

"Why?"

"So the marines don't kill you. I think we ran right into their headquarters."

"Please tell me you're joking," whispered Ed.

"I'm not joking. They're almost on us. Don't make any sudden moves, and do exactly what they say," said Alex.

A diesel engine roared to life, swallowing his voice. A brilliant light whitewashed the green image of figures moving in his direction. He squeezed his eyes shut, not daring to move his hands to flip up the NVGs. A sizable vehicle screeched to a halt in front of him, a large-caliber weapon most assuredly centered on his body.

"Don't move! United States Marines!" they screamed repeatedly.

He had no intention of moving, not even a twitch. He hoped Ed had the sense to do the same. Rough hands yanked his arms back while others groped for his rifle and pistol. He was disarmed in a matter of seconds. His night vision goggles were ripped from his head; then he was thrown face first onto the cobblestone.

The impact jammed the triple-stacked rifle magazines attached to his tactical rig into his chest and abdomen, knocking the wind out of him. He groaned as his face was pushed into the curb. His wrists were squeezed together, pulled unbearably tight by military-grade zip ties. Sharp surges of pain exploded at multiple points along his legs and sides as his gear was stripped with knives. He struggled, but was hit in the lower back with a rifle stock. The flat end of a bloodied knife was jammed against his right eye, the point digging into his temple.

"Stay down, or I'll cut your fucking eyes out," a voice hissed, the smell of wintergreen chewing tobacco inches from his face.

"Can you believe this fucker was trying to ghost us?" someone called out.

"He's a stone-cold killer," said Wintergreen.

"I wasn't trying—"

The serrated blade pressed into his lips. Alex grimaced.

"Nobody asked for your opinion."

He felt the marine's hot, tobacco-heavy breath against the side of his face before everything faded.

Chapter 40

Harvard Yard
Cambridge, Massachusetts

Alex fixated on the steady rumble of an industrial generator. He pulled at his restraints, confirming once again that he wasn't going anywhere. The marines had stretched him prone and mercilessly secured his limbs to the four corners of the bare metal bed frame with zip ties. Moonlight from the room's single window exposed a dark trickle rolling down his blood-encrusted left arm. His captors had tightened the plastic restraint too high on the wrist, digging into the thicker metacarpal bones.

The slightest movement reopened the wound, yet he still gave the zip ties an angry tug every few minutes—or what he thought was a few minutes. He had no idea. He faded in and out with no true concept of time. He knew it was nighttime, but that was about it. He couldn't tell if it was the same night or three days later. He hadn't soiled himself, so he guessed it hadn't been very long.

He stared at the half-illuminated striped mattress lying across the desk next to his bed, one end sagging out of sight toward the floor. Another desk and bed sat pushed against the wall in the opposite corner. The marines had stripped Alex down to his underwear and left him to rot in a sweltering, stagnant college dorm room.

They'd done exactly what he would have done in the same situation: locked him up for later. They couldn't afford to waste any time or energy on vetting Alex Fletcher. The situation in Boston would continue to deteriorate, occupying more of their attention and resources until the city reached a critical mass, forcing the marines to withdraw. He just hoped they didn't forget about him. They'd have little warning when it happened.

He lowered his head onto the metal frame and prayed for sleep. Anything to get his mind off the fact that he had effectively doomed Ryan and Chloe. Best-case scenario, the marines released them without their gear and they returned to the Jeep to gear up and try again. Worst-case scenario, the city fell apart around the marines and they were forgotten—or discarded. He'd let his guard down approaching Sennott Park. A stupid, exhaustion-fueled mistake that could cost them everything. Alex yawned, welcoming the waves of fatigue washing over him.

The door burst open, causing him to tense against the zip ties. Bright lights focused on the bed; boots shuffled through the room. He turned his head to the right, anticipating a vicious punch.

"Get one of the corpsman in here! What the fuck did you do to this guy?" said a gruff voice.

"He tried to ambush us," said a marine hidden behind one of the flashlights.

A hollow snap dropped Alex's left leg to the bed frame.

"Careful with the snips. You guys already did a number on him," said a staff sergeant, leaning far enough into one of the beams for Alex to make a rank identification.

One by one, the rest of his limbs fell to the steel frame. They felt heavy, almost useless. A CamelBak hose was pressed against his mouth, and he turned away.

"It's just water, Mr. Fletcher."

Mr. Fletcher? They must have checked his ID. He drank from the hose for several seconds, letting the excess water dribble down the side of his mouth onto the black-and-white checkered linoleum tile beneath the bed. The hose tasted like chewing tobacco, but he didn't care. He let the hose drop from his mouth and closed his eyes for a few moments, letting the fluid settle.

"You need to drink more."

"You got one that doesn't taste like Skoal?" said Alex. "Just kidding, sergeant. Thank you."

"This is going to hurt a little," said the corpsman, sprinkling powder from a green packet onto Alex's wrist.

He tried to yank his hand away from the intense stinging, but the corpsman held it in place.

"Fuck, Doc. What *is* that?"

"It's a combination of Celox and disinfectant. The disinfectant part stings a little," said the corpsman.

"No shit," Alex groaned.

"I need to rub this in all of your cuts. I don't have time to wrap all of them."

"Sprinkle away, Tinkerbell," said Alex, bracing for the burn.

"No time for that," called a sharp voice from the doorway. "Battalion commander would like a word with you."

"I need to wrap the wrist, sir. Zip ties cut him pretty deep," said the corpsman, digging through his med kit.

"Tidy up the wrist, and get him down to the TOC (Tactical Operations Center), Corpsman." He turned to Alex. "Can you walk?"

"I should be fine, Captain. They didn't hobble me."

"They should have dropped you dead on the pavement. That little disguise kept you alive long enough to generate some discussion with the platoon commander. You stumbled right into one of our platoon HQs," said the captain.

"My lucky day. What about the other guy on the street with me?" said Alex.

"Mr. Walker is doing fine. Enjoying a cup of coffee with the battalion commander as we speak," said the officer. "Get him down to the TOC, ASAP."

"Got it, sir."

⫷⫸

Dressed in his original clothes, which now featured bloodstained, custom ventilation slits along his right thigh and ribcage, Alex followed Doc and Wintergreen through the cramped dormitory hallway. Deep red chemlights dangled from an overhead wire running the entire length of the floor, bathing everything in a muted, monochromatic crimson aura. They passed an information board titled "Hollis Hall." Alex had studied enough Boston-area college maps to pinpoint their location. He reached up and plucked the wire, glancing behind him at the dancing lights.

"Having fun back there?" said Wintergreen.

"Sort of. Did the battalion take all of Harvard Yard?"

"Shit if I know. I'm not an alumni."

"Alumnus," said Doc. "And no, the battalion just took the buildings in the northwest corner of the Old Yard. It was mostly empty dorms when we got here. Six buildings form a perimeter around a courtyard, chapel in the middle. It's about as good as it gets in terms of a naturally defensible position in the middle of Cambridge. We're spread too thin for anything else."

"Doc's one of the smart ones," said Wintergreen.

"Not smart enough to go here," said Doc, opening a door. "Welcome to Harvard, America's oldest institution of higher learning. Now home to 1st Battalion, 25th Marine Regiment."

Alex stepped into the shadowy courtyard. A large tent was set up under the massive bare trees in the center of the courtyard. A flap opened, spilling bright light onto the grass. Two marines dashed toward the gap between Hollis Hall and a building with a small cupola protruding from its rooftop. Harvard Hall. Alex had reoriented himself quickly. Doc's assessment made sense. The buildings formed a perfect rectangle, with minimum space between separate buildings. Half of the perimeter benefited from the formidable wrought-iron fencing along Cambridge Street. The two marines reached the opening and sprinted past sentries barely visible in the shadows.

"Sergeant, he's all yours. I gotta get back to the triage center," said the corpsman, splitting off.

Alex stopped him briefly. "How bad is it out there?" he asked.

"Bad. Every hospital is beyond capacity and barely functional. Anyone in the city exposed to the flash got second-degree burns. Some of the older buildings collapsed. Lots of partial collapses. Anyone who got up to check on the flash got hit by glass or branches. They're saying it wasn't a fucking nuke, but nobody's buying it. This is exactly what they described in NBC training," said the corpsman.

"Then the EMP," Wintergreen chimed in.

"Then that. Something doesn't add up, and nobody's telling us shit," said Doc. "Good luck, man."

"You too," said Alex.

"Battalion TOC is up here," said Wintergreen, leading him across the grass.

"Where is everyone?"

"Half of Comms Platoon is manning the perimeter here and providing security at the vehicle gate. Medical section is out that way somewhere," he said, pointing at Doc's vanishing profile.

"We have a quick-reaction force made up of some Motor T guys and nonessential battalion staff. Everyone else is out on the streets. I'm headed back to my platoon once you're delivered."

"Which platoon are you with?" asked Alex.

"Indirect fire. 81's."

"No tubes?"

"Thank God, no. Only individual weapons. Pretty light."

"Hopefully you won't need any of it," said Alex, amidst the brief, distant pounding of a fifty-caliber machine gun.

"I'm not hopeful." He turned to a marine standing behind the tree near the entrance. Sergeant Evans with Mr. Fletcher," he announced.

"Go ahead," he heard, followed by a quick radio transmission notifying another marine inside the TOC.

Wintergreen, aka Sergeant Evans, opened the flap, releasing the sound of radio traffic and hurried voices, followed immediately by the pungent stench of stale coffee and perspiration. He could use some of that shitty coffee. Alex ducked into the tent and squinted in the bright light.

Modular folding tables—jammed with laptops, radio receivers, digital plotting gear and maps—ringed the tent. Men and women in Woodland MARPAT uniforms and full combat gear crowded the tables. Some in chairs, others standing—all of them speaking into headsets. To an outside observer it made about as much sense as the floor of the New York Stock Exchange. To the initiated, it signified the right amount of controlled chaos necessary to run a marine battalion. Nobody turned to acknowledge his entry.

A sturdier table divided the tent in half, holding up two immense, side-by-side flat-screen monitors, one displaying a map of the greater Boston area. The other focused on Cambridge and the areas north of the Charles and west of Interstate 93. Icons flashed on each monitor. A movie screen hung suspended from one of the tent's center ceiling braces, extending down to the top of the monitors. The words "No Input" flashed in the center of the blue screen. Two marines sat at the middle table with their backs to the entrance. Ed sat hunched over the far end of the table, cradling a metal canteen cup.

"Sergeant Evans reporting," he said.

A few heads turned, but the noise continued unabated. Ed grinned and started to get up, but stopped when one of the marines seated at the center table stood to face them.

"Thank you for not killing Mr. Fletcher, Sergeant Evans. Dismissed," said the lieutenant colonel.

"Yes, sir," said Evans.

"Yeah, thanks for not killing me," said Alex, offering his hand.

Evans shook it quickly, anxious to get out of the tent. The lieutenant colonel's dark brown eyes fixed him with an unemotional stare. The marine looked familiar, but Alex couldn't place him. A long, lateral scar extended from the top of his cheek to the middle of his ear. His head was shaved clean. His skin was weathered and cracked, thick crow's feet extending past the corners of his eyes. He'd seen his share of the Middle East, Africa and Afghanistan. Either that, or he spent his off hours on the beach. Somehow, Alex doubted that. 1st Battalion, 25th Marine Regiment's commanding officer had that undeniable, "been there, done that" look typical of senior marines. For the first time in years, Alex felt intimidated.

"So, what brings the infamous Captain Fletcher to Boston?" asked the lieutenant colonel.

Alex cocked his head and examined the marine's face, finally recognizing it as one of the last faces he had seen in Iraq. Second Lieutenant Grady had taken shrapnel from the same rocket-propelled grenade warhead that had aerated Alex's body. He'd just given Grady a set of medevac orders when the warhead detonated several feet from Grady's Amphibious Assault Vehicle. Mostly protected by the AAV's one-and-a-half-inch aluminum hull, Grady was hit by a single fragment, which opened his face to the bone.

"Sean Grady?" he blurted.

"About time. Am I that ugly now?" he said, rushing forward to hug Alex.

"Beautiful as ever. Careful, the wrist." Alex winced.

"Sorry about that. You're lucky they didn't light you up out there," said Grady.

"That's what everyone keeps telling me. You've met Ed. Hope he's explained things a bit."

Ed stood up with a pained look on his face.

"Sergeant Walker of the, uh…what was it again?" asked Grady.

"3rd Special Operations Department," stated Ed matter-of-factly.

"Yes. Sergeant Walker of the 3rd SOD," said Grady, raising his eyebrows, "hasn't broken character, despite everything I've told him about you. He's still some kind of spec ops technical advisor, and you're his high-speed, ninja escort."

"You've gotta be shitting me? They have your wallet, Ed," said Alex, shaking his head.

"I don't break easy—unlike *some* people," said his neighbor, taking a sip of coffee and leaning back in a folding chair.

"I can see that. They didn't offer you some cookies to go with that?" said Alex.

"He refused a whole assortment of—"

"Colonel Grady! Fire Support platoon commander requests the QRF (Quick Reaction Force)!" yelled a marine. "Someone just drove a bulldozer through one of the concrete barricades at the far end of Western Avenue Bridge!"

"I want Raven coverage immediately," said Grady, pushing past Ed to one of the tables on the opposite side of the tent. Alex followed, patting Ed on the shoulder.

"How's the coffee, sergeant?"

"Shitty," whispered Ed.

"Welcome to the Marine Corps," said Alex, rushing to keep up with Grady.

"Did they try to drive it across?" asked the battalion commander.

"Negative. Pushed the concrete barrier into the river and stopped. Last pass by the Raven picked up a large group massed beyond Soldiers Field Road. They're partially masked from our sensors. Probably hiding in the underpass," replied the marine.

"Define large," said Grady.

"Thirty to fifty, estimated."

"Launch QRF. Put them on the bridge," said Grady, turning to face Alex and Ed. "This has been going on all day and all night."

"Are you guarding the bridges?" asked Alex.

"Hold on," he said, shifting two tables down.

Two marines sat in front of a laptop monitor, watching a live, panoramic aerial feed.

"I want you scouring the areas beyond the bridges connecting to Harvard Business School. Anderson Memorial, Cambridge Street, Western

Avenue, and Weeks. Any vehicles or groups of people on the move need to be tagged and sent to ground units in the area. Get it done," said Grady, turning back to Alex.

"We're loosely guarding the bridges, trying to restrict traffic. No vehicles. Pedestrians are stopped and searched," said Grady.

"Both ways?"

"One way. Nobody is going south anymore. It's not a very hospitable environment. 1st Battalion, 101st Field Artillery Regiment out of Brockton never linked up with our forward elements. We don't think they made it north of Dorchester or Roxbury. I gave it twelve hours and yanked the marines back."

"You're not talking to the 101st?" said Alex, following Grady back to the monitors on the center table.

"We're talking with 1st Battalion, 182nd Infantry Regiment out of Melrose, and that's pretty much it beyond Homeland and a few local law-enforcement agencies."

Grady stopped in front of the rightmost screen, which showed the greater Boston area broken into color-shaded sections. Everything south of the Charles River was shaded red. He pointed at the north shore.

"First off, the 182nd has everything shaded green. East of the 93, up through Salem. We've got everything shaded blue. 93 west to Waltham. We were supposed to connect with the 101st and help them with the areas west of Kenmore Square, but that obviously fell apart. All the better, really. We're spread beyond fucking thin as it is. Take a look," he said, shifting to the other monitor.

"I've split the Indirect Fires Platoon into two platoons. Same with the Large Caliber Direct Fire platoon. LCDF is lighter on personnel, so I have them working areas outside of the concentration zone. Somerville to Medford. Watertown to Waltham. We're talking thirty marines max per platoon, including some of the guys on loan from the Short Range Direct Fire platoon. We called that the heavy-machine-gun platoon in *your* days."

"That's not a lot of coverage," Alex pointed out.

"It's more of a presence mission," Grady explained. "We're driving around with bigger guns than the criminals. It's working."

"So this is the area of concentration?" asked Ed.

"Sergeant Walker is all over this, Captain Fletcher. Better keep him out of danger," said Grady. "I have four platoons working here. The Fire

Support platoon, with a little heavy-machine-gun help, is spread out along the river, mainly watching the bridges. I have overwatch in the buildings and a 'meet and greet' team on the ground level. The other three platoons are stationed around Cambridge. You ran into one of the HQs at Sennott Park. They cover east of battalion HQ to the 93. We're running vehicle patrols 24/7. Limited 'walk and talks' if the intel section thinks we need to dig a little deeper into one of the neighborhoods."

Alex politely stared at the screen, a single question clawing to the surface. "How were you able to get here so quickly?"

Grady grinned. "False flag rumors have everyone on edge."

"You have to admit it doesn't look good. A marine infantry battalion rolls into town within twenty-four hours of the EMP, with working vehicles and communications gear?"

"Who said anything about an EMP?" said Grady.

"Come on. Asteroid strike? Sounds a little far-fetched combined with a region-wide electrical outage."

"The power outage isn't regional. It's nationwide—and the asteroid strike has been confirmed by local sources. There's something bigger going on, no doubt about that, but we don't have shit for information. We have our orders, and that's about it."

"It still looks suspicious. Mobilizing an entire marine reserve battalion within twenty-four hours?"

"Twelve hours, and it was pure luck, really. I had two of my companies at Fort Devens for the start of annual training. H and S was prepping for the rest of the battalion, while Weapons Company was knocking out some of their heavy weapons quals," he said, shaking his head. "The rest of the battalion was scheduled to roll into Devens on Wednesday. Two more days, and I'd have been at full battalion strength. The plan was designed for a minimum of three out of the five companies. I have two."

"If this had happened two days earlier, you'd be stuck in Fort Devens holding your dick. What is this plan you mentioned?" said Alex.

"Category Five Event Response ordered by the Department of Homeland Security. We're supposed to prevent a widespread breakdown in civil order."

Alex looked around. "Is that possible?"

Lieutenant Colonel Sean Grady leaned in and whispered, "Not with two companies. I give it a day or two."

"That's why we hauled ass to get here," Alex admitted, glancing at Ed. "Our kids are stuck over the river."

"I was wondering what dragged my former company commander to Cambridge, Mass, geared up for urban combat," Grady said. He reached under the table to grab a familiar rifle. "We're confiscating shit like this on sight."

"I heard. Category Five requirements?"

"Something like that," said Grady, reluctantly.

"I dropped my son off at BU on Saturday. Ed's daughter is a sophomore at BC."

"That's not good," Grady mumbled.

"That's what we keep hearing, but we don't have a choice."

"Maybe they got out early," Grady suggested.

"Not likely. They had a prearranged plan. Stay in the safest of the two places, and wait for us," said Ed.

"We have to make the trip, Sean. Even if the kids made it out, we have no way to verify it. One way or the other, we're going into those badlands," said Alex, pointing at the red-shaded zone on the monitor.

"You can't walk across one of the bridges. Not with your commando gear. They'll tear you apart."

"What exactly is going on over there?"

"Rioting. Looting. Arson. Personal violence—"

"Rape?" said Ed.

"Everything. Large gangs are staking out territory."

"Drug gangs?"

"Not really. We can't discount a heavy criminal element based on what we've witnessed, but it seems like a typical power grab in the absence of authority. Early this morning, we stopped a mixed group of ten men and women trying to cross the Weeks pedestrian bridge with AR-15-type rifles and semiautomatic shotguns. They had the shit broken down and concealed in backpacks. I felt like I was back in Helmand Province. That group was sent across for a reason, and it wasn't to seek a new life in the mountains of Vermont. We're talking a hardened group of ex-con-looking types."

"Colonel Grady," said the UAV operator, "Raven is sweeping north to south over Harvard Business School. White-hot thermal imaging detected."

"Copy. I'll monitor from here," said Grady. "Watch the screen," he said, navigating to a new screen on his monitor.

A few mouse clicks and the blue screen changed to a grayscale aerial image of the buildings along the northern tip of the business school complex. The screen panned south until a white cluster appeared in the middle of Soldiers Field Road near the intersection of Western Avenue. The camera's crosshairs centered on the cluster, and the image magnified.

"That's why you can't cross the river," said Grady.

At least twenty armed figures huddled under the Western Avenue overpass, hidden from the building-based surveillance teams in Cambridge. The crosshairs focused on one of the individuals, who carried an AR-15 and wore a tactical vest.

"Where are they getting the hardware?" Alex asked.

"Take a guess. The weapons we grabbed were a mix of previously legal ARs and heavily modified Class Three shit."

Ed said, "I thought Massachusetts—"

"The governor's mandatory buy-back program was a joke," Grady interrupted, "and Boston's draconian firearms ban only succeeded in disarming people who followed the rules. The guns never went away. They just shifted into the wrong hands."

"Any way we can get an armed escort?" Alex requested. "You could use the Raven to find a safe route. We'd be in and out in less than an hour. Your marines don't leave their vehicles."

Grady shook his head with a grave look. "I can't justify sending anyone across, Alex. I'm strapped here. It's no longer possible to move anyone, including heavily armed marines, past the river. We've tried it several times, with the same result. We eventually reach a point where we have to engage with small-arms fire to continue. I'm doing everything in my power to avoid that."

"Sounds like the fifty cals are cleared for engagement?"

"Countersniper operations. My posts overlooking the bridges are taking persistent sniper fire. We're only using the fifties when the sharpshooters get cocky and bunch up."

"Fuck it. I'll swim across."

"Not a great idea. It's anywhere from two hundred to three hundred feet across, and I'm sure they're watching the water. It's a full moon tonight."

"I can swim low profile. Combat swimmer stroke. I'll follow one of the bridges across. Swim between supports," said Alex.

"You'll probably get into a knife fight under the bridges. You'll be better off swimming straight across. We'll hold off on popping flares. No guarantee they won't spot you," said Grady, glancing up at the screen. "See that? Another group off Cambridge Street. Hiding out in a parking garage behind the Double Tree."

"Second group, Colonel," said the assistant UAV pilot.

"Got 'em. Nice job, Marines," Grady said proudly. "Wave for the camera, assholes. Split the QRF between the Western Avenue Bridge and Cambridge Street Bridge."

"Passing the order, sir," said one of the operations marines.

"I wish we had some Reapers on station—with ordnance," said Grady.

Alex looked at him. "I thought you were trying to avoid civilian engagements?"

"Trying. If either of these groups crosses with weapons—the trying part is over."

"We should probably get out of your way. What about our gear?" said Alex.

"I'll send it with you to Fire Support HQ. They're set up at the Hyatt, right across the river from the university. Captain Baker has some individual river-crossing gear. Watertight bags. Tow lines. He may have some fins. He'll set you up and get you into the river undiscovered. You're on your own after that. I can't send anyone in after you," said Grady.

"Sounds like a plan. Any way I can grab one of your spare Motorolas to announce my return? Hate to get smoked coming back."

"I can't give you an encrypted radio, but I'll give you an open frequency that we monitor," Grady offered. "You can program it into the radio we took off Sergeant Walker. Yours is sort of smashed."

"Great. What about a new tactical vest? I'm pretty sure your marines cut mine to pieces."

"S-4 will hook you up. They're set up on the first floor of Harvard Hall. I'll let them know you need a—"

"QRF is in position at both bridges," announced one of the radio operators.

"Copy," said Grady. "Tell them to maintain blocking positions on the Cambridge side."

"Colonel, I have both groups on the move! Transmitting data to the platoon commanders," said the UAV pilot.

"Got it," he said, turning to Alex and Ed. "It's gonna be a long night for both of us. If you can't get back across the river by sunrise, wait for tomorrow night. Hostile sharpshooters have been more of a nuisance than anything else—at night. Daytime is a different story. We've had some close calls."

"Got it. You better be here when I get back," said Alex.

"We'll be here. I'll have hot chow and coffee waiting for you and the kids. Lieutenant McGarrity?" he said, scanning the tent.

"Yes, sir," said a stocky officer watching the UAV feed by the pilots.

"Escort these two gentlemen over to the main supply point and arrange a ride to Fire Support HQ. Supply has their gear. Replace anything we smashed or slashed. You better get moving. The situation over there could change in a heartbeat."

"Thank you, Sean. I owe you one," said Alex, shaking his hand.

"Careful what you say. I might cash in on that if you're still handy with one of these," said Grady, returning Alex's HK416.

"I can hold my own," said Alex. "One last thing. Sergeant Walker could use a weapons upgrade," he said, patting Ed's shoulder.

"That won't be necessary," said Ed.

"I'm not taking you over with a Ruger 22. If Colonel Grady can spare—"

"I'm not going," he said.

"That's the first thing out of his mouth that's made any sense. Good luck. Get 'em moving, Lieutenant."

Alex grabbed Ed by the arm and guided him through the tent flap. "I'm willing to take you, if you want to go."

"I can't walk another mile on these stumps right now—let alone try to swim the river," said Ed.

"We'll float you across," said Alex.

"The river isn't the issue. I appreciate you letting me come this far."

"I wouldn't have stopped you," said Alex.

"It's better this way. Trust me," said Ed. "I'll stay here and make sure you don't get left behind." He looked up at the ancient buildings crowded over them. "They have less than twenty-four hours, and Grady knows it."

"I'll get the kids back before it all goes to shit. Just a walk in the park," said Alex.

"Make sure you write down all of our frequencies. I picked something up on my way out of the tent," whispered Ed, pressing something against his ribcage.

"Either that's a radio antenna in your pocket or you're really happy not to be swimming the Charles," said Alex.

"It's both."

Chapter 41

EVENT +44:58 Hours

Hyatt Regency
Cambridge, Massachusetts

Alex paused on the eleventh floor stairwell landing and put his hands on his knees. Taking deep breaths, he fought the wave of nausea that had decided to join him on the seventh floor. Unlike the other landing areas, which were illuminated by a single red chemlight, the eleventh was bathed in green light from three chemlights taped just above the exit-door window.

"How we doing, sir?" said Corporal Rodriguez, his unflagging stairwell escort.

"Better than you," grunted Alex.

"Good. We got six more floors to go," said Rodriguez.

Alex sighed and straightened himself, embracing the fact that he was going to meet their platoon commander with vomit on his new gear.

"Just kidding. This is our floor," said Rodriguez. "You should have seen the look on your face, though. You really going across?"

"My son is at Boston University."

Rodriguez nodded with a blank look.

"You got kids, Rodriguez?"

"Family's in Lowell. We've heard it ain't so bad up there."

"I came through Haverhill. Not much going on in that area. They should be fine," said Alex.

"For now—until this mess spills north," said Rodriquez, knocking on the door and standing directly in front of it. "It's Rodriguez! I got your mystery guest!"

A face appeared in the window, and the door opened. "Get back down to the patio, Rodriguez. We got a situation on the riverbank," said the marine inside the hallway.

Rodriguez disappeared down the stairwell before Alex could say a word.

"You gonna stand there all day?" asked the marine.

"No. Sorry," said Alex, stepping into the dark hallway.

"NVGs," said the marine, shutting the door and casting the hallway into complete darkness. "Fuckers across the river have some night vision capability. We've moved twice already."

Alex flipped his night vision goggles down and followed the marine left. A night-vision-equipped helmet peeked around the corner at the end of the hallway. They slid past the hidden sentry, who reported their approach through his headset, and walked halfway down the long hallway to a door on the left.

"Welcome to platoon headquarters. Stay low, but don't crawl. There's glass everywhere," he said, opening the door.

He followed the marine inside and scanned the room.

"This was your third choice?"

"At first we thought the Rain Man suite would be too obvious. Turns out it doesn't matter where we set up. Bar is to the left—don't mind the snipers," he said. "Captain Baker, our battalion guest is here."

"Bring him out, Staff Sergeant," said a voice from the far right.

A crack shattered the quiet, flaring his night vision. Alex whipped his head left. A sniper team was set up behind the bar, their instruments of long-range death aimed across the room toward the empty windows facing the river. Seated on bar stools, they had adjusted the stool height to perfectly accommodate using the bar as a platform for the rifle and spotting scope. The sniper pulled back on the bolt and ejected the spent casing onto the shell-littered granite slab, sliding another round into place.

"I can't see him anymore. Looked like a hit," said the spotter.

"Busy night?" said Alex.

"Getting busier. Captain is out on the patio."

They walked over broken glass to a wide patio spanning the entire length of the suite. Two marines crouched along the front of the patio wall, scanning the distance through their rifle optics. Three sat against the back wall of the patio under an empty trellis. An array of radios sat on the tile floor, cables snaking out to several tripod-mounted antennas next to the outer wall.

"Over here," said one of the marines along the back wall.

They approached, staying crouched below the top of the patio wall.

"Grab a seat, Mr. Fletcher. The CO speaks highly of you. Sorry to drag you up here, but I have a little problem you might be able to help me with. I'm told you have a thermal scope?" said Captain Baker.

"It's not rifle mounted," said Alex.

"Even better. The battalion's Raven is busy up north, and I think we've got a problem under the BU Bridge. There's an old rail bridge that passes under it. I have a team watching it from the boathouse, but there's still a shitload of intact foliage down there. We've caught some movement on night vision, but I'd like to take a look with thermals before I send a team," said Baker.

"Be my guest," said Alex, pulling his assault pack off and digging into one of the pouches.

"Excellent. It's a little embarrassing, but we have no thermals. It was supposed to go into the response kit, but it never happened."

"Was all of this part of a special kit?" said Alex.

"Comms gear and vehicles, yes. The rest is battalion issue. We didn't have many equipment failures. Everything has been EMP hardened over the past five years," said Baker, taking the scope. "Let's have a look."

They scooted to the forward wall, moving the two marines out of the way. Baker poked his head over the top and aimed the scope down Memorial Drive, toward the Boston University Bridge. He made a few minor adjustments and settled in, leaning against the concrete patio wall. The platoon commander keyed his Motorola.

"Boathouse, I have six thermal signatures about one hundred feet from your position, right along the riverbank. I'm going to roll one of the JLTVs right up Memorial onto them. Make sure they don't slip by the boathouse," he said. "Sniper section, up!"

He heard the sniper team scrambling over to their position along the wall.

"Set up right here," said Baker, patting the balcony wall next to them. "Targets along the riverbank, one hundred feet from the boathouse."

"Copy," said the spotter from behind them.

Alex watched him extend the legs of the Scout Sniper Spotting Scope and position the optic. The sniper joined him, resting the feet of his rifle's bipod on the top of the balcony wall. He started adjusting the AN/PVS-22 night vision scope immediately.

"Six hundred and fifty feet to the right front corner of the boathouse. I have no hostiles in sight. Can I get an IR mark?" said the spotter.

"I don't know if it's worth it," said Baker, turning to Alex. "They can see the mark across the river. We'll start taking fire."

A snap passed overhead.

"Already taking fire," said the spotter.

"Surprise, surprise," said Baker. "Ramsey, send Raider Two-One. We'll mark the targets for them. Fletcher, I'm going to guide your IR laser onto the group hiding by the river."

Alex rose above the top of the balcony wall and leaned forward, resting his elbows on the concrete. Two successive snaps passed nearby, causing him to flinch.

"Nowhere close," said Baker.

"Sounded close enough," said Alex.

The spotter next to him said, "If you hear it go by, you're good to go."

"Funny," muttered Alex, triggering his IR laser.

"Left and down—bring it back a little to the right—down a little—little more. Hold that," Baker directed. "You guys got anything at that mark?"

"Affirmative. Movement along the riverbank, heading away from the boathouse. Range seven-five-zero feet, estimated. Too much foliage down there. Marking targets," said the spotter.

A second green laser reached out from the balcony. The M40A6 rifle barked, drowning out the sound of the JLTV's roaring diesel engine.

"Hit. Range eight-zero-zero."

The rifle thundered again, and all hell broke loose on Memorial Drive. The M240G machine gun mounted to the JLTV's turret fired an extended burst at the terminal point of the IR lasers. Red tracers streamed into the darkness, briefly illuminating the bushes, before ricocheting skyward across the river. The vehicle crept forward, mercilessly hammering the riverbank. The sniper rifle cracked. Adrenaline surged, and Alex's breathing shallowed. His thumb touched the safety and his index finger caressed the trigger. A few muscle twitches and he could put some rounds downrange.

Nothing good would come of it.

"I see one hostile on the move. Headed toward the rail bridge," said Baker. "The rest are down. No movement. Ramsey, have Raider Two-One deploy their fire team to confirm five KIA. We don't need any surprises."

"Got it, sir," replied one of the marines by the radios at the back of the patio.

"We'll mop this up and get you on—" said Baker, interrupted by a long burst from the M240G machine gun.

"Raider Two-One confirms hits to a single hostile trying to climb over the fence at the rail bridge," said Ramsey.

A sharp crack dropped all of the marines to the patio tile.

"That's what we call close," said the spotter.

Captain Baker slowly raised his head back above the balcony wall. A distant metallic ping sounded from Memorial Drive.

"JLTV is taking accurate fire," said Sergeant Ramsey from the back patio wall.

"Roger. Get Raider Two-One back to the staging area," replied Baker, reaching out to grab the spotter's arm.

"Set up inside again. I want you to find whoever is putting those rounds out. Sooner or later, they're gonna get lucky."

"Roger that, sir. Hey, is there any way our guy here might be willing to leave the thermal scope behind? Sure make our job a lot easier," said the sniper.

"I'll trade it for some sniper coverage on my way out," said Alex.

"You headed somewhere?"

"You've seen the three identical buildings across the river?" asked Alex.

"Yes. Stacked up like dominoes. Fourteen stories each. One thousand, four hundred and thirty eight feet to the right corner of the rightmost building."

"My son lives on the sixth floor of the leftmost building. Room 621. Faces the middle building. I'm getting him out of there," said Alex.

"You're not serious," said the spotter, picking up his scope.

"Deadly serious. We got a deal?"

"I can cover you up to Storrow Drive, unless Battalion is willing to break out the fifties," said the sniper.

"Lieutenant Colonel Grady won't bend on that," said Baker.

"Not yet," said the sniper.

"Your .308 will work fine. I just want to avoid a riverside welcoming committee."

"We'll use the thermal scope to find any pickets along the waterfront. My guys will clear a path. We'll also mark any other hostiles with IR laser. Steer you away from any bigger groups. Once you disappear behind the first row of buildings, it's you and that rifle."

"That's all I'll need."

Chapter 42

Hyatt Regency
Cambridge, Massachusetts

"You ready, boss?" Corporal Rodriguez inquired.

"Let's do it," said Alex, taking a deep breath.

Rodriguez rose from a crouch and walked toward the sliding glass doors at the edge of the lobby. The closed doors led to a moonlit breezeway connecting the hotel to the parking garage, where they could access the rear patio and emerge on the western edge of the hotel. The marine produced a set of keys and unlocked the sliding doors, muscling them far enough apart for them to squeeze through. He tossed the keys to a marine standing next to Alex.

"Coming back the same way," said Rodriguez.

Alex looked surprised. "He's not coming too?"

"We can only spare one babysitter for this," said Rodriguez. "Piece of cake."

"If you say so," said Alex.

He plodded through the thick mud that had overwhelmed the entire lobby level of the hotel, feeling the crunch of broken glass between his boots and the marble floor. Like all of the buildings they'd passed on the ride down, most of the Regency's windows had either imploded from the air blast or were shattered from the seismic shock. He squeezed through the door and joined Rodriguez in the muck-filled breezeway.

The marine lowered his NVGs and stepped through one of the shattered panes onto the back patio. Alex did the same, trying to step in the deep impressions left by Rodriguez's boots. They plodded through the middle of the tables and collapsed umbrellas, pushing aside wrought-iron chairs to reach a tall stucco wall beyond a row of bushes.

Spanning the distance between the hotel and the parking garage, the wall formed the western boundary of the hotel. Rodriguez stood next to the wall and interlocked his fingers. Beyond the wall, an office building loomed, its few remaining windows reflecting bright green flashes of moonlight in his NVGs.

"You first. Check the other side for crazies before lifting me up," said Rodriguez.

"I know the drill," said Alex.

"Just checking. Been a while, right?"

"Sixteen years, but I feel it all coming back. Check the bottom of my boots for broken glass," he said, lifting each foot for the marine.

"Good to go," he said, taking Alex's rifle.

Alex stepped onto his locked hands and launched upward, straddling the stucco wall. He made a quick assessment of the dark green shadows on the other side of the wall, seeing nothing out of place. A sea of mud separated the wall from the adjacent building. He reached down with his left hand and pulled Rodriguez up the wall.

"Just like the good ole days," said Alex, taking his rifle back from Rodriguez.

"Not bad for an old man."

Alex dropped to the mud, sinking to his knees. He scanned in both directions with his rifle and pulled his right leg out of the seaweed-encrusted mire with a slow sucking sound. Rodriguez thudded next to him and muttered a few obscenities.

"It's not that bad once you break out of the impact crater," whispered Alex.

"This is some serious-ass bullshit," said Rodriguez.

"Haven't you been out here?"

"Not on foot," said Rodriguez.

"That's encouraging."

"Don't worry, boss. You're in good company. Hand signals from here to the river," he said, stepping forward.

They hugged the hotel's western side, staying behind thick rhododendron bushes until they reached the front corner. Memorial Drive was quiet, the dried mud and debris absorbing the full moon's unfiltered rays. They faced a one-hundred-and-fifty-foot trek across open ground to reach the thick scrub east of the boathouse. Slow ground.

Their other option was to head directly across from the hotel, but the riverbank was bare and would provide no concealment from sharpshooters across the river. Alex would need at least five minutes to stow his gear in the watertight bag and strip down for the swim. Thick bushes near the boathouse would be their best option. Even if they were spotted leaving the hotel, they would disappear in the undergrowth. Alex could slip into the water unnoticed next to the boathouse. He tapped Rodriguez on the shoulder. *Ready.*

"Rodriguez moving to the riverbank," whispered the marine into his helmet microphone.

They started out fast, legs fighting the mud as they shuffled diagonally across Memorial Drive. Alex shifted his rifle across their left flank, searching for any surprises east along the riverbank. A gunshot shattered the quiet, and he ducked. Rodriguez kept pushing across the road. Shadowy green buildings loomed across the river, superimposed over the naked trees. They were in the open and exposed to steel, unable to sprint. He forced his legs to pound and pull at the mud. Another crack echoed above them.

"Friendly fire," whispered Rodriguez, "keep moving."

By the time they reached the nearest clump of bushes, Alex's legs burned. He made sure they were no longer exposed to the tall buildings across the river and leaned against a tree, lowering his body to a sitting position. Rodriguez crouched in front of him, scanning ahead along the water. Both of them breathed heavily. The marine held out his index finger, and Alex responded with a thumbs-up. A one-minute rest was all he would get.

Rodriguez set off at a slower pace toward the dark structure ahead, stopping to point at the thick cluster of bushes at the base of the boathouse's eastern edge. A set of steps, barely discernible under the sludge, led down from Memorial Drive to a gate just beyond the bushes. Looked like a well-concealed place to put into the water. They arrived at the waterline, and Alex went to work.

Five minutes later, Alex waded into the Charles River, towing a rifle-length watertight bag through the mud. He submerged to his chest, inhaling sharply. Seconds later, he was fully immersed, bare feet planted in the river muck. The cuts across his body stung in unison, the pain fading quickly as he moved forward. He gave Rodriguez a nod and submerged, swimming underwater several feet toward the boathouse dock. His feet no longer touched the slimy bottom.

He surfaced slowly, raising his nose above the surface and exhaling quietly. The fixed dock was mostly destroyed. Formerly jetting into the river, thick planks of wood projected skyward in a twisted heap at the far end of the boathouse, casually swept aside by the wave of water travelling inland along the river. He saw no reason to swim any closer. He focused on the massive high-rise directly across the river and started to swim.

He didn't feel the current, but he knew it was there. If he swam toward the high-rise, he'd still end up somewhere several hundred feet downriver. In fact, he counted on it. This would put him directly in front of his son's dormitory building. A gun battle erupted somewhere in the distance. The crackle of rifle fire mixed with the deep, rhythmic thumping of a fifty-caliber machine gun for several seconds, stopping abruptly. They must have tried to cross one of the bridges further upriver.

The short duration of gunfire suggested the marines had put on a temporary display of fire. Enough to turn back the tide, temporarily. The situation was untenable, and Grady would eventually lose the city, no matter what his Homeland Security directives ordered. Alex desperately needed to be on the right side of the river before that happened. He might have to risk a daytime crossing. He'd slipped into the water at 2:46 AM, which didn't leave him enough time to reach both kids and get back across at night. Not even close.

Automatic gunfire erupted from the high-rise ahead, and Alex dove for the bottom of the river, escaping the noise. He pulled at the water with his arms until the towrope attached to his belt yanked him to a stop, buoyed by the watertight bag. He turned left in the blackness and swam further. His lungs burning, he opened his eyes and slowly rose to the surface—blurry red flashes appearing overhead. Alex's mouth cleared the water first, greedily sucking in the humid air. The sharp staccato battle rushed back to fill his ears.

Red tracers arched across the river from the Hyatt, bouncing downward off the face of the high-rise. Small explosions flashed across the building, stitched between the tracers' impact points—fifty-caliber projectiles tearing into concrete and steel. An automatic rifle continued to fire from the high-rise, peppering the boathouse and dock. A single shot reached his ears, and the high-rise rifle fell silent. He kept a low profile in the water and kept swimming. The sudden, furious battle had been focused on the boathouse. Retribution for the massacre near the rail bridge, perhaps.

Halfway across the river, something hard bumped his head. He grabbed the obstruction, feeling a nose and teeth. A dark mass swung lazily with the current, lodging against his body. He kicked and pushed at the corpse, splashing the water for several seconds—until he realized what he had done. Alex submerged as far as the towline would allow, expecting to hear bullets slap the water in pursuit.

Perfect silence enveloped him for the next thirty seconds as he drifted downriver. Nothing. He swam forward and came up for air. The silence continued as he lengthened his sidestroke and angled for the shallow outcropping of land identified by the marines. Landing there would give him a buffer from Storrow Drive and some natural concealment from sharpshooters.

He switched to a frog kick and slowed, taking time to observe the riverbank. Even with a full moon, his vision was borderline useless without night vision goggles. The marine snipers would have to be his eyes for now. A few more strokes brought him in line with the shallow land projection that would give him some room to transition into his combat gear. He could drift the remaining fifty feet and save his energy.

Three heads surfaced near the river's edge, moving slowly into deeper water. He stayed mostly submerged and drifted motionless—eyes pinned to the three men. Did the marines see them? A red dot appeared on the lead man's forehead and disappeared. The red dot reappeared on the second man's head and vanished. The spotter was telling him something. A plume of water exploded in front of the group, causing a gurgled scream.

Alex pulled furiously on the towline, dragging the watertight bag closer. The swimmers reacted, splashing toward him. He kicked in the opposite direction, bringing the bag into his hands. He fumbled with the holster attached to the bag's external webbing, drawing his suppressed pistol just as one of the swimmers reached him. A sharp burning creased his upper left arm, and Alex kicked out hard, turning onto his back. He caught the faint reflection of a knife just above the surface of the water.

The figure lunged forward, and Alex pressed the trigger, snapping his head back. The second attacker swam for the shoreline. Alex took a deep breath, floating on his back, and lined up the glowing tritium sights on the splashing. He fired twice, and the frantic swimming stopped. Alex drifted with the three bodies toward the esplanade, hoping that this had been the extent of his welcoming party. He doubted it.

His feet sank into the soft river bottom, and he pushed off toward the riverbank, clawing up the steep muddy slope. He pulled the black bag through the mud, exhausted, but not daring to pause. Alex opened the zipper and pulled his rifle clear, chambering a round. His night vision goggles came out next, pulled tightly over his head. He swept the esplanade with the goggles, verifying no immediate threats. He dragged the bag to a small park bench, searching the contents for his first aid pouch.

Alex washed his arm with the CamelBak hose and removed a small packet of the same powder the corpsman had used on him in Harvard Yard. He tore it open and dumped it on his upper arm, hastily rubbing it into the deep cut and grimacing. He'd properly bandage later. Right now, he needed to gear up and get as far from the esplanade as possible. He was on the move within sixty seconds, sprinting from tree to tree on his way toward Storrow Drive.

A bullet snapped overhead, and he dropped to the mud. It was impossible to determine who had fired the bullet, and there was nothing to gain by assuming it had been the marine sniper. He scanned forward and saw a figure slump against the side of the pedestrian walkway over Storrow Drive. Alex raised his rifle and ran through the mud, eager to get off the esplanade.

A green laser appeared to his left, marking the base of a tree fifty feet away. A snap passed through the branches above, hitting the metal fence behind the illuminated tree trunk. Alex knelt in the soft mud and thumbed his IR laser, placing the green line at the edge of the trunk. He rested the rifle magazine on his raised knee and eased the laser an inch past the edge of the tree. A dark blob peered around the trunk, and Alex fired, striking the figure in the head. Time to put some distance between himself and the river.

He jogged toward the waist-high, metal picket fence separating the esplanade from Storrow Drive, clearing it with little difficulty. Across the road, he jumped onto the raised concrete wall beyond Storrow Drive, and grabbed the bottom of the chain-link fence above it. He hung there for a moment before pulling himself to the top of the concrete and scaling the fence. His drop holster snagged on the top of the fence, knocking him off balance and pitching him prostrate into the mud. He lay immobile for several seconds, breathing heavily—his eyes heavy.

I could fall asleep here, he thought for a few more hazy moments. The distant sound of a vehicle engine jarred him back into action.

He pulled himself up by the chain-link fence and jogged to the nearest street corner, leaning against a brick wall. An engine roared nearby, somewhere deeper in the city. He glanced around the intersection for a street sign, wasting precious time. Street signs were a rare sighting on side streets in Boston. He considered the GPS, but with the pedestrian walkway behind him, he was pretty sure the street in front of him was Silber Way. The Warren Towers were less than two city blocks away.

A raised pickup truck careened onto Silber Way from Commonwealth Avenue, tearing through the mud. A figure with a rifle swayed behind the cabin, holding onto the truck's utility rack. The truck raced in his direction without headlights, seemingly oblivious to the fact that the road ended before Storrow Drive. Alex triggered the IR laser and aimed at the truck, placing several tightly spaced shots through the front windshield.

The truck swerved into a line of parked cars and rebounded into the street, turning sideways and flipping. Alex pulled back from the wall just as the truck careened past, tumbling over the pedestrian walkway and crashing down onto Storrow Drive.

This was insane.

Chapter 43

Boston University
Boston, Massachusetts

Alex crouched between two cars in the parking lot across from the Warren Towers, waiting for the slow-moving SUV to pass Granby Street. Beams of light randomly stabbed through the darkness above him, gradually moving left through the parking lot and disappearing. He risked a look, catching the taillights turning off Commonwealth Avenue.

Gunfire erupted in the distance—the familiar thunder of a marine fifty cal. What he wouldn't give for some heavy-machine-gun support. Nothing said "everything's going to be all right" like the sound of a fifty. He eased onto Granby Street and approached Commonwealth, pausing behind a low hedge at the corner to visually sweep the wide road.

The four-lane road looked still. He craned his head back and stared at the Warren Towers, noticing that the rightmost tower was crooked, leaning several degrees to the left. Maybe that was just his angle of view. His son's tower, to the left, looked straight, but he couldn't shake the marine's description of the towers. *Dominos.* He had to get Ryan out of there.

Glimpses of flickering green light played across dozens of windows, advertising occupants. Ryan would know better than to give his position away like that. They'd talked about these things. He counted six floors up on Ryan's building and scanned across. Two of the windows shimmered. He had no idea which room was Ryan's. Room 622 didn't mean anything to him from the outside. They'd only visited his room once, and he'd been too busy hauling boxes to pay close attention to the room's location. He couldn't wait any longer.

Alex raced across the street, passing underneath the "T" wires that cut a path down the middle of the wide street. He reached the other side and ducked into a vestibule, checking the street. Nothing moved, though he doubted that his trip across Commonwealth had gone unnoticed. The vestibule contained a door with a key-card reader. He pulled on the handle, which failed to budge the door. No surprise there. All of the external doors would be equipped with the same electronic system, all designed to prevent unauthorized access in the event of a power failure.

He was familiar with two ways into Warren Towers. The parking garage, which he had used to offload most of Ryan's college possessions, required a housing card to access the stairwell or elevator. That left the front door. Not the stealthiest entry point, but the large floor-to-ceiling windowpanes next to the double doors would have undoubtedly shattered, allowing easy access to the lobby. "Easy," of course, being a relative term on this side of the river.

Keeping his rifle pointed forward, he shuffled along the front of the building, his damp, mud-lined pants grinding away at his inner thighs. He arrived at the entrance, scanning the street for any onlookers, then stepped through one of the missing windowpanes. The lobby was empty. The couches and tables he remembered were gone, replaced by a mud-streaked tile hall. He activated the IR designator and probed the room with the green laser, walking steadily toward the escalator bank.

He moved slowly and deliberately up the escalator, watching for signs of an ambush. A head peeking around a corner. A carelessly exposed rifle barrel. The slow movement and concentration triggered a cascade of fatigue. His legs felt heavy and sluggish, barely clearing the lip of each metal stair. He reached the top and crouched in the escalator, contemplating the P-STIM tablets given to him by the corpsman. Eventually, he'd have to pop these. He was approaching forty-eight hours with minimal sleep, which he knew from experience was the "hazy point." He'd start making poor decisions, unaware of the consequences. Without anyone to second-guess him, one of those decisions would kill him.

Alex caught himself staring blankly at the grooved metal stair in front of his face. He rubbed his eyes and peered around the metal balustrade, surprised to find the student union area completely abandoned. Once again, the furniture had been stripped, leaving nothing but scattered papers and broken glass strewn across dirty tile. Maybe the students had barricaded themselves on the upper levels, using the furniture to block the entrances. He hoped not. He was too tired to fuck around with obstacles.

He jogged across the empty student lounge, searching for the central hallway spanning all three towers. He'd made this trip once before, but the monochromatic image cast by his night vision goggles looked alien, giving him no recognizable visual cues. He knew the hallway was located beyond the student union, so he kept moving until he approached the far wall and found several sets of doors leading into the long, empty passage to Fairfield Tower.

The green image darkened as he reached the end of the corridor, indicating a complete lack of light in the area. He flipped his goggles up and triggered the rifle-mounted flashlight, bathing the hallway in light. Small piles of concrete fragments lined the corridor at scattered intervals, the walls above them deeply cracked. He shifted the light to the ceiling, exposing a twisted puzzle of metal gridwork and warped ceiling panels. All bad news for the long-term survival of the building.

Thick streaks of mud swerved out of the hallway into the empty elevator lobby, ending at a door marked "stairs." He switched back to night vision and entered the stairwell, which felt ten degrees cooler. He paused for a moment to examine the long fissures in the cinder-block-wall enclosure. The concrete landing and stairs leading to the next floor appeared undamaged. He took the stairs cautiously, clearing blind corners and paying close attention to the doors leading to each floor.

By the time Alex read the sign "Sixth Floor," he couldn't hear his own thoughts over his heartbeat. Fighting every instinct to yank the door open and run to room 622, he put his back against the wall next to the door and tried to steady his breathing. Once his breathing hit a slow, rhythmic pattern, Alex pushed down on the door handle and tried to nudge the door inward. It didn't move.

He leaned into the metal door with his left shoulder and gave it a hard push, shifting the fire door a few inches.

"Someone's trying to get in," a voice hissed.

"Stab him in the face!" yelled a woman.

"Just shut the fucking door!"

Alex pulled a rifle magazine out of his vest and wedged it through the opening at the bottom.

"I'm trying! It's jammed. Can you see who it is?"

"I don't see anyone."

"I'm here to find my son!" yelled Alex.

"What did he say?" said the female.

"I don't fucking care! Shine a light, and see what's blocking the door!" said the male.

"My son is in room six twenty-two. Ryan Fletcher. I'm here to bring him home!" added Alex, flipping up his NVGs to avoid being blinded.

"Does anyone know Ryan Fletcher?" said the female.

More voices joined them in the hallway, and several flashlights shined through the crack in the door.

"He's got it jammed at the bottom with—fuck, get away from the door! It's a machine-gun mag," said someone.

"Isn't there a roster or something? Ryan Fletcher lives in room six twenty-two. He's my son. Doesn't anyone know him?" said Alex.

A hand fumbled with the rifle magazine at the bottom of the door, and Alex stuck his foot against it, pinning it in place.

"Someone stab his foot!"

Alex backed up in the tight stairwell and front-kicked the handle side of the door, driving it back several inches. Screams erupted inside the hallway. He hit the door again, opening a two-foot gap.

"He has a gun!"

Alex triggered his rifle flashlight, scattering the students. One of the large couches from the downstairs lobby sat against the wall, several feet down, covered by a sleeping bag and pillow. He squeezed through and pulled the door shut, directing the light into a tangle of wooden chairs pushed against the wall. A male student in jeans and a mud-stained yellow polo shirt lay curled up under the chairs, shielding his eyes with one hand. The other arm was trapped under the chairs and looked hyperextended at the elbow. Possibly broken.

"Dude. Is this a rescue?" said the kid, lowering his hand slightly. "Are you, like, Special Forces or something?"

"I'm not Special Forces or the military. Where's room six twenty-two?"

"Six twenty-two is locked," he said. "It's the only one we couldn't get into."

"Where is it?" he said.

"Around the corner. At the end of the hallway. You're not with the military?" he said.

"How many times do I have to tell you? My son lives on this floor," he said, stepping over him.

Alex flashed his light around the corner, seeing the door to six twenty-two directly ahead. Everything was starting to look familiar again. He knocked first, calling out his son's name and trying the handle. Nothing stirred beyond the door. More students wandered into the hallway, muttering about the military.

"Does anyone have a spare key?" said Alex.

"The RAs took off when the bomb hit. We searched their rooms, but didn't find any," said a boy from the dark.

"He kind of disappeared," said another kid.

"What do you mean?" Alex asked.

Someone muttered, "I wouldn't say any more."

"You want to see my driver's license?"

"That would be a start," said one of the girls.

"Shouldn't all of you be hiding in your rooms? I am still holding a rifle, right?"

"Nobody's come up here with a specific name before. You might be legit."

"Might be legit?" said Alex. "Strong SAT scores apparently don't translate into strong survival instinct."

Alex removed a red chemlight from his vest and snapped it, throwing it to the floor. A crimson glow illuminated the weary students. He shook his head and opened a small pouch on his vest, tossing his identification at the young woman who appeared to be in charge.

"He's totally military. Look at the gear," uttered a voice.

"Ex-military," said Alex.

"He could be a merc. Paid to rescue whoever that kid is."

"You guys play way too much Call of Duty," said Alex, pounding on the door while several students examined his license with flashlights.

"He checks out—for now," said the girl, handing his license back.

"Thanks for the endorsement. So where's my son if he isn't here? Can I get the young man who spoke up earlier?" said Alex, knocking on the door again.

"I remember seeing him here late Sunday night. Around eleven maybe? A bunch of us were hanging out in the hall, and he came by. Said something about a girlfriend at Boston College. He was gone after the blast."

"I saw him heading for the far stairwell right after the shockwave hit. He had a backpack and some kind of bucket," volunteered another student.

Alex knew exactly where to find his son.

"Is there a second lock on these doors, maybe above the handle?" said Alex.

"No. Just the handle" said someone.

Alex kicked the door, causing everyone to back away a few steps. The door didn't budge.

"You should shoot the door," stated one of the kids.

"Good idea. Clear the hallway!" he yelled, pointing the rifle at the door and activating the visible red laser.

While the students broke into pandemonium, tripping over each other to get clear, Alex steadied the laser and fired three bullets into the space between the handle and the doorjamb. The hallway fell deathly silent after the last shot, everyone frozen in place.

"Holy shit. Did he really just shoot the door?" said a kid on the ground to his left.

"He totally shot the door! Dude, your silencer doesn't work for shit!" yelled a student hidden in one of the rooms.

Alex kicked the door, knocking it against the interior wall. He took a step and stopped. The room smelled like Ryan. Like their home. Alex deactivated the Surefire light and stood there, remembering everything the way it had been—before. He felt like a distorted time-traveller. The past forty-eight hours expanding over eternity.

"You need this?" said a young woman, holding out his red chemlight.

"Thanks," he mumbled.

"Is everything okay? You don't look...the same," she said.

"I'm fine," said Alex, walking forward.

He swept the Spartan interior with his rifle light. A crumpled blue comforter hung off Ryan's bed, draping the tile floor. An empty plastic bin lay tipped over on the bed. Most of the cardboard boxes stacked on the floor were unopened, his priorities upon arrival clearly focused on a young lady at Boston College. A few books and pictures covered his desk. One picture of the Fletchers and—Ed was going to love this—several pictures of Chloe. He couldn't believe how badly they had underestimated that relationship. He threw the chemlight next to the bin on Ryan's bed and deactivated the rifle light.

Alex sat on Ryan's bed and leaned back against the cinderblock wall, wondering if he could take a small nap. Just the thought of closing his eyes for a few moments caused him to sink down the rough wall to the mattress. He dug into his front pants pocket and pulled out a dark tab, ejecting a small pill directly through the foil into his mouth. Designed to release its contents upon contact with saliva, he held the P-STIM under his tongue for thirty seconds, kick-starting the amphetamine boost. It worked immediately.

He lay there calculating the time it would take him to reach Chloe's apartment, no longer contemplating sleep. Moving cautiously, a 3.1-mile walk through the back streets of Brookline shouldn't take him more than an hour and a half. Two at the most. His watch read 2:37.

Plenty of time.

He took the family picture from the desk and removed the picture from the silver frame, straining to see the image in the dim red aura. He knew it well enough. The four of them in cushioned wicker chairs, on the wide porch at the Chebeague Island Inn. He stared at the picture, unable to put it away.

"Nobody's coming for us?" said a girl standing in the doorway. "You're really just someone's dad?"

The gravity of the situation came into sharp focus, weakening his knees. He'd been so single-minded kicking his way into their lives that he hadn't stopped to consider their predicament. The kids were stranded, waiting for a rescue that would never arrive. He folded the picture and tucked it into the pouch holding his license.

"You need to seriously consider leaving this place," said Alex, brushing past her.

"And go where? What happened out there?" she said.

Alex stopped outside of Ryan's room and glanced around the hallway at the flashlight-illuminated faces. They were just children. He swallowed hard, barely able to meet their stares. How many had shown up for early orientation? Hundreds? Thousands? His thoughts drifted to the parents experiencing the ultimate nightmare just days after sending their babies into the world. They'd said goodbye this weekend, unaware that some of them would never see their children again. The odds were long against most of these students surviving. Without food and water, they would have to venture into the city.

"What's going on in the city? What's wrong with you?" she demanded.

"Nothing," he said flatly. "Has anyone here been outside of the towers? I mean outside of the building?"

"We didn't think it was a good idea. The shooting started yesterday afternoon and got worse all night. That's why we blockaded the stairwells. We figured we'd wait for the military or police to start evacuating us," she said.

"Taking their sweet-ass time, too," said a kid holding a baseball bat over his shoulder.

"You guys don't know, do you? Holy shit," he whispered.

"Know what? What don't we know?" said the young woman, directing her flashlight in his face.

"The power outage isn't confined to Boston. It's everywhere. We've been hit by an EMP," said Alex, pausing. "Nobody is coming for you."

THE END

The Perseid Collapse: Event Horizon, Book Two in *The Perseid Collapse Series*, will be available in the spring of 2014.

Please consider leaving a review for *The Perseid Collapse* at Amazon. You don't have to write a novel. Even a quick word about your experience can be helpful to prospective readers.

Steven Konkoly is the author of *The Jakarta Pandemic, Black Flagged, Black Flagged Redux, Black Flagged Apex, and Black Flagged Vektor*

To sign up for Steven's New Release Updates, send an email to:

stevekonkoly@gmail.com

Please visit Steven's blog for the latest news of future projects:

www.stevenkonkoly.com